Understanding the Alacrán

Jonathan LaPoma

ISBN: 978-0-9988403-0-7

Cover design by theBookDesigners
Cover photograph by Pastor Soto
Interior design by Polgarus Studio
Author photograph by Emilio Azevedo

For more information, contact info@almendroarts.com.
www.almendroarts.com
www.jonlapoma.com

Praise for *Understanding the Alacrán*

"LaPoma obviously knows Mexico well, framing the nation not by its problems but by the hearts of its people . . . the descriptions of Mexican locales are as vibrant, colorful, and illuminating as the novel's unique characters. The author can write about serious things with humor, and Will's tale shows an understanding of Mexico that goes beyond the ordinary."

—Kirkus Reviews

"I loved Understanding the Alacran. Loved. It. . . beautifully written, funny, moving and all-round wonderful coming of age story. LaPoma has done an excellent job in creating characters that his readers will be able to connect with, relate to and truly come to care about. Absolutely read this book. . . My very highest recommendation."

—Chris Fischer, Readers Favorite, 5 Stars

"LaPoma takes time to create a sense of people, place, and why situations evolve; not just how – and these elements are what gives the story added value and impact as the landscapes of Mexico and William's psyche immerse readers in the mental and physical atmosphere of the story . . . an appealing, engrossing story that moves beyond the traditional coming of age approach to add social and cultural concerns into the mix . . . Given the latest state of affairs between the U.S. and Mexico, its undercurrent of social understanding and issues mixed with psychological examination makes it an especially relevant, timely read."

—Diane Donovan, Midwest Book Review

"Unique and accessible . . . brilliant story that explores the evil of drugs, a man's struggle for freedom, and redemption through love . . . the finish is awesome."

—Divine Zape, Readers Favorite, 5 Stars

"I enjoyed the protagonist's journey, the passage from despair to hope, and above all, the search for inner freedom. Readers will also love the compelling characters and the way the author captures Mexican culture, its beautiful setting with its smells and sounds in this inspiring tale . . . a wonderful coming-of-age story."

—Arya Fomonyuy, Readers Favorite, 4 Stars

To Toni and Caro, who read the book before it was written.

And to Mexico, for saving my life.

If you had all the beauty you desired, you could with boldness leave the wood and make your way among mankind.

-Petrarch

Chapter 1

I was twenty-three when it happened. While that may seem late to some people, to a lot of those people it never comes—no matter how many lives they threaten to prove it has.

I'd been traveling by bus through Mexico for nearly two weeks with two German friends and my girlfriend, Luz, who left us at our last stop, Veracruz, to spend the rest of the Christmas season with her family. We woke that morning in a hostel in the cool mountain town of San Cristobal de las Casas and set our sights on the Mayan ruins of Palenque.

I was the first to the road, pulling ahead of the sluggish Deutsch Duo. A cab rounded the corner.

"Taxi . . . TAXI!" I waved frantically and though it was slowing, I almost ran in front of it.

The Germans lumbered behind.

"Hurry the fuck up!" I said.

The morning was peaceful, but I wasn't. We'd missed our buses in two other towns, and I'd be damned if we missed another. Our group leader, and my best friend, Luz, wasn't there to cool my nerves, and the fresh morning air could only do so much.

We hopped in the cab. "Bus station, please," and the cabbie took us on a complementary tour of the town for our fare. The bus was leaving in an hour, buying me time to enjoy the scenery: Spanish colonial architecture with the Sierra Madre de Chiapas just beyond. Beautiful.

Though Gretel had only come to Mexico for this particular trip, the other German, Mica, and I had already logged four months in the small Pacific coast city of Lila. Lila was one of the oldest Mexican cities west of Mexico City and was known for its brutal tropical heat and humidity.

I rolled down my window and breathed in the fresh air. It was nice to get some relief from the heat. The weather resembled a beautiful spring day in the US city I'd tried to escape, drawing my thoughts to inevitability. No one truly leaves Buffalo.

The cabbie dropped us in front of the bus station, and we walked inside. I was exhausted. I was always exhausted. Sleep was just a temporary delay in one endless and grueling day. My eyes were only opened wide enough to find the ticket counter, my wallet, and a plastic seat in the waiting room where I relieved my legs of their duty.

I'd noticed another difference between San Cristobal and Lila, other than weather. San Cristobal was a tourist town; Lila wasn't. I looked up and saw a mix of pasty white gringos from—judging by accents—Australia, the US, Britain . . . All the clowns I'd tried to leave behind. For a moment I was no longer in Mexico, until someone with a remote turned on the small TV mounted to the wall in a darkened corner, shattering my tranquility with the rhythmic blast of a banda music video. Banda was basically a Latino version of polka and, along with mariachi, was teeming with cultural significance for the Mexican people.

I didn't even look up. Hearing banda in Mexico was nothing new. I'd been poking fun at it for the previous four months for its trite lyrics and almost ludicrous instrumentals, and tried to tune it out when I heard it.

On that morning, however, I believe I felt the true message of the music for the first time. It wasn't the music itself that caused this change, but rather the reaction of all the gringos in attendance once they'd been jolted awake by the forceful blast of trumpets and piercing grito of the mustached lead singer.

I kept my eyes on the floor until I heard a rumble of laughter that spread throughout the room. It didn't seem intentional, but it happened. I sat for a moment as a tidal wave of thought broke in my mind. Soon, we hopped on the bus and everyone took their seats. Most shut their eyes, but I spent the next six hours fully awake and deep in thought as we twisted and turned through the mountains and countryside in one of Mexico's poorest, yet culturally richest states, Chiapas.

I'd arrived in Mexico four months earlier. The trip was long and an experience in itself. I flew from Buffalo to Cleveland to Houston to Guadalajara, and in Guadalajara I took a wild cab ride to the central bus station where I boarded a bus to Lila. The bus ride was peaceful and helped to dilute several of the nagging voices of 'reason' I hoped to dissolve in whatever solvent the Mexican people had to offer. The bus itself was comfortable and would have been empty if not for the two giggling girls sitting to my right.

My attention, however, was focused through the window to my left. It was late, but the dying amber sun held on just long enough to cast a bronze hue on the lush fields and jagged mountains beyond them—a cordial greeting for this strange white man. For hours I stared at the small fruit stands and taquerias and auto garages that lined the highway. The dusk had drawn the people from the protective cover of their homes. Shoeless jugadores played soccer matches on dirt fields lit by streetlights, while others worked on cars and smiled. Others stood talking, laughing over god knows how many beers, while elderly men and women sat in lawn chairs, quietly basking in the company of those around them. There were great fields of tall grass with fires burning in the distance, flames leaping off the world like brilliant, localized solar flares. There were big gorgeous mountains on the horizon, and every so often a moonlit river would cut through a forest of towering palms as if for nothing other than to please the hungry eyes my inadequate soul had been so longing to satiate. The girls to my right would shoot me intermittent glances, then whisper and giggle. Their hushed words weren't necessary. Even if I could have understood them, I don't think I would have paid them any attention.

I arrived in Lila around ten p.m. The night was humid and the heat oppressive. I wiped the sweat on my brow, grabbed my big blue bag and guitar, and headed into the bus station. Sal was there as he'd said he'd be, along with our other college buddy we called Cletus. I'd known Sal for the better part of a decade, but we'd only been friends for the last few of those years. We grew up in the same town, went to the same high school—he was even friends with my older brother. But it wasn't until college that our lives had aligned. He told people he was in Lila studying the Volcán Rojo, Mexico's most active volcano. This was true. He was a grad student at the Universidad de Lila's School of Volcanology. But I already knew he was there for the same reason I was—whatever that reason could be . . .

Cletus was an adventurous, well-intentioned chap but was prone to mood swings and self-loathing. Perhaps it was due to years of everyone calling the poor fucker Cletus? Cletus was only halfway through a two-week vacation but was ready to go home.

"Hey, William, how was the trip?" Cletus said.

"Long."

"How've you been? I think it's been over a year now, huh?"

Just hearing those words aged me some calculable degree. "Good." What the hell else can you say to someone you haven't seen in so long?

Sal made a call on his cell phone, and soon a blue hatchback came tearing around the corner. The driver, a beefy Mexican named Marco, stopped, got out, and popped the hatch. I laid down my guitar and big blue bag, closed the hatch, and piled in the back seat with Sal and Cletus. A husky German named Jorg sat shotgun. He shook my hand, and gave a jovial "Hello," then turned his attention back to the road. The other guys continued talking among themselves.

I preferred not to speak to anyone. I wanted to take in the

sights. Lila was a gorgeous town. Its stucco houses and cobblestone streets were something I'd hoped to see. Sal had described the city in his fervent recruitment efforts to get me to move down there, and now here I was rearranging all the misplaced colors and shapes of my own fantasy.

We took the main road, Madrid del Rio, past the university's sports complex, the Club Deportivo de Lila, and swung a left just before an elementary school. This road, unlike the paved main one, was cobblestone and it led downhill, dumping us at the only house at its dead end. A white tile walkway led from the curb through the gated front door and spread out into every room in the stucco house, which looked as though it was a giant rock structure forced upward through the earth's crust by some great lake of magma just below the surface. In front of the house and to its right was a thick stone wall at least fifteen feet high that spanned the enormous perimeter of the city's cemetery, or panteon. With the exception of the neighbors sharing our western wall, that house stood apart from humanity.

Marco pulled the car under a series of almendros, or almond trees, out front, and we followed the walkway inside. Conversation could only take us so far, and soon we were back on the cobblestone streets in search of drinks. We set out on foot, following the panteon's wall to the nearest Arce, a Mexican liquor store chain. We each shelled out twelve pesos for a caguama, or a liter of beer, and the guy behind the counter dunked his hand into a large plastic tub, navigated the waters of melting ice block, and fished out the glass bottles. We returned to the house, sat on uncomfortable handcrafted furniture, and gulped our beers. Now true introductions could be made.

"I'm tellin' you, chicks here are prude." Sal spewed this crap as if he actually believed it. "They're all traditional catholic. It's gonna take you at least six months to get in anyone's pants, *if* you can get past their fathers."

Marco said, in English, "The girl I have been seeing, it takes me long time, maybe seis months?"

"Damn, you gotta step up your game, man," I said.

Marco inhaled deeply and gave me a look as if to say, "That shit ain't gonna fly here," then let it go. He wasn't the kind of guy you wanted to piss off. He stood about six feet with broad muscular shoulders and face-poundin' fists. But he seemed equal parts lover to fighter. He was a handsome dude who put a lot of thought into his style, which was built on tight designer clothes and lots of hair gel for his mullet. Despite the tough guy bullshit, Marco was personable and enjoyed drinking, fighting, shredding guitar, and getting laid. I liked him right away.

"I think I would have to disagree with both of you. It doesn't take me long to," Jorg smiled like some dumbass kid, "make it with the ladies." It was a surprising statement. Jorg was a bespectacled twenty-nine-year-old grad student, and though he was a likeable guy, he wasn't the best looking of characters. Jorg, like Sal, was in Mexico to study volcanology. He divided his time equally between the volcano, the Universidad, and parties. Though still husky, he'd lost considerable weight since his arrival in Lila nearly four months previous, most likely due to the high-altitude fieldwork he'd been doing on the volcano.

Sal and I broke out our guitars during a lull in the conversation, but I stopped playing when I heard Marco repeat a word while speaking with Jorg.

"What's alacran?" I said.

Sal smirked as Marco answered.

"Alacran means scorpion."

Sal couldn't wait to bust in. "You better be careful, boy. This house is infested with yellow scorpions, and those are the most dangerous kind. If you get stung, you got like twenty minutes to get to the hospital or you'll start convulsing. You could even die."

"Fuck!" I said.

"Yeah, I see three of them just last week," Jorg said. "I shished them out the door with the broom. Just be sure to always wear sandals."

"Yeah, and check your bed each night before you go to sleep," Sal said.

"Man, I'm glad I'm leaving here soon," Cletus said.

Christ! I laughed off their comments but knew I'd be dealing with their aftermath later. I gulped my caguama.

"Just wait, Willy," Sal said. "You'll be seeing a lot of wildlife around here. Snakes, tarantulas, rats, mosquitoes carrying malaria. There are enormous bats that hang in the almond trees out front. One flew right into my chest the other night as I was coming home from a run. It's crazy."

Soon the conversation wore itself out and most decided on sleep. Despite the exhausting journey, I wanted to explore the city. Cletus was the only one to accept my invitation to grab a few beers, and we set off down the cobblestone streets in search of a place still open. We found a bar advertising two-for-one beers and sat at a wobbly plastic table outside. A waiter came over and tried explaining something but soon gave up when the cold blank stares on our faces never warmed. He tossed down a couple of menus and wandered away. Cletus had visited a number of bars in the past week and laughed when he saw the prices.

"What?" I said.

"They offer two-for-one beers here because they're double the price."

"Man, this fuckin' place, huh?"

The waiter came back, and Cletus and I pointed to what we wanted on the menu. The waiter left and returned with four Indios. Despite our inability to communicate with them, the bar staff was friendly. The guy who looked to be the owner came over to introduce himself. He was a gregarious chap who didn't stop flapping after introductions. He very well may have been telling us how great our mothers sucked cock, but he did so with such cordiality we couldn't help but think he was on our side. He tossed down a plastic bowl of spiced nuts before waddling away.

Cletus had an uneasy look about him.

"What's wrong, Cletoid?"

"Eh, not much." He took a sip. "It's just that I've been here for a week now and haven't done shit. Sal promised to take me to the beach, to Guadalajara, to the top of the damn volcano. But we never do anything. He wakes up at two, jerks off for a few hours, then we sit around and get drunk until it's time to pass out again. I haven't seen a damn thing outside of these bars."

"Yeah, that does suck."

"And he's such an asshole on top of it. Just the other day we went out to eat with his girlfriend, Paz. Halfway through dinner he chucked a hot tortilla in her face and stormed out."

"That's crazy. Why'd he do that?"

"You know him. Everything was fine until she offered me a spoonful of rice, and he went insane."

"What a lunatic!"

"Yeah. You really should just get away from him. Go explore Mexico on your own."

"Yeah, but he's not *that* bad."

I knew the words were a lie before I even said them—but I still said them. Sal was a mercurial beast. No one knew when he was going to blow, but blow he did, and often. Cletus knew this better than anyone. The two were roommates in college. One night, Sal got upset with Cletus for something trivial like not washing a dish after using it, so he kicked down Cletus's door while Cletus was asleep, jumped on his bed, and slapped him hard across the face. And the abuse wasn't just physical. Cletus once made the mistake of bringing a cute new girlfriend over to the house. Sal asked her if Cletus had a small cock. She just giggled. Sal said he was sure his was bigger, so he called Cletus over and told him to whip it out so she could compare. Cletus obviously refused, but Sal persisted. Sal pulled his out, and she indeed confirmed it to be the bigger of the two. Then she started touching it. Cletus did nothing. He and his girl broke up soon after.

This abuse wasn't just directed at Cletus. I'd taken a good brunt of it as well but not the physical stuff. I think Sal knew not to push me like that. But the mind games . . .

In the summer of 2005, we took a road trip together: six weeks across the country, from Buffalo to Denver to Seattle, then down to

LA, Vegas, and the Grand Canyon and straight back to Buffalo in a thirty-hour marathon of driving—a feat I wouldn't recreate even if Salma Hayek was giving roadhead the whole trip. In those six weeks, we'd experienced some great highs, but none could even out the lows. With Sal it was one sadistic game after the next. We spent most of the trip camping in state or national parks: Yellowstone, Glacier, Mt. St. Helens, Crater Lake. He'd do things like pack up his tent in the twilight hours of morning while I was still asleep in my own, then start the car, stick his head out the window, and say something like, "If you're not packed up and out of here in five minutes, I'm leaving you." It might have been funny if it weren't true. He did leave me once, and I had to walk several miles with all my gear to catch up. I could go on, but there'd be no room for any other story.

And now here I was, sitting in some small bar in some small Mexican town, drawn there by the exact same promises that were so ruthlessly unfulfilled for Cletus. Was I a fool? I knew the answer to that question and ignored it.

Sal had moved to Lila in the fall shortly after our road trip. For months he'd been asking me to move down there with him. He'd call with stories of crazy parties, hikes up the volcano, bus trips to other cities. But I always refused.

I studied education in college and began student teaching that same fall. It was one of the most difficult periods of my life. Each day I went to school, I felt worse than the previous. I hated teaching, and schools, and ties, and pants with pleats, and people sitting around faculty rooms discussing prime-time TV and their boring-ass kids. But I hung in there. It was something I had to do or society would have shamed me even deeper into myself. And each time Sal called with another story about gorgeous Mexican women and lively cultural festivals in the town square, a large part of me wanted to hang up. I knew if I said yes, maybe I'd never be able to say no to anything ever again. I was doing bad—worse than I think even I knew. I was getting fall-down drunk every moment I had away from school. A lot of heavy drugs were being passed my way, and each time I refused them I felt less resolve to ever do so again. One night in particular, I was hanging out with a friend addicted to heroin—didn't drink, didn't smoke reefer or cigs—just shot H. I watched him cook up, pierce his skin, milk blood, and empty the evil liquid into his arm. He pulled out the syringe, removed the needle, licked it, and threw it behind his couch, then he took off his shirt and gave some contrived speech about the superiority of the human body on heroin, followed by an intense flexing session. After, he grabbed a small scooper, dipped it in the bag of China white, and presented it.

"Who wants some of this?"

"Willy'll do it," said a friend.

"Yeah, don't be a pussy," said another.

I was stoned and drunk and already living at the limit of sanity. I thought long and hard, then said "Sure" as casually as if he'd asked me if I wanted a bag of mixed nuts. But right at the final moment, as the scooper was a deep breath from my nostrils, I glanced at a husky friend lying on the floor—Junkyard Jake, we called him—who was barely conscious.

"Uh, Junkyard'll do it," I said.

I didn't think he'd agree, but Jake shrugged his shoulders and snorted the powder meant for my nose. I don't know what would have happened to me if I'd taken it. Maybe I would've liked it? Maybe I would've made it part of the routine? Maybe my dick would've grown six inches, and I'd be able to dunk a basketball with my nuts? Who knows? But what I did know was that ol' Junkyard wouldn't always be around to save me from myself.

Sal called a few days later: "Hey, you gotta get down here. I'm drinking a beer and walking around the streets in nothing but my underwear, and nobody's saying shit. The cops just drove by and kept right on going."

Goddamn it! I wanted to believe. But I thought of our road trip. I thought of the time he slammed me face-first on a bar alley street after we got into an argument over Iggy Pop's real name. The times he threatened to poison my food with magic mushrooms before I had a test or a class presentation. The times we'd stolen bikes or cars, took 'em for joy rides, and brought them back in the middle of the night. The houses we'd broken into just to prove we could . . .

"I'm in."

"Excellent! You should wire me the cash so I can pay the landlady for your room. This way it'll be ready before you get here."

And so it went . . .

Chapter 2

We followed the panteon walls back to the house. Cletus claimed the couch, and I walked into Sal's room. He had a king-size bed made of two twins put together but had split them up before Cletus and I left for the bar, and I lay down on the far half. This wouldn't have been necessary had the landlady honored my rent payment. But she'd taken my loot then rented the room to some German two weeks before I got there. I could take care of all that tomorrow though. For now, sleep, but only after checking the sheets for scorpions—my new bedtime routine no matter how desperate I was for slumber.

In the morning, I met the pale German occupying my room. He sat on the handmade loveseat in the living room, typing on a laptop and sucking the guts out of a cigarette. His name was Matthew, but we called him Mica after some miscommunication, and the name stuck. He didn't care either way. Mica donned similar style glasses to Jorg and even came from the same town in Germany, Essen. In his twenty-two years of life, Mica had already spent a year in Australia, where he became fluent in English, three weeks in Hong Kong, and several months wandering through Europe. Though he was German, he preferred speaking in English. This made my life easier. Since I was lowest in the house rankings, I asked Sal if he'd bring up my predicament to the reticent German. He complied.

"Hey, man," Sal said, "it looks like Maria rented out the same room to both of you. William already paid for it before you got here so he'd be all set up when he arrived."

"Oh, how unfortunate. Perhaps we should pay her a visit to amend the situation?"

Though I felt uncomfortable causing a stir, it was only right. The woman screwed us both. I hoped this wouldn't be the same for all future business deals in Mexico. Sal, Mica, and I set off for the landlady's house, and Cletus stayed home. We walked in the blistering heat and followed the panteon walls around the block. When we arrived, Sal tapped a key on the iron gate.

Maria called to us from the house, but I had no clue what she was saying. Mica's Spanish was as green as mine. He'd taken a yearlong prep course at a university in Essen before joining the study abroad program, putting him at about the same skill level as me. I'd studied Spanish for seven years through grammar and high school but hadn't taken a single class since.

Maria fumbled through the door and shuffled to the gate. She wore a light cotton dress, which hung from her wilted frame and flowed like her long unkempt gray hair. Two short fat dogs with matted fur followed behind, barking incessantly. She waited until she arrived at the gate to start speaking but didn't open it. She said something at us in Spanish, and only Sal responded.

Salvatore Juarez was a half-Mexican, half-Italian who grew up on the streets of Buffalo. The Mexican half of his family was from Guadalajara. Before beginning his studies with the Universidad, Sal knew about enough Spanish to converse with them—which was about the same that I knew. As he spoke to Maria, however, it was clear to me that he'd become near-fluent in the nine months he'd been in Lila. This gave me hope.

I tried my hardest to understand the conversation. Though I picked up several words, I had no idea how to piece them together. The more defeated I felt, the more my eyes wandered—and they found a feast. Maria's house was like an alternate Noah's Ark for all those creatures too strange to be granted permission to board with ol' Noah. Two balding rail-thin cats lounged on a window ledge just above a shirtless man sitting in a fold-out chair and staring into space. The man looked emaciated, and his torso revealed an abacus of ribs. His gaze was distant, likely taking him well beyond our frivolous matters with Maria and transporting him to another place entirely. He looked to be in his mid-fifties, but it was possible he was younger and had aged beyond his years. Judging by the sunken lines on his face, tremors in his hands, and intense distant gaze, I couldn't help but think this man was an addict or recovering addict of something.

The dogs kept barking long after we'd walked from the house.

"So, what'd she say?" I said.

"She said we'd have to take care of this on our own."

"That's it?" Mica said. "Seemed like she had a lot more to say than just that."

"She did mention that she had a few other properties she was renting and that we could check those out."

"I wouldn't mind moving if I had to," Mica said.

"Goddamn it!" I said. "She probably makes a killing screwing foreigners."

Sal got a phone call, spoke, and hung up. "That was my friend Jose. He wants to know if you guys wanna to go to El Campo today. There are some ruins there worth checking out."

"Well, my day is ruined anyways . . ." I said.

Sal laughed.

"I've got a lot of work to do, so you can count me out," Mica said.

We stopped by the house to get Cletus, then hiked up the dead-end hill, crossed Madrid del Rio, and hopped on a bus just outside the deportivo complex. The bus took us down Madrid del Rio through the commercial heart of town. We passed posh clothing stores, sushi bars, a megaplex movie theater, and a Super Walmart. We got out at the corner just before Walmart and waited for another bus. Soon, a rickety old blue jalopy came sputtering around the corner. We hopped on when it stopped, and it took us north. Though we passed some more businesses, this was mostly a residential area. Most homes were modest stone structures like those I'd already seen. Others, however, were gargantuan mansions resembling small palaces and were usually located behind high, thick stone walls with armed guards at the front gates.

We passed a main highway and left progress behind. We continued onto a dirt road and were enveloped with vegetation. The tree cover here was thick but thinned away, revealing great pastures just beyond where cows grazed and bulls rested. The road was full of potholes, some the size of a bathtub, and the driver made frequent turns to weave around them as we sputtered and bounced along. Our speed reduced as the scenery improved. We passed a terraced farm with three levels, each with soccer nets at its ends, just beyond a small stone farmhouse. In the distance was an enormous tree that towered over everything but the mountains beyond. The tree stood alone with strained limbs sagging toward the earth. Its massive branches grew from its trunk like trees of their own, and each spread out for a good fifty-feet before opening into a brilliant display of lush, green leaves.

The gorgeous countryside soon met a small rural town, which seemed frozen in time, and continued through it as though it were a lazy green river. We passed a shrine to the Virgin Mother decorated with flowers and strands of Christmas lights wrapped around its concrete frame. Several men rode by on horses, exchanging casual greetings with their townsfolk. The dirt road ended on the edge of town, and we were soon on cobblestones again. These stones, however, were in much more need of replacement than those in Lila. The town's name was El Campo, and it was unwittingly built over the buried ruins of an ancient civilization that weren't discovered until 1945. Though some of the town had been dug up to expose these ruins, there was only so much they could dig without having to evict the town's current residents.

We hopped off the bus at its first stop and were greeted by a tall, thin Mexican man named Jose. Though reserved, Jose wasn't the least bit shy. There was a subtle confidence and warmth about him, making him easy to like right away. We exchanged handshakes and hellos. I overheard Sal whisper something to him, and Jose nodded.

"Hey, Will," Sal said, "say 'quiero' then 'ver' and 'gas' all together."

"What's that mean? I want dicks or something?" I had a lot of experience with practical jokes and was pretty keen to them as they were unfurling.

"No, no, it means, 'I want to see gas.'"

"Why the hell you want me to say that?"

"Just do it."

"What the fuck: Quiero ver gas."

They started laughing.

"What the hell does it mean?"

"Verga is slang for dick. You just said, 'I want dicks.'"

"You guys are pretty classy."

Jose led us through the gate and inside the ruins. There was an entrance fee, but his aunt ran the town so we got in free. As a kid, Jose would come down to the ruins and seek out white foreigners in hopes they could teach him some English, which Jose spoke fairly well compared to the rest of the Mexicans I was soon to meet. He had a natural hunger for knowledge, which invigorated me. He guided us through the ruins and interrupted our inane chatter with interesting and informative stories about the pyramids, altars, and ball courts.

The sun was almost directly overhead and cooked my skin and even though I loved a challenge, the heat was too much. But it wasn't just the heat that got me. The humidity was brutal too. Cletus was feeling it as well, and soon we rode the rickety blue bus back to Lila.

The bus was hot and full of riders. Some teenage girls in catholic schoolgirl uniforms giggled and stared at us for the length of the trip. When we got off at a sandwich place, they followed behind, giggling and shouting words like "guapos" and "hermosos." I knew enough Spanish to smile at those words. They continued to shout words at us as they walked down the street. Day number two, and almost every girl I'd seen had been thus receptive to my pasty-white ass. I felt as sexy as a middle-aged Marlon Brando.

Regardless of any minor successes, I knew I'd need to figure out my living situation. Mica was typing on his computer when we got back.

"Maria stopped by while you guys were gone," Mica said. "She said she'd be by tomorrow to show us her other properties."

"Sal, we're going to the beach tomorrow, right?" Cletus said.

Sal didn't even look at him. "I wouldn't mind checking out houses tomorrow."

Cletus sighed.

That night, Sal, Cletus, Mica, and I went to Crystal, a trendy club teeming with teenybopper socialites looking to scale Lila's social hierarchy. We walked in after getting patted down at the door and headed for the bar where we were told we had to order from a waitress who'd bring us drinks. We flagged one down and made good use of the all-you-can-drink deal that came with the cover.

I scanned the room while sipping a Cuba Libre. Both stories were filled with ass-shaking Latinos. We were the only gringos in the crowd.

It didn't take long before we were dancing and didn't take long after that to find some girls. A tall one took a liking to me, and I ground sloppily on her leg.

"That is not how girls dance in this country," she said.

We kept downing Cuba Libres and the room kept spinning—clouds of fog, cheap laser lights, mirrors covering the walls . . . I was drunk on the moment. We got tired of dancing, ditched the girls, and headed back to the house to slug some caguamas.

I woke up the next morning to the sound of Sal and Cletus arguing in the living room.

"Can't you guys check out the houses tomorrow? You said we'd go to the beach today!"

"If you wanna go to the beach, take the damn bus."

"But I'm leaving *tonight!*"

"Nobody's stopping you from going . . ."

I could already tell it was gonna be a long day.

Maria stopped by a little while later and drove Sal, Mica, and me to another house. Cletus stayed behind, citing a bad stomach. I didn't blame him.

We drove along the panteon walls, made a turn at a small street taco stand, parked in front of a large pink house, and walked inside. It was huge—double the size of our current place. It had three bedrooms, a sizeable backyard, garage, washer and dryer, and my favorite feature: a dining room that looked as if it were dug into a cave. Sal did the talking.

"How much she say?" I said.

"Fourteen hundred pesos a month."

"That's cheap!"

"It's fourteen hundred per person."

"Isn't that standard?"

"It'll be fourteen hundred per person, for six people."

Ahh, there was the bullshit. She wanted to cram two sausages in each room.

"Or you could pay four thousand pesos and have your own room."

I laughed. I'd be out of cash in two months paying that much. Sal's reaction was similar. Mica, however, wasn't so hasty to decline.

Maria drove us back later. Cletus was on the uncomfortable sofa when we arrived. I sat next to him, and he handed me a note scribbled on a piece of graph paper.

"What's this?" I scanned it.

"That girl you were dancing last night with stopped by while you were gone. She wanted to see you. She left her phone number and email address."

"Christ, *I* don't even know the name of our street. How'd she find me?"

"She said you told her you were at the bottom of the dead end near the university."

"Crazy."

Just then, a clumsy fellow in a shirt and tie wandered up to the house. He held a briefcase in one hand and a bible in the other. I was the only person to acknowledge his presence; I met him on the sidewalk.

"Hello," he said.

"What's happenin', padre?"

"Do you believe in the lord jesus christ? If not, you must repent . . ."

I stared at him blankly. I could only make out a few words here and there. Normally, I would have sent the prick away. But I encouraged the conversation.

"Sorry, man," I said, in English, "I don't go for that guy like you do. We had a pretty ugly breakup."

"Here, take one of these. Read it every day."

He opened his briefcase, pulled out an annotated bible, and handed it over. I thumbed through it while he continued to speak. The images were rough crayon sketches that seemed to have been drawn by a precocious third grader. I could hear the guys cracking open beers in the living room. I kept flipping pages and stopped on a picture of christ carrying the cross—blood everywhere.

"I'd seen enough of this shit, man . . ." I tried handing it back to him, but he refused to take it.

I wanted to walk away but remained still. There was something about the man's demeanor that set me at ease. I knew I could fail a million times at conversation, but he wouldn't leave me hanging. We spoke like that for a good fifteen before the guys pushed out the front door, and he left.

Sal handed me a beer. "Who the hell was that?"

"The hell, that's who . . ."

We sucked down a few under the almond trees before dropping Cletus off at the bus station. The kid had the travelin' gene. I knew it wouldn't be long before he was in motion again. He ended up in Thailand a few months later after picking up a teaching gig there.

I wished him well before he left.

Chapter 3

When we got back from the bus station, Mica told us about a party going on that night at a fellow German's house. I was in, but Sal wasn't: "Paz's been ridin' me to take her to that new Julia Roberts flick . . ."

Mica and I drank a few caguamas under the almond trees before the party. The bats were out, and huge, and darting in and around us as we spoke—a few times almost making contact.

"Damn, fuckin' Bela Lugosi!" I ducked, almost spilling my beer, then bent over and scratched my legs.

"I've been thinking about that new place the inept one showed us today," Mica said. "I think I'm going to take it."

"Seems like a good place. I just don't trust that bitch." I kept scratching.

"Yeah, she does seem quite aloof. You know, you can use the washing machine whenever you'd like."

"Thanks, man, I appreciate that." I couldn't stop scratching. I examined my legs. "Goddamn, these bugs are eating me alive." I had at least fifty red bumps located mostly around the ankles of both legs.

"Yeah, the bugs are terrible. I've been here for two weeks now, and it's starting to slow down. I think they just like fresh blood. I've had some time to process the Mexican food through my system, and they're not biting as much."

"I hope that works 'cause I can't take much more of this shit."

We slugged through our caguamas. Mica finished first.

"Damn, you must be thirsty."

"Well, you know what they say: 'The German body runs on beer.'"

I laughed, caught up, and soon we were following the panteon walls to the party. Mica's friend lived a few houses from Maria. His name was Hans, and he was twenty-five and in Mexico on a vacation that never ended. Hans was swinging in a hammock under an awning in his driveway and chatting with his girlfriend, Daniela, when we showed up. I was envious of Hans for two reasons: the hammock and his girl. We must have been early because we were the only guests there. We slugged some caguamas as we spoke.

"When will the others arrive?" Mica spoke in English because we all at least knew some of it. Hans was quick to correct this error.

"We are in Mexico, please speak in Spanish." He said this in English, mind you. Hans spoke it well but practiced a "No English" policy, as did so many other English speakers in Mexico who would piss me off in the future. I valued the exchange of thoughts and feelings above a need to conform to trends. He replied once more in English, "They'll arrive soon. The party doesn't start for another half hour." He gulped his caguama, nearly tipping it back at a ninety-degree angle, then dragged on his cigarette. For some reason he was shirtless. He exhaled as he asked us, now in Spanish, "Have you met my girlfriend, Daniela?"

Mica and I shook our heads. We said hello to Daniela, and in our minds we all agreed—Hans included, I'm sure—that she was far too beautiful for him. Dark hair, cute face, great body . . . Hans lay there like a worm wrapped in a rainbow cocoon. He continued to suck at his cigarette. We banged our way through an awkward conversation before guests started to arrive. Hans kept mentioning something about the "extraneros." I asked what the word meant, and he said, "foreigners" or "foreign exchange students." Apparently, each semester brought with it a new wave of exchange students to the

Universidad, and this particular group loved to party. There were about forty in total. Most came from Central and South America, but there were a number of Germans, Brits, a Canadian, and a Nigerian. None, surprisingly, could claim the US as their home country. I liked that.

The extraneros showed up to the party in waves. The first I met were two lovely Colombian girls. They both had fair skin and round pretty faces, which I got to see up close when they each leaned in and kissed my cheek to say hello. This was a custom I could get used to. We sat together on wooden chairs outside and patiently struggled through a conversation, relying more on carnal instinct than a definitive verbal language. Neither of them spoke any English, so they were in no danger of breaking house rules.

My Spanish, however, was coming back to me now that I had a motive to remember it. The girls told me stories about Colombia. I understood every few words and through patience and hand gestures was able to pick up on the gist of what was said. Patience was key. Here I couldn't awkwardly machine-gun through a conversation just to finish it as I did back in the States. Anxiousness was to be expected, and patience was already built into the conversation. This set my mind at ease. I could focus more on the words I was saying than on how I was saying them, and I used those words I knew to tell the girls about myself. They asked what I was doing in Mexico. I smiled. That was a question I don't think I could have answered even in English. Soon I was throwing out words and phrases, and verb conjugations I hadn't used since fifth-period Spanish with Sra. Rodriguez. The human mind was a fascinating entity, and I was glad I hadn't yet completely destroyed my own.

Party people kept coming as the Colombians and I kept conversing. I met Peruvians, Argentines, a cluster of Germans, an Ecuadorian, more Colombians. They pushed into the house carrying bottles of liquor and beer, smoking cigarettes, and conversing in celebratory tones. When the music started, it didn't stop all night. My conversation with the Colombian girls ran dry at about the same time as did my caguama, so I followed the extraneros into the house to see what could be afforded. I did half a lap around a giant circular table separating the living room dance floor from the kitchen, and a cute girl handed me a glass filled with some kind of punch.

"What is this?"

"Ponche. You drink it."

I shrugged my shoulders and took it down the hatch. "ES FUERTE!" I shouted to match the party's energy.

"Jes, I know. You take more."

She shoveled back in the punch bowl and poured me another glass.

The crowd was multiplying on the dance floor. I pushed through it and found one of my Colombian princesses. She didn't mind me grinding on her. I could feel her body warming. Thank god I'd made it through the question and answer round. This one took far less energy. Though I felt an intense freedom dancing with that gorgeous girl, I couldn't help but feel trapped in some new and specific way. There was no way to really know her, and there was no way for her to know me—at least, not in that moment. I chugged the rest of my ponche.

The Colombian and I got separated between bathroom breaks. In my drunken wandering, I met a Mexican girl named Juana. She spoke some English.

"Hola, gringo, how are you?" she said.

"Bien. What's that word, 'gringo' mean?"

"Someone from the United States."

"Well, how'd you know I was from the United States?"

"Only a gringo wears his hat backward."

"I don't think I like that word."

"Is not bad. Just means 'foreigner,' really. Nada feo."

"So, this must be a gringo party, then?"

"Jes, and they are the best! The gringos party harder than anyone else! I prefer for to be with them."

Though she spent most of her time with the extraneros, she

wasn't one herself. Juana was a full-blooded Mexican born and raised on the cobblestone streets of Lila. She wasn't the only local I'd met who hung with such a transitory group. These Mexicans who were drawn to foreigners intrigued me. These who made friends with the fleeting, who invested time in the transitory, energy in the ephemeral. What did she stand to gain from a group who'd likely be gone in a college semester? Was she onto something here? I knew the answer to that question and did my best to ignore it.

Juana was a fun and personable girl even though she was prone to whining. There was a spark to her—a desire for something more but nothing resembling greed. Something about her put me at ease but also provoked my inner devil. I liked Juana right away.

Mica and I were some of the last guests to leave the party. We walked together along the panteon walls and were soon home. I felt good about my minor success in communicating with the Colombians and in meeting some new people. There was still so much to learn. I wished I could fast-forward a few months to where I could at least speak Spanish at a conversational level, but I allowed those thoughts to rest. I checked my half of Sal's bed for scorpions and went to sleep.

Mica moved out the next morning. He didn't have many possessions, just an old leather suitcase and his computer, and after a half hour of packing, not a trace of him was left in the house. Sal and I wanted to help him move, but we had other matters to attend to that afternoon. It was Paz's twenty-fourth birthday, and we had a lot to prepare. Jose's aunt owned a bar in El Campo, and she closed it to the public that night so that we could hold a proper fiesta. Sal's friend Javier, who was also friends with Paz, said he'd drive us around to pick up what was necessary for the party.

Javier showed up just past noon. He hopped out of his truck and staggered up the front walk. Javier was a small man with sharp facial features. He exuded energy and carried a perpetual smile, which seemed his default expression. It was as if he'd consciously blocked out sadness and had himself convinced he could achieve this impossible goal simply by smiling. And Javier was smiling, and smiling hard as he staggered toward us. He looked drunk, and judging by the full forty-ounce bottle of Sol he was carrying, it looked as if he planned to stay that way the rest of the afternoon. He walked up to Sal and gave him a big hug.

"What's *up*, cabron!" Javier said.

"Chillin', Javie. How you been?" Sal pulled away from Javier's clutches.

"Eh, you know . . . So this must be Will!" Before I had time to object, Javier grabbed my arm, pulled me to him, and hugged me. "Cabron!" It was clear to me this was his catchphrase.

We squeezed inside the cab of the small truck, and Javier grabbed some plastic cups off the floor. He gave one to Sal and one to me, and filled them with his caguama.

"This is the way to start an afternoon!" I said before taking a gulp.

"Get used to it. It's not illegal for passengers to drink in a car in Mexico," Sal said.

We brought our drinks together for a festive "Salud!" then hit the road. I could get used to this.

We sped along the cobblestone streets, swerving every so often as Javie gulped his beer. We stopped first at a pasteleria to check out some cakes. Though Sal had his wallet set on the cheapest one in the display case, the pretty woman behind the counter guilt-tripped him into buying the most deluxe confection in the place. People often seemed perplexed by those who swung between the extremes, but they made perfect sense to me. Sal was one of those cats who'd just as soon max out his credit card to stay in a five-star hotel's penthouse suite as he would sleep in a cardboard box in the alley out back. Maybe that's why we were friends?

The lady wrapped up the overpriced hunk of sugar, and we set off again in our rolling bar. Our next stop was for the piñata. We drove to el Centro, or the town center, and stopped in front of a small stone house with a dirt floor. We walked inside and were enveloped in weirdness. There, hanging from the wooden rafters, were several dozen piñatas swaying in the breeze. It looked as if some medieval king had just put down a rebellion, and we'd stumbled upon the gallows after sentencing. But instead of people, this rebellion seemed to to have been led by frogs, and pigs dressed like princesses, and a giant apple. Sal approached the man as he was pasting up the guts of an elephant, and soon we walked out of there with a chiva, or goat.

On the way to the truck, we passed a hardware store, and I asked Sal and Javier to follow me inside. I sent Sal to find the thickest plastic tubing in the place while I went for their biggest funnel. I paid for both and explained to Javie what they'd be used for on the way back to his truck.

Javier dropped us off under the almond trees, and Sal and I went inside the house. I boiled some water to assemble the funnel, and Sal grabbed his guitar. When I finished with the funnel, Sal told me to grab my guitar too. He wanted to play a song for Paz that night and needed me for rhythm while he did a solo. We'd played in a band with a few other guys during our senior year in college—Sal on bass, me on rhythm guitar. We'd just started to hit our groove when graduation tossed us, and our instruments, out on the street. It was one of the most potent time periods of my life, and I still didn't believe it to be completely over.

Sal started with three simple chords, which didn't change through the song: E minor, C, and G. Then the words: "I see you at my door/I know just where you wanna go/But night falls down/And can't this wait another day . . ." The song had a great rhythm and melody.

When we finished, we put the guitars down.

"You write that?" I said.

Sal shook his head.

"Who did?"

Sal said nothing and walked away.

I put my guitar away and decided to settle into my new room. I unpacked my big blue bag, put new sheets on the bed, and hung up my clothes in the closet. The room was small but had a high ceiling on the far end that sloped down to the wall near the door, making it feel larger than it was. There was a jalousie window in that wall, but all the glass panels were missing, leaving a big opening between my room and the hallway. There was a clear shot from that window to another across the hall leading to the outside. None of the windows in the house had glass; all but mine were simply large openings with security bars around them. Anything small enough to fit between those bars could slither its way inside. I hadn't noticed this until that afternoon. I checked under the bed just to be sure . . .

I could hear Sal playing guitar in his room. Though the door was closed, and he wasn't playing loudly, I could hear all his words: "Can't this wait another day . . ." He finished the song and started it again. Then came the music from his speakers: "Can't this wait another day. . ." I knew that voice. It was Ian Warsaw. Ian went to high school with us in Buffalo and was Sal's best friend. After high school, Ian tramped it out to California. He lived on the streets in Venice Beach and started to make a name for himself playing his songs at local bars. The kid had a golden voice for rock—raspy and soulful with just the right amount of desperation. He signed with a major record label that asked him to assemble a band. Ian asked Sal to join before asking anyone else. Sal played a mean bass and would have done the group justice.

But Sal said no. And he never gave a reason why—at least, he never gave *me* a reason. Ian's group got pretty big in 2002. Their first album sold over four hundred thousand copies, and they had a few songs move up the Mainstream Rock chart. But this never seemed to bother Sal—a kid who lived for music. He just stayed there in his bedroom that afternoon, playing along with that song over and over . . .

I fell asleep in my new bed and woke when a driver started honking out front. Sal poked his head through the open space in my wall.

"Yo, Marco's here to bring us to the party."

"Wha—Okay, gimme a few minutes to take a shower."

"No, man, the party's starting soon. We gotta get going."

"But you didn't tell me he was coming, and I look like hell." It was true. I was in nothing but a sweat-stained yellow t-shirt and a pair of cotton gym shorts.

"You look fine—let's go. Grab your guitar."

Marco laid on the horn.

"Fuck it." I hopped out of bed, put on a hat, grabbed my guitar and the funnel, and we hit the road. We picked up Mica, then drove down Madrid del Rio and made a right just before the Super Walmart. The sky drizzled, as it had all day. Marco took us past the posh boutiques and row of mansions, and soon we were swallowed in the dark void leading to El Campo.

When we emerged from the darkness, we parked in front of a pair of heavy wooden doors attached to a high brick wall. We pushed through the doors and entered an open space alongside a covered bar area. Jose waved at us from behind the bar, and we walked over.

Paz and her guests were seated around a long series of tables that had been pushed together. There were maybe twenty-five guests in all, but more came in behind us, all dressed nicely. I looked down at my gym shorts and sighed. Sal looked at them and laughed.

Paz sat at the head of the table. She was a petite morena with sharp facial features and deep, dark eyes which were somehow pronounced even amid the rest of her natural beauty. She was a business student at the Universidad and wanted to open her own clothing store in Lila when she graduated. For someone who studied business, she should have seen a bad deal as it approached, but she just sat there as Sal walked over and gave her a kiss.

Sal introduced us, and we kissed cheeks, then Paz introduced me to a group of her friends. Marta had kind eyes, but it seemed that could only remain so by her refusal to ever look at a single thing ugly. I kissed her cheek and said hello. Sofia was tall and pretty. I'd seen a picture of her on Sal's wall before that night and couldn't wait to meet her. She seemed kind too, but in a similar way to Marta. I kissed her cheek as well. Tito was lively and loud but underneath the celebrative exterior had a quiet dogmatism that threatened to erupt into ruthless contention at the slightest hint of a challenge. There was something about that quality I admired. He seemed the type who'd never be taken alive without a fight. I leaned forward to kiss his cheek, out of rote and nervousness, but stopped myself before planting one. He smiled. Javier arrived later with a notably thin, almost emaciated, man named Edgar. Javier introduced us, and we shook hands.

Sal sat beside Paz at the head of the table among the heaviest concentration of guests. Mica and I walked to the opposite side and found our rightful place separated from the rest of the party. Marta broke from the group and sat next to me.

Mica scanned the menu. "What's a michelada?"

"A michelada has beer, chili, ice, and salt," Marta said.

"Is it any good?"

"You should try one."

Mica and I each got a michelada, which was served in a large Styrofoam cup with a lid and a straw. I took one sip and nearly spit it on the floor.

"God, that's like spicy ocean water."

"It's not so bad." Mica took a big slurp.

"Do you want some?" I pointed my cup in Marta's direction.

"No thanks, I don't drink."

"Like hell you don't." I shot her a smile.

She shot back. "Okay, maybe I'll just have a beer."

"Yo, Jose, two beers!" My Spanish was coming around . . . I set my michelada in front of the thirsty German, and it soon disappeared.

Time passed, and the empties piled up on the table. I looked to its far end. Civilization. There was a gap between us as if two separate parties were going on: one in Spanish and the other in terrible Spanish. We kept ordering drinks. I'd forgotten about the funnel but pulled it out from under the table after Marta accidentally kicked it and asked what in the hell it was. I explained how to use it and took a beer down as an example. Marta's eyes lit up. Soon, she was on her knees and sucking plastic. Then Mica went. Then me again. Some other guests saw us and wandered over curiously. I initiated several more people to the way of the funnel before a dance contest began on the dance floor. First, the girls danced. There was no standout among them, but one girl was sexy as hell, so when the crowd voted for the winner with their applause, the men gave her a standing ovation.

Then it was the guys' turn. Neither Mica nor I made any motion toward the floor. We knew our place at the party. When the music started, the guys took off. They all knew what they were doing—but Tito knew it best. Sometime during the previous week I'd heard Sal mention something about Tito's supreme dancing ability but had no idea the extent of it. Tito lit across the floor like a firecracker. He spun around, stuck his ass in our direction, and shook it at a speed that would make even Ricky Martin blush. The crowd quickly voted the others away, and the finals fell between Tito and the goddess he most likely cared nothing for standing beside him. When the music started this time, Tito worked himself into such a frenzy that his rival stopped dancing and just watched him in awe as he twirled and ass-shook his way to certain victory. To celebrate his win, Tito did a split, but in doing so kicked the legs of a table behind him where two of the more elegantly dressed guests were seated, sending their drinks and tapas into their laps. Tito smiled, then quickly walked away. He was definitely my kind of people.

The music started and everyone danced, this time Mica and me included. I'd occasionally stop dancing to get another beer for the funnel and present it to the crowd. Someone would always drop to their knees and take one down. I approached Marta with one, but she waved me away. I pulled a coin out of my pocket and said, "Heads you drink, tails, me."

She nodded, and I flipped the coin. I caught it and put it on the back of my hand, but before I could see its face, Marta took it from me and said, "This is a twenty-peso piece. These are rare."

I decided to do the funnel myself. When I finished, I asked

Marta for my coin. She just stared at me blankly. Jose walked over and mentioned something about me owing three hundred pesos for all the beers I'd washed through the funnel, and I pretended not to understand and walked away.

The party continued to get rowdy until Jose stopped the music. He said something to the crowd, and they gathered around Paz and started singing as Jose brought out the fancy cake. He held it carefully, but when he stepped on the dance floor, he slipped and dropped the cake on the ceramic tile. Sal yelled out "Fuck!" while the rest of us laughed. One of the other bartenders, a big teddy bear of a guy, scooped the cake off the ground. He carried it to the back where I assumed he'd throw it out, but minutes later he came around the opposite side of the dance floor with it still in hand. He snuck up behind Jose and smashed it on his head. Everyone laughed again, this time Sal included. Jose picked up a piece of cake and chased after his coworker, inducing an all-out cake fight. Everyone was clawing at the cake, ripping out huge chunks to throw or smash in someone's face. I grabbed a piece and approached Sal, but when I extended my arm to smash it in his hair, I slipped on some frosting and punched it in his eye. He shouted, "Son of a bitch!" then scooped up a piece with both hands and dumped it on my head. The floor was slippery, and people started falling in huge chunks of cake and spilled beer. Though everyone was covered in frosting, no one seemed to care.

When people tired of the cake fight, they walked to the open area where the chiva was tied to a tree. Jose put a blindfold on Paz, spun her around, and handed her an aluminum broom handle. She took a big cut and hit the piñata, but not enough force to spill its guts. Next up was Tito, but he missed each time he swung. He handed the broom to one of the girls. No success. They passed the broom around like that, and soon it came to me. I took a big cut and connected, coming down on it as if I were chopping wood, but while I didn't break the piñata, I did split the broom handle in half. I picked up the other half from the ground and took another swing. Again nothing. I felt a sharp pain in my hand, which started gushing blood. I looked at the broom handle in the bloody hand and noticed a sharp edge where it had been split in half, and right where I was holding it. I walked to a table, grabbed a napkin, and held it in my hand.

"Let me see it," Jose said.

"No, it's fine. It was a clean cut," I said.

"I insist."

I removed the napkin and showed him. He called to the teddy bear to grab the first aid kit. The crowd started to back away from me while looking on with dreadful eyes. I could hear them whispering, see them pointing. They acted as though my hand had been chopped off, and I was holding it in my other. Someone whispered to Sal, and he roared with laughter as he approached me.

"What the hell's going on, Sal?"

"Yo, you're not going to believe this," Sal said. "Apparently, Cletus told everyone that you have SIDAS, or AIDS. They don't know what to do."

"Tell them it's a lie!"

Sal addressed the group, assuring them I was free of SIDAS, and soon the party resumed. I was angry at Cletus, then remembered the time in college when Sal and I picked the lock of Cletoid's bathroom door and took turns upper-decking his toilet. I smiled.

Someone broke the piñata with the untainted half of broom, and the masses dove at its bounty. After, we returned to the bar area to watch Paz open her gifts. Sal and I broke out our guitars, and Sal sang to her. The moment passed quickly, and I put my guitar back in its sarcophagus.

The drizzle had been coming down all day but suddenly turned into a downpour. Sofia was the first in the rain. She dashed out to the open area and let the water wash away the cake. Marta, Tito, and Paz joined in. A part of me wanted to join them but another remained still. I stood there and observed as the party moved from the bar to the muddy grass area. The well-dressed partiers had traded cake for mud as an adornment to their clothes. They wrestled and danced and slid through the grass on bare feet as if they truly were children of the earth. Paz held her hands up to the sky as the clouds dumped everything they had. She'd tried multiple times to get a visa to visit the US. She had family in Denver she hadn't seen in years. She also wanted to meet Sal's family in Buffalo. But each time she was denied. The same with Marco, and Marta, and Sofia. All denied. They filled out the paperwork, went through the proper channels, paid the hefty fees . . . and here I was drinking their beer and eating their food. As much as I wanted to, I couldn't join them in that storm.

Eventually the muddy people made their way back to the bar. I filled another funnel and presented it to Marta. She looked dizzy.

"Here, this'll help clear your head."

She pushed it away. "My mother will be so upset that I'm drunk."

"Your mother's probably sucking tube right now too." Big mistake. I said that just as the song ended. Several people heard me and gave me the worst looks.

"Oh, sorry . . ." I said.

Marta just stared vacantly. I got another round of evil-eyes from the partiers, but soon the smiles returned. I think Sal could see that everyone was letting it go, and he stepped in.

"Did he really say, 'Your mother is sucking tube?'" He walked to the center of the action and addressed the crowd like some fucked-up politician, never even looking at Marta. "What's wrong with this guy? Your mother's a nice person, and she doesn't have to put up with that."

"Hey, man, why don't you cool it with that shit. I said I was sorry."

Marta's dry eyes began to moisten, and she ran into the women's room. Paz followed behind.

"Yo, man, that ain't cool," I said. "You made her cry."

"No, *you* made her cry. You need to learn two rules to survive in Mexico: one, don't talk about someone's girlfriend, and two, *never* talk about someone's mother."

Marta and Paz emerged from the bathroom about twenty minutes later. The party was dead. Jose again approached me about my tab.

"You drank thirty beers. That's four-hundred and eighty pesos."

"Hey, I didn't drink 'em all." I pointed at Marta as Marco carried her out on his shoulder. "You want your money, you can get it from her. I know she's good for at least twenty pesos."

I forked over two hundred, and we called it even. Marco took Sal and the girls home, leaving me, Javier, Edgar, and the German behind.

"Hey, cabrones, you want to continue the party?"

"Do Mexican chicks love denim?" I said.

Mica laughed.

Javie stared at me. "What does that mean?"

"It means yes, cabron," I said.

"Where we going?" Mica said.

"You'll see . . ." Javie said.

I went to the bathroom to wash the cake off my face, and then we took off into the night. Javier's truck was too small for four passengers, so I volunteered to sit in the bed. The stars were full and brilliant in the sky, casting a dull glow on the mountains and fields below. The grass towered over the truck bed's walls, dripping rainwater inside. I fought the urge to leap out and run screaming into the wilderness. What the hell was I doing? Where the hell were we going? I lay in the bed to rest my mind.

Soon I could see neon lights. Javier parked behind a building, and we got out. I was still covered in frosting, but so was Mica. We walked to the door and got patted down by security, then walked inside. The place was nice: AC, flatscreen TVs above the bar, twenty-foot stripper pole—not what I would have expected based on the shit I'd seen in the movies.

We sat at a table and ordered a cubeta, or bucket of beer. Javier called a well-endowed woman in a bikini over, and they had a brief conversation, periodically pointing at me. I could only guess their words:

"So, it's this guy's birthday, huh?"

"Yeah, you should give him a free dance."

"Why's he covered in cake?"

"He likes to party."

"Looks like it . . ."

Or maybe he was asking about a dance for himself in the back room? I wondered if Sal and the others were wrong about him. But I didn't have much time to think about that. The woman approached me and said something too quickly for me to understand. I looked at Javier for assistance, but he just kept nodding his head and smiling. She said something again, and my head nodded as my eyes followed her bouncing breasts. She hopped on the table, took off her top, and started dancing. Fuck! This was going to be expensive. Might as well enjoy it. She bent down and slapped my face with her tits.

When the song ended, she hopped down from the table, said something to me, and held out her hand. Again, I looked at Javier.

"She wants you to pay her," Javie said.

"How much?" I said.

"One hundred pesos, cabron."

"Hey, man, you called her over. We should split this."

"You pay."

"Bah . . ."

I forked over the loot, and she walked her hourglass ass away. In a couple of hours, I was out three hundred pesos. There was no way I could keep this up. I needed to make three hundred last a week.

Javier drove us home a short time later. I was angry at myself for not taking better care of my finances. I unlocked the front gate and door and walked inside.

Something about the house felt different. I walked to my new room and undressed. Though exhausted, I searched my sheets for scorpions. None. Then under the bed. Nothing. I turned out the light and hopped into bed. Then it began: Are you sure you checked under the bed? Those things are small, man, you might have missed one. What about inside the pillowcase? Or the closet? Lots of hiding places there . . .

Fuck. This wasn't good. The evil thoughts were back and rushing me all at once—perhaps to punish me for trying to get away?

Scorpions can climb, Willy. Keep your damned hands away from the walls. And, fuck, the bedframe! You're not safe here, man. No matter how thorough your inspection, a scorpion can climb up that frame at any time and snuggle with you all night.

The room was pitch-black. I held my hand an inch from my face, but I couldn't see it. Everything started spinning. The bed gave out and fell into the void that had grown around me. I wasn't whole. I wasn't human. I was a nervous fucking cloud of dark energy, expanding and collapsing on itself.

Don't touch the cool parts of the sheets, man. A scorpion might have crawled there since you'd moved your leg . . .

I heard a noise that sounded like someone tapping their keys on the front gate.

Did I lock the damned door?

But, fuck, Jorg said not to. If there's another earthquake, we're gonna need to get out in a hurry. And what if the volcano blows? How much time would we need to get away?

I drifted inward—always inward. My whole life stuck inside. Then it hit me: you've got nowhere left to run. I couldn't sleep. I couldn't think. How could anyone live like this?

Chapter 4

In the morning, my brain felt crippled and ready to seize like a car engine running without oil. It seemed that any movement would only bring me a step closer to total collapse. But I thought of Paz's party and the beauty surrounding me in Lila, and I got out of bed.

Sal was cooking in the kitchen.

"What up, Barry Bolognese?" he said.

"Not much, Gruce Gruber," I said.

Sal and I called each other random names sometimes. We just started doing it one day, and it took off from there.

"Gruce?" he said.

"Yeah, like 'Bruce' but with a 'G.'"

We both laughed.

"What are you making?" I said.

He showed me the box of a frozen pizza. "Want half?"

"Sure."

Sal opened the oven door and unwrapped the pizza—but he didn't put it inside. Instead, he rolled several paper towels like tortillas and slid them through the hole in the broom cap. He lit the paper towel roll with a match and turned on the oven, then he backed away and stuck the flaming paper wad inside. Nothing happened. I could hear the hiss of gas filling the oven.

"Just watch . . ." he said.

Suddenly, a fireball shot six feet into the kitchen. I could feel its shock wave.

"Goddamn, man," I said, "was that thing designed by Lockheed Martin?"

"No, the pilot light doesn't work, and this is the only way to heat it."

"Doesn't that waste a lot of gas though?"

"Probably. We're almost out now actually. I'll call the gas company to fill us up—"

"What do you mean, 'fill us up?'"

"There's a tank on the roof. When it runs low, they drive their truck over and fill up the tank."

We ate our pizza in the living room. Sal turned on the TV, but it wouldn't stay on.

"Damn it. This piece of shit hasn't worked since someone dumped a beer on it at our last party."

"What's the problem?"

"It turns on, but doesn't stay on."

I got up and studied the TV for a moment then took a toothpick off the coffee table and wedged it in the On/Off button. The TV went on and stayed on.

"Mystery solved, Sherlock Columbo."

Sal tossed a disc from his *Simpson's* Season Two set in the DVD player, and we watched while we ate. When the episode finished, we put our plates in the sink, which was filled with dirty dishes. A team of ants worked together to pick them clean.

"Fuckin' Jorg, man!" Sal said. "He always makes this nasty-ass macaroni and beef shit but never does the dishes. I should put these on his bed."

"Let's do it."

"He locks his door."

"When has that stopped you before?"

I'd seen Sal pick a number of locks but never with intent to cause any serious damage or to steal anything of importance. It was usually just for kicks—for practical jokes or to prove he could do it.

"Naw, fuck it. He's going back to Germany soon anyways." He washed Jorg's dishes. "You should get ready. My friend Herb is coming by on his lunch break to take us to find jobs."

"That the dirty, old man?"

"The one and only."

This was great! Sal had told me several stories about this guy, and I couldn't wait to meet him. Herbert Goldberg was born in Chicago to a life of wealth and privilege. His grandfather made a fortune selling steel during World War II. Though Herb could have had anything he wanted, six years back he gave it all up to stuff into a studio apartment in this small Mexican town where he was well-known for being a scumbag. Herb knew every gutter in Lila, every whore by name, every secret handshake and special knock. He'd been thrown out of countless parties by Paz and her friends for telling dirty jokes or starting fights or showing up with toothless prostitutes. And despite this horrid reputation, ol' Herbert held one of the most respected jobs in town. He headed the English Department at the prestigious Academia de Lila, an exclusive private high school where the progeny of Lila's privileged class studied. He was the guy to know if you wanted to make connections. And he was using his lunch break that day to help us do just that.

I had to get ready, so I lit the pilot light on the water heater out back, waited a few minutes, then hopped in the shower. The heater didn't have much time to do its thing, but the sun had been beating down on the water tank on the roof, so the water wasn't too cold. After I toweled off, I put on my nicest clothes: a light cotton button-down shirt I'd gotten at Goodwill, some old, ripped jeans, and my only pair of dress shoes.

An old lime green Buick crept down our dead-end street and stopped under the almond trees. A large, middle-aged man, who was bald in front and had a long ponytail in back, got out. He sucked the last drag of a cigarette, tossed it on the cobblestones, and approached us. He looked as if he'd been styled by a cashier at a truck stop outside of Albuquerque. He wore a purple t-shirt with an iron-on wolf in the center over some faded blue jeans and Velcro sandals. He had the size of a guy you'd expect to reminisce about the good ol' days playing second-string defensive tackle for a high school football team but now had a bad back and solid gut, pushing the wolf ahead of him as he walked—but that was the only spot on his body where fat seemed to collect. In fact, if you looked at the guy from behind, you might think he was actually in shape. He moved calmly, with no sense of haste. At first glance, I thought he might have just been a tourist. Perhaps he'd stopped to ask for directions? All he was missing to complete the getup were some socks under the sandals, a wide brim hat, a fanny pack, and a spread of zinc for his pink schnoz. Certainly this couldn't be the man who caused Paz to shudder when Sal'd mentioned his name at the party the night before?

"Javier told me you give the best roadhead out of all the fairies in Lila, Sally."

This is the guy!

Herb moved his head from side to side as he spoke as if he were trying to avoid the recoil of all the hideous things shooting from his mouth.

"I bet that makes you jealous, doesn't it, old man?" Sal said.

"Well, handjobs were really always my forte."

They both laughed. Herb was a man of contradictions: self-righteous yet tolerant; aspiring yet indifferent; disgusting but oversexed. He was a tie-dyed, aging flower child—a Deadhead who'd seen over a hundred shows while Jerry was still rockin'. But he was also an old-school Chicago hardcase who had no problems smacking the shit out of anyone who got too far out of line for his liking. I liked him right away.

"How was the party yesterday?" Herb said.

"It was good," Sal said.

"Paz still got those knees locked tight?"

"Don't worry about that, you horny old fuck."

Herb looked at me. "So, this must be your buddy Will." He stuck out his hand. "Nice to meet you."

We shook.

"Nice to meet you too. So, what's the plan today?" I said.

"Well, I figured I'd take you guys around to apply at some language schools. There aren't many people here who speak English, so you've got an advantage. The only problem is that most schools just started their fall semester last week, so they've probably already done their hiring."

"Shit, I hope we find something," I said. "I only have enough cash on me to last the next few months."

"How good is your Spanish?" Herb said.

Sal laughed.

"Not so bueno," I said.

"It might be difficult for you to find anything given your limited Spanish. And, if the employer wants you to, you also might need to get some special papers signed to work here legally. Sal, you got your papers, right?"

"Papers? I'm a citizen." Sal showed Herb his pasaporte. He had dual citizenship. If it came down to one job opening between us, I don't think my teaching experience would put me ahead.

We piled inside Herb's Buick, which he and Sal referred to as "Abuelita," and took off. We headed down Madrid del Rio, made a right before the Super Walmart, and passed the row of mansions.

"What do you think places like that go for around here?" I said.

"I don't know. Probably a coupla mil US?" Herb said.

"There seems to be a lot of money in this town."

"Well, Lila's one of the wealthiest cities and states in Mexico— one of the safest too. There's an excellent standard of living here."

"What's the main industry?"

"Drogas, whey. You can't build a house like that on a teacher's salary. Hell, not even a doctor could put up the cash for one of those palaces. It's either drug dealers or corrupt politicians building those. Lila is fairly well-known as being a sort of retirement community for narcos. They play the game elsewhere, make the big bucks, then move to places like Lila to get away from the filth and violence, which is why it's one of the safer spots in Mexico. There aren't many kidnappings or murders here."

"I guess sometimes it's best to erect condos in the lion's den, huh?" I said.

Herb laughed, then pointed to a wall just after the row of mansions.

"There are probably some sick mansions behind that wall too, only you can't see 'em. That's a big difference between the US and Mexico. People up there are lookin' to max out their credit cards and show off everything they got, especially when they don't got shit. Down here, people feel more ashamed to flaunt their wealth. There's probably more hidden money around here than you'd expect." He pointed at a row of hip bars and posh boutiques on the other side of the street. "See those places?"

"Yeah," I said.

"See anybody inside?"

I took a good look. "Nope."

"If you looked again tomorrow, it'd be the same thing. Same thing with next week, next month, next year. Those places were designed to fail. The narcos buy 'em with dirty money and use 'em as a front to launder it. There's so much happening right beneath the surface. You just need to know how to look at it."

Herb pulled in front of a small language school, and Sal and I hopped out.

"Yo, you're gonna have to carry this conversation," I said to Sal. "I don't want them knowing how bad my Spanish is."

"Yeah, whatever, I'll take care of it."

We walked inside, and I was in it. Sal approached the front desk, and I trailed behind. He spoke with the cute girl behind the counter for a few minutes before she pointed for us to sit. Soon, a middle-aged woman in a business suit called us to her office. We walked inside and sat in front of her desk. I was so nervous I had difficulty processing, "Como te llamas?"

"Uh, W—Will."

"Nice to meet you, Will."

That was it for me and the conversation. I was down for the count a few seconds into the fight. Sal answered all her remaining questions. While this allowed me some relief, it also made me nervous. What if he took the only job they had?

I fought this fear by pretending to participate in the conversation, which I did by mimicking Sal. When he smiled, I smiled; when his eyes lit up, I twinkled mine; when he furrowed his brow, I followed. I picked up words here and there, and based on those and the general feeling in the room, I could tell we were out of luck. The interview lasted a good ten minutes, and soon we were walking back to Abuelita.

"So, what did she say?"

"She said they started their semester last week, and they didn't need any more teachers. She also said we'd probably hear the same thing anywhere we go."

"Damn it, Herb was right."

We piled in the car and informed Herb of our defeat.

"It's gonna be tough, man, but there are still a few places we can try. I know a school downtown we could check out," Herb said.

Herb drove us to el Centro. The buildings were gorgeous—the cathedral, the old palace, the shops around the village square . . . In the center was a gazebo surrounded by large shade trees and wrought iron benches where couples sat, both old and young, to share each other's company.

Herb continued driving south, just past the city center. This was a different scene: junkies and prostitutes everywhere.

"The people here are proud to say that Lila is The Lime Capital of the World," Herb said. "But what they won't tell you is that it's also The Meth Capital of the World—or of Mexico, at least. Something like forty percent of the addicts here are crankheads. It's nasty stuff. The Chinese ship the chemicals through the Port of Zambulla, then the narcos cook it in labs in the mountains. It's gotten so bad, workers at department and hardware stores won't let you buy more than a coupla light bulbs at a time."

We stopped at a red light, and an emaciated woman covered in skin lesions approached the car. Herb waved his finger at her and rolled up the window.

"Fuckin' tranny whore."

"How'd you know she was a tranny?" I said.

"The hands, man. They don't lie. Small hands, she could be legit, but big hands, no chance of a clit. That dude got the old snip and tuck. This town's crawlin' with trannies, man. Sometimes it's tough to sniff 'em out."

"Sounds like you got a confession to make, huh, Herby?" Sal said.

"Hey, trannies are people too," he said.

We pulled in front of another school, got out, went through the same charade, and came out with the same result. We piled back inside Abuelita and took off. We passed another school with the name *Lengua* written on a sign out front, but Herb didn't have time for us to go in, so he kept driving. Soon we rolled down our dead-end street, and Herb dropped us off below the almond trees. Before I got out of the car, Herb gave me a piece of paper with his number on it. "If you ever want to see the way things really are, give me a call. I'll show you the underbelly of Lila."

I got out, and Herb drove away. I wasn't sure how a man in Velcro sandals could be so damned self-assured in his strange take on life. Perhaps his was some form of perverted messiah complex? Herb left me with many questions but the most pressing seemed to be, did Herby reject America, or did America reject Herb? If I was going to find answers to any of those questions, I knew I was going to have to change the way I saw things.

The sun was bright and gorgeous in the sky. I thought of the endless possibilities, of all I could and should be doing that afternoon. But the sun was also intense. I walked in the house and put on a movie. I'd figure out something. But there was little else for me to be doing that afternoon.

Chapter 5

That night, Sal and I headed over to Mica's new place to help him celebrate his move. On the walk, we passed our neighbor's husky, Beethoven, who frequently patrolled the neighborhood. Beethoven was kind but terrified of humans. Whenever we tried to pet him, he'd always run away.

We continued up the street past the loncheria and came across a large wall spanning several lots. I peeped through a gap between two iron doors attached to the wall, and on the other side was a sprawling mansion hidden from the street. Its grounds were all done up to the nines with colors and landscaping and exotic birds flying over misty rainbows. Across from that wall was a row of well-kept houses, but one lay in ruins. Sal saw me staring at the rubble.

"In two thousand three, a huge earthquake rocked this town, and they're still rebuilding."

Sal bent over and grabbed a stone off the street when we approached its end.

"What's that for?" I said.

"You'll see . . ."

Just then, a large and vicious dog started barking at us from someone's front yard. It lunged forward and Sal cocked his arm, but he dropped the stone when he saw the dog was chained.

"You should always be ready around here. That dog's insane,

and it's not even the worst I've seen roamin' these streets. The people down here don't know how to care for their pets."

We turned left on Ignacio Sevilla, a palm-lined main road running perpendicular to Madrid del Rio. There was a billboard above a business on that road with a picture of a smiling Brad Pitt. As I passed that sign, I often wondered what Mr. Pitt thought about having his likeness spread thin across the world in so many places he'd likely never visit. We walked down that street and made a right at the taco stand on Mica's corner.

We picked up the German and walked to the Arce near his house to grab some caguamas. Sal had called Lengua earlier that afternoon and got us an interview at eight the next morning. They had several available teaching positions and wanted to see our chops. We decided it best to buy only one caguama each.

The evening began rather tamely. We sipped our caguamas while watching TV. We finished the first round at about nine and decided on a second. When we got back, we put on some music . . . then we started wrestling. We made another trip to the Arce, then came back and chased mice around the house. We went back to the Arce at midnight and it was closed, but Sal knew a secret spot that sold beer after hours so we followed him to a house across the street from a drug rehab center. Sal tapped his keys on the front gate, and a man carrying some *Phantom of the Opera* candelabra came down the steps. He said a few words, passed two sixers through the security bars, collected the loot, and soon we were up on Mica's roof howling at the moon.

We finally decided on home as the clock rounded four a.m. Sal and I stumbled along the panteon walls to the house, unlocked the front gate, and parted ways when we got inside. I checked my bed for scorpions and set the alarm on my cell phone for seven.

Sal tore into my room the next morning around ten thirty, half-frantic, half-giddy.

"Should we even go?" I sat up.

"I guess we could tell them we had car trouble or something?" he said.

"We might as well tell them we got kidnapped by aliens."

"We should at least give it a try."

We discussed our plan for another ten minutes before deciding to give the interview a shot. We were both well-intentioned chaps but were lacking in direction. We threw on our best attire: ripped jeans, stained button-down shirts, and worn patent leather shoes.

We walked the mile and a half to Lengua and arrived around noon. The school was small and built above a bank. We went to the side door, walked up the stairs, and strolled to the front desk. Lengua was run by three women: Ines was the brains of the operation. She spoke fluent English with a British accent. Neta handled the loot. She spoke no English—only rapid Spanish. Coco was the trio's Curly. She spoke no English and poor Spanish.

Neta stood behind the counter as we walked to it. She said something to Sal, then pointed at some wicker furniture. Sal and I walked over and sat. Ines emerged from a classroom about ten minutes later. I was elated when she conducted the interview in perfect English.

"Hello, gentlemen," she said. "Thank you very much for meeting with me today. Did you find the place okay?"

"Uh, yeah," Sal said. "Sorry we were late. We had some car trouble."

"Oh, that's okay. I didn't get in until about fifteen minutes ago, so this works out great. So, what brings you two to Lengua?"

"We're both interested in teaching English," I said.

"Do you have any experience?"

"I taught Global Studies in an at-risk school in Buffalo for a semester."

"And you?"

"Well," Sal said, "I gave Spanish lessons at an international business in Buffalo, so I have some experience teaching languages."

"And why would you like to teach English?"

I took that one on. "I enjoy making connections with people, and communication, both written and verbal, is essential in achieving that goal. I think I would do a good job of teaching English at any level. I love words. I love people. And I'd really love the opportunity to work here." It was much easier for me to bullshit in English than Spanish.

The conversation continued like that for another ten minutes or so before it actually went anywhere.

"Well, gentlemen, we only have one position available right now, but we expect to be starting some new classes within the next few weeks, so we may be needing several new teachers soon."

"How many students would be in the available class?" Sal had a hint of fear in his eyes.

"Just one. And you wouldn't be giving your classes here. The student is the president of the Coca-Cola bottling factory in Fundido. You would need to go there every Monday, Wednesday, and Friday from nine to ten a.m. so it would require a car."

"No problem, I'm actually getting one tonight," Sal said.

"I thought you said you had car trouble this morning?" she said.

"Uh . . . well, my friend who was going to drive us had car trouble." Good job, Sal!

"No matter. So long as you have a car," she said.

It was true. Sal'd bought a supercharged Passat from some dipshit in Houston and was flying up to the Lone State that night to pick it up. Sal had some friends in Houston, so he planned to stay for a few days, then drive back to Lila. He'd be gone for a week.

"Great. I'm offering the job to one of you. Please decide who will take it and let me know as soon as possible. Cheers."

We walked down the stairs and back out into the blazing heat. There was little point in discussing this . . .

"Hey, man, I think I should take the job. You don't even have a car, and you're an illegal immigrant."

"Yeah, yeah, whatever."

When we got home, we both undressed and hung our sweat-soaked clothes on the uncomfortable handcrafted furniture to dry. The kids in the elementary school on our corner were out playing soccer. It made me uncomfortable just watching them. I tossed Sal the toothpick, and he put on a movie. We had about seventy titles between us. This would become my routine on those stifling afternoons. I felt like a goddamn prisoner—but one with access to great films.

When the movie finished, Sal packed and hailed a cab. I'd walked to Madrid del Rio with him and wandered back downhill when he was gone. The sun was already setting, limiting the possibilities of the dying day. A bat swooped low, just missing the side of my face. He'd be my only company that night.

Chapter 6

When Sal left, I lost my translator and only link to my previous life. This concern, however, quickly gave way to a satisfying mix of unencumbered freedom and burning curiosity. I'd been wanting to do some exploring since my arrival, and now there was nothing stopping me. Though I still wasn't sure why I'd come to Mexico, I did know a large part of it was for exploration—to push the boundaries. And I didn't see any reason, other than prison, not to do just that. Jorg was usually at the geology office or in the field, so I often had the house to myself.

The pressure to learn Spanish was building along with my need to explore. In sixth grade, we were forced to study Spanish, but I think I still would have chosen the course if given a choice. Though I was a white kid born in burger-eating, Big-Game-worshipping, aw-shucks America, I'd always clung to Spanish and Hispanic culture as if it were a life preserver. All the Peruvian pictures and Mexican music and Colombian celebrations—it looked as if life was actually happening somewhere, and I knew I had to be there.

And now I was . . .

But studying it and living it were two different things. And walking through this town, I felt like I was in the middle of a constant lecture, frantically taking notes while a thousand professors rattled off words that fractured in midair before hitting my ears. Sometimes a few would make it through to my racing mind, easing it slightly, while other times the words passed through my auditory system like a sandstorm.

Every day was a challenge. I had victories small and large but failures of the same magnitudes. But despite the failures, I felt my skills were improving. Some days, my capacity to learn felt endless, while others, I struggled with the simplest of greetings. My goal was to learn three new words each day and work them into my active vocabulary. This goal gave me a purpose, helping me through those lonely, blazing afternoons and long, hazy nights.

Mica and I were at about the same level with our Spanish. Everyone else I knew was either fluent or conversationally fluent, putting Mica and me at the bottom of the communication hierarchy. But Mica had a knack for language. He'd learned English in about a year, and with the exception of some misused prepositions ("in" vs. "on") and demonstrative adjectives (exchanging "this" for "that" and vice versa), and the use of some outdated expressions ("it's quarter past two"), he'd achieved fluency in that short time.

Learning a new language made me think about communication in general. I was intrigued that by creating a string of sounds with my oft-strained tongue, I could get me a response from the outside world. A code was released and interpreted, connecting me with another human being. It was reassuring. That through the power of words, I didn't have to be so alone. I felt peace and accomplishment after every successful conversation I had in Spanish. I wanted to be beyond the translating stage. I wanted to see eggs the moment someone said *huevos* without having to translate consciously. Herb once said, "You'll know you're fluent when you start dreaming in Spanish." I couldn't wait to be shouting "Chingan tus madres!" at the cops always after me in dreams, rather than just telling them to fuck their mothers.

I used Spanish words to get around town that week. I used them at the fruteria to get bananas and oranges, at the llaveria to get a new house key made, on the bus to ask the driver where the hell he was going. And each time I used these strange sounds and got what I needed, I recognized the power of knowledge. That something I'd studied so long ago was literally helping me to survive. Sometimes long lines grew behind me while I struggled to find the right words, but no one seemed impatient or upset. No one rushed me through my questions or explanations or pushed me aside so they could get by. I was one of the few gringos in town and one of the even fewer who wasn't a student at the Universidad. The only other person I could think of that fit that same description was Herb.

I wasn't the only person alone at this time. Mica still didn't have any housemates, and we spent a lot of time drinking caguamas in his empty house. He started throwing parties, and his house soon became one of the fiesta-hotspots in that tiny town. He threw his first party that week. I stopped by early in the afternoon with some caguamas, and we finished a few of them before guests started to arrive. A car parked in front, and a large guy and two girls got out and walked to the door where Mica and I greeted them. The one girl was plain—nothing noteworthy about her: style, movements, energy . . . The other girl, however, caused me some newfound, but welcomed, inner agitation. It wasn't her words or body or the way she moved— those were trivial matters. No, here what mattered was her face. She was gorgeous in a way that shook me to my core. But even swept up in the magic of introduction, this reaction seemed extreme. I felt as if I knew her . . . as if we had a history . . .

I shook the guy's hand, then kissed the plain girl's cheek and made a big fuss about how wonderful she looked. Then I kissed the gorgeous girl but gave her no compliment. This wasn't instinctual—in fact, it went against my better judgment. It was, rather, a strategy taught to me by a friend from Buffalo who was successful with the ladies. He advised, "When introduced to a group of girls, always make a big fuss over the ugly ones first. That gets the pretty girls thinking, 'Why isn't he saying these things to me?' and once they start thinking that, you in, man. They'll fight for your attention." I hated these tricks. I hated the fucking games people played with one another—all this goddamned mental masturbation. But this was the world I lived in, and if I needed to play ball to succeed, then ball I would play.

As part of my strategy, I walked away from the pretty girl and played cards in the dining room with Mica and some of the extraneros, who'd started showing up in big groups. We played Soko, some Finnish variation of five-card stud Mica had learned while trekking through Scandinavia, and turned it into a drinking game. We raised each other drinks, though it was the loser of each hand who had to drink them. Anyone who folded had to pound half a beer. The game started to grow as ambassadors of several different countries sat at the table. Though many spoke English or German, we stuck with Spanish. Those who weren't playing were dancing to Manu Chau and Daddy Yankee in the living room. I broke concentration from the game intermittently to check out the girl still dominating my thoughts. She sat alone on a windowsill, so curiously apart from the chaos around her. Everywhere people were shaking their asses, dumping drinks down their throats, smoking joints, screaming, slamming down beer-soaked playing cards . . .

I decided I'd had enough of silly games. I cut through the noise and approached her. She patted the empty space beside her and shifted over, and I sat. For some reason, the Spanish flowed from me better than it ever had in my life.

"Why aren't you dancing?" I said.

"Sometimes I just like to watch."

"I understand. In fact, I think I *always* prefer to watch."

"Why?"

"Because somebody has to, or maybe it will all disappear."

She smiled. "What are you doing here?"

I held up my caguama.

"No, I mean in Mexico."

I thought about that for a moment and set my caguama down. "I don't know. What about you?"

"I am the manager of a gas station in la Villa del Lado."

A few bad jokes came to mind, but I let them pass . . . gas . . .

Her name was Ximena. She was twenty-six and a few months out of a nasty divorce. She'd married her high school sweetheart but after ten years couldn't fake the passion any longer. The early twenties were such a battleground for relationships, and hers, she said, was too battered to ever mend. While she spoke of loss and despair, the life and desire never left her face. And it was that very face that drew me—a beauty that could cut through any chaos without losing a hint of resolution. I could dance however I liked but I knew that after all my foolish movements there would only be that face, clear and beautiful, guiding me . . . teaching me . . .

Ximena and I exchanged a few moments of our lives cleverly wrapped in a half hour conversation. She caressed my thigh while telling me how much she liked it. I wasn't always one to pick up signals, but I knew if I missed that one, I deserved the dull ache in my loins.

"Would you like to accompany me to pick up another friend? She wants to come to the party," she said.

"Sure. You drive?"

"No, my friend did, but he doesn't mind if you come."

We walked outside, leaving the chaos behind. The guy hopped in the driver's seat, and Ximena opened the rear door.

"You can sit in front if you'd like." I went for the passenger side handle.

She shook her head; she sat in the back seat, shifted over, and patted the spot beside her. "No, I want to sit with you."

I sat, shut the door, and we took off. I had no idea where in the hell we were headed, but I didn't care. Ximena was clawing at my thighs and running her hand under my shirt, feeling my bare stomach and chest. She kissed my cheek and buried her head against my neck, breathing heavily. I could feel it rise a little higher, a little harder, each time she exhaled. The driver said nothing the entire trip. It was strange, but I didn't care. When we arrived at the "friend's" house, the driver got out, walked to the door, went inside, and returned a few moments later, alone. He started the car, and we headed back to the party.

On the trip back, the driver stopped at a red light just below a street lamp. The lamplight filled the car and illuminated Ximena's face. I put my hands on her cheeks to keep her in frame. She was every bit as real and beautiful as I'd been imagining. Fuck! Fantasy was becoming harder to imagine now than reality. I allowed the floodgates to burst open and the repressed chemicals to race through my body—I was in it now. But I contained myself. And once I got a taste of control, I realized how much I liked it.

When we returned to the party, the plain friend stormed out of the house with tears in her eyes. "WHERE WERE YOU? YOU LEFT ME!" I couldn't understand all of her words but assumed what she was really saying was, "This party isn't filling the endless void inside of me. You shouldn't have left me to face that terrifying realization in the company of strangers, whose faces all became mirrors the moment I discovered you were gone."

But Ximena ignored her friend. She got out of the car, pulled me to her, and kissed me. But this was no friendly besito. Ximena and I went at it as if we were about to rip each other's clothes off, then get down in the grass—something I might not have passed on given my BAC. We embraced each other as teenaged lovers about to be ripped back to our separate worlds by the hand of time and were desperately trying to extract the most feeling from each kiss. Ximena was cool. She had a coolness that, by its very nature, she probably didn't even realize she had—a coolness that made me want to follow wherever she led. Though I was old enough now to know that these things didn't always work the way they should, I didn't attribute lost love to fate. Fate was something old people created to justify the mistakes they made in life. I couldn't believe in fate—to fall back on the shoulders of that Great Mother. She'd surely carry me to my death. No, this was a coincidence, nothing more, and could develop just as easily as it could vanish like a shallow puddle under the stifling midday sun that would most assuredly beat down tomorrow. All I wanted was something to keep me wet until then.

The frantic friend did her piece to pry Ximena from my face, but Ximena fought her bravely and only moved when her friend grabbed her arm and jerked it away from me. But this meant not capitulation. Ximena broke free, as spirits tended to do, clung to me, and whispered in my ear, "I want to see you tomorrow. I will come to your house and give you carinosos."

"What's a carinoso?"

"You will see. What time will be okay?"

I knew damn well that I had some serious celebratory drinking to do that night and that I probably wouldn't be up until at least noon the next day.

"How about one?"

"One is good. Where do you live?"

"Among the dead."

She gave me a knowing smile. "Which street?"

Good question. There wasn't a sign on the corner nor a number on the house, so, unlike most preschoolers, I didn't know my address. "It's at the bottom of the dead end by the deportivo complex. You know where that is?"

She nodded. "I will see you tomorrow at one."

She kissed me deeply, then broke away from me with a wisdom I hadn't yet had time to extract from the earth. She got into the car and it left. I had no phone and hadn't thought to get her number.

I wanted to believe I'd see her the next day, but the nagging voice of cynicism disguised as reality told me it was already over. I broke myself from her spell and did a victory lap at the party, dumping as much crap down my gullet as possible. I was a drunk volcano ready to explode.

When the party died down, I said my goodbyes and set off for my casita. I was drunk and relied on the panteon walls to guide me. I thought of Ximena and of my life back in Buffalo. I was far from any scathing critic or unsolicited piece of half-baked advice. It was just me and the wall.

I'd staggered about halfway home when a car pulled over next to me. The driver rolled down the passenger window and said something I didn't understand. I peered inside. The guy looked familiar.

"Do you want a ride, friend?"

Ah! He was my neighbor—Beethoven's owner. At least, I thought he was. Either way, don't be rude, Willy.

"Uh, yeah, sure."

I hopped in and knew immediately this was not my neighbor. He pulled away from the curb and took off.

"Where you live, friend?"

"Make a right at the next street."

Without hesitation, he grabbed my cock and said, in terrible English, "I like your penis."

I pushed his hand away, opened the door, and jumped out while the car was still moving. He continued down the street.

What a fucking creep! I grabbed a stone off the street and checked over my shoulder. *You gotta stop doing dumb shit like this, Will!* What if that guy had a gun? Maybe you woulda tasted your first cock tonight. Why did you get in the car? They teach you this shit in preschool! But, they also teach you in preschool to be good to your neighbor . . . Fuck! I wanted to blame the driver, but it wasn't his fault.

I made the conscious decision on that dark street to never knowingly violate my good sense again. I took another look over my shoulder and figured he wasn't coming back. I dropped the stone and walked the rest of the way home. I could feel my brain's chemistry changing. That night, I felt like a moving science experiment.

Chapter 7

As planned, I woke up the next morning around noon. Though I couldn't call her, I could feel Ximena moving closer to me. I lit the water tank, took a shower, ate, and popped in the first disc of my *Led Zeppelin DVD*. I cranked the volume, seeing as how most of my neighbors were dead. Twelve forty-five came, and I felt anxious. But at one, my instincts kicked in. Soon, a rusted station wagon rolled downhill and stopped under the almond trees. I was so excited to see her that I left the TV blasting.

Ximena got out of the car and gave me a hug. She was every bit as beautiful as the night before. She grabbed a bottle of Johnnie Walker Red out of her back seat and led me inside the house John Bonham was currently shaking.

"Sorry, I can lower it."

Ximena didn't answer. She stared at the TV and whispered, "Que padre," or "How cool."

"Do you like Led Zeppelin?"

"I never heard of them before."

"Have you heard of *music*?"

"I don't understand . . ."

"Never mind. So, what would you like to do today?" I said.

Ximena continued to stare at the TV. "Can we just watch this?"

Holy shit! "Yes!"

"Do you have any glasses?" She waved the bottle at me.

I grabbed two blue-rimmed glasses and set them on the coffee table. I sat on our uncomfortable couch and Ximena on the equally uncomfortable loveseat. She poured drinks while focusing on the TV. Her phone rang several times, but she ignored each call and eventually just shut it off.

Though I was nervous, I was also glad I had the house to myself. Jorg was at the office and wouldn't be back until later. Ximena, however, was present and unconsciously destroying several of the unwanted stereotypes I had of women that had been involuntarily programmed into my brain—destroying the misguided advice that had worn me down to a neurotic incoherence whenever a girl was present in a situation. The same advice that must have worn down my buddy Doug's Uncle Steve. In high school, a group of my friends and I always used to hang at Doug's house. We were chugging beers and bullshitting one night when ol' Uncle Steve, who was drunker than any of us, staggered over and addressed the group. He was a sad, lumpy old man but still full of that good ol' boy "charm."

"You know what, fellas?" He addressed us with this well-intentioned, bald sincerity, as if he were some esteemed platoon sergeant comforting his beloved troops on the night before a suicide mission. "Girls don't want guys like us. It's science." He started feeling his nose and cheekbones while pacing the floor. "I read all about it in some fancy magazine. Women only want men with sharp facial features. They'll never want any of you unless you're rich." He started pointing at each of our faces. But instead of telling him to go to hell, we all sat there with these terrible, heavy looks of despair in our eyes and took his words for gospel. It was as if those words were cement being dumped deeper and deeper inside each of us, filling those almost-impossible-to-reach holes, way deep down—and then that slow and grueling process of hardening . . . None of us needed any extra weight. None of us were especially good with the ladies already. And when he pointed at me, he might as well have done so with a pistol. Ol' Drunk Uncle said he was doing us a "favor" by setting our fates and reading our fortunes. But I didn't need his damned fortune or anyone else's for that matter. I designed my life around avoiding fate at all costs—even death. I had no money, no status, no defined facial features, nor fancy things. All I had were my cock and balls, and a remote control. Yet she was still there. These Mexican girls, man . . . these delightful darlings stayed with me!

Ximena and I sat there and drank whiskey on the rocks, and when the first Zeppelin disc was up, I popped in the second. We talked and flirted and sipped more whiskey. Each time my glass approached empty, she grabbed it, walked to the bag of ice melting by the door, bent over, tossed in a few cubes, and poured in more whiskey. She filled those baby blue jeans, torn around the knees, and knew just how to swing those hips.

There was a moment after she poured me another whiskey and returned to the loveseat when the question that had been pestering my subconscious found its answer. The light hit her face just right, revealing a faint cluster of freckles scattered across her upper cheeks. It was then I realized how much she resembled my dream girl from elementary school—the girl who'd consumed my thoughts for so many of those formative years. She was Julia, the dark-haired Italian girl who ruined my good sense. I'd spent years chasing after her in vain, but then in seventh grade I heard she liked me. I asked her out, and she said yes. I took her on our first date, and my first ever . . . to the YMCA . . . to play basketball. Some people just didn't have it. Julia didn't like me much after that.

But now here she was, buzzed and warming in my living room. All I had to do was be. The day was magnificent; the sun was bright, but I didn't feel its wrath. As the second Zeppelin disc ended, I threw in the *Song Remains the Same.*

I was nervous but poised. I'd drawn pocket aces, and all I had to do was place my bets against whatever she was holding. I put my leg up on the coffee table and shot her a smile. When my glass approached empty, she grabbed it, walked to the door, and bent over. I couldn't take it anymore. I shot over to her, lifted her doubled over body until we were both upright, and kissed her.

Jorg came home around six and found Ximena and me with our hands in each other's pants. Ximena buttoned up and led me to my room—TV still blaring. She pushed me on my bed, shut the door, and turned off the lights. Though I'd hung a tapestry over the hole in my wall, at any point Jorg could have gotten a free peep show with nothing more than a push of his fingertips. I didn't care if he wanted to watch, but he didn't.

Ximena then did the impossible. She slowly removed her shirt—disproving Sal's claim of the chastity of "all" Mexican women—leaned in, and whispered in my ear, "Do you have protection?"

I guess that *was* the question, wasn't it? Suddenly, the bed broke free and fell into the same abyss it had a few nights earlier. I'd been with plenty of girls, but penile penetration of the va-juicy was something relatively new to me. I was raised catholic christian and had gone to a catholic school where a horde of nun-teachers had successfully burned their vision of hell into my curious and impressionable young mind. Puberty and control weren't a healthy mix, and after absorbing several consecutive years of unchecked dogma, I couldn't even scope a luscious pair of tits without seeing fire and brimstone beyond them, scorching my sexual horizon. I knew most purveyors of this horseshit meant well, but forcing religion onto a kid was nothing more than child abuse.

So I avoided penetration at all costs, throughout my horniest of years. I'd done everything else but didn't give up the real goods until about a year back. I'd quit the church during high school (ironically, just after my confirmation), but the scars persisted. By college, I figured maybe it was a good thing I hadn't done it. Then I could save it for someone special.

But the more life tried to beat the purity of that idea out of me, the stronger I clung to it. It finally happened one night while I was out with a girl I liked. I mean, I really liked her. She was this beautiful Israeli girl, intelligent and kind. She was into art and poetry and dance—things nobody else I knew seemed to be into—and she told me things I'd never heard anyone before say. We were at a bar together that night. I'd been drinking the entire day, as was fairly normal for me. I told her I needed to use the bathroom and walked away. En route to the men's room, I bumped into a girl from one of my history classes. She said something like, "Hey, Will, wanna come back to my place? I've got a coupla cases of beer." I grunted a response, and soon I was making out with her in the bed of someone's truck. Then I was in her bed where she pitched me the same line:

"Do you have protection?"

"Uh, no . . ."

"It's okay, I'm clean. I've only been with one guy, and he was my boyfriend." (It was funny, though, she didn't seem too concerned about how clean I was.)

I couldn't fight it anymore: "Eh, whatever . . ."

In and out with my bare dick for about an hour but with nothing doing. Hell, it didn't feel like much of anything really. And this was what I'd been waiting my whole life for? This was the disappointment that assured my eternal damnation in hell? Even when I stopped believing in the fairytales, it was hard for me to say "yes." It was as if I'd said "yes" to one girl, I'd have to say it to them all. The Israeli dancer never spoke to me again after that night. Maybe that was how I wanted it . . .

"Do you have protection?" Ximena said again.

"Uh . . . yeah."

She moved aside, and I stumbled to Sal's room, hard dick slapping my thighs like a jockey's whip. I reached into a bag of condoms and brought a handful back to my room. I found something that looked fruity and fun and wrapped it on. I got on top of her and worked my way in. She was ready for me.

Then came the voices: "You gotta be careful with those Mexican girls down there. They're all diseased." "All they wanna do is distract you so they can steal your wallet." Dumb fucks! You don't know what the hell you're ever talking about! Shut the fuck up! LEAVE ME ALONE!

I started slowly, then gave a deep thrust and held it inside, pressing against her with all my might. I could feel Ximena's body give under me. She cried out, "Ahh, papi." That was all I needed. Now faster and harder. She bit her lip. The quicker I moved, the more control I felt. The chemicals raced through my drunken body. I grabbed her, spun her over, and pushed her on top. She sat on me and shifted her hips to take it as deeply as it could go. She moaned and clawed at my chest. Jimmy Page broke into that sultry and stolen riff in "Since I've Been Loving You." The air turned purple, and the light aged to a deep golden brown. Ximena hit her rhythm, keeping in time with JPJ on bass. We rocked that bed with no concern for heat, or hell, or alacranes. I flipped her again, pushing her face-first into the pillow. I lay on top, conquering her body—taking her from behind. She screamed out. I pulled her up onto all fours. Our bodies came together in perfect rhythm. The chemicals surged, and all systems prepared for release. I was a fucking animal, but that was about all I knew of myself. I pulled her onto her feet. Ximena staggered to the table in the corner with me still inside her. She braced herself on it and presented from behind. Our bodies poured sweat. I licked her back, tasted her salinity. She reached out and turned the fan onto her. I grabbed her hand and guided it back to the table. I put my hand on top of hers and took a good look at it . . .

Goddamn, those hands! They weren't quite my size, but they were big enough. Oh fuck, *is this a dude?* You've got to be fucking kidding me! Okay, be reasonable, no man could have those curves— but don't hormone injections work some miracles nowadays?

What these thoughts did to me is basically the opposite of what Viagra does to a penis. I'd never had that problem before. In fact, I'd always had the opposite, pitching a tent at the most inconvenient times throughout my life: at church right before lining up to receive the eucharist, at the beach just before wanting to exit the ocean, in school before being called to the board to diagram a damned sentence. I used to think the teachers at catholic schools were trained to know when a young guy was thinking more about the new tits on the blonde sitting next to him than factoring equations. I must have pulled the tuck-n-waddle a hundred times during school. I thought I invented the move until I'd discovered later it was standard procedure.

Ximena caressed my cheek. "Many guys have this problem."

Gracias, baby, I feel all better . . .

Ximena grabbed her purse and turned her phone back on. She listened to a voice message while getting dressed. "They need me at work."

"I'm sure they can water down the gas on their own."

She looked at me as a mother would look at her sick child before heading off to work. "I have to go." She kissed my forehead. "I'll come back later tonight. I want to sleep with you." She handed me a piece of paper with her phone number, then headed out the door. Her cards turned over with her engine, revealing a flush made on the river, beating my pocket rockets. I knew she wasn't coming back.

I crept into the corner of the bed. There I sat naked and alone wearing nothing but that damn jizzless, fruity condom and contemplating what had happened to the light. That afternoon was so bright it was almost blinding as we teased, and laughed, and drank together. But the night had crept in unnoticed, sliding inside, riding on the waves of Jimmy Page's Les Paul. I sat in the solitude of the moment feeling isolated—lost for a confusing and overwhelming jumble of reasons that I knew I had no power to untangle. Ximena dug a hole behind her as she left, and I fell inside, willfully wrapping myself in the darkness.

Chapter 8

I woke alone the next morning. I was right about about Ximena. She didn't come back and never would. The sun was ruthless that afternoon, beating me into the darkest, coolest corner of the house where I remained obediently until dusk. Mica sent me a text: "Party at the Canadian's!" I took a shower, buttoned up, and set out along the panteon wall. When the wall ended, I was on my own to navigate the streets of Lila. I walked Ignacio Sevilla for several blocks, then cut down a side street where Sal had shown me a shortcut to the neighborhood south of the panteon. I found the shortcut, a sidewalk between two colorful rows of stone houses, and strolled along. These homes were well-kept—gardens, fresh paint, smell of tamales wafting through the opened windows . . . Every time I passed through, a cute pit bull puppy chained to a front porch would jump to its feet and alert its masters of the possible threat I posed to the general balance of things. I always said hello when I passed him and did so that evening as well. That walkway led into a small park square like a stream flowing into a lake. I could hear the celebratory commotion long before arriving at that concrete collision.

There was this moment whenever a group of people got together for the first time, whether it be in college dorms, or on the road, or wherever, where I'd think, maybe this will be our time. Maybe now we'll be able to strip ourselves of all the bullshit and create something beautiful—something where the group serves as a means to inspire and energize and heal and spread unity while respecting the individuality of each member. And I'd thought the same the first time I met the extraneros. But soon, just like every other time, rules systems and sexual politics and a social hierarchy emerged, and spending time around those fuckers began to feel as oppressive as all the shit driving us to places like Mexico.

Regardless, I continued walking across the park toward the party that was so massive it not only filled the small house but also a quarter of that huge square. I recognized a number of faces. The Canadian was a leader among the extraneros. He'd come to Lila to study for a semester at the Universidad and had promptly signed up for another once the first ended. His was the first face I recognized. He was talking to a small and pretty Mexican girl in the square. I imagined he'd been telling her how he planned to sign up for another semester once the second ended—promising her he'd be around long enough to justify her acceptance of his courtship but not so long as to cause her any kind of concern.

I felt a particular resolve that evening, and my feet followed along. As I approached the chatting couple, the light dimmed in the Canadian's eye, telling me all I needed to know. He introduced us, then made an excuse to check on something in the house. Some people just didn't have the heart of a champion.

The girl was prettier up close than from a distance. Her name was Izel, and like Paz she was a petite morena with sharp features. We spoke in Spanish at first, then flipped to English after she told me she spoke a little of it. She was being modest. In no time, we were strolling along the panteon wall. When we arrived at my house, I unlocked the front gate, and we walked to my room. I didn't turn on the light; instead, I lit two candles on the table. We lay on the bed but not with lustful intent. With her, I knew I had time. The candlelight filled the void in that hollow space, revealing a beauty in her I hadn't yet detected. It was as if she was designed to be best seen by firelight. She wore a flowing white cotton dress embroidered with a floral pattern around its collar and had a blue ribbon tied in her hair. I could tell she wanted to look nice that evening. Izel began the conversation—she had to. I was too busy studying the outline where she met the chaos of night. She caught my attention, however, when she grabbed a notebook and pen from the table and wrote something.

"These are Mayan characters. I'm studying them in school. I can trace my lineage back to the Maya. It makes me happy to know about my ancestry and where I came from." She showed me the characters. Simple but powerful sketches. "This one is 'Sun,' a symbol for enlightenment, and this is 'Night,' a symbol of balance."

"Nice." I didn't know what to say. I was impressed but felt my words were nothing compared to hers.

"My family is proud to be part Mayan, but they didn't know any words until I taught them. They said I'm a good teacher." She smiled and flipped through my notebook. "Are you a writer?"

I thought long about the question. "No."

"Well, you have written through this entire book. Read me something?"

"I, uh, don't think—"

"My English isn't that great. I probably won't even understand. I just want to hear your words."

I looked in her eyes. She was sincere.

"Okay." I opened the book and found something I'd written years ago. "This one's called 'The Beasts We Allow in our Homes:'

> I walked out the door
> After I'd kissed my mother,
> And realized—I'm
> A monster's son.
> My claws felt heavy at
> The ends of their long, tired,
> Muscular arms—

To be human,
With nothing to hold onto.

I looked through the window
And saw a
Tear streaming down
My mother's face
A moment before my mind
Could curse her out.
I could hear her
Crying as well—

To be human,
If only for a day.

I think there are times
When even she can see
There's a human being
Inside of us all.
And, those are the times
When we walk away
And cry
The loudest
For what we've done—

To be human,
If only for a moment.

To be human—"

"Wow, that's a beautiful poem."
"It's not a poem. Just something I wrote."
"It sounds like a poem. There's a rhythm."
"You can add a rhythm to anything and call it poetry."

"I like poems that rhyme, but yours is very pretty."

"Well, maybe I'll write you something that rhymes, but it won't be a poem."

"Saying it isn't a poem doesn't make it so."

"Nothing is nothing, not poetry."

"Just because you don't commit to something doesn't mean you're doing nothing."

I thought about her words; I said nothing.

"You say you are not a writer but you write. You are not a poet, but you see the poetry in everything around you."

"They got a Mayan character for nosy?"

She smiled. "Do you have any other notebooks?"

I reached under the bed and pulled up four more.

"You *are* a writer. You just don't see it yet."

I leaned in and kissed her. She accepted my lips and warmed to my hands. I pulled the cotton dress over her head. Her body trembled; I pulled her close and it stopped. She pushed me onto my back and got on top.

"Tell me about your family." She kissed my cheek.

"I don't want to talk about that."

"But you just read me a poem about your mo—"

"That's different."

"How's it different?"

I slapped the wall. "I said I don't want to talk about it!"

She looked concerned—but not for herself. "Okay, we don't have to talk about that. I just can't imagine being so far from my family."

"Well, I can."

"Okay, I'm sorry I brought it up." She sounded sincere.

"Why don't you tell me about the Canadian?"

"What would you like me to say?"

"Is he your boyfriend?"

"No."

"How do you know him?"

"We met at Crystal last weekend."

"Do you like him?"

"He is very kind."

"But do you like him?"

"I don't know."

"'Cause you left him pretty quick back there . . ."

"What are you trying to say?"

"Never mind. I'm sorry I brought it up." I smirked at her.

"All you boys think that girls like macho guys. You'd be surprised how much we appreciate nice and respectful boys. No girl likes to be treated bad."

"No boy does either . . . Look, I'm sorry, okay?"

She nodded and kissed my cheek, and we got back to it. I slipped my hands inside her panties, rubbing fingers over prickly mountains and deep into river valleys. I felt my wet fingers up her spine and stopped at her head. For some reason, I started to untie the ribbon in her hair but did so clumsily.

"Ouch, that hurt."

"Sorry. I'll be more gentle." I continued to untie the ribbon but got my finger tangled in her hair.

"That hurts. What are you doing?"

"I don't know. Just stay still." I tried to work my finger out, but it wouldn't come.

"Ouch, PLEASE STOP!"

I didn't respond well to loud noises. "Don't yell at me!"

"I'm sorry, but you're hurting me."

I finally freed my finger from her hair, but the damage was done. "Well, maybe if you didn't tie it so damned tight—"

"I think maybe I should go."

"I think that's a good idea!"

"Don't yell at *me*!"

"Here, take your dress." I picked it off the floor and tossed it to her. She didn't say anything—just slipped it over her head, put on her shoes, and walked out.

"Wait, where are you going?"

"I'm leaving. Maybe it was a mistake coming here."

"Maybe . . . At least let me walk you home."

"I live in the next town over."

"How'd you get here?"

"The Canadian picked me up in his friend's car."

"Fuck. Well, let me at least buy you a cab."

We walked to the road, and I hailed a taxi. I opened the door, and Izel got in. I closed the door and stuck my head in the window.

"Look, I'm sorry for yelling. I just have a hard time controlling myself—"

"It's okay, Will. Keep writing. Maybe someday you'll realize your 'nothing' is really something beautiful."

"Will I see you again?"

She thought for a moment, then reached into her bag and grabbed a pen and paper. She wrote down her number and gave it to me.

"I want to hear my poem."

I dumped some change in the driver's hand, and he took her away. I stumbled back downhill and into my bedroom. The candles were still burning. I sat on my bed and could feel a dull ache in my groin, so I released some pressure. Then I looked at the table. I grabbed the notebook and read Izel's characters. She wasn't the only one allowed to write. I uncapped a pen and vomited some lines until the convulsions stopped, and I felt temporary relief. I threw the notebook on the table, checked my sheets for alacranes, blew out the candles, and fell into a deep, satisfying sleep.

The first thing I noticed when I woke up the next morning, other than the scent Izel'd left on my pillow, was an overpowering pain in my testicles. It was as if Buddy Rich had snuck into my room during the night and played a drum solo on my nutsack. I tried to get up, but pain shot through my stomach and into my brain. My legs gave, and I fell on my bed. I needed something to distract me from the pain. I grabbed my notebook from the table and read what I'd written the night before:

> Just enough time for the party tonight
> To see the last girl out the door.
> Small, yellow bumblebee
> Taking my night's love far away from me.
> Cigarettes and stale cologne,
> Pitch-black room, can't see the floor.
> But why unlock these feelings tonight?
> We got Sunday afternoon or Tuesday at night.
> Red, swollen cheeks,
> Crusted over eyes,
> Case-hardened shell,
> Withered insides.
> And all I ever wonder
> Is whom I'll end up being tonight?
>
> Blue, tangled ribbon,
> Fragile as brittle bone,
> When it falls to my feet,
> The world will be gone.

The sun shone through the window, burning my hand. I tossed the notebook back on the table. The light always brought so many damned possibilities. I wished it was already night.

Izel's crumpled phone number was on the table next to Ximena's. I figured that morning was as good as any to buy a phone. I tried to get up and again fell back on the bed. I forced myself up, got dressed, and headed out the door.

There was a Telcel store on the corner of my street. Herb had mentioned that Telcel's owner, Carlos Slim, had a monopoly on the Mexican cell phone industry. Herb despised predatory capitalism, as did I, but he also owned a Telcel phone. Plus, the store was air-conditioned . . .

I stood in a long line, propping myself up on the next barrier post each time we moved. The dull ache was still with me and didn't seem to be losing any intensity. When it was my turn, the man behind the counter called to me. I staggered to him and braced my arms on the counter. Perhaps it was due to the progress I'd been making with Spanish, but for some reason I didn't even consider that I'd have to communicate with this man in Spanish until he spoke it to me. But, despite a few setbacks, I maintained a successful conversation with him and walked out of there with an activated phone. I punched the two girls' numbers into it as I walked, and the pain seemed to shake from my body. It was gone by the time I got home. I sent both girls texts, but neither responded. I was already making quite an impression on that small town.

Chapter 9

The days passed quickly, and the permanence of my trip began to take hold but never really solidified, like wet gelatin placed in a recently unplugged refrigerator. It'd been nearly ten days since Sal left, and though I was unsure of my place in it all, some part of me felt that the kingdom was now mine. I didn't know how I'd take to his return.

One hot, sunny morning, a cherry red, supercharged Passat with Texas plates rolled downhill and stopped under the almond trees. I walked outside as Sal got out.

"How was the trip, Bobby Waterloo Sniffbelch?" I said.

"Pretty good, Mudmeat Stevens—except for the potholes. You gotta have a death wish to drive any Mexican highway at night."

"How long did it take?"

"Shit, about thirty hours. It woulda been faster if they had more direct routes, but it's a mountainous country. Help me with my bags."

I grabbed a suitcase from the trunk and rolled it in the house. Part of me was glad to have him back. But then I thought of Izel and Ximena. Maybe it was best that they didn't return my texts.

"Anything happen while I was away?" Sal said.

"Jorg fell in the volcano and was shot out in a plume of smoke. He's riding some enormous luggage in the Pacific right now. But other than that, not much."

He laughed. "I see you got your room all set up now." He moved aside my tapestry with his finger. "I'm gonna throw shit at you while you're sleeping."

"Sounds about right . . ." I said to myself.

Sal dumped his bags in his room then went to the kitchen to make some lunch. "Hey, I've been thinking about that job in Fundido. I'm gonna take it. I mean, you don't even have a car."

"I think they needed someone last week."

"Please, no one else would take that job. I'm sure it's still available."

"Whatever."

"You should call up Jose. His aunt basically runs El Campo. He said she could get you a job teaching English lessons there."

"I don't know. It's a long trip."

"It's only two buses. Besides, what else you gonna do?"

He was right. My savings were quickly depleting, and at the rate I was spending, I'd be broke within the month.

"Hey, what the hell happened between you and Marta at Paz's party?" Sal said.

"What do you mean?"

"I asked her why she stole your twenty pesos, and she went ballistic. She said she never stole your money and that you're a horrible person."

"Well, what the hell'd you tell her for anyway? I don't even care about the money. I only told you because I haven't seen a twenty-peso piece since and wanted to know if I was just imagining it."

"Either way, she's pissed at you. She says you're giving Americans a bad name."

"Well to hell with her then. The fuck do I care what she thinks anyway?"

Sal made a sandwich and ate it at the coffee table. He picked up my new cell phone between bites. "This yours?"

"Yeah, I bought it a few days ago."

"Yo, I'll give you Jose's number so you can call him. He's got a cousin in town too who'd like to get in on the lessons. You met him at Paz's party the other night."

"Franklin?"

"Yeah. He was born in El Campo but grew up in LA. I think his real name is Carlos, but his mom gave him an American name when they moved. Chicanos always pick the worst names, like Franklin or—"

"Salvatore?"

Sal laughed. "Fuck you, Sour Krautowski. Didn't your grandparents float across the Atlantic on a kielbasa?"

"Yeah, well didn't your dad dig a tunnel a little too far and end up in Buffalo?"

We both laughed. I speared the TV with the toothpick and tried to find a channel that wasn't fuzzy.

"That's it, I'm sick of not having anything to watch." Sal got up, walked to his room, and returned with a pair of pliers.

"Follow me."

"Where to?"

Sal climbed the front gate and pulled himself up to the roof. I followed. We walked past the water tank to our neighbor's roof. Sal crouched down low so no one could see him from the street. He put a splitter in their cable connection, then walked to the edge of our roof, grabbed our cable, and connected it to their feed.

We hopped down to check it out. It wasn't perfectly clear, but we now had cable. I looked outside and saw the Jehovah's Witness dude walking downhill. Sal saw me looking, and looked himself.

"Why do you even talk to that wack-job?" Sal said.

"I don't know. He just seems lonely, and he likes to talk."

"His face lights up like a retarded toddler whenever he comes by here."

"Maybe he thinks he's making a difference?"

"The only difference that guy is making is that by coming here he's not pestering someone else."

"Eh, he's all right. I mean, he can't hurt me here."

"You know what we should do?"

"What?"

"We should keep the door closed until he gets to it. Then, when he knocks, let's open it slowly, but be waiting on the other side with our asses hanging out."

I laughed.

"And not just our asses. We should drop down to our toes to give him the whole fruit salad—balls, tip, and all, and rub 'em while moaning like whores."

"Sounds good."

The dude came knockin', and sure enough, we put on the sphincter show. He never came back after that.

I called Jose a short time later. He told me to come down that afternoon to speak with his aunt.

"Yo, Jonathan Horsetrash, could you take me up to El Campo?" I said.

"Fuck that, Charles Cordon Bleu, I ain't wastin' gas on you. Take a cab."

"I don't have the cash."

"Then take the bus."

I walked up the hill and waited in front of the deportivo complex for the number twenty or twenty-four bus. There were college girls everywhere, and I threw smiles in all directions. I was a novelty and enjoyed the D-list celebrity status I felt each time I went into public. When it came, I took the twenty to the corner before the Super Walmart, then got out and paid five pesos for the rickety blue bus ride into El Campo. I rode through the entire town before getting out. When I did, I saw Tito wearing an apron and sweeping the floor inside a corner convenience store. He waved and showed me where to find his aunt (he and Jose were cousins).

I took off down the street and stopped in front of a one-story brick building surrounded by a tall iron fence. I walked through the gate, up the stairs, and into the building. Several women were running cloth through sewing machines inside.

Jose called me over to the corner where his aunt was speaking with Franklin. Though much older than I'd expected, she had a youthful vibrancy to her. She was throwing her arms this way and that in what looked to be an instruction to Franklin on how to work with the idiosyncrasies of the room. Franklin stood there nodding and furrowing his brow. He was a tall guy with a muscular build and had a quiet confidence that seemed to come more from having lived a hard life than from the size of his frame. I liked Franklin. He was bilingual and quite social once he felt comfortable with someone, and hearing his perfect English brought me a sense of security in that small town.

When I approached her, the aunt addressed me, but she spoke too quickly for me to translate. I just nodded along and waited for her to talk herself out—but she just kept going. Eventually, she said something to the sewing group and left.

"Okay, so there's a chicken living in the bathroom?" I said.

Franklin chuckled. "Not quite . . . She said we could use the place every night at seven after the women are done with their sewing group. She said the place wasn't much, but we could do what we wanted with it."

I looked around. There were only three tables, all different sizes, and each was covered in graffiti and gum. Several of the chairs surrounding the tables were missing backs or had loose legs. There was a chalkboard, but half of it was covered with some sticky residue that wouldn't wash off. Above was a ceiling fan that shook so violently when powered on I feared it would bring down the section of roof it was attached to. Out back was a large volleyball court surrounded by a twenty-foot-tall chain-link fence. Chickens and stray dogs occasionally ran past, and often a pack of spirited kids trailed behind with smiles on their faces and dirt on their clothes. The kids were everywhere—climbing the fences and roof, playing tag, running over stones with bare feet. But the main attraction was the volleyball court. The kids didn't seem to know the rules, but that didn't stop them from grabbing any ball they could find—beach, soccer, volley—and starting up a game.

"That it?" I said.

"She also said there was a large demand for English lessons. I figure we can fit about thirty students in the room comfortably. If we charge ten pesos an hour and do two hours of instruction each day, we'll make three hundred pesos a day each." He ran the numbers through his head quickly.

I was more concerned with watching a chicken on the street dodging a stray each time the stray lunged.

"Uh, that sounds great," I said. "You think we could really pull in that many people?"

"Depends on how well we recruit."

With fifteen hundred pesos a week, I could live like a king.

"We should take the bus into Lila so we can buy supplies and come up with some lessons." Again, Franklin was the man with the plan.

"Fine with me. When's the bus come through here?"

"Every half hour, and the last one leaves at eight thirty, which means I'll have to teach the final half hour of class each night so you don't get stuck here."

We stood by the road and waved down the bus as it approached. It was packed with riders of all ages. Some were young students in their school uniforms and others were parents with their small children. There was a girl who looked to be about twenty, oozing sex like a pungent perfume. She sat just beyond Franklin. I kept saying stupid shit to him so I could glance past his eyes and catch her perky breasts shaking as the bus jerked along the cobblestone street. God, she was fucking sexy. Her skin was dark and inked in several areas. I wanted to lick every inch of it. I started to feel that warm sensation in my loins, and the cobblestones made it impossible to control; every time we bounced up and down, another lustful thought exploded in my head. I shot her a few glances, but each was in vain. Her eyes were stuck dead ahead. At one of the stops, Franklin got up and signaled for me to follow. I pulled the tuck-n-waddle and walked past her on our way to the street. I wanted to talk to her—try to get her number or something—but I just kept following behind Franklin. Either way, a part of her stayed with me. She was dripping sex and I was wet, covered in her allure.

Chapter 10

Lila was always hot. I'd usually get up around noon right when the sun was at its zenith, burning and beating everything it touched into submission. I spent most of my afternoons tucked inside my concrete cave watching movies and waiting for the earth to cool. I still didn't know many people, and most of those I did were at work or school. The afternoons were mine. Sal and Jorg were normally at the office or in the field, and when they came home they'd usually take a nap. On weekday mornings, our quiet dead-end street would fill with parked cars. This modest bustle was my only source of entertainment besides TV and fucked-up imagination. After getting up, I'd usually eat a bowl of Zucaritas, or Mexican Frosted Flakes, then lie on the uncomfortable sofa and watch TV. Now we had cable, which meant I could watch more than just the news. But that more was usually crappy Mexican soap operas and talk shows. The only station that seemed to be of any worth was the one playing Mexican music videos. I'd often clean the house just to pass the time while blasting music. I swept the floor even though I didn't mind the dirt. Every time I swept, the dirt found its way back inside anyway, clinging to the soles of shoes or blowing in on a gust of wind. It was my hamster wheel, and it kept me from going crazy inside my scorching subconscious prison.

I'd make a ham or turkey sandwich sometime around two or

three to cut my film/music/cleaning session in half. I'd try to prepare foods that didn't need to be cooked. I'd almost set a bag of garbage on fire the last time I used the oven, and I preferred not to burn the house down. Sometimes, I'd sit in a plastic chair under the almond trees and watch all the insanity surrounding me. Crappy cars constantly whipped around the corner—cars so beat up they looked as if they'd been resurrected from the junkyard by some automotive messiah. There was one in particularly bad shape—a rusted orange Lazarus whose owner temporarily abandoned it in front of our house each day. This pissed off Sal, who saw the spot as his. Each day after Sal would leave for the Coca-Cola plant in Fundido, Lazarus would creep around the corner and pass out in Sal's spot. One day, Sal used some sticks to pick up a soiled diaper from a pile of street trash and put it on Lazarus's windshield. The guy didn't park there again after that.

The dead end attracted curious characters, and I'd often see suspicious cars parked outside. Couples, who'd arrive in separate cars, would meet in one of the vehicles and not come out until it stopped a-rockin'. I often saw cop cars parked at that end too, and they'd remain there for several hours as civilian cars would pull up beside them, then pull out a few minutes later. This shit usually happened at night, but I suppose daylight wasn't too strong a deterrent because they also happened frequently on those long afternoons.

It was always gorgeous outside while I was in. There were two seasons in Lila: the summer and winter. The summer season was the wet season. Every day would start out perfect and sunny, then it would start pouring the moment I'd step foot outside to take the bus to work. Thick, dark, low-lying clouds lumbered through the atmosphere around four or five daily. The darkness and rain were one of the few consistencies in my life.

When the time came, I'd dress as nicely as possible, pack my book bag, and trudge uphill to wait for the bus. I had to leave the house around five thirty to make it on time for my seven o'clock class in El Campo. This usually meant I'd have to trek through the wall of water that dumped on the small town each late afternoon. I wore the oversized rain jacket Sal gave me several years back and hoped for the best. The streets had horrible drainage and would often turn into shallow, raging rivers during a good storm. The tributaries would run together to the main river, Madrid del Rio, and that would seek its lowest level, flowing downhill, carrying with it all the trash and sediment and dumping it in front of our house. When the water evaporated, all that remained was trash, littering the site of future drug deals and adulterous affairs.

There were always pretty college girls waiting in front of the deportivo complex for their buses. Each time I'd get on my bus, some girls would stare or giggle. Some never gave me a look, but no one could ever win 'em all. I felt a shallow peace every time I sat on the bus. I always tried to grab a window seat so I could watch the town as we crept through it. This commute was the most peaceful part of my day, despite its length. This was the only thing I had going for me. I was a gnarled ball of nervous energy that always threatened to erupt. But the moment I sat down, my job was done. Now, it was up to the driver. There were always so many damned possibilities—so many things I hadn't yet done or seen. Every minute I felt as if I was wasting life. But on that bus, the possibilities were limited. I always hurried through everything: cleaning, dining, speaking, daydreaming, feeling . . . I wanted to see the whole world all at once, spread myself thin across continents and oceans—all right now. Life was so complex, but what I wanted was simple: to know everyone and know them well. I wanted to say hello to people on the street, and mean it, and be invited to dinners where we had real conversations about things that actually mattered. I wanted to do away with synthetic emotions like embarrassment. Guilt was different. Guilt was healthy. Do something wrong, feel bad, correct your error, then move on better than before. But embarrassment was something else, something we created. Shame was something we heaped on one another to make up for it having been heaped on us. It was a wretched fucking cycle I couldn't get out of. I didn't want much—just to know people and make music and feel okay. There were so many people out there throwing away their talents and values—goddamn, I didn't want to think about it. Just stare out the window . . .

The twenty or twenty-four would take me down Madrid del Rio. We'd pass hip furniture stores, posh boutiques, and strategically empty bars and restaurants. There was a church about halfway down the street, and each time we passed it, most passengers would sign the cross. Sometimes, I felt my right hand move out of rote, but I'd force it back down (in time, I'd just sit on it). Next to the church was a narrow building in ruins—a stone heap of what had once likely been a business or house before the earthquake. Each time I saw that lot, it reminded me of the tent my brother and I'd bought when we were kids. We were paper carriers and saved up for months to buy it. We got up every weekend morning at seven, were back from any friend's house after school by four. It was a tough gig, but we wanted that tent. It was huge—ten by sixteen. We wanted the biggest one they had. We had a big family and it was something we could all share—someplace that would maybe make us all happy, even if for a moment—someplace I could go to get away from the screaming and smashing. We put it up early one summer when I was twelve or thirteen, and I slept in it for several days straight. I bought all the accessories: a cot, sleep bag, camping pillow. Then one day a torrential rainstorm blew through Buffalo and knocked the tent over. A day passed, and no one picked it up. Another day passed and the same. Another, and it was still down— no one even mentioned it. I wanted to pick it up but just couldn't. I'd stare at it through the window but couldn't go near it. A week passed, and it still lay there. A month, the same thing. Then, at the end of the summer, I knew I had to do something. I walked to the end of the yard, picked it up, and confirmed what I already knew: There, torn into its side, was a hole big enough to serve as another entrance. My brother and I dragged it to the curb, and the garbagemen took it away the next day; no one ever mentioned it again. I felt as if that tent represented my entire life. And each time we passed that rubble, it reminded me of the futility in everything.

The twenty or twenty-four would stop before the Super Walmart. I'd get out, and it would keep going into la Villa del Lado. I'd walk north about a hundred yards and stop at the next parrada, or bus stop, and wait for the blue bus. This parrada was in front of a small café built about five feet off the ground on a thick bed of concrete. I'd walk up the stairway and sit on the edge of the concrete under the awing, dangling my legs over the side facing the street. I sat with my face to where the dying sun would beat down if not for the thick cover of dark clouds. There was an aerobics class in a gym above the café, and it ended at about the same time I arrived every day. Women in spandex would wander down the stairs and out into the street while I sat kicking my legs over the side of the concrete and listening to music. I had thousands of songs with me—some I'd never even heard before. I'd downloaded many unknowns to give my mind ample room for growth. This strategy fulfilled more than it disappointed. I'd sit there, listening to music and reflecting on my thoughts while waiting for the next bus to take over responsibility and carry me safely to my next moment in life. This was the best part of my day.

Sometimes I'd wait there for forty-five minutes before the blue bus would round the corner. It'd scoop me up and take me past the castles with junkies wandering around outside their gates, and soon we'd be in the wild. The bus would follow El Campo's square road plan before returning to Lila. Though my stop was first, I always rode it through the entire town before getting out. I loved to watch the people working in tiny corner shops or sitting in the small restaurants or bars. Children would play eighties-style arcade games like *Frogger* in front of the convenience stores while men sat under palapas, gulping beers and laughing. Elderly men and women would sit with them and talk or stare off into the distance. I often wondered if they were looking into the past, present, or future.

We'd continue down that road and make another left onto another lined with two-story homes. A woman who rode that bus with me almost every day would get off at the end of that street. She had two dogs that would start barking and wagging their tails every time they saw that bus coming. The woman would get off and walk right by her adoring pets without so much as a head pat or a "Good boy," then open the door just wide enough to slide her ass through and walk inside. The dogs always shot to the door when it opened but usually didn't make it inside before it closed. Sometimes the little one would, but I never knew whether to smile or frown.

We'd then make the final left and creep down the cobblestone street leading out of town. Franklin's grandparents' place was only a few houses down. I'd signal to the driver, and he'd let me out. Tito worked at a small shop across from his grandparents and would often wave when I arrived.

Franklin's grandparents lived in a beautiful ranch-style home with a chicken-wire fence surrounding it. I'd walk up to the door and knock. There were always different extended family members sitting around the living room, talking or watching TV. Someone would greet me at the door, then call for Franklin. Seeing him was always a relief. He could fill the gaps in conversation in that small room. If I was early, we'd sit and talk before walking to the schoolhouse.

"Jose, Tito, and I used to go down to the river behind the house and swim, or try to catch snakes. I was happy here, but my mom wanted me to grow up in America. I'm only back for the summer. I'll be starting college in the fall. I've been here for six months now, and while it's great to see family, I can't wait to get back home."

He also shared a number of interesting stories about his grandparents:

"My grandmother would always prepare us food, but I was scared to eat it. One day, I saw her kill a chicken by picking it up by the head, then swinging it around until its head came off in her hand. Then there was another time when we were halfway through lunch. I made some comment about how good her tacos were. When I asked her what they were made out of, she replied, 'Iguana.' I literally threw up on the floor. My grandfather is a tough old man. When I was younger, I remember watching him pick scorpions off the walls by their tails, then place them outside. I asked him why he didn't just kill them, and he said, 'I don't have the right.' I used to be scared of them, but I'm not anymore."

Sometimes his grandmother would offer us something from the kitchen, but I'd invariably decline if there was any meat in it. Her rice and beans were incredible though.

We'd walk the cobblestone streets as trucks passed by. The drivers would usually honk and wave, and we'd wave back. The town only had about eight hundred residents, and most families had been there for generations.

We'd stop by Franklin's aunt's house to get the key to unlock the front gate of the schoolhouse. The second we'd unlock it, kids would come flooding in from all directions. Soon they were climbing the fences, playing on the roof, and bumping soccer balls on the volleyball court.

Sometimes it would still be raining while we set up for class. The roof had the consistency of a cheese grater, and water poured through it as though someone had turned on an indoor sprinkler system. On our first day, Franklin and I spent fifteen minutes before class sweeping big puddles out the door. Sometimes the lightning killed the power, and we'd sweep in the dark. Just before the start of class that first night, the lights flickered and went out. A little girl ran outside and around back, and I followed. She opened the fuse box, and before I could object, grabbed a rock and stuffed it inside, propping up a cluster of wires. The lights in the schoolhouse came back on.

Kids started showing up that night around six fifty. The first we met were two adorable young girls ages six and ten. The younger, Lupita, wore an embroidered cotton dress and carried a large backpack over her shoulders. The older, Emma, carried a notebook tucked under her arm. The girls were cousins and were there of their own accord. They wanted to learn English and were always well-behaved and attentive. The next student to show was Jose. Jose was a twelve-year-old who dressed and carried himself like an experienced pitchman who went door-to-door pushing food storage containers or some other shitty wares that he truly believed in. He wore a short-sleeved button-down shirt buttoned all the way up to the last one on the neck and a pair of dark slacks. He carried a satchel filled with loose-leaf paper and pens. He was a quiet kid who smiled no matter the situation. The older kids were the last ones to show. Ernesto was a chubby and gregarious thirteen-year-old who never stopped asking questions, which was usually a good thing. Most teachers appreciated an engaged student, but his questions were ones like: "What does 'fuck' mean?" "What is 'shit?'" Ernesto also never stopped singing the chorus to that James Blunt song. Every ten minutes, he'd belt out a "You're beautiful!" Ignacio was the town's tiny tough guy. He was a twelve-year-old with the strength of a grown man. He spent his days running with a group of other tough guys who rode their bikes around and picked fights with other boys. He was one I'd frequently find on the roof of the schoolhouse yelling and throwing things. Julietta was also twelve. She was a smart and funny girl who frequently cooked up curious schemes to get me to stay in El Campo after class: "My mom cooked a large pozole that we'll never finish. You should come by for dinner." One day before class, I saw her driving a truck around town. She waved and smiled when she saw me as though there was nothing unusual about it. I smiled and waved back. There were a number of other kids who came and went as the weeks passed, but those were the core students. They were great kids, and I enjoyed their company.

The first day's lesson centered on some basic questions: "What is your name?" "How old are you?" "Where are you from?" Franklin and I took turns leading the instruction. Most of the kids participated.

"I haf twell years ode."

"I am fum El Campo, Meh-hico."

None had more than the most basic understanding of English, making it difficult for me to communicate with them. We often taught in Spanish. I usually let Franklin take the lead with this, but sometimes I still gave it a shot. One day I gave an instruction in Spanish, and the students all laughed. I asked Franklin why.

"You just told them to fuck their papers."

"I thought *cojer* meant 'to take?'"

"Yes, it does mean that—in Spain. In Mexico, *cojer* is 'to fuck.'"

I didn't think I'd have to worry about the media crucifying my ass for such an error here as I would in the States though. The kids would frequently correct my grammar when I spoke with them in Spanish. I think they got a kick out of teaching a teacher.

That first class was supposed to go until nine, but by eight, the kids had already lost focus. People from the town kept sticking their heads in the windows to see what was going on. Outside, kids were playing volleyball and climbing the fence. Every so often, someone's mother would pop in and say something like, "Julietta, you need to come home and clean the dishes." Or a chicken would run into the room, and one of the little kids would chase it outside. Franklin and I used volleyball as an incentive. If the students performed well that evening, we'd end class early to play a game. I usually played with them. They made the mistake of teaching me the Spanish word for spike, and I'd yell "CLOBBER!" as I smashed the ball on the other side of the net. We'd run around outside playing tag or wrestle with the boys. I enjoyed the hour I spent with those kids each night. Sometimes this was the only time during the day I'd speak Spanish. After games, the kids would usually crowd around me and ask questions: "Do you have a girlfriend?" "What is it like in America?" "What does 'fuck your mother in the dirty asshole' mean?" These press conferences helped improve my Spanish immensely. I didn't feel any pressure to answer quickly or correctly. Because of this, I usually spoke my best. Kids were incredibly patient if they cared to hear what you had to say and were usually quick to forget your mistakes. All they wanted, it seemed, was to spend time with you.

A little before eight thirty, the kids would alert me when they heard the bus coming. Even after a month, I couldn't tell the difference between the bus and a passing truck, but they could, and they saved me a lot of frustration. The Q & A sessions would sometimes continue all the way to the bus stop as the kids crowded around me, only letting me go when the bus was there. They did this some nights even in the rain. I really liked those kids. It was nice being able to spend time with them outside the judging eyes of principals, and supervising teachers, and miserable parents. There, in that ancient town, I was free to make mistakes and still retain my pride.

Sometimes I'd miss the bus, despite the kids' warnings—usually if I was having a little too much fun on the volleyball court—and I'd have to hitch a ride back into town. The drivers were all different: some talked non-stop the entire journey, others were silent, some wanted me to ride in the truck bed. One guy even asked me to correct his English in exchange for a trip. I didn't complain. I was just thankful for a ride. Those trips back into town were always peaceful. I'd ride back shortly after the rain had ended and clouds had cleared away. We'd travel through the damp fields just in time to watch the sun disappear behind the mountains, making a shadow of the great tree in the distance. The Virgin Mary statue was always lit with colorful strings of Christmas lights and surrounded by the tall grass, still dripping rainwater.

During the first few weeks of school, I'd get off at the first stop in Lila, in front of a new fitness center always filled with sweaty, protein-shake-swollen young socialites pumping themselves full of New World Culture, then hop on another bus that would take me down Madrid del Rio. But as my bank account balance diminished, I started opting to walk the few miles home to save four pesos, or about thirty US cents. I'd usually get home around nine thirty or ten. I spent about four hours going to El Campo and returning each day, but I hardly ever took home any loot. We charged each kid ten pesos per class, but few of them ever paid. How was I going to bounce kids with holes in their shoes from school because they couldn't pay?

I was okay with walking. I had music. It gave me time to think and take in the town. When I got home, I'd make dinner then head out the door. There was always a party somewhere. The extraneros went hard nearly every night. Sometimes I'd go just as hard, while other times I'd just sit around and chat with Mica over some beers and a spliff.

As the weeks dragged on, so did the time. With the exception of school, I wasn't doing shit with my life. After a month, I'd watched almost every movie we had—and with the seventy-plus titles between Sal and me, this was quite a feat. It was too hot during the day to accomplish anything but sloth. I so desperately wanted to see Mexico. I'd come for an adventure. I'd come to see the beaches, and the mountains, and the volcano. But I still hadn't accomplished any of those simple goals. Everywhere was potential, but I had no money to realize it. It was fifty-six pesos for a bus ride to the beach, but I didn't have it. The clubs were packed with girls who paid more attention to me now than ever before, but I didn't have the cash to take them out, much less to pay the cover to even get inside. Goddamn, I could make enough working part-time at Taco Bell in the States to survive here comfortably, but even that modest dream was out of reach. I was becoming desperate. I tried following Herb's advice: "When you want to save money, buy what the locals buy." I bought tortillas, and rice, and beans, and pasta, but I also bought caguamas and weed. I considered dragging my guitar down to el Centro to busk for change but never did. The darkness had made its way back in full force. It was crippling and consumed me whole. I'd gotten away for a short time, but when it caught up again, it hit me with an extra viciousness— perhaps to punish me for running. Nobody truly gets away.

Chapter 11

Fifteen hundred pesos. That's all I'd need per week to stay alive—that is, if I'd been born in that moment. I'd deferred all my student loan payments after college, and the juice alone on those loans would claim a good chunk of that weekly sum. But I didn't need to think about all that just now . . .

I needed a job. But I was illegal. This didn't necessarily preclude me from employment, but it wouldn't make things any easier. Luckily, I was able to take over Sal's class in Fundido. The ladies at Lengua had given Sal another class to teach, and it was at the same time as the one with the president of the Coca-Cola factory. This was good for me because it gave me a steady cash flow, and it was good for Sal because it gave him someone to split the gas with. Both classes were for employees of the Coca-Cola bottling factory in Fundido. Sal was to teach the factory's administrators, and I its president.

I got up early the first morning of class and ate a few bowls of cereal before we got in the car. I was excited. This was the first time I'd traveled west of Lila and the closer we came to those mountains in the distance, the closer I felt to myself. I longed to travel again. To see the ocean, other cities . . . But I felt like a damned failure. I'd come so far only to be stuck in the same crippling inertia.

The carretera was everything the highway had been for me back home. I'd slit its vein, slide inside, and ride the juices until they all dried up. But there was a particular freedom on this road unlike the others I'd traveled—a particular freedom in seeing bus stops along the highway and truck beds filled with not-so-eager workers cruising beside us. We passed several sprawling ranches set below fields of towering palms where cows grazed leisurely, enjoying the warmth of the rising sun on their backs. Soon, we saw the only familiar sight: "Coca-Cola" written on a factory wall.

Sal pulled off the highway and parked in a dirt lot. When I got out, I almost fell over. Sal, Mica, and I were up until late drinking again. But I wasn't hungover; I was drunk. I could tell Sal was feeling it too. He had that, "Just-don't-mention-alcohol-in-my-presence" look on his face. We staggered to security, showed our credentials, and passed through. We were both exhausted to the point of giddiness. The guy watering the garden out front accidentally sprayed his shoes, and we couldn't stop laughing. We were able to pull it together by the time we made it to the rear entrance. The woman at the desk was friendly, but I was surprised she could smile with the inch-thick caking of makeup she'd spackled on her face.

Sal and I parted ways, and the secretary guided me to a large office in the back. She rang a buzzer, and the door unlocked. She opened it, gestured for me to walk through, and I stepped into the enormous space. An older man stood behind a large wooden desk and spoke on the phone. Though I had no idea what he was saying, I could feel his command of the situation. He looked at me, smiled, held up his index finger, and continued the phone conversation. He said a few more words, then hung up. He spoke with me only in English.

"Hello, so you must be my new teacher!" He walked around the desk and over to me.

"Uh, yes, I will be your new teacher." For some reason, whenever I spoke in English with any foreigner, I'd initially avoid contractions and emphasize my syllables—usually until I realized the person I was speaking with wasn't four years old.

"Good! I am glad for to meet you. My name is Gabriel. I am

the president of operations at that company." We shook hands. Very firm . . .

"Well, it is a pleasure to meet you, Gabriel!"

"Let's have a seat." He pulled out a chair and gestured for me to sit, and I obliged. Gabriel was a short and fit man in his mid-fifties. It looked as if he took care of himself. He had a youthful appearance despite his smoky hair and the thin lines running across his cheery face. Gabriel was a gregarious chap, and if not for his loquaciousness and confidence, I would have had to pull off the herculean task of carrying the conversation that morning.

"What I would like for to do today is to speak to you and you to tell me about my English."

Thank god! This I can handle . . . This is about *all* I can handle. "No problem, Gabriel."

"I have been the president of these factory for ten years. Is a good place, the people are nice. I have been to United State for many meetings. I want for to improve my English so I can communicate better with other members of my company around the world . . ."

He went on like that for our full hour together. I corrected his grammatical errors and pronunciation when it was called for and was happy not to do much else. The room was spinning. I didn't know how he could continue to look at me with respect. Didn't he realize what was going on? I must have stunk of booze, and my eyes were bulging so far out of my head they threatened to pop out on that table and roll onto the floor.

". . . and my daughter also is learning the English . . ."

Gabriel was a good guy. He was never short on stories. I could tell there was a reason why he was the boss man. Something about being in his presence, though, caused a great stir inside me. I felt freedom going toe-to-toe with the president in my condition, but after seeing what a good guy he was and how much he appreciated my knowledge and instruction, that freedom seemed to cost so much that it wasn't worth it.

At ten, we shook hands and parted ways. I walked to the lobby where Sal was sitting on a couch and gently stroking his temples. I gestured to him, and he struggled to his feet. We exchanged goodbyes with the secretary, walked past the gardener and security guard, and took off down the carretera. Though we were late to that job by about fifteen minutes each day, Gabriel always greeted me with a firm handshake and a smile. Maybe he wanted to learn English so badly he'd put up with anything. Or maybe he'd also had a rough go earlier in life and just got that shit . . .

Either way, Gabriel always made me feel as though I had something valuable to teach.

Though I'd just started a new job, I feared that the money train would derail at any time. Each day brought new challenges, which built upon those I was already struggling with. Every few days I walked the mile round-trip to the water filtration stand to fill my two garrafones, or ten-liter jugs. The walk there was swift; the return wasn't. There was a leak in our water heater's pilot and it passed gas like an incontinent old man. We cut the line to it to save gas and usually took cold showers as a result. This was quite invigorating at midday, but a pain in the ass once the sun went down.

Maybe I hadn't noticed it before, or maybe I'd initially taken it as something of a novelty, but now I was fully aware of the anti-gringo acts perpetrated against me, whether subtle or outright. I was a shining white target anytime I strutted along the streets of Lila—and strutted I did. Once every few days or so, some driver would yell something like, "Go home, gringo!" as he passed. Sometimes they'd throw things too. One day, some asshole pegged me with a half-full bottle of Sprite and followed that by showcasing his middle finger. I rarely had time to respond to such acts with something appropriate, and I'd usually just shout a few swearwords in English. In time, I just shot up my middle finger—no need for translation there. But doing that shit didn't satisfy my anger. Each time one of those assholes pointed and laughed or spit in my direction, the anger grew exponentially, building on top of that already boiling inside me.

Mica had bottles thrown at him too while assholes told him to "Go back to America!" He was walking down Ignacio Sevilla one rainy day when some young prick driving a Porsche slowed down and changed lanes just so he could drive through a puddle and splash Mica. The asshole pulled over, pointed, laughed, and kept going. Mica identified the Porsche one day as we were walking through a mall parking lot. I picked a large stone off the street and handed it to him. We debated the point for several minutes before deciding it best to just walk away.

Once I was aware of them, these situations occurred over and over. I was grocery shopping with Sal one day when some prick started following us with his girl and small kid. The bastard kept pointing his damned finger and laughing hysterically. He followed us through the produce section, the cereal aisle, the pharmacy—he even pulled his cart up to the checkout next to ours where he continued to stare and laugh. Sal was cool. I was ready to kill. I stared at the prick while I unloaded groceries on the conveyer belt and said to Sal, loud enough for everyone around me to hear, "What the fuck is this guy's problem? Doesn't he realize if he keeps laughing at us like that I'm gonna split his damned lip?"

"He's laughing at you, not me."

"You're a gringo too, dumbass."

Sal searched for someone to meet his eyes, but the only taker was an elderly woman a few lanes over. When she looked at him, Sal pointed at me and gestured to her as if to say, "This guy, huh?"

The asshole followed us into the parking lot. Sal and I loaded the car, got inside, and started for the exit—but the fucker continued to laugh.

"That's it," I said, "pull over."

"You sure?"

"Pull the fuck over."

I stormed out of the car and got right in the guy's face. "Who the fuck do you think you are?" I grabbed him by his shirt. "Who the fuck do you think you are?" He continued to laugh, unaffected by my aggression. A crowd started to gather. I tried addressing him in Spanish: "Que tienes, pendejo?" Still, nothing. The kid tugged on his shirt. I looked at the kid and let the prick go. I got in the car, and we drove off. I could feel all my dark energy aligning. I felt enough strength to punch right through his head. But I knew one punch would lead to two, then two to three. Maybe I'd keep punching until there was nothing left of either of us . . . That was my fear—one of my greatest. And if these pricks kept pushin' me . . .

But still a part of me knew I couldn't commit a crime because I didn't really exist. I left no traces of life behind—no fingerprints, no DNA, no witnesses, memories, or love—just small piles of ash that threatened to blow away the second the wind kicked up again. And it would blow. That was certain.

These sticks and stones and words presented themselves in other ways, as well. I was over a month into this adventure and still had less than a conversational ability to speak Spanish. This tormented me more and more as the days passed. I felt trapped by language, words locked in my own internal prison. I was helpless to defend myself against slick businessmen, or corrupt cops, or the general machismo horseshit. But far worse, I couldn't speak with anyone and be understood or understand clearly. The scorpions still haunted my good sense, and my fear of this very real specter was only intensified by new stories of disease-carrying mosquitos. Sal burst into the door one hot afternoon: "Yo, we gotta get some bug spray. I just drove one of the girls from my department to the hospital. She thinks she has Dengue Fever. It's all over town. It's the headline in every newspaper."

"What's Dengue Fever?"

"She called it 'breakbone fever.' She said she had it a few years ago. She spent fifteen days in the hospital, and the pain was so intense she wanted to die. She said it felt like her bones wanted to explode inside her body, and the slightest touch to her skin caused her horrific pain."

"Is it a communicable disease?"

"No, mosquitoes carry it and pass it when they bite. We gotta get some bug spray, man. Spray down this whole fucking house."

I probably had a hundred insect bites on my ankles. I was surprised I hadn't had it already.

2006 was an election year in Mexico. There were signs for Obrador and Calderon posted all around town. Calderon would eventually win and launch war against the drug cartels. Though this war wouldn't begin for several more months, the drug violence had already been escalating. Five severed heads were dumped in a packed disco in a nearby town that October. This shit was everywhere—not just the border towns. Drugs were all over Lila. Here, the kids had the money for them. Everywhere I went, I couldn't help but feel as if there was one big secret about that town that no local would ever tell me—a secret shame they shared and would dutifully take to their graves at the expense of their own peace and security. Everything was always "mi casa es su casa," until I'd ask a question about the drugs or political corruption, then the conversation would be forced to something more pleasant, like futbol or food, if it even continued at all. I knew I could never be on the inside, no matter how long I spent there—no matter what darkness I helped it perpetuate. In Oaxaca, the military and police were murdering unarmed civilians protesting for education reforms and an end to political corruption. I'd been told by many that this spot was one of Mexico's gems but that it wasn't safe right now to even travel through. People were the goddamned worst every-fucking-where you went . . .

There were bats, and scorpions, and snakes, and now, Dengue. Sal and I launched a feverish campaign to mosquito-proof our house. We swept away puddles of standing water and burned huge piles of leaves in the street. We shopped at Walmart, despite our moral objections, and bought poison to kill the buggers. Nearly every time I looked down, a cluster of bloodsuckers was circling my ankles. They were relentless. I found myself constantly swatting my legs, oftentimes in rote without even looking at them—even if no bugs were there. I wrapped myself in blankets at night, despite the heat, to make penetration more difficult, preferring extreme discomfort to potential disease.

I couldn't think of any good reasons why I was still in Lila. The vacation was over; the fever returned. Every minute of every day I was plotting my escape in the same way I always had. I went over it compulsively in my mind, subconscious so preoccupied with the task it had little time to enjoy anything pleasant. I could go east to the Gulf. It's beautiful there, right? Or maybe south into Guatemala? My plans were always so needlessly complex, often with conflicting details, rendering me unable to take a step:

With fifty-six pesos I could bet the farm on a ticket to the coast—head to the port of Zambulla and stow away on a ship bound for Shanghai. The open sea, the sunshine, the complete reliance on the ship's captain and navigation system . . .

But wait, you don't speak any Mandarin. What the fuck would you do when you got there? And what the fuck do you know about stowing away on a ship? Do you find a quiet place in the hull and munch on potato skins while crossing the Pacific? Do you assimilate into the crew and start mopping the deck while singing a merry tune?

No steps here . . .

At some point though, Lila was what I'd wanted. I owed it to myself to explore what was here.

Chapter 12

Herb was a hard worker and an even harder partier. Each week, he'd start his celebration shortly after work on Friday and keep it going until the sun dropped on Sunday. He'd usually head over to our place after classes with a couple of six-packs of Barrilitos, and we'd pass the time on plastic chairs under the almond trees. Occasionally, someone would get up, pluck another lime off the tree, slice it, and pass it around.

"So, you boys ready to take a walk on the wild side?" Herb asked late one afternoon with a smirk on his face. He opened a new beer, wiped the top with his shirt, and wedged a lime inside.

Sal shook his head and walked into the house. I could tell by his quiet exit he'd already seen the underbelly and wanted nothing more to do with it.

I, however, was all in.

We killed the Barrilitos and hopped in Abuelita. Herb drove into el Centro and parked along a city street, and we started walking.

"So, where to, Unkie Herb?" Sal and I'd added the "Unkie" to his name in honor of the *Simpsons* and dishonor of the Herbster.

"The Rock Bar."

"Not that place again!"

I'd been to the Rock Bar too many times already and couldn't handle another. It was one of the few dives in town with live music—

something I had no aversion to. It was the quality of music at this place that unfit the bill.

We walked through the uneven streets until we were close enough to hear the echo of too-much-fucking reverb bouncing off the ancient stone structures surrounding us.

"Can't we go someplace else, Herby?"

"Quit your bitching. We'll only stay for a few drinks and move on."

We walked through the entrance, and Herb sat at a table in front of the band. The leader singer and guitarist, Rudi, shot us a smile mid-song. Herb smiled back and waved. I searched for the barmaid.

The place was crowded, as usual. Rudi was something of a local rock legend—a distinction I figured had more to do with a lack of competition than raw skill. The girls batted their eyelashes and called out his name and unrepressed all those gnarled emotions now dripping from the air like water at a saturated dew point. The group was a trio who slaughtered their way through covers of both English and Spanish tunes. Individually, they weren't so bad. But, apparently, they must have missed the second half of the saying, "All for one . . ." The bassist kept rhythm that no one followed, and Rudi seemed more interested in playing the part than mastering the craft. He always wedged a lit cigarette between the strings on the headstock of his guitar while he played, then took a histrionic drag after the coda. There was a different drummer each time, ala *Spinal Tap*, and the quantity of my discontent usually depended on him. A good drummer could at least keep the music respectable. But a bad one—Check please!

The band only played a couple dozen songs, which they clunked through repeatedly in a playlist that never seemed to end. Rudi's father owned the bar, giving Rudi and his group center stage seven nights a week. I empathized with the neighbors.

Herby and I ordered some drinks just as they were wrapping up "A Lotta Blick ina Wral." The beers arrived in enormous frosted glasses and were set down beside a few bowls of spiced nuts. I cringed when Rudi hit the E minor opening "Zombie." "Zombie" was one of the handful of English covers that nearly all Mexican bar bands covered. Others included: "Creep," "Roadhouse Blues," and "Break on Through." Though I loved all four tunes, they were played out to their deaths here, often by bands more excited to touch the notes than live the music.

"C'mon, Herby, let's jet after these brews. The night's callin' my name."

"Just relax. We'll grab another beer and take off."

When "Zombie" ended, they started into "Eleanor Rigby."

"Okay," Herb said, "it's time to go."

We got up, waved to Rudi, and walked back to Abuelita. Herb drove us south of el Centro onto some country road I hadn't yet traveled. He slowed and pulled behind what looked like an abandoned airplane hangar, but there were nearly a hundred cars parked there in the grass.

"What the hell is this place?"

"It's like a big dancehall. You'll see . . ."

We walked around front where two large men frisked us.

"A dancehall, you say?"

Herb didn't answer; he was too busy getting his balls patted down. I was overcome with weirdness when we walked inside. The room was enormous and lit by black light. There were about fifty small, circular tables set around a wooden dance floor in the center. Everywhere were people dancing, drinking, and celebrating life. A full banda ensemble performed on a raised stage equipped with house lighting and a curtain. Above the stage was a neon painting of NYC's skyline, which shone in the black light. That scene somehow made me feel at home. The word "Pati's" was written to the right of the skyline. Herb and I sat at an empty table and ordered a cubeta. We each popped open a brew, wiped the top with our shirts, and slid a lime wedge inside.

"So, is this like a school dance for withered old fucks?"

Herb didn't respond. He just sat there lost in the scene with a wide smile curling up his face. I studied the dance floor. Something about this place just wasn't right. Pretty young girls danced with hideous old men. Perhaps this was an alternate universe? Herb saw me staring at the dance floor.

"Why don't you go out there? Find a girl . . ."

I shrugged my shoulders and got up from the table. I figured I could do better investigatory work from up close anyway. I stepped onto the floor and started moving. The banda group broke into a swingin' new groove: "Corazon, te amo mi amor . . ." (the words "corazon" and "amor" were lyrical staples in many traditional Mexican songs). I figured it'd be softball to rip one of these luscious honeys off the cadavers they were currently latched on to. After all, I seemed to be having a way with the ladies here . . .

But none of these bit. They stayed with their men and hardly paid me a casual glance. I tried to dance my way into their hearts, but it was no use. On my way off the floor, I walked by some facially hirsute stiff tonguing a sweet, young thing.

"I struck out, Unkie Herb."

"Hey, you don't win 'em all, killer." He popped open another beer, wiped it down, and handed it my way. I watched some young lady lead a decrepit old man outside.

"This isn't a dancehall, is it, Herb?"

He didn't answer. Some chick was busy calling him over with her finger, and soon he was up and gone. Fuck. At least I had the beer bucket. Occasionally, girls sat and tried to make conversation, but I quickly shooed them away. I didn't have the cash or patience for their company.

Soon, Herb was back at the table. He was sweating and smiling.

"Damn, that Pilar has one serious ass. I could munch Thanksgiving dinner out of that thing."

"Yeah, after she's eaten it . . ."

Herb laughed.

"Let's get the hell out of here," I said.

"Relax, I just ordered another bucket. This place is filled with pussy. Man up, and go find something to stick your dick in."

"I'm not paying to fuck any of these whores. I don't play that shit." It was true. I'd made a pact with myself back in Buffalo when things were at their darkest, that no matter what else I got into, I'd never touch hookers or blow. I could probably find a way to justify stealing some rich dude's wallet or selling a garbage bag full of marijuana and still retain some dignity, but I couldn't touch hookers or blow. This had nothing to do with religious morals or respecting social conventions—I just needed some limits. After all, a crook without limits will soon start stealing pieces of their own heart and soul until there's nothing left but animal.

For the remainder of the night, I did what came natural in times of discomfort and uncertainty: I receded inward. The colors, the smells, the sounds—they all took shape of their own. There was a strangeness about it all that poked at me—teased my curiosity. What forged all this? This black-lit temporary reality highlighted several hideous neon memories surrounding me—memories that were always with me, but that I'd been able to hide in the brightness of daylight. In the brightness of school or work or holiday celebration.

But there was something satisfying about the strange. Something appealing of the abnormal. And each time I indulged in my desire to greet this darkness, I felt both more and less alive simultaneously. And each of those things strange floated like portals I could step through. Each had its own weird world on the other side. There was something so appealing about stepping into the darkness, the unknown, and letting it wrap around me, caring for me like an evil mother. I wouldn't have to worry anymore; she'd take care of me and show me the way. All you have to do is close your eyes, relax, and flow . . .

"C'mon, Herby, let's get the hell out of here."

"We're only half finished with the bucket."

"I'm gonna be fully finished if we don't go somewhere else."

"I got a place in mind, but we gotta finish these beers first."

"All right, hand one over."

He did. I popped, wiped, slid, and took it down double time. Soon we were at the door. I turned and looked once more at the neon skyline of the city I'd cursed so many times in my youth. It represented everything I'd wanted—everything I'd feared.

"They don't frisk you on the way out, do they, Herby?" I loved to say that guy's name. It fit him so well.

"Not unless you slip 'em a coupla bills."

On our way to the car, a pack of young tough guys stared Herb down as they passed. They rounded the corner and continued to the entrance.

"You pay to fuck one of their sisters?" I said.

"Don't worry about those cholos. They're just street trash."

We piled in Abuelita, rolled through the grass field, and onto the carretera.

"So, where to now, old man?"

"You'll see. This next place makes Pati's look like a church."

"Yeah, I guess some of the girls in there did look like nuns . . ."

Herb laughed.

"It's not another whorehouse, is it?"

"Pati's isn't a whorehouse; it's a dancehall."

"Sure it is, Unkie Herb."

"I call this next place The Star Wars Bar, and you'll soon see why."

Herb drove down a city street and parked in front of a seemingly normal bar—until we walked inside.

Herb had been dead-on with his description. The whole place was overcome with a festering rot, which, if not for the motion of its decrepit denizens, would have entirely camouflaged the variety of weirdness inside—and this sight did make Pati's seem reasonable. Everything looked to be melting to the floor: the tables, and chairs, and jukebox in the corner were lumps, indistinguishable shapes with some dreadful deception about them. They invited you to sit, and sleep, where they could wrap around you and begin that slow process of digestion before you even realized you'd been had. But the creatures inside didn't seem to mind. They seemed to have some kind of symbiotic relationship with the rot, which they shuffled around like a moving Ralph Steadman. Their bodies had morphed to adapt to the disease and filth surrounding them. They were some brand of mutant species that would no doubt find a way to survive through world war or nuclear winter. There was nothing their eyes hadn't seen, no chemical their bodies hadn't processed. This elite species fed off tragedy like maggots on rotting garbage.

Herb and I walked to a table. I hesitated to sit, pondering whether STDs could crawl through denim. We ordered a couple of beers and scanned the room. I knew I had a set time limit before the chair juices would start to digest me.

"What time is it, Herby?" I shifted in my chair, allowing each ass cheek to bear my weight for only so long before switching and holding it above the scabies-infested seat again.

Herb didn't answer. He was busy staring at some lumpy creature in the back corner. "See that skeezer back there?" His eyes never left her. "She's truly something special."

She was hard at work, chatting to some mustached superhuman across the room, when she saw Herb. Their eyes locked. They both smiled. She flirted with her body, then shimmied around lumpy tables and chairs on her way to her favorite client. Though she was probably in her thirties, time had not been kind to her. She clenched a cigarette between her pointer and middle finger and held a glass of what could have been toxic waste with the other three digits.

Still, Herb smiled and blushed when she kissed his cheek. They exchanged hellos, and she leaned in for a private conversation. Herb was fixated on her and she on him. I didn't know if Herb was a friend or former client, or both. It didn't matter either way. It was nearing four a.m., and I was exhausted. Every bit of my waning energy was now focused on one goal: making it safely back to my bed.

Soon the woman shimmied away, and Herb watched her delicately. There was some bridge of respect between them. I realized I'd missed something important.

"Who was that beast?"

"That right there," Herb smiled like a dumb kid, "is the best dancer in Mexico. She moves like an angel."

"And sucks like a whore."

"Have some respect, sonny boy. Whores are people too."

"I thought you said this wasn't a whorehouse?"

"It's not. Some of these skeezers are whores. Some are just regular girls."

"Yeah, and what kind of 'regular girl' hangs out in a whorehouse?"

"Don't get so cocky. You still got a lot to learn." Herb scanned the room and found a pretty girl sitting with a broad-shouldered young man. "There. I bet that girl isn't a whore."

"Well, she does look pretty respectable, but that doesn't preclude her from employment in the sex industry."

Her male friend sat with his back to us, so Herb and I indulged in a few glances throughout the night.

"So, what's the deal with this place? Is it a bar?"

"Yeah, it's just a bar where people come after Pati's closes."

"How long have you been coming here?"

"One of my buddies turned me on to the place shortly after I moved down here."

"I bet you've got some stories."

He smiled. "More than you'd want to know about."

"Care to share?"

He thought for a moment. "A few years back, there was this fight out front between two whores. They were really goin' at it, givin' each other hell. A crowd of guys slowly gathered around, cheering them on. They were scratching, and punching, and clawing big chunks of hair out of each other's heads for a good twenty minutes, and nobody stopped it. These guys just stood around howling like a pack of hyenas. Finally, the one bitch knocks out the other and just wanders off right before the police arrived. The cops didn't ask any questions—just scraped the bloodied, unconscious whore from the ground, and tossed her, stomach down, into the back of their truck like she was a bale of hay. She came crashing down with a dull thud. I'll never forget that sound. The guys disappeared as quickly as they came, most likely out to satisfy whatever fix they were searching for before the fight. I stood out on that sidewalk alone and watched the cops haul that bag of flesh away. There were huge puddles of blood and piles of hair on the sidewalk. It was really a dark night."

"That's too bad," I said. "Why didn't you do anything?"

"It's just not my place. I hate the corruption and general police thuggery here, but it's just not my place to complain."

"Well, where is your place to complain?" I said.

"Uh—"

The dancer returned. This time she acknowledged my presence.

"So, who's this handsome young man?" she asked Herb.

"This is my nephew Will from Chicago."

I smiled and shook her hand.

"And what are you doing in Mexico?" she said.

"Just visiting my Uncle Herpies. I only get to see him once or twice a year."

Herb laughed. "Why don't you two dance?" Though he'd said that to us both, he was looking at me.

"I, uh, I'm tired . . ."

"Just give it a go. She's a real princess."

I rose to my feet, nearly comatose, but was pulled into her orbit by following her swaying hips as she backed toward the dance floor. Herb was no liar; she could move. And though I had no capacity to judge dance moves, I knew her every movement was entirely her own. She grabbed my hand, jolting me awake, and twisted me around her body. I had no idea what was going on, but I momentarily allowed myself to ignore the judging eyes of the other creatures surrounding me. My body and spirit were tired, but they permitted me the use of just enough stored energy to make it through the song. When it was over, I returned to my seat much more attentive to my surroundings. She walked up beside me and kissed my cheek. I smiled and blushed (and hoped I wouldn't be billed).

Herb and I shared a few more stories, then decided to leave. It was nearing five a.m., and the sun was threatening to cut through the darkness, casting us all in its revealing and blinding light. I slapped some cash in Herb's mitts, and he walked to the bar to pay our bill. I waited by the entrance and pondered my strange existence. Just then, the broad-shouldered man walked by with the pretty girl, and as he passed, he whispered in my ear, "Chinga tu madre," and walked through the door.

Words formed in my gut and rose upward but got detained in my throat under orders from my brain's translator, which wanted to double check their meaning before release. My anger, however, erupted from deep inside, forcing these words through without proper inspection, and I started screaming random swear words in both English and Spanish: "Puta!" "Fucker!" "Mierda!" "Tu abuela sucks dick!" I followed behind after he walked out the door but felt a hand pull me back by the collar of my shirt. I turned and saw one of Herb's pasty sausage-fingers wagging in my personal space.

"You're in *his* country, man." He said this with supreme self-assurance as if it was the punch line to some fucked-up fable he'd been desperately trying to convince himself actually had some merit.

"Fuck! That doesn't give him right to talk shit to me!"

"Well, we were checking out his girl all night. That should make it even."

"That doesn't even begin to make anything even! I'll fucking kill that bastard!"

"Just calm down. You don't want to get in a fight down here. They'll lock you up for a week. I know, 'cause it's happened to me a few times. And if it's a white guy versus a Mexican, you can almost guarantee you'll be the only one behind bars. It's not worth it. C'mon, I'll take you home."

We rode Abuelita through some unfamiliar streets before I identified the panteon wall. The sun's first rays had broken over the horizon, fulfilling the promise that a new day would indeed arrive. I was piss drunk and had been drinking for well over half a day. My whole body hurt; it was under such pressure my blood felt as if it could burst through my skin. All I hoped for was a quick escape once I hit my sheets.

Chapter 13

I went to a party at Hans's house the following night with Mica and Sal. We'd started drinking early that afternoon and were already lit up by the time we got there, which happened to have been before everyone else. We were firing on all cylinders as the waves of extraneros began to show. I sifted through the crowd and saw something beautiful—a tall, fair-skinned gal who was with two other girls and two guys. The beautiful girl crushed my insides. I knew I'd have to talk to her or I'd regret it eternally, even after the next girl came along. And she just so happened to have walked over and sat beside me . . .

Though I was nervous, as a gringo I could mask this nervousness with my "cute" struggle to speak Spanish, allowing me to focus more on my words than on how I looked saying them.

"I haven't seen you around any of these parties," I said.

"I don't really like to go out very much. I prefer to spend time with my family instead." This was something new to me. It wasn't that girls in the US didn't enjoy spending time with their families, but Mexican girls took it to another level. They had no problem forgoing a night of debauchery to spend time braiding grandma's hair. It was something I really admired.

"Well, that's nice. Family is important." I threw a few platitudes at her beautiful head, and she smiled. My anxiety melted away.

The conversation took over for itself, leaving us free to explore each other without needless worry. The girl's name was Flor, and she was a great ambassador for the moniker. Her whole body lit up with talent, and charm, and beauty. I liked her, I really did. Sometime later, we moved to the living room dance floor where the extraneros were breaking it down to some reggaeton. Flor pressed her body against mine, grinding her warming area on my own. We locked together, and I slid my right knee between her legs, and she massaged herself on it as we moved. She bit her lip and kissed my neck. Her body released a pleasing scent, driving me wild. I could feel a wetness in my boxer shorts.

We left the dance floor after a few songs and returned outside hand in hand. Marco approached me.

"Hey, man, I was just at the Arce, and these pendejos were pushing me to fight. Will you come with me? They're probably gone, but if not, I think we can hurt them too much."

"How many are there?"

"Only five or six. But they are weak."

"Why don't you ask Sal?"

"He left with Mica to buy some mota."

I looked at Flor, and she looked back. There was something reassuring about her gaze—as if her attention span could last more than the half hour necessary for my departure and return.

"Listen, I'm not lookin' for any trouble," I said.

"Me neither. I just want to flex some muscle and buy some beers. I'm not going to another place just because of those assholes."

"All right, all right, I'll go with you. I need some beer anyway. But I don't want to fight." I looked at Flor. "You want anything, hermosa?"

She shook her head and kissed my cheek.

"Look, cutie, I'll be right back, okay?"

She nodded and smiled. We walked to Marco's car and got in. He drove to a different Arce than we usually went to, but there was nobody outside.

"So why'd these guys fuck with you?" I took the last gulp of my caguama.

"I was in line, ready to buy a bottle of whiskey, and the one pushed his friend into me. I told them to watch what they were doing, and they surrounded me. So, I walked away and told them I'd be back."

"Well, I don't see anybody, do you?"

"No, they must have left."

We walked up to the Arce, bought a bottle of whiskey and some caguamas, and drove back to the party. Marco took an alternate route back in hopes to see the punks, but he didn't. He looked disappointed.

"You know what you say to a guy if you really want to fight?" he said. "Vete a la verga."

"What's that mean?"

"Go to the dick. If you say that to someone, you'd better be ready to fight."

I nodded. Now I had a little more ammo to throw at the world should it peg me with another Sprite bottle.

We'd only been gone for about twenty minutes, but that must have been too long for Flor because she was in the corner laughing it up with some German shithole named Ferd (who we obviously called Turd). Turd was a loud, scrawny, sickly pale, golden-haired, wannabe pretty boy—and Mica's enemy. Mica hated Turd's need to be in control of every damned conversation and to know every girl present by name—his need to speak with Mica in Spanish despite the fact that they both spoke fluent Hochdeutsch. He hated Turd's constant need to scream and throw up his hands in celebration every time he took a damned sip of beer. But even in celebration, Turd's eyes were dull and lifeless. He was a creature devoid of individual thought—a rolling mess of every party cliché that could be scraped from the walls and floor of a college frat house after alumni weekend. But until that party, I had nothing against him.

I sat in a chair outside and sipped my caguama in hopes to cool my warming blood. I didn't want to seem jealous or blow the situation out of proportion. Maybe they were friends just catching up? After all, Flor did say she didn't get out much. Maybe she didn't see me come back? I decided to test this hypothesis. I got up and strolled past her. Nothing. Her eyes remained on the German's. She was either playing games or simply not interested. I decided to allow her to continue her game if that's indeed what she was doing. Turd threw up his hands and screamed like a prick several times during the conversation—and she smiled. She smiled? Was she even worth it?

Ten minutes passed, and they didn't break from each other. Twenty minutes, and still together. Each time that asshole shouted it pissed me off more and more. After a half hour, I decided to walk straight over and push him out of the way. It had nothing to do with her anymore. I just hated that prick.

I got up and started after my target. But en route, a gorgeous, short-haired morena bumped into me. Her name was Serafina, and I'd met her before. Serafina and I'd had a long conversation a few parties back, but I tried to keep myself in line because I knew she had a boyfriend—fucking Turd. How wonderful was this!

"Hello, Serafina, how are you?"

"I'm good. It's nice to see you again."

We couldn't advance the conversation past banalities. Our minds were focused on other endeavors, limiting our casual access to witticisms and charm. We both shot intermittent glances at the subject of our subconscious unrest.

We eventually took the conversation onto the dance floor. Serafina was a wild girl. She was one of the few girls who could pull off the short-haired look, and she was grinding on my knee in no time. I could feel her whole body moan as we danced. I was beginning to forget about Flor.

Later, we walked back outside, and they were still talking. Serafina grabbed my hand and led me right past the scratchable itch onto the cobblestone street out front. I knew Turd saw us walk by. He looked right at her.

"I don't know why he always does this. Am I not pretty?" Tears streamed down her cheeks.

"You're a knockout. He's just a tourist, honey. He doesn't know what he's doing."

I outlined her face softly with my fingers, then my lips to her mouth. I could feel her whole body give; she molded into my arms. I pulled back to study her face. She was gorgeous. Her face was soft and adorable and sexy as hell. I savored each kiss, taking her in slowly. Kissing was usually just a gateway to other things, but with Serafina, kissing was the thing. I kissed her nose, her cheeks, her ears, her neck . . .

I'd look up occasionally, and he was still there, talking to Flor. But with significantly less swagger. What the fuck did anyone see in him? The guy was hideous through and through—a fucking pock-faced weasel with a soul of ash. He spoke Spanish in a nasally German accent. There was nothing attractive about him other than that he was something entirely different—just like me. Fuck . . .

He looked over at one point, and I stared his weak eyes down. All my life I'd always done my best to avoid those eyes. There was something about them that terrified me. But I never understood why.

But staring into that shithead's eyes helped clarify part of that mystery for me. After staring him down, he started looking at us with less frequency even though he seemed less focused on Flor. I could see the suffering in his eyes. I was kissing all over his girlfriend's face right in front of him. And he did nothing. There was something about his weakness that enraged me. What was holding me back from exploring these feelings before? What previously had kept me from indulging in these dark powers?

Part of it became clear to me: I was no longer among anyone whose judgment had any consequence on my actions. I had no one to explain a black eye to. No one to call me evil for using my fists. No one to call me selfish for standing up for myself. No one to condemn me to hell or purgatory or any other fictitious place for following my god-given instincts. These fucking priests and nuns and godparents and patron saints, all staring me down all the fucking time, judging my every weakness and failure: "God is watching you!" "Santa is watching you!" "The IRS is watching you!" Well, I wasn't going to keep these instincts in check any longer. I wasn't going to hold my rage inside, where the magma and pressure had been building for too long, weighing me down and scorching everything good I carried with me. Every time I kissed that gorgeous Mexican girl, I could feel the magma preparing for release. Could feel its fucking sheer power inside of me. Maybe the eruption would destroy the entire town, but I couldn't hold it in any longer. Couldn't fear it. Couldn't let them keep a lid on it. There was nothing wrong with fucking. There was nothing wrong with fighting. There was nothing wrong with feeling life at least once before its next close.

Herb's words about prison kept echoing through my mind. But this German was a gringo, just like me. If he attacked . . .

But he didn't. An hour went by, and he just stood there. Watching. That was enough of a victory for me. I could feel my anger subsiding. Besides, I had this gorgeous girl under my arms who still hadn't left me. Even after an hour, I hadn't tired of kissing her. I could have gone on all night, all week, all life . . .

But, suddenly, Serafina stopped. There was an element of distress in her eyes.

"C'mon, baby, let's take a walk."

"I don't want to walk, I just want to kiss you." I pulled her close, but she pushed me away.

"No, please, let's just go for a walk."

She grabbed my hand and started pulling me along. We got halfway down the block when I saw her looking at something over my shoulder. I stopped and turned around.

There, charging up behind me, were three man-shaped silhouettes whose steps seemed far too deliberate to imply a peaceful encounter.

"Just keep walking."

"Fuck that!" I broke from Serafina's grip and stood my ground. The silhouettes stopped. A street lamp lit their faces: three Mexicans I'd never seen before. The guy in the middle threw some aggressive concoction of words at me, but I didn't care to translate. I knew what they meant. Part of me wished to find a peaceful solution to this situation. But the other part of me won. I started moving toward them. Two of the fuckers turned and walked away while the other one remained. He said in English, "You are lucky, man, he don't want to fight you."

"Vete a la verga, cabron!" I waited—but nothing. The last punk turned and walked away too. Wow, that was easy. That was the moment I first realized I was a king. If only I'd known years ago . . .

Serafina tried to kiss me, but I was through with that shit. I started back to the party. Serafina grabbed my hand and tried to restrain me, but it was useless. What were those punks after? I didn't recognize any of them. Maybe I'd done something to one of them before? Sal and I had been pretty rowdy in the beginning of the party. It was customary in Mexico to slap someone's hand, then follow that with a light bump of the fists. Somewhere along the way, Sal and I thought it funny to punch those fists as hard as we could. Several guys there were clutching sore knuckles. But I don't think we'd said hello to any of these fuckers . . .

I saw the punks sitting on a car hood in front of the house. I walked over to them. Sal saw me and got there first. He started talking with the boss punk. Their Spanish was too fast for me to translate. When they were through, Sal turned to me. "He said you elbowed him in the stomach during the party."

"Bullshit! I've never seen this bitch before in my life. Ask if he's friends with the loud German."

Sal said something to the guy, and he responded.

"No, he says you hit him."

"Well you can tell him I'm game if he is."

Marco must have caught the scent because he stormed over. "What's going on here, fellas? Do we need to break some noses?"

Sal stood between Marco and the asshole. "Relax, Marco, nobody's throwing any punches. Will, he just wants you to apologize."

"Tell him to go to the dick!"

"What the fuck are you talking about? Just shake his hand, all right?"

I looked at Marco. He seemed ready to release some aggression.

"Fuck it." I shook the clown's hand, and he and his posse walked back to the party. Sal was a pit bull and Marco a bulldozer. There was little doubt we could have taken half that party if needed. But it wasn't. I later discovered the guy I'd supposedly "elbowed" had a pretty serious crush on Serafina.

I lost Serafina in the chaos of things and later saw her crying in the German's arms. She was foolish but human. Something big had changed in me that night. Some switch had been turned on that I knew I'd never be able to turn off again. If I invited violence into my life, I'd never stop fighting. But there was no way I was ever letting someone push me around again. I'd spend a week in prison if I really had to.

I discovered several months later, while chatting with Mica over some drinks, that Turd had hated me from that day on. But he still always smiled and shook my hand when he saw me. Fucking tourist.

Chapter 14

Near the end of September, I begged the ladies at Lengua for more hours so I could continue surviving after my savings ran dry—a rapidly approaching reality. I asked about extra classes, substitute gigs—even cleaning the damned bathrooms. My strategy of relentless pestering eventually paid off when they gave me another student who came Tuesday, Wednesday, and Thursday afternoons from eleven to one. Those six extra hours a week would provide me enough cash to cover my weekly grocery and alcohol bills. With just a few more classes, I'd be sitting pretty.

My new student's name was Guadalupe. Guadalupe was eighteen and had just started college. Her goal was to become a lawyer, and she wanted to learn English to help with this pursuit. She came from a life of privilege, and her father saw to it that she had her fill of all the trendiest clothing and latest technological gadgets the boutiques and department stores of Lila had to offer. Guadalupe was a nice girl but rarely said anything more than she had to.

I'd never taught English solo before and was insecure. Though fluency gave me an advantage to succeed as an English teacher, this wasn't the only prerequisite. Being a good English instructor also required the skill to explain why a certain word was used instead of another or why one tense was better to use than another tense or ten million other things I wasn't quite sure how to explain. I think this exploration of my own language helped me in learning Spanish, which is something I found pleasantly serendipitous.

It was also nice to be a part of something. Lengua was a reputable school, and Ines seemed like a good leader. She was intelligent and dynamic and seemed to run a tight ship. She kept the building well stocked with the standard pedagogical paraphernalia: whiteboards, DVD players, workbooks . . . It also had air conditioning and a water cooler. I'd usually arrive early for classes just so I could sit in the AC and thumb through *National Geographic* magazines or check my email at the computers. Teaching Gabriel in Fundido was rewarding, but getting that gig with Guadalupe made me feel as though I'd finally made it.

The ladies at Lengua also gave Sal a class in that building. We assumed they thought they owed us for shipping us off through the mountains three days a week just to teach a one-hour class. I didn't always understand what they were telling me, but I didn't care. This new job came with perks. Sal and I would often bring several empty bottles and fill them at the school's watercooler, cutting down on my trips to the filtration center with the garrafones. We also used their phone to make local calls, and Sal swiped one of their DVD players so he could watch movies in his bedroom.

Life seemed to be improving. Sal was an avid runner and, for years, had been trying to convince me to join him. And for years I'd said no. But I said yes one day after Sal described an unbelievable view of the volcano he always got on one particular leg of his route. He said the best time to go was just after seven when the sun was setting beyond it.

I'd been an athlete my whole life. I could play games of football or basketball all day with no problems. But running was a different beast. There were no quick shifts or breaks in play or players to defend. In running, it was just me, the road, and all my hideous thoughts. I didn't know how this would turn out.

We started up the small hill and made a right on Madrid del Rio. We ran down that main road for about an eighth of a mile, passing the deportivo complex, biblioteca, and several small shops.

We made a left at the Kiosko just before the carretera bridge, which separated Lila from la Villa del Lado. We ran up a slight incline along the carretera for about a mile. This was the road that contained the gorgeous view of the Volcán, which towered over the horizon like a craggy, earthen god. The view was so clear and the volcano so vast, it looked as if it were only a few hundred yards away. I felt as though I could run right up its base, touch its rim, and slide back down.

There wasn't much around us here except for the goats grazing in the tall grass between us and the highway. The volcano in the distance inspired me to continue running despite my aching knees. This was a part of Lila I still hadn't seen, and I was amazed that my own feet could provide me such an excellent vehicle.

Sal warned me of some vicious strays that always hung out in front of the auto garage we were about to pass. He picked up a stone from the road and advised me to do the same. I grabbed a big one, but the dogs never came.

We continued running up that road for about a mile, taking us through a peaceful residential neighborhood just before a grassy field. But the peace filtered away through the tall grass, and the only element of humanity passing through was a sordid dust, which gathered in colorful heaps in the fields beyond, taking the form of a row of strip clubs and whorehouses.

"Yo, Rocky Sixteen," I said, "I'll see you back at the house."

"All right, later, Little Roger Donkeysamples."

I ran the whole way back and returned home about forty minutes before Sal. He was a record-setting long-distance runner in high school. Running was his poetry and release. When he finally got back, we sat together under the almond trees in plastic lawn chairs and discussed plans to run more often. I felt a particular freedom in finally committing to something.

I was beginning to feel more comfortable in Mexico. I now had over a month there and had significantly fewer bite marks around my ankles. I was washing the dishes and feeling pretty good about life one sultry afternoon when the landlady's daughter came tapping on the front gate.

"Come in!" I yelled from the sink.

She opened the door and stepped inside. The woman was large and burly with the hulking build of a trucker, square jaw of a lumberjack, and fashion sense of a construction worker. Mica referred to her as 'the man-lady,' and she didn't fuck around.

Her visit that afternoon was no warm hello. She had a stone-cold agenda and delivered a message far too quickly for me to decipher. She slowed it down and tried several times to clarify herself, but I still couldn't understand. I gave her a blank stare, and she finally returned to her default pissy tone. Sal and I were always doing things around the house that she deemed wrong, so I just nodded a few times and smiled.

"Tienes escoba?"

"What? I don't know what that is."

"ESCOBA! TIENES?"

She scanned the kitchen, grabbed the broom, then went outside and started sweeping the leaves. I drowned out that racket with the sound of a steel wool pad on Jorg's macaroni surprise. The pot was covered in burnt ground beef. Fucking Jorg!

About fifteen minutes passed before she came back inside. She said some more indecipherable crap while shoving an empty plastic milk jug in my face. I'd assumed she was reprimanding me for littering.

"I'm sorry," I said. "It must have fallen out of the trash."

But that wasn't good enough. She continued to push it in my face. There was something chunky in the bottom of the jug that I initially mistook for curdled milk. But a tremendous wave of anxiety twisted up my spine when I heard her repeat the word, "Alacran!"

Oh, don't tell me . . .

That was the first time I saw one—one of the mythical creatures that had ravaged my thoughts and sense of security. Until then, I still could have convinced myself that these beasts were as likely to cross my path as a shark would while swimming in Lake Erie. But now

I had a recent kill being showcased mercilessly before my watering eyes. She spoke again, and I understood.

"I've killed four or five of them in the past ten minutes," she said.

"Is that normal?"

"I've lived in Lila my whole life, and I've never seen such an infestation."

FUCK! "What should I do?"

She motioned for me to follow her outside. Curiosity got the better of my fear, and I walked through the door.

"Where'd you find them?"

"They are all over. Mostly under piles of leaves. You should really keep this place cleaner."

She swept a leaf pile under one of the almond trees, and a scorpion ran from her like a coward. She crushed it under her sandal. She swept several more piles, and each time a scorpion would appear.

All my fears and stereotypes of scorpions were rearranging in that moment. Before, I would have just assumed that scorpions would stand their ground and fight to the death in an epic struggle for survival. But these little fugitives were nothing more than common arachnids, running like cockroaches from the orange glow of a fluorescent light. Perhaps these creatures weren't hunting me?

The landlady's daughter was now a hero of mine. Her actions were swift, confidence resolute, and justice delivered ice-cold.

She swept a pile under a different tree, and a yellow scorpion ran directly at me. In one quick motion, she flipped the broom and speared it with the handle. I did a little jump, but it was inspired more by excitement than fear. By the end of that cleaning session, she had at least six confirmed kills, and despite her concern about our extreme scorpion infestation, I felt significantly less fear to ever come across another. Some of my Mexican friends had only seen a few alacranes their lifetimes. But I saw six in one afternoon.

The woman left later and walked ten feet above the sidewalk, which was made from the same material as her nerves.

That night, I lit the candles on my table, sat on my bed, and wrote the following:

I read the story of the alacran.
I saw its picture on TV.
I heard the tale of the man who died sticking his hand in a hole
    inside a tree.

When I first entered the land of the alacran,
Teeth gnashed tight and cold, sweaty hands.
Fear paralyzed the night and brought time to a stand.

I now have over a month in the land of the alacran.
It took four weeks for me to understand.
In that afternoon, the sun shone upon the land,
And washed away the darkness like a soapy, damp rag.

In that afternoon I could finally see,
Not one, but six villains as I was raking the leaves.
But instead of attacking their home's destructor, they fled like
    cowards
With their backs to the breeze.

Yet they were slaughtered like criminals
To prevent the rape and pillage of other cities—
Their power respected to the end.
And my jaw relaxed and hands dried knowing how to fight their
    friends.
It was then I'd realized that the man should have kept his hand
    out of an
Unknown place.

Tonight, I might accidentally put on my shoes in the dark.

I want to be ready.

Chapter 15

In late September, Lila had a number of visitors. Sal had been smiling all week after hearing that his older brother, Cisco, was ditching his bohemian hideout in Brooklyn to join us on our well-intentioned romp through North America's last remaining Wild, Wild West. Cisco was an intriguing character. He was an artist with tremendous talent. By age twelve, he'd already had several paintings hung at the Albright-Knox Art Gallery. He moved to NYC after high school and established quite a reputation in the underground scene. I was excited to see him again. Part of that excitement was due to his company. He was just a cool dude. The other part was because he was the only person I'd ever met who could calm Sal during one of his fits.

Cisco arrived at our dead-end house one sunny afternoon with a canvas duffle bag over his shoulder. His eyes were hidden behind black Ray-Bans, and his dark hair was slicked back with something stronger than its own natural grease. Cisco was tall with a medium frame, and like Sal, wasn't laden with muscle, but he had a combination of power and dexterity that left little doubt that any punch thrown would punish its unfortunate target. And he was someone who hit first and didn't stop to ask questions. Cisco was free-spirited but also ruled by the same old-school discipline that drove Herb to bitching any time a conversation centered on a topic like "kids these days."

It was an intriguing juxtaposition and kept life interesting. I liked Cisco and found his presence refreshing on those long, stagnant Lilan afternoons.

Sal quickly absorbed his brother in his slipstream, and soon there was nothing else surrounding him. For the next few days, Sal's long, late-afternoon naps were replaced with blood-only tours of places I hadn't yet seen in Lila. Apparently gas prices were only an issue when Cisco wasn't there, and Sal's cherry red Passat hit every nook and cranny in that small city in the short time the two brothers were together.

When Sal was in the office, however, Cisco spent several late-mornings and early-afternoons discussing life with me under the almond trees.

"There's no place like New York in the whole world," he said. "Everything's there. There's no better city for artists. San Fran is a close second. I'm tellin' you, man, if there's anything you want in life, you need to just go after it. I wanna spend the next few months hitchhiking through Mexico, stowing away on trains . . . You know, there's a port town nearby here. I'm sure you could find a way to work onboard a ship in exchange for a trip someplace else. They could probably take you right down the coast if you wanted."

I loved and hated his words. Cisco tossed one of his mix CDs in the boombox, and we played it over and over. Those afternoons were filled with Morrissey's baritone bravado, and Peaches's casual detachment.

"You know where I wanna go?" he said. "Puerto Vallarta. Get a job working on the beach and just be for however long I feel like being. You should come with me."

"I don't know. I just got a decent job here. Besides, I think this city still has something to offer me."

"Well, that's where I think I'm heading next. I'll give you my number in case you change your mind."

"Cool. Maybe I'll take you up on that . . ." I really wanted to but knew I shouldn't. It just wouldn't help my situation. Still, it was nice to hear some can-do positivity again.

Sal and Cisco's cousin Eduardo and his friend Andre paid us a visit from Guadalajara that weekend. Eduardo, or Lalo, as they called him, and Andre were both intelligent and well-traveled recent college graduates who spoke a myriad of languages and could hold conversation on any number of topics. Both spoke fluent English, and Lalo was now studying Swedish. His current girlfriend was also a Swede. This was no coincidence. His advice: "The best way to learn a language is in bed." I guess it made sense . . . (and what a great pedagogy for a language school: "Here's your 'tutor' for this weekend. Study hard!"). But if it were true, he should have been able to speak dozens more languages. He resembled Javier Bardem, and Sal often spoke about how much the ladies loved him.

Lalo, Andre, Sal, and Cisco were sitting on our uncomfortable furniture and drinking caguamas early that Friday evening when I returned from teaching in El Campo. They'd been discussing music and our tastes overlapped. I dropped my book bag in my room and opened a caguama. Sal and Cisco went to Sal's room to get ready for the evening, and Lalo, Andre, and I sat on plastic chairs under the almond trees. We'd been speaking in English, but the conversation quickly rolled over to Spanish, and I didn't even realize it until Sal and Cisco came back outside. Maybe it was due to the nature of the conversation and the company I was in, but I finally saw those huevos in my head, and they looked and smelled delicioso. I can do this!

The bats were flying all around us, darting to and fro. One swooped and missed my face by about an inch. I didn't flinch. I really think I can do this . . .

Sal's family members weren't the only visitors we had around this time. Jorg had also been talking nonstop all week about a friend from Germany coming to Lila. Jorg went to the airport that night to pick him up, and shortly after, he and his friend were getting out of a cab under the almond trees. And goddamn was he tall—and gangly. He looked like a great, great, great, great, great descendant of Ichabod Crane.

"Hello, fellas, this is my friend Ekkehard."

None of us would ever remember that name.

Ekke opened his mouth as if to speak, but his words seemed to have gotten caught up in his giant fucking Adam's apple. He looked to have given up, then upchucked a guttural, "Hul-oh."

"What up, Icky Shuffle? Welcome to Meh-hico!"

Ekke turned red and said nothing. Dude was the definition of awkward.

"Don't mind him, fellas," Jorg said. "He doesn't speak any English or Spanish."

Ekkehard said something to Jorg. None of us knew any German, but we could tell he even spoke that awkwardly. Ekkehard had signed up for a three-week stint in Mexico—an eternity for someone so seemingly unsure of his decision to come. Jorg was almost always busy at the office or in the field, but he promised to show Ekkehard a good time. Ekke dropped his bags off in the house, then sat with us out front.

"So, what's the plan tonight?" I said.

"Me, Andre, Lalo, and Cisco are gonna head up to The Limit to shoot some pool. You're all welcome to join," Sal said.

"I could go for some pool," Jorg said.

"Dr. Josh and some of the new geology grad students are coming too. They're on their way over now," Sal said.

Soon, a car rolled downhill, and five young adults got out. They were an earthy crew: worn sandals, and dirt-stained cargo shorts, and t-shirts with iron-on nature scenes or logos of obscure bands. Dr. Josh was among them. I'd hung out with him several times at parties or the geology office while visiting Sal. He was a twenty-seven-year-old Scot who grew up on a farm just outside of Glasgow. He was a practical guy who made best use of whatever resources he had. Sal loved to tell the story about how he once saw Dr. Josh drink the oil from a can of sardines while doing fieldwork because it was "packed with energy." Dr. Josh had already spent over a year in Lila studying the Volcán. He'd earned his doctorate in the amount of time it took most people to figure out what in the hell they wanted to do with their lives. He was a brilliant and dedicated geologist who spent most of his free time surfing or climbing the crags of Lila. The guy had a lust for life and was a crowd favorite anywhere he went. In the year he'd been here, he'd become fluent in Spanish, and he shared stories and interesting facts with an always-interested audience. But I think the real reason why everyone liked him is because he was the only person there who ever seemed like he knew what the fuck he was doing. And I felt safe knowing he was a leader on the team who would alert the town should the volcano show signs it might blow.

He was helping a new group of recruits learn the ropes. Only a few had shown up to our house that night, but I'd met the others while eating lunch with the good doctor a few days earlier. Most came from Europe, but a handful were from Canada and one from the US. Most were cool, but a few were preachy, idealistic assholes.

The recruits soon faded into the background except for one character: Dan—the only one from the US. Dan was an asshole. He was born and raised in Iowa where he'd lived until he was twenty-nine, but because he'd spent the last few months in Hawaii, that's where he told people he was from. Dan was a self-proclaimed intellectual and took every available opportunity to dispense irrelevant facts to an always-uninterested audience. Dan was Dr. Josh's foil, and I felt sorry the Doc had to take him under his wing. Because Dan had also spent some time in Canada and the Philippines, he decided he was too good to use standard US measures.

"My car gets twenty kilometers to the liter."

Fucking asshole . . .

Dan spoke no Spanish, and his English burned the ears of most who heard him. Despite the nearly unanimous thumbs down he got from everyone else, I liked Dan right away. Not necessarily for his charm, but for his zest for life, bubbling way deep down, forcing all his awkward words to the surface long before they'd been given the once-over by his atrophied good sense. Despite his social deficiencies, Dan held his head high. I found something noble in that.

A number of personalities were at my house that night, which was something that could often be volatile.

"So, Sally, I see you got some Texas plates there," Dan said. "Nothin' but steers an' queers, right?"

Don't say it. Don't say it!

"And you don't look like a steer to me . . ."

Ahh, you fucking douchebag!

Sal tried to laugh it off, but Dan wouldn't let go.

"You know, I spent some time in the ol' panhandle there back in the summer of ought-three. Let me tell you, you think it's hot here. It got damn near forty-degrees Celse somedays."

"What the hell are you talking about?" Sal said.

"Celse—forty-degrees Celsius." He said "Celse" with this smug tone as if he thought he deserved a goddamned Noble Prize for Brevity.

"That's great. Look, I'm not from Texas anyways—"

"Where you from?"

"Brooklyn," Sal said with an aggressive pride.

"Fuhgeddaboudit. New York sucks."

Cisco strutted over. "Hey, I'm from New York too. You got a problem with that?"

Dan scanned up and down Cisco's forearms. "Wow, you got a lot of tattoos. Those are permanent, you know."

"Who the fuck is this clown?" Cisco asked Sal.

I think Dr. Josh could sense the tension because he ushered Dan away. "Hey, Dan, have you met so-and-so yet . . ."

Both Sal and Cisco were heated. They decided to head over to The Limit with their cousins. The geology crew saw them leave and decided to head over themselves. This left me, Jorg, and the Ekke-bopper alone under the almond trees.

"You guys gonna head over too?" I said.

Jorg said something to Ekkehard, and Ekkles responded.

"No, I don't think we will go," Jorg said.

"Great . . ."

I finished my caguama, walked uphill, and caught a cab. A song I recognized came on the radio.

"Hey, can you turn this up?"

"*Si!*"

The song was on a disc Sal brought with us on our cross-country road trip, and there was one night in particular where it affected me deeply. We'd stopped in Denver on our way to Yellowstone and had made some friends there. We were all at a bar one night. None of us had eaten dinner, so we ordered some food. I ordered first and asked for a hot dog. Sal shot into character: "Hey, Will," he said *my* name but was addressing everyone else, "remember that time you bought a hot dog at a gas station in Louisiana? Check it out, guys, Will eats station dogs."

They all pretty much ignored him. In fact, several asked for hot dogs themselves. But rather than give in to defeat, Sal upped the ante: "Hey, Will, remember that time you found that lump on your nut, and I had to drive you to the hospital?"

I left the bar, and my dog, and walked to Sal's car. I'd been driving earlier and still had the keys. I opened the passenger door and sat inside. I put on the CD, scrolled through the songs, and stopped on that one. I had no idea what the woman was saying, but she said it with such emotion. I needed to get away. I wanted to go to wherever she was singing—to find the place where I'd be free to learn how to express myself as she did. But, even with the keys, I was just a passenger in that car.

"Do you know who sings this song?" I asked the cabbie.

"Yes, this is Julietta Venegas. She is from Tijuana. I think the song is called 'Lento.'"

"Thanks." I added Julietta to the list of people I needed to hug before I died. Julietta released a new album right around the time

I'd arrived in Mexico, and the radio was full of her beautiful voice. Julietta, if you're out there, look me up—you got a hug coming your way!

When I arrived at the bar, I could feel the tension before I even went inside. I saw the guys sitting at a long table in the back, but Sal was missing and Cisco was pacing near the bar. He looked ready to hurt someone. I walked past him, and he didn't notice me. I sat at the table.

"Where's Sal?" I said.

"He and Cisco got in a fight, and he took off," Lalo said.

"Like a fist fight?"

"No, just yelling at each other."

"Fuck it . . ." I ordered a forty-ounce Sol Brava. The shit tasted like fermented goat piss, but it was six percent alcohol and only cost twenty pesos.

Cisco cooled down and sat beside me at about the same time my beer arrived. Lalo, Andre, and I tried to continue our conversation about music, but we didn't succeed.

"What's your favorite guitar solo?"

"I love George Harrison's work on 'Something.'"

"Me, I can't think of anything finer than, 'Black Magic Woman—'"

"Santana sucks," Dan said from across the table. "A real fan of music would never pick Santana."

"Yeah," I said, "just like a real fan of dick would never pick yours."

Lalo and Andre laughed.

"It's just," Dan didn't know when to stop, "Mexicans should stick to soccer and leave rock 'n' roll to us Americans."

"Mexico is a *part* of America," Andre said. "You mean to say 'us in the United States.'"

"Please, you ain't a part of the U.S.A.," Dan said.

Andre stood and pointed in Dan's face. "Mexico, Peru, Honduras, Brazil are all America!"

Dan smirked at him.

"Argentina, Colombia, El Salva—"

"Just forget about it. He's an idiot." Lalo put his hand on Andre's shoulder, and Andre calmed down.

Cisco didn't. "What the fuck is this guy's problem?"

"He's just a dumbass," I said.

"He's already made fun of my city and my heritage. You got anything else to say, puto?"

Cisco's aggression didn't deter Dan. I think this had less to do with bravado and more to do with Dan's complete obliviousness in social situations.

"I'm just saying that no good music comes out of Mexico, that's all."

"Oh, that's *all?*" Cisco said.

Cisco cocked his arm but relaxed it when Sal returned.

"Hey, I'm sorry for blowing up before." Sal walked back to the table.

"It's fine. Let's get the fuck outta here. I'm gonna break this dude's face."

"Hey, don't get mad at me for tellin' it like it is," Dan said. "You New Yorkers get so bent outta shape whenever somebody challenges you. When it comes down to it, you're all a bunch of know-it-all pussies."

"Say one more word!" Cisco got right in his face.

Dan opened his mouth, then shut it. I think he finally understood.

"Let's get the fuck outta here," Sal said.

The family crew got up, leaving the geology crew behind. I got up too, hid my forty under my shirt, and walked out with them. We piled in Sal's car. Cisco sat in front.

"Does that dude know what an asshole he is?" Cisco said.

"I don't think so," Lalo said.

"It's shitheads like that who give Americans a bad name," Cisco said. "That dude should be shot out of a cannon straight into a brick wall. No helmet. Those are the fuckers I'm trying to get away from."

"Me too," I said, "but they're fucking everywhere . . ."

We spent the rest of the night at the Rock Bar crushing through beers as Rudi crushed my will to live. He was thumping the open E for "Roadhouse Blues" when we walked in. I couldn't take much of this.

The next morning, Herb came by and took Sal, Cisco, Lalo, Andre, and me to some vegan buffet in el Centro. We got our fill of beans, and rice, and fresh fruit, and tortillas, then Herb dropped us off under the almond trees. Lalo and Andre were leaving that afternoon, so they packed while Sal and I played our guitars in the living room.

"Yo, that dude Rudi sucks," I said, "but everyone sweats his nuts like he's frontin' Morris Day and the Time. We should start another band." I started playing "Purple Rain."

Cisco laughed. Sal shook his head.

"C'mon, man," I said, "we could get Marco—he shreds the guitar, and his cousin kicks it on drums. We could be *the* band . . . we coulda *been* the band, man, in high school."

Sal started laughing as I broke into a simple C Am F G progression punctuated with hammer-ons. It sounded something slow and nostalgic, a gloomy dream straight out of 1950s small-town America. Then I started riffing with the words:

"You know, we could have been the band
in high school—
in high school.
We could have found a place to stand
in high school—
in high school.
But days pass by, and still I'm wondering why
I'm sleepin', and I'm not waking anytime soon."

Sal kept rhythm by tapping an empty beer bottle on the coffee table.

"Hey, that's pretty good." Cisco broke the silence.

I stopped playing. "Oh, I was just, uh, dickin' around."

"You guys should get something together."

"I don't have my bass," Sal said.

"I'm sure we could find you one somewhere," I said.

"I don't know. I'm busy with work and school, and Marco can get annoying . . ."

"C'mon, I bet we could make some cash on the novelty alone—a coupla gringos slammin' on guitars—"

"You wanna start a band, then start a band. Nobody's stopping you."

"Fuck it . . ." I continued playing:

"When I grow up, I want to be in the band
In high school—
In high school . . ."

The day passed by, and the Guadalajarians and Cisco were gone. Cisco was northbound, and his tales of Vallarta were about to be written. He reminded me once more before he left, "If you ever wanna come up, just give me a call."

I tried to ignore his invitation, but it took several days for my brain to stop sending signals to my restless legs. Sal, Jorg, Ekkes, and I were the only ones left in the house on the dead-end street. Jorg had taken Ekkehard up to the volcano and to a few other spots around it, but most of Ekkehard's time was spent around the house with me. He was an awkward dude, but I enjoyed his company. He spent most of his time reading, and he brought an interesting weird presence to our already strange house. My only complaint with the dude was that he sucked down the water from my garrafones with the thirst of a winded Thoroughbred, yet he never offered to get more water. I knew he was having a rough time with his trip, so I let it go.

Ekkehard spent most of his three-week vacation on our uncomfortable couch. He was there alone one Friday—his final night in Mexico—when I returned from a party. The day before, I'd found a fat, tightly rolled joint in the breast pocket of the button-down shirt I'd worn all day—through my classes with Guadalupe at Lengua and later those with the kids in El Campo. I had no idea where it came from but knew where it was going. Mica and I'd given it a good go while watching Sal's *The Last Waltz* DVD the night before, but we'd hardly put a dent in it. It was like some magical endless joint.

I was double drunk that night and fumbled through my closet looking for the second half of my doobie snack. I found it, lit it, ripped it, and fell into my happy place but was called back to reality by a hysterical German.

"WILL! WILL! WILL!" He repeated my name, even when I met him in the living room. "WILL . . ."

"What's the deal, Sticky-Icky?"

"Something bite me . . . BITE ME!" He ripped off his shirt and showed me a red mark on his shoulder.

"A wise guy, eh?" Something inside of me turned on. I dug into the sofa, tossing off the cushions and checking its guts for the creep who bit the Ickster. "Nobody fucks with a guest in my house! Where are you? Show yourself!" This would be my showdown with the beast. I wanted to find one. I wanted to rip it apart, then chew it up and swallow it. "Show yourself, you coward!" I continued throwing upholstery around the room for a good five minutes, and just as quickly as it began, it ended. "Sorry Ekke-baby, I couldn't find anything." I think I was sorrier for myself. "If you feel like you're dying, just come wake me up, and I'll find a way to get you to the hospital. If you see anything else, just tell it to 'go to the dick,' okay?"

Ekkehard looked more shocked than ill. He got bit by something all right, but it probably wasn't a scorpion. Though I didn't find one, I was proud of myself for not backing down when the Ekke-bopper really needed me.

Ekkehard was curled up on the couch in a seemingly pleasant slumber as Sal and I walked by him on our way to work the next morning. I didn't think to put a mirror to his nose. On our way to the Coke plant, I told Sal what'd happened the night before. When we got home, Ekkehard was gone. I never saw him again but assumed he didn't die. Our house was quiet again.

Chapter 16

I was having a particularly shitty afternoon one day in early October. I hopped on the twenty or twenty-four, rode it to the Super Walmart, got off, and sat on the raised concrete under the awning. The day was overcast and threatened rain, and I caught several angry glances from assholes as I waited for the bus. Even though this commute was often the most peaceful part of my day, the late afternoon was generally the hour I felt the shittiest. I wasn't quite sure why. Maybe because the day's possibilities were becoming more limited as it aged. By night, I was usually able to make some peace with a blown day. But those afternoons were often like torture. What the hell was everyone else doing with their lives? I wanted to join the circus. I wanted to run off to the South of France and become a gypsy. But dreaming almost felt like a waste of time. I wanted out of my own skin. I wanted someone to destroy me with their own sense of justice, relieving me of any duty to fate . . .

My heart was racing and thoughts colliding when I caught a glimpse of a beautiful girl sitting solo in the bed of a truck. She found my eyes and held them as the truck continued down the street. Then, just before the truck reached an intersection, she threw up her arm, smiled, and waved. I knew that face . . . she was the bus girl—the one dripping sex! I threw up my arm and smiled just before the truck rounded the corner. Most of my anger was gone.

A few days later, I rode the blue bus back from El Campo and contemplated my life situation. I was a few stops away from walking distance home when the bus stopped, and she got on. Our eyes met, but before I could find the words to say, she'd approached me, leaned forward, and planted a kiss directly on my lips. No words—just a kiss. She sat beside me, and we stared at each other with nervous smiles. Neither of us said anything. I dug my hand in my pocket for my phone, but before I could even get it out, she reached in and grabbed it away from me. She typed in her number.

"I'm Yurizan. I have seen you before."

"I've seen you as well."

She kissed me again and wrapped her arms around my neck. I was warming to the situation when the bus stopped, and Tito boarded. He shot me a disapproving glance and sat across from us— watching. He said nothing but continued to stare, judging me with his eyes. Goddamn, couldn't these fucks just leave me alone?

I got off the bus several stops past mine and walked the several miles to Mica's to cook the can of soup in my backpack for dinner. We were out of gas again, but Mica had plenty of that, and beer.

Though I enjoyed the time I spent in El Campo, I had to do something about my financial situation. Only a few of the kids ever paid for their classes, and it was costing me more money to commute there each day than I was making.

Franklin had gone back to LA at the end of September, and I decided to end the classes. I organized a pizza party for that final day. The plan was to watch a movie in English with Spanish subtitles while eating two party pizzas from a place offering a two-for-one deal. I got there earlier than usual that day to set up. But so did the rain. Ernesto's dad had offered to let us use his TV, but the ceiling was pissing water, so that was out. The power had gone out several times as well, and the rock-job wasn't bringing it back that night.

The delivery guy showed up around seven with the pies. I paid, tipped him, and set up the greasy buffet in one of the room's few dry areas.

The kids all got there at seven, but because there was no movie they just ran around the wet room eating their pizza and driving me crazy.

At about seven fifteen, a pretty head poked through one of the windows. It was Yurizan, and she was soaking wet.

"Hello, Will!"

"How'd you know where to find me?"

"You said you gave English classes in El Campo. I live right there." She pointed to a small house across the street.

"Oh, wow. You have a TV we could borrow?"

"No, no TV." She looked sad when she said that. She walked through the door and slowly approached me.

"Would you like some pizza?" I reached for a slice.

Yurizan said nothing. Instead, she pushed me against the table and started running her hands all over my body. When the kids saw this, they erupted. Ernesto started chanting, "PUTA! PUTA! PUTA!" while running around the classroom, and the others followed along.

Yurizan rubbed my thighs and buried her head in my neck. Julietta ran to my aid. She pushed the pizzas aside, climbed on the table, wrapped her arms around my chest, and pulled me away from Yurizan with such force, I fell back onto her lap. Yurizan buried her face between my legs.

"What the hell are you doing?" I said.

The kids continued running around the wet room chanting, "PUTA!" Ernesto, however, was now singing, "You're beautiful!"

Yurizan lifted her head and tried to kiss me, but Julietta pulled my head back each time Yurizan lunged. I didn't know what to do. I thought back to my teacher training but found no solution for this situation. My mind made a decision without me. I broke free from Julietta's grip, pushed Yurizan aside, and locked myself in the bathroom where I stood sweating in the dark for several minutes until Yurizan left.

The kids were still screaming when I came out. Thankfully the rain had ended, the lights had come back on, and the ceiling was no longer dripping.

"Ernesto, do you think your dad would still let us use the TV?"

"Yes."

"Can you go get it?"

"Yes."

He took off. I called Jose.

"Yo, can you come down to the classroom to monitor my little pizza party? It's almost eight, and I gotta catch the bus back soon."

"Sure."

He arrived at about the same time Ernesto came back with the TV. We popped in some shitty Pixar flick, and they finished off the cold, wet pizza.

"Yo, you'll never believe what just happened. This girl Yurizan was down here—"

"Yurizan Badillo?"

"Oh, I don't know her last name."

"Does she live right over there?" He pointed to her house.

I nodded.

"That girl is a prostitute. She has problems with smoking the meth. She's had sex with almost every guy in town. You should stay away from her."

"Well, prostitutes need lovin' too, Josecito."

"Her father was very bad to her. He did some terrible things. It's very sad . . ."

Eight thirty came, and the kids told me when they heard the bus. They stopped the movie to follow me outside and wait. The Q & A session continued: "Have you ever seen a horse?" "Have you ever met Robert de Niro?" "What does 'Suck the cum out of my asshole with a straw' mean?"

When the bus came, I started up the steps. But Julietta wrapped her arms around me and pulled me back to her. I fought her embrace for a moment before relaxing and allowing her emotion and spirit to pass through to me. She was a cool girl, and I knew she'd find a great guy sooner or later to share mama's pozole with. I walked up the steps and found a window seat. I looked down from the window, and they were there below me. No matter what I thought, no matter how disgusting or broken I felt, at one point in our lives, they were my students and I was their teacher. I was going to miss those kids.

As the bus took off, I could hear Ernesto belting out, "You're beautiful!" We took the dirt road through the wet grass. I pulled out my phone and almost cried as I erased Yurizan's number. I'm sorry, babe, I know you got your problems. But I've got my own . . .

Chapter 17

October seventh was my birthday. I shared it with Desmond Tutu, Thom Yorke, and Vladimir Putin. Unkie Herb was the only family I had in town, and he showed up with some Barrilitos after work on Friday the sixth. Sal was busy with Paz, and Mica was out of town on some extranero excursion. That night, it was all me and the weird old man. He again presented me with the "Underbelly of Lila" pitch.

"Eh, what the hell . . ." and soon we were in Abuelita, cruisin' Lila's bumpy streets. We followed Sal's running route down Madrid del Rio, then left at the Kiosko, and drove up the road that gave the incredible view of the Volcán.

Herb slowed and parked behind what looked like an abandoned circus tent in a brown field between life and the carretera. We got out and walked around the front. There was a dead dog by the street—the same dog that Sal had warned me not to step on during one of our runs. A few weeks back, it was bloated like an inflated birthday balloon. Now it was flat like a deflated birthday balloon. It still stunk of death.

Though it was early, the place was already full of depraved creatures. The first thing I saw when we walked in was some gray-haired man sucking a young whore's chubby tits while she straddled him and looked on unaroused. I got lost in the detachment in her eyes. I continued to stare until the flamboyant singer of a banda group playing in the corner won my attention. He upstaged the weirdness with his spasmodic movements and sparkling silver jumpsuit. The group broke into a new song as Herb and I sat at a reinforced wooden table in the center of the action.

Naked flesh everywhere. Some strippers danced on tables, others served drinks with their titties hanging out, and others performed on the enormous oval stage in the center of the place. Herb ordered a cubeta and scanned the room.

"Where is she?" he said to himself.

Herb had been talking up some girl all night who supposedly had an "epic asshole" that I just *had* to see. Now, I loved nearly everything about women, but a sexy poo hole just didn't do it for me. Regardless, my head nodded a perfunctory "Si" when Herb found her and called her over.

"This is my nephew. It's his birthday today." I bet she'd never heard that one before. "How about a dance?"

She nodded, then hopped on the table, wishing me a happy birthday by intermittently slapping me in the face with her tits. She kept rhythm with the banda group, then dropped down on all fours, presenting us with her exemplary brown eye. Herb's eyes lit up. He wet his pointer finger, then began several unsuccessful attempts to jam it in there. Each time he got near, she pulled her sphincter away. She must have been using some kind of sixth whore sense because she wasn't even looking at the salivating old fuck as he tried to spear her. She just kept lunging forward in rhythm with the thrusting of that chubby, moistened digit. The banda group ended the song, and soon the "epic asshole" was off in some other sick fucker's face. Herb slipped her some bills before she shimmied away.

"Damn," Herb said, "I'd let her fart in my breakfast cereal."

I laughed.

"Ya know," Herb said, "I love chicks with a dumper so thick, the cheeks don't entirely separate when she bends over. Which one you wanna fuck? It's on me tonight."

"I already told you, old man, I don't pay for sex."

"Hey, these girls are just doin' some honest work. They made choices just like anyone else."

I scanned the room and saw the whore with the chubby tits snort a line of something off the bar. She threw her head back and had that same detached look in her eyes.

"You know, Herby, I've read that some seventy-five percent of whores were sexually abused when they were little girls. Kind of makes you wonder if this was really a choice."

"Well, we've all been fucked over in one way or another," he said.

The banda group kicked into a powerful new song. Herb recognized it and started to clap. "This is my jam!"

"How could you like this crap?" I said.

"It's an acquired taste." He put his hand on my shoulder and leaned his head toward me. "I once thought the same thing, but it's really grown on me. Banda is all about pride and love and loss—all universal themes. It's kinda like Mexico's version of country, and it's nearly sacred to the people here. There's something very masculine about it despite its peculiar sound. It takes a while, but once it gets inside you, part of you becomes Mexican forever. You just need some roots, boy."

The sparkling singer belted out a piercing, "AYYAYAHAHAHA!" while the tuba player kept beat.

"You think the tuba player gets as much trim as the rest of the group?" I said.

"I don't know."

"I mean, I know chicks dig singers and pianists and shit, but you think an ugly dude ever got any snatch just because he blew a mean tuba?"

"Why don't we do a little research?" Herb called over a half-naked barmaid. "I have a question for you. Would you ever have sex with an unattractive guy just because he was a great tuba player?"

She thought about the question then shook her head. "Saxofon, si; tuba, no. Do you want more drinks?"

"No, we're good, dear. Thanks!"

Herb and I watched her wiggle as she walked away.

I scanned the room again. I didn't know whether these people were pariahs or Lila's doctors, lawyers, and teachers on a brief break from a long reality, but I let those questions fall to the dirt floor where they belonged. I got up, pissed in a dirt hole out back, and returned to my seat just as every stripper in the place hopped on stage and started jiggling and bending in some great fleshy dance number.

"Yo, let's jet, Herby. This place is depressing me."

"Well, it is your birthday . . ."

We piled in Abuelita and rolled over the grass toward the road. I caught a glimpse of the volcano. It was so vivid, so beautiful. The sun was setting just beyond. I wondered if Dr. Josh was up there sucking down sardine oil in preparation for a long night of dealing with both the volcano and Dan.

"Where the hell are we going?"

"You'll see . . ."

I didn't like the tone of his voice.

Herb drove us through the sleepy town and into its heart, el Centro. He parked on some side street, and we started walking. Soon, I saw the sign for the Rock Bar.

"Aw, goddamn it, Herb!"

"What? We'll only be here for a few drinks."

We walked inside, and Rudi shot us a smile from the stage. He and his group were halfway through Molotov's anti-corruption protest tune, "Gimme Tha Power," which was part of the group's usual set list. The place was packed, so Herb and I had to stand in the back. Herb said something to a waitress, and soon the bar's owner, and Rudi's father, approached us with a bottle of tequila and three shot glasses.

"How are you, Daniel?" I said.

"I am well. So, I hear it is your birthday? How old are you today?"

"Twenty-three."

"So, we do twenty-three shots in your honor."

"We can try, Danny-boy . . ."

Daniel poured us each a shot. Bottoms up, and he poured another.

"Drinks are on me tonight, friends."

Daniel poured us one more shot. We did it, and he walked away.

"Damn, he's awful friendly tonight. What's the deal?"

"Well, we bring enough business to this place. I think he also may have a chubby for gringos."

Rudi and the group finished "Gimme Tha Power," and began "Break on Through."

"Ya know a day da da da do. Nice diwides da day."

"How can you stand this crap, Herb? You've heard good music."

"Eh, Rudi's just doin' his thing. Let him groove."

Herb quoted guys like Robbie Robertson, Willie Dixon, and Dylan. He'd seen countless blues shows in Chicago nightclubs. But this . . .?

". . . he's Kind," Herb said.

"What?"

"He's Kind. Are you Kind?"

"The hell you talkin' 'bout, old man?"

"It's a lyric from 'Uncle John's Band.'"

"Yeah, so what about it?"

"The reason why I loved The Dead so much is because of the experience. It wasn't just about music, it was a way of life. Jerry was asking, 'Are you Kind?' to weed out those who were from those who weren't. If you were Kind, then you were one of us. You were welcome to live, and love, and be free among a massive family of people who genuinely cared for you. But those who hurt, and killed, and hated, and oppressed weren't welcome." Herb stuck out his middle finger as if someone from afar had just called his mother a fat, commie-fucking pig. "All those hate-mongering, jingoist shitholes can go fuck themselves!"

Herb dropped his pants and pulled his tighty-whities up over his pasty left hip, revealing a tattoo of the word "Kindness." He slapped it while he repeated, "They can all go fuck themselves!" I wondered how he still had so much life left inside him.

Daniel came running out from the backroom. "Herb, I've told you before that you can't drop your pants in my bar. Please, pull them up!"

"Uh . . . what? Oh, okay, sorry!" Herb pulled up his pants, and Daniel offered another shot, which we took.

"You going to be good, Herb?" he said.

"Yeah, I'm good, Daniel."

Daniel laughed and walked away.

"Blake on thru to dee odder sid . . ."

I thought about Herb's words. "Are you Kind?" I was pretty sure I was but wasn't certain. There was still too much darkness on my horizon. All I wanted was to answer with a sincere and emphatic "Yes!" without any doubts, but that didn't seem as if it'd ever be possible.

My pocket vibrated. I pulled out my phone and checked the screen: Ximena.

"Holy shit!"

"What's up?" Herb said.

"This girl I haven't heard from in like a month just texted me. She wants me to meet her at Crystal."

"Fuck that place. All my students hang there. I got a better spot . . ."

I knew what place he was referring to. And I knew where I wanted to go. But I still followed him out that door and inside the car.

We pulled behind the airplane hangar, parked in the grass, got frisked by security, and walked inside the black-lit "dancehall." It was just as alive as it was the last time.

Herb and I sat at a plastic table near the dance floor and ordered a cubeta. A cute, young woman kept smiling at me from across the room. Herb noticed. "You should go talk to her."

"I already told you I'm not fucking a whore."

"And I already told you not every girl in here *is* a whore."

She was sitting at a table near the guys who'd stared Herb down the last time we were here. They were staring again.

"Who the fuck are those guys?" I said.

"Don't worry about them. They're just some street trash punks."

They walked over. There were four of them. One was about Herb's size, but clumsy looking, and the rest were smaller than me. Herb stood his ground.

"I thought I told you not to come here no more," the leader, and smallest of the four, said.

"I go where I want to go," Herb said.

"Well, maybe we have to teach you a lesson, maestro?"

"I don't think an illiterate naco like you has very much to teach."

"Why don't we have this conversation outside?"

"I'm here to celebrate, not fight." Herb gestured to one of the security guards, and he came over. "Carlos, can you show these punks the rear exit?"

"Are they bothering you, Herb?"

"I think they just need to learn some manners. If you want to put a fist into the little one, be my guest."

Carlos ushered the four away, and we got back to the cubeta.

"Yo, Herb, fuck this place. Let's go to Crystal. I don't want to fight on my birthday."

"Crystal blows. Why don't you go talk to that girl? She's still staring at you."

"Look, man, you know I got your back if you need it, but I don't need any extra bullshit in my life."

"There are no problems here, man." Herb wiped the rim of a brew, slid a lime inside, a pinch of salt, and handed it my way.

"So, you know the bouncers here?"

"Know 'em? Carlos and I tag teamed some toothless skeezer in the men's room last weekend."

"You're a sick fuck, you know that?"

"She was a squirter too. Ruined a good pair of sandals. They stink like rotting halibut now."

"Herb, I *will* throw up on you."

We finished the bucket and got another, and eventually shut the place down. Dirty old men had claimed most of the women and only a few single girls remained—including the one who'd been staring at me all night. Herb and I left when they turned on the lights, and she followed us out the door. Herb lit a cigarette, and I leaned against the sheet metal wall. She wandered over and said something to us, but I didn't respond. Herb, however, did, and they had a long conversation that I ignored. Soon, Herb and I were back in Abuelita and parked in front of the Star Wars Bar.

I immediately realized the error in walking through that door. On my first night there, I was a novelty. The whores probably figured I was just there to satisfy some curiosity.

But the second time? Now I was fair game . . .

Herb walked deep inside the cave of weirdness and sat at a table in the back. I dragged behind him. He ordered a cubeta. I was exhausted. We'd been drinking heavily for over half a day, and I fought with all my strength not to pass out and let my head touch the table. I just wanted my bed.

I was drifting in and out of consciousness but at some point had inadvertently locked eyes with Mexico's greatest private dancer. She smiled. Normally I would have smiled right back, but I didn't given the circumstances.

The girl who'd been staring at me all night walked in and sat at our table. She and Herb struck up an inane conversation that I tried to ignore, but the shit she kept saying was too much for me. She was a maudlin mess and kept repeating, "I make my beans and tortillas with love!" while dripping puddles on the table. I assumed Herb was a former client and let him do his thing. But then she tried engaging me. "What's your name?"

"Han Solo—hey, Herb, let's get the fuck outta here."

She said something to Herb in a whiny voice, and Herb relayed the message. "She said she wants you to talk to her."

"Well, tell her I'm too tired to talk."

I laid my arms on the table and rested my head on them. I could hear her whining again. She grabbed my arm and tried to pull me to her. Mexico's greatest private dancer must not have liked that because she was over from across the room in a flash. She pulled my arm away from the girl, grabbed my head with both hands, and licked me from my lower jaw to my ear.

"Ahh, what the fuck are you doing?" I pulled away from them both.

Herb chuckled. "I think she's marking her territory."

"I'm glad you're amused, Herbert."

The old skin-bag wanted me to dance with her again, but I pulled my arm away from her each time she grabbed for it. The other girl kept whining to Herb as tears streamed down her face. At one point she opened her mouth widely, revealing a few missing teeth in the back row.

"Herb, I'll never ask for another birthday wish for the rest of my life if you just get me the fuck home right now."

"Okay, okay, calm down, man, we'll go."

I got up and walked to the exit. Herb dragged behind, and the girl followed him out the door. She continued to follow us to the car. When we got to Abuelita, Herb asked if she wanted a ride.

"Si!"

I opened the passenger door and sat, but before I could close it, she was on my lap. She started to cry again.

"Why's she crying?"

"She said you were mean to her."

"Really? I wasn't . . ."

"C'mon, Willy, you said her beans weren't fit for a burro."

We both laughed. I wiped a tear from her cheek with the back of my finger. "I'm sorry, okay?"

She nodded. She started kissing my cheek then my neck. She was pretty cute despite the missing chompers.

"Herb, are you sure this girl isn't a whore?"

"Has she asked you for any cash? Believe me, man, they're up-front with that shit."

"Yeah, maybe with sick, old, tighty-whitey-wearing, stage-seven-male-pattern-baldness-having fucks like you."

"Trust me, she's not a whore."

I decided to believe him for the same reason a man solicits a whore in the first place.

She breathed into my ear. It moved. Herb dropped me off under the almond trees. The girl got out first and bent over in my face. I made the game-time decision, and soon we were in my room. She pushed me on the bed, then stood back, pulled a few levers on her whore-suit, and it fell to the floor. I got up and turned off the lights, and soon my clothes were on the floor beside hers.

We skipped the kissing; she went right for my man parts. I figured this best, seeing that the new day's light had already begun to fill the dark room. She started down south, sucking on my swollen amigo and moaning as if she were the one getting pleasured. A few times her knees buckled in wild bouts of ecstasy. I would have liked to cite my salami as having been sexy enough to evoke such an effect, but I couldn't ignore the missing teeth and gnarled emotions, and had to assume her pleasure was being multiplied by some chemical she'd smoked, snorted, or swallowed earlier that day.

Soon, she went souther, past the base of the shaft, then the balls, and into no-man's-land. She licked every inch of that desolate, hairy patch and kept going until her tongue found the deepest, darkest spot of them all. I'll never forget the awkward position my body froze into the moment an inch of that girl's tongue penetrated my asshole. It was a new sensation, and I was an explorer, so I let her play ball for a few minutes before I caught a whiff and had to call the game. I pushed her head from my crack, rushed to the bathroom, and took a quick shower. I dressed myself from head to toe, wrapped her naked body in a bedsheet, and slept as far away from her as possible.

Then her phone started ringing and didn't stop all night. She got up several times to puke and each time she closed that bathroom door behind her I considered digging in her purse, grabbing out her cell phone, and smashing it on the tile floor. Herb had given her my number, and I knew after that night I'd never want to see her butt-munching ass again.

I woke around nine a.m. to her repeating, "You've got to come see my kids!" while pulling on my arms and legs.

"No, *you've* got to see your kids. Why are you staying out all night anyway?"

"You've got to see my kids!"

"I don't have to do shit, psycho, except sleep and wake up by Monday. It's my birthday, and I don't plan to spend it with your damned children."

"You've got to see my kids!"

I could see this wasn't going anywhere, so I got up, got dressed, and said, "Vamonos!" We walked uphill, and I hailed a cab. I opened the door like a gentleman and let her go in first, then I shut it, dumped the driver some change, and told him to "Drive, please drive!" He took off, and I rolled back downhill. Mica and Jorg were in the living room when I got back. Both had backpacks over their shoulders.

"Hey, Willy, we're going to Guadalajara for the weekend. Care to join?"

"Sorry, fellas, I'm low on cash. I can barely afford to breathe."

"Who was that girl?"

"My worst fucking nightmare. Don't ask. I'm going back to sleep."

And like that, they were gone, and I was back in bed.

I woke up a few hours later, and Sal was in the kitchen trying to light the oven. I felt like death.

"Happy birthday, Blaine Scaldo! I heard about your little misadventure with Herb last night."

"That right?"

"I also saw that girl you led out this morning. Where'd you say you picked her up again?"

"Didn't."

"Don't tell me you took home a Pati's whore . . ."

"Herb says not every girl there is a whore."

"Yeah, and you're gonna believe that guy? You know he smokes meth, right?"

"Really?"

"Are you kidding me? That dude's as sick as they come. You better be careful around him. He hangs out in the nastiest places in town. Pati's is like a petri dish. It's a well-known breeding ground for AIDS."

"I don't wanna hear that . . ."

"About a decade ago there was this really sexy model who was already famous in Lila by the time she was like sixteen. But for some reason she started turnin' tricks at Pati's. She caught AIDS and died when she was twenty-one. That shit's everywhere there. That Star Wars place too . . . You fuck that girl last night?"

"Naw, she just sucked me off. I don't think you can get AIDS from that, right?"

"Hell yeah, you can."

"Oh god, and she had her tongue up my ass too. What if she had some sores or something in her mouth?"

"That's disgusting! You're a sick fucker, you know that?"

"Fuck you, man."

"You know, the ass is one of the most absorbent barriers in the body. Why you think gay dudes are always droppin' dead from that shit?"

"Yo, I don't wanna hear any of this. You think I should get tested?"

"Well, you need to wait at least three months to get tested. I just did, and I'm clean across the board."

"I can't wait three months. This is gonna drive me insane. Maybe she doesn't have AIDS? She probably doesn't, right?"

"How the fuck should I know? That's your fucking problem . . . You know Herb's got a kid too?"

"No, I didn't."

"Yeah, he knocked up some Pati's whore like five years ago. He's got a little girl, but the family won't let him anywhere near her. They hate Herb, and the whore's brother wants to kill him."

"Is he a little guy, crooked nose?"

"Yeah."

"He tried to fight Herb last night."

"You'd better stay away from him. Those guys are lookin' to put the hurt down on Herby, and I'm sure they wouldn't have any problem taking down some random gringo if he got in the way." Sal put something in the oven.

"Yo, I'm done with that guy. I don't want to see him ever again. You really think that girl was a whore?"

"I'm absolutely positive."

"'Cause I didn't pay for her?"

"You see Herb talking to her at all?"

"All fucking night."

"You don't think it's possible he could have set this whole thing up?"

"C'mon, man, he said she wasn't a whore . . ."

"He probably bought her as a birthday gift for you."

"This is fucked up. This is so fucked up! What should I do?"

"Why don't you call him and see what he says?"

I got my phone and called him. "Yo, Herb, are you sure that chick last night wasn't a whore?"

"Whoa, hello to you too. No, she wasn't a whore."

"So you didn't buy her as a gift?"

"Fuck no, man. Did you see me hand her any cash?"

"No, but that doesn't mean you didn't."

"Hey, look man, she wasn't a whore. I didn't pay for her. Who's telling you all this? Sally?"

"Hey, you got a kid, man?"

"You know, you really shouldn't believe everything he tells you. A few weeks before you got here, I caught your buddy Sal stealing weed from my friend Tyson. I had to talk Tyson off the ledge from beating Sal's ass. Sal still says he didn't do it, but I saw him with my own eyes."

I put the phone aside. "Hey, Sal, you steal weed from a dude named Tyson?"

"That dude's full of shit."

"I think you're both full of shit." I put the phone back to my ear. "Listen, man, just tell me one last time she wasn't a whore."

"Will, she wasn't a whore."

"All right, Herby, I'm running out of minutes. I gotta let you go."

"Happy birthday, man!"

"Yeah, yeah . . . bye."

I hung up and locked myself in my room. I'd felt the darkness all my life. It was something natural to me, and I'd learned how to coexist with it. Despite it, I was still always able to make friends, and go to school, and hold a job. But the darkness I felt that morning was worse than any I'd ever known. It crushed down on me from all angles. It blinded me to any of my redeeming qualities, silenced any of those pleasant internal voices offering comfort and reassurance. The thought of any happy memories crippled me, any hope just highlighted the inevitable. I was past writing therapy, beyond any comforting by friends. The light that had always been with me, even during my worst times, had gone out. I felt like a creature. I hit rock bottom. For those of you who think you possibly might have hit this point at some time in your life as well, I tell you this: there is no mistaking it. If you hit it, you absolutely know—there are no maybes. I was at the fucking bottom. And that was the closest I ever came to doing it. If this continued . . .

Chapter 18

Eventually, I unlocked my door after finding new motivation to continue: the dire resolution that I needed to change. I had no idea what that change looked like—if I did, I wouldn't have been in the situation I was in. But it gave me a reason to continue—something to be sure of in a world ruled by blind faith and fear—some fucking bedrock to stand on. I was the only thing standing between me and death, and I was a pretty fucking unreliable defense. I needed to beef that up. I'd broken a fundamental promise to myself. I was no better than any of those whores or junkies wandering around el Centro. But I made a new promise: I wasn't going to spend any more time with Herb.

This was enough fuel to get me dressed, fed, and off to an Internet café to check my birthday greetings from family and friends. I didn't want to see anything they'd written. Their words reminded me of the arduous journey separating me from life.

I spent most of that afternoon alone watching movies in my scorching death cave. Sal came back from the geology office around six.

"Yo, Jumbledear Squigglewatt," Sal said, "we should head over to Javie's soon. His birthday is tomorrow, and he's throwing a party tonight."

"All right, but I'm not drinking anything."

Sal and I headed over around eight. There, playing dominos in his driveway, were Javie and fucking Herb! A bottle of rum stood beside them on the table. The air thinned, and I felt dizzy.

"Oh, goddamn it! Yo, Sal, let's go someplace else." I took deep breaths but couldn't get enough oxygen.

"C'mon, man, forget about all that shit this morning. You know Herb's all right."

Talk about pulling a one-eighty.

"Fuck it . . ." I could never keep a promise to myself—at least, not in this world—so I did what I did best: recede inward. Suddenly, I could breathe again . . .

"Hey, Willy!"

"Happy birthday, cabron!"

We sat and played dominos. I'd never played before so Herb explained the rules. They were all standard except for one modification: the loser of each game had to do a shot of rum. I was determined not to drink anything that night, so I put all my focus into winning, which I did for several straight games.

"Yo, Herb, I gotta ask you again. You sure you didn't pay for that girl last night?"

"Man, I already told you like sixty fucking times. No, I didn't pay for her."

"Will, you need to relax with all that," Sal said. He leaned toward Herb and Javie. "He's been going on like this all day."

"Fuck you, man . . . Yo, you guys wouldn't believe that shit. She kept trying to get me to come home with her to see her kids."

"Maybe you shoulda gone back with her," Herb said. "I hear she makes some damned good beans."

"Fuck her beans, and fuck you too."

"You guys know she cleaned Will's cornhole?" Sal said.

"She just rim it or dart inside?" Herb said.

"She's a darter," Sal said.

"This was some fucking traumatic shit!" I said.

"Hey, it saves you money on toilet paper," Herb said.

"God, why the fuck'd you have to give her my number?" I said.

"You looked like you needed a good time," Herb said.

"Yeah, well, it was a nightmare."

We kept playing, and I kept not losing. By the time guests started to arrive, I hadn't touched a drop of rum. They came in groups: well-dressed and respectable couples in their mid-to-late thirties. These were Javier's friends—young married professionals celebrating life sensibly. I felt uncomfortable around them right away.

One of the guests, however, was a loud, mercurial young man, who was drunk and ready to take on the world (aka, my kind of people). He overheard Sal say something to Herb in English, and he sprang into action: "YOU ARE IN MEXICO! SPEAK IN SPANISH!"

To which Herb responded in Spanish, "You just spoke in English yourself," much to the amusement of the sensible guests.

The drunk said in English again, "I CAN UNDERSTAND YOU! I AM PSYCHOLOGIST! I CAN UNDERSTAND YOU!"

Again, Herb came back at him in Spanish: "Well, that's great, Doc. Why don't you take a nap and psychoanalyze some of your dreams?"

The doctor staggered around for a few minutes before finding a seat next to me at the table. He promptly passed out face-first on the plastic. I continued my streak of not losing any games of dominos and was feeling pretty good about myself. I poured a glass of soda and reached for the ice bucket near the doc's head. When I picked it up, he shot awake: "I CAN UNDERSTAND YOU! I CAN UNDERSTAND EVERYTHING YOU SAY!"

"Whoa, relax, Doc, I didn't even say anything."

He got in my face and squared off as if he was about to start swinging. "I CAN UNDERSTAND YOU!"

I looked to the group he came in with and asked them to take care of their friend. They ushered him inside where he paced the living room floor and continued to shout, "I CAN UNDERSTAND YOU," while pointing at me.

"Why do I always attract these lunatics?" I said.

"It's because you actually listen to 'em. You need to just ignore them like everybody else," Sal said.

I didn't respond. I thought about his words.

Some familiar faces showed a short time after the doc had passed out on the couch. Tito and his cousin Yesenia arrived with a bottle of tequila. Tito insisted I do a shot with him.

"It's your birthday, whey!" he said, ignoring all the previous lectures he'd given me about my drinking.

I fought it at first, but, considering a member of society was offering me the sauce and not some fucking depraved creature, I took one down the hatch. This was the beginning of the end. I sat back down to dominos and swiftly lost several games in a row. The rum swirled with the tequila in my stomach. More familiar faces arrived and more birthday tequila shots were demanded. The world started spinning. People kept handing me drinks, and it became impossible to discern which came from the members of society and which came from the mutants. I tried to focus on the well-dressed guests, but they became a blur as well. I receded deeper into my tainted subconscious.

At some point, I walked over to those well-dressed guests and pointed at each one individually while saying, "No eres importante," or "You're not important." My words were neither sloppy nor elevated. They were, rather, controlled and powerful like bullets leaving a sniper's rifle. And when I'd finished with those guests, I pushed through the wrought iron gate and walked into the neighborhood, casually strolling up to houses and shouting at the people inside, "You're not important!" "You're not important!" "Go to the dick!" People came out of their homes. Members of the party started walking into the street. Somewhere during the night, Herb had managed to get as drunk as I was, and he laughed hysterically each time I called another one of those people out. After taking a few videos and pictures of me, Sal came to my aid.

"Hey, man, people are talking about calling the cops."

"You're not important either."

"What's wrong with you?"

"This isn't working. This isn't working for me . . ."

"C'mon, I'm gonna take you home, okay?"

"They hurt me bad. Sal, they hurt me bad."

We piled in Sal's car and took off, and Herb was still laughing in the street. Had the doc gotten under my skin? I knew I was going to get arrested sooner or later. Maybe I just wanted to get it over with . . .

Sal woke sometime in the middle of the night and found me sitting naked on a plastic chair under the almond trees. A stray had been barking at me for some time, and it woke him up. He brought me back in the house, and I put on some clothes. I remember trying to sleep, but the bed was spinning. I went to the kitchen and purposely grabbed the pot Jorg always used for his macaroni and beef surprise just in time for it to catch the last of the rum and tequila mixture inside me. I woke up the next morning with my head inside the pot and my hair covered with crusted puke.

"C'mon, man. Herb's picking us up soon. It's the Bills versus the Bears. We gotta show that good ol' boy what Buffalo's made of."

I looked in the pot, then staggered to my room and threw on my red, white, and blue Zubaz pants, my Bills t-shirt, and my hat. I was in serious pain. I no doubt had alcohol poisoning but knew the hospital couldn't do shit for me that I couldn't just do for myself, so I dealt with it. I walked to the kitchen and drank some water but it came up. It hurt to stand, hurt to sit—all I wanted was to fast-forward to Wednesday. I didn't want to sleep, I didn't want to lie around watching movies. I just wanted to stop existing for a few days.

Herb picked us up and took us over to his first-floor studio apartment to watch the game. After it was over, and our Bills had been inevitably defeated, Herb dropped us back off at our place, where I continued to count down each second of the day. Later that night, I felt a satisfying sense of accomplishment for having survived the day. Wednesday was coming . . .

Chapter 19

The next few days were relatively ordinary. I was sad I'd quit my teaching gig in El Campo but knew I'd made the right decision. This freed up my late afternoons, and I used this time to run or work out in my room using the garrafones as weights.

Everything was going well until I was woken up by a call late one Wednesday night. I answered the phone, but when I heard the whiny voice on the other end, I screamed "Ahh!" shut the phone off, and went back to sleep.

I dreamed I was driving an old convertible through West Texas. The cops were after me as I headed south for the border. But the car kept making this hideous sound. At first I couldn't make out what it was. Then it became more and more distinct.

"WILL! WILL! WILL!"

I woke up, and that sound was the bridge between the dream world and reality. I looked through the hole in my bedroom wall and saw a silhouette in the hall window.

"WILL! WILL! WILL!"

I knew that voice. It was the toothless Pati's whore! Was she back for more? Or was this revenge for not seeing her kids? I was paralyzed by fear. Maybe she had a gun, or a knife, or a jar of well-trained attack scorpions . . .? And fuck! I'd left my tapestry open, giving her a clear shot if she wanted it. Eventually Sal rushed outside. I mean, she was really screaming . . .

"What the fuck are you doing? Do you know how late it is?"

"I'm here to see Will!"

"You need to get the fuck outta here before I call the cops!"

She didn't listen. Instead, she tried to squeeze her pizza dough head through the window's security bars.

"Okay, I'm gonna grab my phone, and if you don't leave in two fucking seconds, I'm callin' the cops." He was an asshole, but in that moment, Sal was *my* asshole.

She left the window but spent the next twenty minutes running a wire clothes hanger under the door. We assumed she was trying to break in, but eventually she gave up and left.

I fell back asleep but got no rest the remainder of the night. I woke up the next morning feeling shell-shocked. I kept looking over my shoulder thinking she was there behind me watching . . . waiting . . . Sal and I discussed the night's events all the way to Fundido.

"What the hell are you doing hanging around these psychopaths?" he said.

"You make it seem like I *asked* her to come."

"Alcohol doesn't do that to a person. That bitch is smoking crystal."

"Well, you don't know that."

"Well, you're a fucking idiot."

I checked my phone. She'd called at three-thirty. She must have been at our house around four. That bitch *must* have been on drugs. I drank, and I'd never do that. I called Herb again.

"Yo, that whore came back last night. She a fucking meth head?"

"Whoa, man, she probably just wanted a little sausage—relax."

"No normal person does that."

"What would you like me to say?"

God, he was right. Nothing he could say would have calmed me down. I spent the next few days checking over my shoulder everywhere I went. I kept seeing shadows behind bushes and in corners. I made sure to lock the door whenever I was in the house. This was no fucking way to live. I was a fucking prisoner.

I went to a party at Mica's the next day, and Juana invited me to an art festival in Guanajuato that she was going to that weekend with Mica and the extraneros. At first I said no due to my lack of cash, but then I thought of those bushes and darkened corners and knew I had to get away. I gave Juana the loot, and she made the arrangements. All I had to do was wait. My savings were almost gone. I had no idea what I was going to do when they ran out, so I tried not to think about it.

Soon, the weekend came. Mica and I met at the end of my street so we could split a cab to the bus station where Juana was waiting for us. We boarded our bus and took off on the eight-hour trip through the mountains.

We rode the carretera far beyond anything I'd yet seen in Mexico. We headed northeast, past Guadalajara, to the city and state of Guanajuato north of Mexico City. I'd never heard of the art festival, Cervantino, but didn't care. I knew there'd be drinking, and music, and celebration, and I was all in. I felt peace being in motion again. I was staring out the window at the great, green earth when I saw a truck pass by with the Canadian and his purple-haired girlfriend in its bed. Some of the extraneros had decided to hitch their way up north, and these fuckers were doing it . . .

The bus drivers usually played movies for the passengers on these trips and that day was no exception. He put on a subtitled copy of *Mission Impossible*, and when that finished, he put on *MI:II*. It was too much Tom Cruise for me to handle. I couldn't wait for the second waste of celluloid to finish, but halfway through, the driver stopped the DVD and replayed it from the beginning. Shit! Mica and I wondered if he was fucking with us. We arrived in Guanajuato shortly after the driver had restarted the first *MI*. I guess I couldn't complain. If I was driving buses, I'd probably do the same.

When the bus stopped, we got out, grabbed our bags, and walked to the road. The sun had just set, leaving the sky several shades of dark orange and red. I had no idea where we were going but continued to follow our clueless leader, Juana, who'd made all the plans, but had no idea how to execute them in a non-assbackwards manner. Mica and I followed her to the road and then onto a sidewalk.

"Are we looking for a cab? Our hotel? What the hell's going on?"

We knew she could hear us, but she didn't respond. We continued down the sidewalk, and I stopped just before an enormous hole in the sidewalk swallowed me whole.

"Goddamn, can't they put up a warning or something? That shit's like five feet deep!" I said. This would never fly in the US, the land of lawsuits. But I felt a distinct freedom in knowing that my own instincts had kept me from falling in rather than some government-mandated barrier. Some atrophied part of my brain had finally gotten some exercise, saving me from injury. Perhaps this combination of vigilance and exercise was the real price of freedom?

Juana stopped walking and hailed a cab, and we took it to the center of town. The city was achingly beautiful. Rolling hills, cobblestone streets, Spanish Colonial architecture. The Spanish had discovered silver in the mountains of Guanajuato in the sixteenth century and spared no expense in building, perhaps, the most gorgeous city in Mexico.

The cabbie dropped us off short of the celebration in the city center, and we walked to our hotel. My god, was I glad I'd come. Life pulsated from every direction. At the festival's edge was an opera house filled to capacity with a massive, hushed crowd, caught up in the power of some epic symphony, which filled the mountains and valleys with beautiful, deliberate sound. The streets were packed with thousands of visitors from all over the globe, who shared the space with live bands, artisans, comedy troupes giving live performances, vendors, mimes . . . Most faces were brown but a lot weren't. The night concealed endless possibilities.

We arrived at the gorgeous stone hotel, and all the extraneros were already there waiting in the lobby. Juana had made the reservations with her credit card, and they needed that to get in the room.

"Where have you been? We've been waiting for hours!"

That seemed dramatic considering we'd all left Lila around the same time. Juana presented her card, and we walked the four flights of stairs to the roof, which we had all to ourselves. There were two enormous rooms filled with double beds. I claimed one bed, set my bags down, and walked onto the balcony. What a fucking view! The houses on the hill in the distance looked like a black garbage bag filled with glowing air, then poked at random with a blunt ice pick. My eyes climbed the easy slopes and dipped into dark valleys.

I remained on that balcony while the hitchhikers washed the bugs from their hair, and I watched as three young men below unloaded a truck and carried cases of beer inside the hotel's bar.

"C'mon, guys, let's hit the town!" I said. But the group was too big for its own good. Indecision, whining, politics . . .

I could hear people singing in the streets. It sounded like the football chants at the end of Pink Floyd's "Fearless." I needed to get out there. I recruited a small group—Mica and one of the cooler Ecuadorians—and we hit the town.

Life was here. I'd been looking for it everywhere and found it on those streets. Groups of people threw celebrations of their own among the grander one uniting us all. They chanted, and danced, and drank, and tossed each other in the air. I wanted to run into the crowds and let them absorb me into their energy. But it just didn't work that way.

Before leaving Lila, I'd been warned by several people that this festival was known to turn into an orgy of violence once the lights went out. And gringos were easy targets. But surely these people wouldn't hurt me if they knew I was one of them . . . Right?

We found a lively bar, walked up to the second floor, and sat at a table overlooking the city. We asked the barmaid for a round of their cheapest beers and ordered a second when she brought the first. Beautiful women filled the voids wherever I rested my eyes.

It started to rain and didn't stop all night. We left to meet up with the others. They moved slowly through the streets—far too slowly for me. I gestured to Juana and Mica, and we left the group behind.

But as I navigated those narrow streets, I was overcome with dizziness. Mica and Juana walked back to the hotel with me. I opened a beer and tried to drink it, but it didn't go down. I walked out to the balcony and doubled over. The people were shouting louder now than before. I was so fucking close, but I'd never be able to touch it . . .

We got up early the next morning to make it in time for brunch. I was feeling better so I joined the rest of the extraneros, who were already eating at a long table in the hotel's restaurant. I sat and said something to Mica in English, and Turd gave a hollow, "We are in Mexico, speak in Spanish!"

I stared him down, and he surrendered. After brunch, Mica, Juana, and I hit the streets. Juana had taken a lot of shit from a lot of people in the last twenty-four hours. Because she had organized the trip, everyone decided to take out their every grievance on her: "Juana, the bathroom's out of TP." "Juana, my towel has a hair on it." I could tell she was stressed, so I laid off her. I was glad she'd taken on the leadership role for the trip. As disorganized as she was, at least she'd gotten us there.

We walked the streets with intent to check out the Museo de las Mommias, or Museum of the Mummies, and hit several of the town's highlights along the way. My favorite was the Callejon del Beso, or Alley of the Kiss—a street so narrow the balconies on both sides were close enough for a couple standing on the opposite sides to kiss.

The line to the museum was out the door, so we just walked the streets taking pictures. Mica liked to snap candid shots but felt uncomfortable sticking his camera in people's faces, so I pretended to pose for him as he snapped pics to my right or left, zooming in on street vendors and kids playing and old women sitting and staring into the unknown . . .

We walked the city for most of the afternoon, stopping in cafés and watching street performances. I was feeling better so I suggested we get some brews to lube the gears. We popped in a small ma and pop convenience store and bought some caguamas. A group of cops in full gear walked in while we were in line, then walked out just after we had, and they were carrying several bottles of top-shelf liquor. A little, old woman ran out after them, shouting, "OIGAN! OIGAN!" One of the puercos turned and blew her a kiss without stopping. They rounded a corner with the bottles and were gone. The woman wilted and walked back into her store. Perhaps *this* was the true price of freedom . . .?

The sun set, but the party lost no intensity. We wandered to the opera house in hopes to catch some grand symphonic performance but instead found a crappy Swedish folk group busy putting the crowd to sleep. I wanted some Wagner. I wanted some death from above but left unsatisfied.

Mica got a message from one of the extraneros requesting we meet them in the disco beside the hotel. We flashed our hotel wristbands and were soon inside. I had low expectations but was overwhelmed by the number of people shaking their asses in the packed two-story disco.

We did a lap before Mica and I gravitated to the bar.

"C'mon, gringos, let's dance." Juana shimmied around us.

But neither I nor the German were giving up our spot at the bar. We worked through drinks as Juana continued to whine, so we switched from Spanish to English to subtract her from the conversation. It was at that moment I realized I'd been speaking in Spanish nearly all weekend—and quite well, I might add.

The dance floor was alive and packed with sweaty bodies. Reggaeton blasted from the speakers while young men and women danced in step. Then the DJ tossed on some banda, and I started laughing. It never failed to amuse me seeing young girls aged nineteen, twenty, twenty-one years old, in the prime of their I'm-hotter-than-you-so-piss-off years, breaking it down to what was essentially a Mexican version of the polka. The tuba player really laid a good beat: Bump bump bump badada . . . Mica started laughing as well. Juana didn't like this.

"You know it's disrespectful to laugh at my culture like that."

"Yeah, yeah, Juanita, outta my face . . ."

Mica and I headed to the dance floor without our whining travel companion. We tried unsuccessfully to infiltrate a few groups of dancing ladies before we found ourselves back at the bar.

The DJ played "Gimme Tha Power." The once-dancing Mexicanos were now raising their fists in solidarity. Juana joined her brothers and sisters and pointed her fist at me.

"You Americans are so greedy. You want all the oil, all the money, all the power."

"Hey, you got the wrong gringo, sister. I've been wearing the same pair of underwear for the past seven years."

She pointed at Mica. "Both of you—your countries are so greedy. You need to learn how to live with what you have. And you send your disease to all other countries. I can't go one block without seeing a KFC, or Burger King, or pinche Walmart! And don't even get me started on NAFTA . . ."

"Relax, Juanita, I'm on your side. But greed and corruption aren't entirely a white man's game."

"Yes, but you're certainly winning."

"Or losing . . . I need a drink."

I walked to the bar, but they'd run out of alcohol. It was just past midnight.

"Goddamn it! Well, it's too bad the bar owners weren't a little greedier when they placed their drink order for the night!"

We left the disco. Juana went upstairs to sleep, but Mica and I walked the streets in search of food. Juana's words stung worse than I'd thought they would. I considered her a good friend, but no matter what I did, she'd always see me as a gringo first and a person second. What chance did I have of shedding the calloused skin of nationalism to become an autonomous human nation if even a friend wouldn't recognize my authority? But, maybe she was just having a bad night . . .

Mica stood in line at hot dog cart, and I waited for him in

the street. I'd hardly been standing there for two minutes before I'd experienced a typical week's worth of aggression. Three Mexican guys passed by, and one of them said, "Chinga tu madre, pinche gringo punitero," and they kept walking. Some shirtless drunk asshole stormed right up in my face and repeated, "Gringo? Eres gringo?" I stared directly into his eyes and wanted to say something but was overcome by a sudden and total feeling of exhaustion. I said nothing, and he left. Another asshole walked by, threw a handful of ice at my chest, spit near my feet, and continued walking. Mica was still in line. I looked down the street and saw a cop ushering along a shirtless, handcuffed drunk. The drunk must have said something the cop didn't like, because the cop headbutted him, splitting open the drunk's eye.

Mica finally walked over with a plate of hot dogs.

"Let's get the fuck out of here," I said. "Something evil's about to happen."

We walked back to the hotel and sat in the empty lobby. Mica munched his dogs. He offered me one, and I declined.

"What the fuck am I doing here?" Mica said.

"That's a good question . . ."

"My father has money. He offered for me to study anywhere in the world. And I picked the Universidad de Lila. He's got a job lined up for me back home, but I don't think I'll ever take it. I have no idea what I want to do. I just want to keep traveling. My goal is to see the whole world before I die."

"I'm with ya there, Mikey."

A young boy slept against a window just outside. Mica pointed him out to me, but we said nothing about him. A wristband was all that separated that kid from either one of us. Mica scarfed down his dogs, and we walked to the roof to go to sleep. Either of us could have written a weighty tome about the shit that pissed us off. But neither could write a fucking sentence about something real we wanted.

We left Guanajuato early the next day. I was glad I was on a bus. I was in no mood to go thumbing in the streets with the other vagabonds. The ride home was nowhere near as special as the one there, but it never was. As we neared Lila, the image of that frantic, toothless Pati's whore came screaming back. I did get some mild relief, however, when the driver put on a movie staring Salma Hayek and the much sexier Cruz, Penelope. And there was this killer lingerie scene . . .

Chapter 20

When I transferred to Conesus University in the spring of '03, I became friends with a girl named Diane. We shared a class, Western Humanities, which quickly became our favorite. We could talk Voltaire or Goethe for hours and used their works to try to paint a better world around us. Diane was a writer. She wrote poems, and short stories, and song lyrics in her notebook during class, and she wasn't afraid to show me her work. I was impressed. Her words had such power and grace; they weren't the typical rambling journal entries many college kids tried to pass off as poetry.

Her poems were usually dark, but that was what I knew, so there wasn't much need for translation. One day during an otherwise normal Humanities lecture, Diane turned and presented me with a new poem along with a breezy preamble: "I wrote this one about the guy who raped me freshman year." After class, she gave me the rest of the story: loved the bastard, too scared to go to the police, wasn't sure if she'd brought it on herself . . . I assured her she did no such thing and begged her for the guy's address. I began obsessing over how I'd take him down—a baseball bat to the kneecaps, a tire iron to the shoulder blades—and felt there to be something poetic in that. But she never gave him up.

I walked to Diane's dorm one warm spring day and saw her

lying in the grass out front and writing something in her journal.

"So, how do you know what to write?"

"The animals come. I chain some and allow some to roam free. Others, I try to chain, but they break away—often before I can even make out their images—and others chain themselves even though I'll never look at them. It's a combination of taming, observation, sorrow, joy, and acceptance all mixed together. Sometimes the words leave the pen as a bullet leaves a rifle. Other times they fall softly as a shredded pillow of down feathers, tossed over a cliff into a still valley. There are no real rules except the ones you create to break or follow or just plain ignore."

"Christ . . . I never know what to say. I'm no artist."

"And the rose is no flower . . ."

Diane and I shared the same affliction. We were petrified to have to stake some sort of claim soon in this life that had tried to destroy us on so many different occasions. Diane's problems grew exponentially as the semester came to a close. She'd discovered that her uterus was damaged from the rape, and within a few years she might not only develop cancer, but she could also become sterile; she didn't know which was worse. One day before the start of the next school year and Diane's sudden withdrawal from school, she stopped by my dorm and gave me a blank blue journal with one instruction: "Let the animals come." Simple words. For years, I'd thought about writing but never felt I had permission until that moment. I filled the book within a month. I got another and kept going. I'm fairly confident that writing is one of the few things that's gotten me through many of those very worst of times. Diane is now healthy, married, and has a young son. I credit the gift she gave me as having an incalculable role in saving my life.

I was exhausted and still a little sick the Monday after our weekend in Guanajuato. One of the ladies of Lengua called me that afternoon to ask if I'd like to sub for a class that night at seven. I didn't feel like working but accepted. Sal's other college roommate—and our mutual friend—Aaron, had signed up for a two-week stint in Lila, and his plane was scheduled to arrive at eight-thirty that night. I wanted to be around when he came, but I needed the cash.

I'd arrived at Lengua several minutes early despite my lack of inspiration to work. I was in the back corner thumbing through a *National Geographic* when someone ascended the stairs with rhythmic and graceful steps. I looked just as a dark-skinned beauty finished that final step and rounded the corner into the room. At first, I mistook her for one of Sal's students. But a fourth and fifth glance confirmed that I'd never seen this girl before. My god was she beautiful—beautiful in a way unlike I'd yet seen. She exuded an air of maturation and subtle sophistication, which heightened the quality of any room she entered, and her beauty looked as if it'd been aged in handcrafted oak casks—some great family secret recipe, passed down through the generations and uncorked that night on a premonition. It was a Monday night, nothing out of the ordinary. But who was I to determine such things? I prepared myself for battle—even if that meant sudden, emasculating retreat.

I tried to play it cool but couldn't stop looking at her. She was doing the same with me. My senses heightened and fired signals in all directions while the chemicals in me raged like monsoon rains. I fell into myself, deeper and deeper into a state of almost pure energy, my consciousness and fears dissolving away. The magazine fell through my hands and clothes passed through my body. I began to pulsate, beating to the rhythm of the room—the rhythm she kept . . . the rhythm of nature. The memory of all other women rarified and floated to the heavens. If I'd never spoken to her, I'd still have loved her—loved her if for nothing more than bringing such intensity to an otherwise dull moment—for nothing more than bringing a smile to my face when my whole being ached. I was in no way prepared to approach her. But time, in its ever-morphing form, had taken the shape of Neta, who reached out and touched what was once my shoulder, jolting me from a trance and returning my body's fragile, physical form.

"Will . . . Will! This is Luz. There were eight students scheduled tonight, but the other seven canceled. She's the only that showed."

Christ! What the fuck was I going to do? I'd been eye-marrying-and-growing-old-with this young girl for Buddha knows how long. She probably thought me a classless pervert.

"Are you sure no one else is coming?" I said.

She shook her head and called Luz. Luz walked over, shook my hand, and said "Hello" in English. I wanted to enjoy her touch, the sound of her voice—but the walls had eyes.

Neta showed Luz to the classroom. I grabbed some whiteboard markers and followed behind. Neta left and Luz sat at a desk. I put the markers on a table and realized I'd forgotten the eraser and radio, so I went back out to get both. When I'd returned with those, I realized I'd forgotten the textbooks. Somewhere in the shuffle, half of the markers once on the table were now back outside. So, I again had to excuse myself to grab them—quite a first impression.

"So how long have you been in Lila?" she asked in adorable English.

"Uh," I fumbled with the radio and a dial fell off, "almost two months now." I picked it up.

"Where are you from?"

"New York . . . Buffalo, New York. Have you heard of it?"

"Jes!" She smiled—her whole body radiated when she smiled. "I am from Zambulla. My father is the head of Aduana's . . . how do you say it?"

"Oh, I don't know . . ."

"Customs? Jes, customs. I love for to surf, play the futbol, spend time with friends, go to the beach, scuba dive with my family . . ." She was so full of life, it couldn't help but spill out onto her gorgeous exterior. Her every gesture, expression, intonation were all her own. She moved as she pleased, unencumbered by both the subtle and blatant demands of anyone around her—unencumbered by the needless restriction of steel-woven social fabric. Luz wore a playera over some skintight pants the same color as her long, wavy black hair, which twirled down her back like thin, dark grapevines reaching toward the earth. She had terra cotta skin, a beautiful broad nose, and full reddish-brown lips concealing a mouth lined with pearly whites.

I'd never had a conversation with a girl like Luz before, and I didn't want it to end. She was so full of life, and passion, and beauty. Yet something about the purity of her words unsettled me. And it was precisely these words, tossed freely in English, that reminded me I was getting paid to mend them. We'd spent the first half hour conversing. I felt tremendous shame in wasting so much time. I could feel the eyes watching me, fingers wagging in my direction, newspaper headlines ready to print . . .

I couldn't tell whether we were flirting. If this were a party, I would have been certain that was indeed what we were doing. But we were in school, and there was an entirely different set of rules.

Sal popped in about halfway through class with some ridiculous excuse: "Is your AC unit working properly?" which sounded more like a fucked-up setup to a kid's phone prank than genuine concern for our comfort. He took a long look at Luz, and I showed him the door. He continued to watch through the glass. I had this strange suspicion he was more focused on me than her, just waiting for me to do or say something stupid.

The two-hour class flew by. And when it ended, Luz hesitated to leave. She got up and walked to the door, but she didn't pass through it. It was as if she was waiting for me to say something. So I did . . .

"It was nice to meet you!"

"It was too nice to meet you too!"

An awkward silence—but still, she didn't leave.

"Well, goodbye," I said, sealing my fate.

She smiled and left.

I couldn't ask for her number. I wanted to, but just couldn't. I knew if I did, it would only bring pain. Some girls came and went. But others . . .

When Luz finally walked out that door, I pushed her far out of mind—but did nothing of the sort.

I got home just in time to see Sal pull in under the almond trees. He'd wrapped up his class early to pick up Aaron, or A-bomb, as we called him, from the airport. A-bomb moved like a calming breeze. He was a tie-dyed, well-worn, and warm old soul who always knew how to bring peace to any situation. He was intelligent and sociable, well-traveled and wise—a rolling combination of all the best qualities of man. A-bomb could be hanging over a cliff by one arm, but he'd remain calm as he lifted himself to safety all while comforting the hysterical spectators too fearful to help—and he'd do it all with a smile on his face. A-bomb was visiting from a mountain town outside of Denver, where he'd gotten a job locating oil for some big fuel company. He was living in a company trailer close enough to Denver to enjoy the city but was paid for as much as he wanted to work, so he rarely went. Like Sal, he'd studied geology at Conesus, and the two had become good friends. Though he'd recently broken up with his longtime girlfriend, Delilah, he seemed to be in good spirits. He and Delilah were as close to a perfect couple as I'd seen— she a wild, earthy rebel, and he a strong, steady breeze. She'd cheated on him with one of her professors when she went to grad school in NYC. I was surprised to hear it. I remember A-bomb once describing her as his "Zest." It didn't seem possible that someone who could earn such a wonderful description could ever cause pain. Though he smiled, I knew he was hurting. Within a week of deciding to come to Mexico, A-bomb was already there with us under the almond trees.

"A-bomb, how's it going, man?" I said.

"Holy crap, Will? I didn't know you were visiting too."

I sneered at Sal. "I've been living here since August."

He looked at Sal. "You didn't tell me Willy was here. That's a great surprise!"

"Uh, yeah, well I guess I forgot," Sal said.

A-bomb dropped off his bags, and we met up with Mica for some drinks. As much as I tried, I couldn't keep Luz out of my mind.

With A-bomb around, I again had someone to fill those blinding midday voids. We sat under the almond trees the next afternoon listening to the Talking Heads and Flaming Lips albums A-bomb had brought with him. A-bomb was like Dr. Josh in that he knew so many interesting facts on so many different topics. He was the guy who knew butterflies tasted with their feet and that film directors used the pseudonym Alan Smithee when they wanted to take their name off an abomination they directed.

Later that afternoon, Sal left school early to show A-bomb around town, and I snuck on the tour. We headed to el Centro, and A-bomb's curiosity with it all reinvigorated my own. I wanted to learn all about Lila's history, and celebrations, and culture. I wanted to meet every person, know everyone by name—but there was never enough time, and people would only allow you to know so much.

Other than relax, A-bomb had only two goals while he was in Mexico: see the beach and the volcano. Sal had refused to take me to the volcano whenever I asked, just as he'd done to Cletus, but I knew he wouldn't deny a fellow geologist. A-bomb was in the club—on the inside. He knew the lingo, and secret handshakes, and all the other trivial crap so important to Sal. Sal was, after all, the kind of guy who got embarrassed if, while sitting beside him in a foreign restaurant, you mispronounced something to a waiter. But with a geologist at his side, Sal was free to blaze any trail without worry that the person with him would cause him any shame.

In his first week, A-bomb met most of the crew. Though he'd taken a few Spanish courses in high school, he'd only retained about enough to ask for a beer or the bathroom. Despite this, he had no problem making friends. Time and time again, I've seen body language to be a far more effective form of communication than words when it came to attracting friends or mates.

People were always stopping by the house. Mica and some of the extraneros came by one night with some caguamas and weed.

We smoked and talked out front for about an hour before I grabbed my guitar. I played some requests, but soon my own material seeped into the mix. I didn't tell anyone the songs were mine. The Mexicans didn't understand the words, and A-bomb wasn't one to judge. I'd never played my own songs for anyone other than band members, but I let them fly that night for a good hour. Everyone was grooving in their respective worlds. I only received recognition when I finally put the guitar down, and that came from A-bomb. All he said was a cool, "Nice . . ." I thought that adequate.

Chapter 21

A-bomb and I were hanging out under the almond trees and enjoying some brews one late afternoon when I got a call from Sal. "Yo, you gotta get down here." He was at Lengua teaching a night class. "That girl is here and she's absolutely fucking unbelievable. She's wearing this shirt . . . god—you just gotta hurry up and get down here. If you don't ask this girl out, you're a fucking fool."

Fuck! It wasn't just me who thought she was gorgeous . . .

"Well, uh, me and A-bomb are a little drunk right now. Besides, we were about to go see a movie."

"I'm telling you, man, you are a serious fucking fool if you don't ask this girl out. She's unlike anything I've ever seen."

"All right, well, I gotta go. The movie's starting soon."

A-bomb and I had planned on seeing a movie at the Soriana supermarket/department store/movie theater in la Villa del Lado, and it was approaching time. We walked up the hill, hopped on a random bus, and were relieved that it took us where we wanted to go. We got off at the Mexican version of sprawling, shameless capitalism and walked inside.

The movie didn't start for another forty-five minutes, so we walked from the theater to the supermarket. A-bomb bought a bottle of wine, and we sat at a table in a small food court in the front of the store. A-bomb pushed the cork inside the bottle, and I grabbed a few plastic cups from a corn dog stand, and we gulped down that fermented grape juice double-time. We still had a good twenty-five minutes to kill, so I bought a six-pack, and we finished it on schedule. But when we walked back to the movie theater, the doors were chained shut.

"Eh, fuck it. Let's just grab some caguamas and head back to the house."

We hopped on a bus heading west and got off at the deportivo complex. We rolled downhill and plopped ourselves down in the plastic chairs under the almond trees. I put on some music, and the bats started dancing around us overhead.

"Hey, man," I said, "I'm sorry to hear about Delilah. She was quite a girl."

"Don't worry about it. I'm okay, really. It just wasn't our time anymore."

I knew he believed what he said, but nothing could hide the tension in his face as he was saying it.

"It's just crazy to think about. You two were the perfect couple. It just makes life seem so pointless."

"It can seem that way. The quest for peace and love is fleeting and hopeless. You can't go looking for those things. You need to just surrender to them . . . Only then can they exist."

"You're really livin' on the edge there, aren't you, Bomber?"

"That's the only place worth living."

I wanted to believe his words. But it seemed far too risky.

But, so was the other way . . .

Sal came roaring down the street a little while later. He shot out of the car and stormed up into my face. "Yo, why was your girl kissin' all over some other dude tonight? You blew your fucking chance!"

"Well, maybe she's got a boyfriend?"

"Well, maybe you're a fucking idiot! Why do you even like her anyway?"

"I don't know. She seems cool."

"Cool? That's the stupidest answer I've ever heard."

"Look, man, I don't wanna fight. We were just relaxing out here."

"Yeah, well, *relaxing* just cost you, didn't it?" He stormed into the house.

"Is he more upset that you missed a chance or that he did?" A-bomb said.

"Who the fuck knows . . ."

"You don't have to take his shit, you know."

"Naw, it's all right. I can get him to calm down sometimes. I kinda feel bad for him. You know his dad got locked up when he was young?"

"Heard something about it."

"I never got the whole story, but he talks about it sometimes when he's drunk. I think he was involved in some bad shit."

"That sucks."

"Yeah, Sal got a bum rap. I figure maybe I can help him out."

"Doesn't look to me like he wants any help."

"I don't know. It just feels so shitty when I do help though. I mean, helping's supposed to feel good, right?"

"Maybe that means something?"

"Fuck, maybe something inside of me's broken? I don't know. What I do know though is that I wouldn't be here right now if it weren't for him. I guess I owe him."

"He didn't carry you here, did he?"

"I wouldn't be surprised if that fucker'd run across two countries with some dead weight on his shoulders."

"Me neither."

We both laughed.

Fuck it. And Luz? So, she had a boyfriend . . . Actually, that was a good thing. Now I didn't have to try. This girl was killing me already, and I'd only spent one night with her . . . as her teacher!

I almost walked into Luz the following evening at school. I was coming up the steps as she was walking from the water cooler to a table in the back.

"Sorry," I said.

She didn't even look up. She just kept walking and sat next to a girl friend. I sat in one of the wicker chairs in the front and tried to read a magazine, but it was no use. I looked at the pictures in *National Geographic,* then up at that beautiful girl. I was hoping she'd be hideous. But that was a hideous and hopeless life philosophy. In fact, she looked better than the other night—and the shirt she was wearing. Goddamn! I didn't notice those things the night before. Perhaps due to my unwavering professionalism . . .

Boyfriend or not, I knew I had to try, and I forced myself into motion before I could give myself time to think it through. My resolve, however, shattered when I was about halfway there, but I gritted my teeth and kept moving with Sal's voice replaying over and over again in my mind: "If you don't ask this girl out, you're a fucking fool!"

"Hi."

She looked up. "Hi." None of the previous charm.

"How, uh, are you?"

Her friend started to giggle.

"I'm good." She wasn't rude, but it was clear she didn't want to talk. One last try though . . .

"I, uh, think my friends and I might be going to Zambulla this weekend."

"Zambulla?" That was the tamale. "I will be in Zambulla this weekend too. Why don't you give me your number?"

I fumbled in my pocket for my phone and almost dropped it when I pulled it out. She grabbed it from my shaking hand and punched in her number.

"I am going snorkeling with my family. Maybe you and your friends will come?" That's my girl!

"Uh, yeah, sure, that'd be great!" I was terrified of going deeper into the ocean than my nipples but would have screamed "Yes!" to scuba diving with bloody steaks in my wetsuit if it meant I could spend time with her.

She smiled, and I smiled, then her friend smiled, and Neta coughed. It was a magical moment. I wandered away and taught the shit out of my night class (which, by the way, I'd recently been given—more on that later though).

It poured that Friday night, so the guys voted against the beach. I was surprisingly okay with it. I thought it might be best to go slow with this one. I tended to self-destruct when not given ample time to plan my every movement, and I needed to be in top form at all times with this girl.

Sal, A-bomb, Mica, and I went hard all weekend. I was invincible. I could do anything. We played Soko, and chanted, and chased mice, and ripped a gravity bong on Mica's roof. Mica had gotten two roommates, an Ecuadorian named Eduardo and a Honduran named Hugo. Eduardo didn't mind us partying there. In fact, he frequently went just as hard. Hugo, however, constantly bitched about the noise—until one night when Sal kicked down his door and challenged him to a fight. Hugo never complained to us after that.

Luz sent me a text early Saturday. "Where are you staying?"

"We didn't end up going. I'm still in Lila."

"I will be back on Monday. We should get together after class."

Ha! Fuck you, Life!

A-bomb's visit also coincided with the Feria, or fair, which was in town for two weeks beginning on the first of November. I was told that this was a huge event that nearly everyone attended, usually multiple times. All the major bars and discos, and restaurants, and car dealerships did most of their business those weeks in tents scattered inside.

Paz, Sofia, Jose, Sal, A-bomb, Unkie Herb, and I went to the Feria that Saturday night. We piled into two cabs and headed east into la Villa del Lado. Herb had given me several warnings about being on my best behavior. According to him, people got their asses beat there every year, and we'd be targets. He also warned me that Juan Q Lawsito would be everywhere and ready to crack me over the head and haul me away should I get out of line. I scoffed at his comments and sucked down a Barrilito as we drove. About fifteen minutes later, we pulled into a dirt field filled with parked cars. Across the street was some huge stone prison straight out of Alexandre Dumas's imagination. I took one quick look at the gun turrets atop a high wall and set down my beer in the gutter.

The Feria was enormous, and looked like a typical US county fair—only less classy. The games here included: break the beer bottle by hurling a rock, and kick the soccer ball past a drunk guy tending goal. The prize was usually your choice of beer from an assortment of cans in an ice-filled cooler.

The place was packed and crawling with sexy ladies. I didn't mind watching them wiggle along the dusty paths. There were signs everywhere advertising some Queen of the Feria contest along with pictures of the contestants. None had an eyelash on Luz.

All the major discos were set up in one area in the back near the rides. Hielo and Crystal both had tents filled with sexy young people. Each disco tried to out-gimmick the other. One had a beach theme and its ground was covered with sand, and the other had some shitty foam machine.

The men in the crew grabbed cheap beers from one of the dive bar tents, and the girls went to search for deals in the boutiques. We all met up in the dining area about an hour later. We pushed a few tables together and sat. I wasn't in the mood for Mexican food. After two and a half months of eating the same shit, the thought of more tacos or quesadillas made my stomach gurgle and whimper. I searched the place and saw a pizza stand. When I looked at it though, I was overwhelmed with a horrendous sensation. I zoomed in on the girl tossing dough behind the counter. Even from about fifty yards away, I was sure I could see those missing molars.

"Hey, Herb."

"Yeah?"

"Do you think—never mind."

Then she saw me—and didn't look away! Oh fuck . . . She dropped the dough on the counter and started walking over.

"Oh, jesus christ . . ."

"What's wrong, Willy? You eat some bad tacos?"

"It's her!"

Herb looked up just as she passed the table. She said hello to him and smiled, then continued to the bathroom, completely ignoring me.

"Goddamn, man! This can't be happening . . ."

"I think she just went to pass the last of the corn she licked out of your ass."

"Fuck you and your rhymes, Herb!"

"Relax, Willy. She'll probably clean your sphincter again if you ask her nicely."

"That's not funny! I got this new girl I like—I mean, I really, really like her. I can't have this beast haunting me . . ."

"Look, she's a twenty-six-year-old single mother of two. She's already an old maid in this country. She's poor and most likely an addict of something. I'm sure she once had beautiful dreams just like anyone else. She may be a train wreck, but she's still a person. And she's not out to get you. She probably just really likes you and doesn't know how to show it."

"Fuck, you're probably right." Maybe I wasn't the only one tortured by our relationship? I quickly made my peace with the situation and was over it by the time she left the women's room. I didn't say anything to her as she passed the table but wished her well.

We hit some of the disco tents later but called it an early night. There'd be plenty more Feria for future nights.

Chapter 22

Monday came and the very real possibility of seeing Luz carried me through that sunny afternoon. I fought the urge to call her that morning and waited until later in the day.

"Would you still like to get together after class tonight?"

"Jes!"

The ladies at Lengua had given me a new student who came Monday, Wednesday, and Friday nights from seven to nine, and I had a class with him that night. I took a shower at five thirty to give myself ample time to get ready for the night. I didn't want to get my hopes up, but I did allow myself to strut on that walk down Madrid del Rio. I had no idea if this was a date or just two people getting together, but either way I was just glad I'd get some private time to spend with Luz without Sal barging in: "Are your drinks cold enough?"

My new student's name was Joaquin. Joaquin was a middle-aged man from Mexico City where his wife and two kids still lived. Joaquin had moved to Lila at the request of his employer, some supply company from the big city. Though he didn't want to leave his family, he also didn't want them to starve. Joaquin was gregarious, like Gabriel, but unlike Gabriel, he never spoke about deep sea fishing on yachts or staying in fancy foreign hotels. Rather, Joaquin talked about sports, and beer, and food. He had a swollen stomach, which he'd pat when nervous, a knack for conversation, and a quick wit that left me always looking for a punch line. I enjoyed the time I spent with him. Joaquin was born in D.F. but easily could have been from North Buffalo.

As much as I liked working with Joaquin, he frequently canceled class—at least, that's what the ladies at Lengua told me. I didn't know whether they were fucking with me, but I had my suspicions that they were. Several times, I'd shown up to work and walked into this type of conversation:

"Excuse me, I was told I had a new class to teach tonight at eight, but there's no one here."

"Oh, that class is starting next week."

"But you told me yesterday it was starting today."

"No, next week."

Or they'd wait for a half hour after I'd arrived to tell me, "Oh, your student called this morning to cancel."

"You do have my phone number, right?"

And that night with Joaquin was no different.

I'd arrived about fifteen minutes early, and those Lengua dicks let me sit there thumbing through magazines until seven thirty before approaching. "Oh, your student Joaquin called this afternoon and said he couldn't make it tonight."

"I've been here for forty-five minutes! Couldn't you have called me this afternoon?"

I was starting to get angry; then *she* walked in—and my was she beautiful. She'd done up her hair, put on makeup. She hadn't put in that kind of effort before. I felt really special just looking at her. My anger seemed to melt away.

"Hello, Lucecita." I loved to say that name. It rolled from my tongue like a wave. I told her about my class being canceled but assured her I'd be back by nine to pick her up. I walked down the stairs and onto the street with a smile exploding across my face. I started for home but got redirected when I saw Mica and A-bomb coming up the other way.

"Hey, we're headed for some beers. Care to join?" the German said.

"Does the Pope eat bear shit in the woods?" I said.

He laughed.

We walked to the two-for-one spot and ordered a round. I knew a few beers would settle the nerves but also knew too many could confound them. I decided to stop at four. I wanted to have use of all my faculties to take in that delightful beauty waiting for me. We sucked down our beers, devoured several bowls of nuts, exchanged embarrassing and humorous anecdotes, and soon I was back on the street, bound for glory. I waited until around nine to leave the bar so that I'd be about five minutes late—a stupid trick I'd learned was necessary to get what I needed from life.

Luz was waiting outside when I arrived. And so was everyone else. All the night classes ended at nine, so everyone—students, teachers, and the Big Three—was all scattered on that street waiting for rides and saying goodbyes. I walked past Sal's students and strolled up to Luz. She smiled confidently despite the wandering, judging eyes of the masses. I put out my hand, and she met it. I kissed her cheek, and we were off, walking the gauntlet hand in hand. I couldn't care less if those idiots fired me on the spot. Sal's students looked on as if my balls were dragging on the sidewalk. I already knew I was a king. Now everybody else knew it too . . .

"Where would you like to go, hermosa?" I let out a few endearing terms despite my uncertainty of the nature of our relationship.

"I have no place in mind."

"What about there?" I pointed to a bar across the street that was posh and, most importantly, empty. The waiter seated us at a boxy white table lit up from the inside like a glowing sugar cube, and we sat on white chairs. I ordered a Negra Modelo (though pricey, it was time to celebrate), and Luz got a whiskey and soda.

"So, you like to surf?"

"Jes, to surf is my favorite in all the world. I love the ocean and the sun and the waves."

"What's your last name?"

"Corta. You?"

"James. How old are you?"

"Diez y . . ."

Wait? Diez means ten. Fuck! This was the kicker. This chick is a kid.

". . . nueve . . ."

Okay, which one is nueve again? Nueve is good, right? Nueve is nine! Okay, nineteen is better than twelve.

". . . but I will be twenty in January. How old are you?"

"I just turned twenty-three. I'm a quarter of my way through life."

"What do you like to do?"

"God, I don't even know. I don't have any defaults like you do with that surfing stuff. I like to travel, if that counts. I mean, you don't really travel on a regular basis as you would dance or sing or play an instrument—oh yeah, I like music . . ." Good, William, reward yourself with some beer. You're working really hard in there.

The conversation continued like that until Luz released a stinger: "I am a model for bikinis and clothing." Most chicks would lead with this kind of information, but not Luz. "A man from *Playboy* saw me surfing in Zambulla one day and offered me money to pose for them. But I said no."

"Was this a moral objection?"

"I have no problem with the body. It's just not what I want to do. I am in business. I want to open a hotel on the beach someday that accommodates surfers."

Later, I found out that this girl was not only a bikini and potential *Playboy* model, but also the valedictorian of her high school class, and now university, where she was the reigning beauty queen for the last two years. I already knew she was smart before I'd heard all that. Her English had improved in the short time I'd known her. I was in over my head—almost so much so, I decided not to worry about it. I was going to ride this thing out and see where it went. I saw how the waiter looked at her. How the guys checked her out as they passed on the street. It overwhelmed me, yes. But that's the price you paid for taking out the queen. And I fucking loved a challenge . . .

Luz got a call about an hour into our—by that time I felt safe to say—date.

"Would it be okay if my friend and her boyfriend joined us? He is an American just like you."

Oh, goddamn it . . . "Uh, yeah sure."

"From Texas."

Double goddamn it . . .

Soon a white hatchback came tearing around the corner and stopped out front. A light-skinned Mexican girl and an enormous white boy got out and walked into the bar. The girls hugged and exchanged hellos while I sat back and read their vibes.

Everything was cool—even the gringo.

"This is my friend, Luz," my Luz said. "She has the same name as me. Everybody calls her Luz Blanco because she has light skin, and me, Luz Oscura."

I said hello and kissed her cheek.

"This is Kyler. He is Luz's friend. He is from Texas, U.S.A."

I shook Kyler's massive hand. He was a gentle giant, a double-wide almost too goofy and uncoordinated to be threatening. What a waste of such god-given size! But I was relieved not to have to be dealing with an All-American Tough-Guy. Steers and Queers, baby, woohoo!

"How do you do, Kyler?" We shook. A wet noodle (tsk tsk, big boy). Kyler worked at the Academia de Lila.

"Hey, Kyler, you know a cat named Herbert Goldberg?"

"Yeah, he's the head of my department. All the kids seem to really love him. I think I can learn a lot from him."

More than you know, Tex . . .

Kyler and Luz Blanco sat on one chair, and my Oscura queen and I shared the other. The waiter kept coming with new drinks. I pulled out my music and found a song. I stuck a headphone in my ear and one in hers just as "Two of Us" began.

"Do you like it?"

"Jes!"

With each drink, she warmed deeper into me. Next, I played "Golden Age" by Beck. I'd first heard the song on a trip back to Conesus from Buffalo. Sal drove us in the Toyota Corolla that would later carry us over the Rocky Mountains and along the California coast. I wanted to put my hands on the wheel, but the world was so bleak, so snowy. The earth did nothing special in Western New York until it started to wrinkle near the Finger Lakes. We were baked, and even with the guidance of that song, my mind couldn't find a safe spot to rest.

But sitting next to that Mexican angel . . .

I cranked up the volume and ordered more beers, and soon we decided to hit the Feria. On the way out the bar, I saw a familiar face walking in. It was Ximena, and she was with a group of girl friends. I put my arm around Luz's waist and pulled her to me. When she'd warmed, I kissed her cheek. Ximena pretended not to notice. I really didn't care.

When we got to the car, my Luz opened the back door. She got in, reached out her hands, and pulled me to her. I put the headphone back in her ear and played some early Elvis. I tested the boundaries, and she allowed me to kiss her cheeks and neck. I was swollen and ready, and wanted her right then.

We pulled into the dirt parking lot and got out. The parking lot attendant started giving Luz Blanco some crap about where she parked her car. But Luz Oscura got out, batted her eyes, and soon the prick was spreading open a cut section of chain-link fence and waving us through. This girl was good!

When we got inside, she wrapped her arm around my back, and I did the same to hers. Our bodies fit together perfectly. Holding her took no extra effort—in fact, we leaned on each other, somehow lightening the other's steps as we moved. She was so fucking cool.

I was living a dream when someone suggested we go on rides—the same rides I'd avoided the night before because of their outrageous prices. Goddamn! Had I forgotten that girlfriends cost money? How long was a girl with *Playboy* knocking down her door going to last with this romantic gypsy? I'd figure something out . . .

"Hey, wouldn't you guys rather go back to my place? I mean, if it's games you want, I've got plenty of rocks and beer bottles . . ."

They continued toward the rollercoaster, the most expensive death trap at the fair. I tried laying on the sad eyes when Kyler opened his wallet to pay for his Luz, but he left me hanging, and I passed sixty precious pesos (a quarter of my week's grocery bill) through the ticket window on the chance that this girl could be *the one*.

The chick behind the counter didn't even smile when she handed me the two tickets. Luz and I hopped in the front car, and Kyler and his Luz sat behind us. There was nobody else in line—most likely because there were two maintenance guys fixing something at the top of the first hill. The guy at the main switch put his fingers to his mouth and let out a piercing whistle, and the two maintenance guys slid down a metal support pole without any safety harnesses or net below them. Christ, I was gonna die.

"Listen, hermosa, if we make it through this thing alive, I get to kiss you, okay?"

She just smiled. I took it as a "Jes!"

The rusted car lurched forward, and I sincerely feared for my life. Luz threw up her hands and laughed. God, didn't people get killed on these things even in the overly litigious country I hailed from? I wasn't going to make it . . .

But I did. And I got my kiss! On the cheek though—she turned her head at the last second.

"Let's go on the twisty cups next!" My Luz beamed.

I had to think fast. "Uh, those twisty rides make me sick." I assumed it was better that she thought I was a pussy rather than broke. "Why don't we grab some drinks instead?"

They all agreed, and we headed to the Hielo tent. Every guy watched my Luz move through the entrance and past the bar, and stared at her ass until she sat. We ordered drinks. My Luz knew the guy working behind the bar, so we got a discount. If I was going to get sick, it was better to have been from booze than fucking twisty cups.

The girls wanted to dance, so we hit the floor. Again, all eyes followed my girl. Some of these eyes also gave me aggressive looks. I assumed these fuckers didn't like seeing brown on white love.

I quickly lost focus on those penetrating eyes as Luz pulled me into her gravity. Her movements were cool, rhythmic, and controlled, and every bit her own. She pulled me near, enormous chest heaving against mine. I was heaving as well. I knew she felt it; she grinded on it hard. I'd never been so close to cumming with my clothes on. I almost would have been okay with it if it hadn't been the start of my laundry cycle.

The song ended, and we found ourselves back out among the games and tents. I'd pitched a pretty sizeable tent myself but did the tuck-n-waddle before leaving Hielo, and soon it was back to neutral. I gave in to the tired dating cliché of trying to display manliness to impress the girl and paid the five pesos to play the rock game. I'd played baseball most of my life and knew that, while they had me at soccer, I could one-up most Mexicans at the hurling sports. But after three tries, all bottles remained intact. The guy working the booth let me have a beer anyway while smiling and repeating, "New Jork Yanquis!"

Luz wrapped around me once more despite my inability to prove my manliness. We pushed through the opening in the chain-link fence and were soon wrapped around one another in the back of Luz Blanco's white hatchback.

Blanco dropped me off under the almond trees. I kissed my Luz's cheek and told the other couple goodbye. I then locked myself in my room, released some pressure (only took a couple of tugs, then . . . wow!) and fell into a deep, satisfying sleep. This was the girl, man—I could feel it!

Chapter 23

I woke the next morning elated. Though I'd learned that no such thing existed, I could no longer deny the stinging notion that this just might be my time. Stars were aligning, birds were singing, oil tankers were remaining afloat . . . I decided to jettison all doubts before they could capsize the ship. All I needed were my wits and strength. The impossible part was over. I was pretty sure she liked me. Luz called me early that morning, and we made plans to get together that night.

Jorg had finished his studies at the Universidad and was heading back to Germany. That night was his despedida, or going away party, at Dr. Josh's apartment in el Centro, and after, Jorg was taking a red-eye home. Herb came by after school with some Barrilitos, and Sal, Mica, Jorg, A-bomb, and I sat with him under the almond trees and drank them. Soon we were walking through el Centro in search of Dr. Josh's house. Sal had been there before but couldn't remember where it was. It was hidden from the street by a large wall that had several doorways cut into it. Sal guessed correctly, and we entered an impressive courtyard below a two-story stone building. The second floor was packed with people overflowing onto a balcony and the rooftop of the hardware store connected to the apartment. This was the place, man, if there ever was one.

We walked upstairs, and I was stopped by three large, surly Mexican guys on the balcony. "Eres gringo? Eres gringo?" Everyone else I'd come in with kept walking inside the party.

"Well, I prefer to call myself Will, but I'll play ball." I was feeling a bit frisky that night.

"So you *are* a gringo?"

"As Cesar Chavez . . ."

They surrounded me. I backed against the balcony railing.

"Why did you elect George Bush? Why do you want to put up a wall?"

"Well, friend, in fact, I drove an hour back home from college to vote for the other guy. And while I have done some hardscaping and brickwork in my life, I've had nothing to do with *the* goddamned wall. For all I know, they're gonna seal me in on the other side."

"Why do you hate Mexicans?"

"Would you like a kiss? Would a kiss on your lips prove to you that I don't hate Mexicans?"

"Are you a gay?"

"Sure thing, boys. Now, if you'll excuse me, I'm going to go grab something fruity and fun from the bar. Tootles!" I blew each a kiss and walked into the kitchen where I approached Mica, sitting at the table. He grabbed a caguama from the fridge, popped its top with the end of an orange lighter, and handed it to me. I walked through the kitchen and onto the rooftop of the hardware store, which was like a huge balcony to Dr. Josh's already enormous apartment. The place probably went for two thousand pesos a month—a fucking steal for anyone living in some closet in New York, or Chicago, or San Fran and paying thirty times that. Sofia, Paz, Tito, and Jose were on the roof, as was Herb, who was standing alone in a darkened corner and smoking a cigarette. I approached him.

"Would you take a look at those dudes," he said. "That guy Jose is as queer as a three-dollar bill."

"Herby, you think everybody's gay."

"Hey, if the assless chaps fit . . ." He gave a self-satisfied chuckle.

"And look at Paz with her other girl friends. All the guys they hang with are either foreigners or gay."

"Maybe they like it that way?"

"Or maybe they're just a bunch of outcasts in their own country."

I thought about that for a long moment before saying, "Fuck."

"What's up?"

"If they're outcasts, then we're the outcasts of the outcasts."

"I'll drink to that." Herb and I did a "Salud," then tipped back our beers.

Sometime later, Javier staggered onto the roof. I hadn't seen him in weeks, and that night he looked to be on something stronger than alcohol. He left a trail of offended people behind as he snaked his way through the party. He walked over when he spotted me.

"Cabron!"

"Hey, Javie, long time no see."

I stuck out my hand to shake, but he ignored it. Instead, he locked around my waist and started humping me like a dog.

"Yo, get off me, man." I pushed him away, and he moved on to Sal. He did the same thing, and Sal pushed him off. Same with Herb. Javier staggered toward the three tough guys who'd grilled me about Georgie Porgie Put 'em in a Kevlar (or not, in far too many cases).

"Stay away from those guys, Javier!" I said.

He didn't listen. He continued toward them. This was going to be bad.

"Hey, Javie, you can hump my leg if you'd like!" I said.

But before he reached them, he stopped, whipped it out, and took a piss straight on the roof. The stream splattered off the tar paper and splashed onto the legs of nearby party guests, who ran from him as if he were radioactive: "GUACALA!"

Javier gave a sinister laugh, then he zipped up, staggered back down to the street, and took off.

Mica approached me. "Javier threw a condom in my face and told me to come to his bed. I said no, and he just laughed like a maniac and took off."

None of us ever saw Javier again after that night—not even Herb. He just disappeared. And nobody ever really spoke about it either.

Luz sent me a text: "I'm at the Feria. Come and meet me!"

"Hey, anybody wanna head over to the fair?"

Sal, Mica, and A-bomb all nodded, and soon we were exiting a cab and stepping onto the dusty field. Luz said she was in the Hielo tent again. Just knowing where she was set me at ease, so when we passed a beer tent selling five-peso cans of Tecate, I had no problem with stopping for a few drinks. But soon the entire plastic table was filled with empties. Luz sent me several texts asking where I was. Each time I responded, "I'll be there soon." Then someone would buy another round. That game continued for about an hour before Luz came to me.

I looked up, and standing there like the angel in some old drunk's recurring vision was the one from my own. When she moved, I knew she was real. Luz approached with Luz Blanco. My Luz wore a low-cut white shirt, which was incapable of controlling her massive endowment. The fact that she wasn't wearing a bra didn't help. She sat on my lap. Luz Blanco scanned the sausage selection and cozied up next to the Bomber. The girls had left a group of friends at Hielo but neither cared to return. Instead, they chugged beers with us.

I noticed Sal's prolonged glances each time Luz leaned over to set an empty on the table. Eventually, it happened.

"So, Luz," he said, "what are you doing with this loser?"

She ignored his question.

"I mean, his Spanish is horrible. It sounds more German than anything."

"Hey, fuck you, man," I said.

Again she ignored him.

"Last week," she said, "I was scuba diving with my family in Zambulla, and we saw una ballena."

"What's that?" the Bomber said.

"A wha—"

"A whale," Sal said. "Zambulla's sick. Those beaches are disgusting."

"Maybe you are the one who is sick?" She looked him dead in the eye.

He didn't respond.

Eventually we walked to the Hielo tent, which was packed. There was a long line out front, but my Luz walked over to some beefy bouncer, and he let us in the side entrance. I instinctively started for the bar, but Luz took my hand and led me to through the crowd to the dance floor in the back. The place was a blur of familiar faces, though none were distinct. I had brief visions of the extraneros, students from Lengua, Paz and her crew, and people I'd met at parties—and saw their glances, whispers, fingers pointing in my direction. I was with the girl, and they all knew that I knew they knew this. This was also our first public appearance as a couple. I walked proudly beside her.

It could have been easy to wander, but Luz led me through it all. When we hit the floor, she lit up. She put on a brief display before pulling me to her. Guys tried, but none succeeded. They tapped her shoulder and moved in between songs, but each time she rejected them without the slightest hesitation.

Sal and the other guys wandered to the dance floor as well. Between songs, Sal grabbed Luz's hand and started to grind on her. She pulled away and clung to me, saying "I only want to be with you." It would have been easy to just let the crowd sweep her away. But she fought against the current and held onto me for what seemed like dear life. She wrapped tightly around my neck and leaned her head into mine. I did the same with her, and we locked around one another in an impenetrable defense against the world. The tempo of the song was fast, but we remained slow, swaying to our own beat. I started kissing her cheek, then her head warmed and turned, presenting me the lips. But they only came halfway. I gave in, and leaned, and met those soft, full lips with my own. It was sweet and slow. Our first kiss. I felt connected to her energy, plugged into her spirit. Then she pulled her head back and repeated, "I can't believe my teacher just kissed me."

"Whoa, go easy with the t-word, all right?"

"I can't believe I am drinking with my *teachers*."

"Hey, that was just the one night . . . You're free to go at any time . . ."

She put her hands behind my head, pulled it down to her, and kissed me again—this time deep and long. I could feel Sal and Turd and others looking on. Something special was happening here. I wrapped around her, and she around me, and we were whole again.

Sal and the others took a cab back, and I rode with the Luz's in Blanco's white hatchback. My Luz sat with me in the back, despite an available passenger seat, and it took minimal convincing to get her to come in with me when we got to my house. Luz Blanco had apparently come in too, but I was far too wrapped up in my moment to realize it. A-bomb showed her to the sofa.

My Luz followed me into my new bedroom and lay on the king-size bed. When Jorg moved out, Sal took his old room—the biggest in the house—allowing me an upgrade as well. I closed and locked the door behind me. There were no wall openings or two-way mirrors here—no, here, I was allowed to be man. I'd already done the impossible: *the* girl was lying on my bed . . . and slowly undressing.

"Turn around," Luz said playfully, but also with a stern directness. I obeyed her command, knowing full well my eyes would soon see what they were currently being denied. Luz pulled the white shirt over her head and cradled her breasts with her arms.

"Do you have a shirt I can wear?" she said.

I reached into the closet and pulled out my most comfortable: the worn blue "Buffalo Athletics" t-shirt I'd gotten at a summer basketball camp when I was twelve. I tossed it to her. She slid it on, and it hung just past her panties. I walked to her and ran my hands over all the softness of her body—outside, then up and under the shirt, which soon found its way to the floor. She continued to repeat, "I can't believe I drank with my *teacher*," as I ran my hands over her breasts and kissed her neck. She removed my shirt and unbuckled my belt, pulling it off me slowly. She unbuttoned and unzipped my pants, pulling them down and off my legs, then pushed me on the bed and pulled off my boxers. She sat on me, rubbing her warm spot on my own, slid off her panties, and took the tip inside her.

"Wait . . ." I shot over to the closet, grabbed a rubber, and slid it on. I led her to her back, got on top, and slid inside. She was gushing and warm and accepted me with eager invitation.

"Ay . . ."

She bit her lip and rested her head on the pillow, then furrowed her brow and clenched her teeth. I knew I'd hit a spot and continued to work it until I'd extracted all its worth. She came on me, leaving a thick, white crème all over my dick. The sight of it drove me wild. I flipped her over to her stomach, pulled her on all fours, and guided her to the edge of the bed. I stood on the floor and our bodies came together at a perfect proportion. She came again, then pulled me on top of her, flipped me to my back, and got on top. She dug her claws into my wrists for support and gave me everything she had. After about an hour, it was over. We'd drained each other of everything we had and lay on that bed locked in each other's embrace.

"Baby, you are the fucking best I've ever had."

She just smiled.

"Have you ever gone for so long?" I said.

"I have never done this before. That was my first time."

"Bullshit! No virgin works her hips like that. Besides, isn't there supposed to be blood or something?"

"I told you what I am!" She got up, put her clothes on, and walked to the door.

"C'mon, it doesn't really matter either way . . ."

She unlocked the door, opened it, and left. I fell asleep.

I woke the next morning to the sound of Luz Blanco banging on my door.

"Luz! Luz! I have to go to work!"

My Luz must have come back in the middle of the night because she was sound asleep by my side. I tapped her shoulder to wake her, and my movements sent streaks of pain through my arms. I examined my wrists, which looked as though they'd been used as a perch for a large bird of prey. Goddamn, if that's what my wrists looked like, I couldn't imagine what the girl had done to my—

She woke up.

"Good morning, princess." I kissed her lips, but they were cold and uninviting.

"What time is it?" she said.

"I don't know, but I think Luz wants to take you home."

My Luz popped out of bed and put on her shoes. The life, the passion, the vulnerability had all been lost in the night. She walked to the door with none of these. She hardly said goodbye before turning the doorknob.

"Wait! Please don't go—"

She smiled with enough sincerity to make me believe I was still in the game, then walked through the door. I wanted to believe, but I knew it was over. We'd put ourselves on display far too early—a relationship sin that was far too often immune to acts of penitence. I rubbed the opened wounds on my wrists. The fairytale had been tainted. It was an explosive end to a refreshing ride that was nourishing yet fleeting, as was everything else of worth in this life. I felt hollow but thoroughly vindicated.

Chapter 24

I didn't see much of Luz over the next few days. We both waited just long enough to respond to each other's text messages to suggest that something had changed between us. We'd write that we wanted to see each other, but neither of us made an effort to do so. I'd been preparing for this moment for years and wasn't going to let anyone get the best of me. I spent most of those days getting drunk with the guys and tried to erase her from memory.

For a week, Sal had been planning to take A-bomb to the volcano, but the conditions hadn't been desirable. A-bomb cared more for the experience than perfect conditions, so Sal finally gave in to his requests and decided to take us one hazy morning. The night before, Sal told me, "We need to get up early tomorrow. It's a long trip to the volcano and a long hike to the top. If you're not up by six thirty, I'm gonna leave you."

I knew Sal and was up at six the next morning. I'd had time to make breakfast, wash the dishes, pack, and watch a movie before Sal finally left his room at ten. He didn't want to take his car up the rugged volcano road, but we didn't have another, so we piled in and took off down the carretera. We drove northeast for two hours, always with the volcano in sight—sometimes it was dead ahead, other times along our side. There were two: el Volcán Rojo, the active one, and el Volcán Azul, its dormant brother hidden behind Rojo.

Despite the distance to Rojo, it always looked as though we were only a few hundred yards from the bottom of its slope. There was a smoking plume shooting from the crater above—proof that inside, the earth was indeed still alive. We stopped in a nearby town and bought provisions (I get to call food "provisions" here because I was about to hike a fucking volcano).

There was an official entrance with an overhead sign welcoming us to the volcanoes. The road was paved and coiled counter-clockwise around the volcano. There were markers every kilometer indicating how many we'd already traveled, and with each marker I grew a little more nervous. On several occasions, I'd heard Sal and his fellow geologists speak about the altitude sickness they'd gotten the first few times they hiked to the top of Azul, which was the volcano we were ascending (Rojo was too dangerous), and I didn't want to spend the trip puking. Our destination was a small lab at the summit of Azul, and from there we'd have a clear look at Rojo smoking just a few kilometers away.

Driving conditions began to deteriorate around the seventh kilometer. Both the slope of the road and the number of potholes increased. Sal cursed each time he hit one, bottoming out his car, and scraping its undercarriage along the dusty road.

Each time we wrapped around the north face of that magma-mountain, the Cuidad Humo looked farther and farther away. Kilometers thirteen, fourteen, and fifteen were still all right, but sixteen was the one that finally claimed Sal's patience.

"Fuck this. We'll walk the rest of the way." Sal pulled over, and we all got out.

"Don't forget anything," he said. "Remember, it gets like thirty degrees cooler up there, so if you forget your jacket, don't blame me."

Sal shielded his eyes and looked to the top of Azul. "See that small box up there?" He pointed at a shimmering light on the peak, which looked to be a thousand miles away.

"That thing all the way up?"

"Yeah, that's where we're headed. It looks farther than it really is. It's only twenty-five kilometers to the top, and we've already done sixteen so we're not too far."

We started hiking. I had a backpack filled with two liters of water, a sweatshirt, sweatpants, and a knit cap. The first section of road was the worst. Though only about a twenty-degree angle, it seemed to go straight up. It took a lot out of me, and I could see it did the same for Sal and A-bomb, but I knew nobody was going to admit it.

The scenery changed as we continued. The tree cover started to thin and those that remained were mostly evergreens. Though the angle of the road had decreased considerably, we were all short of breath. I was winded, but I thought of all the running I'd done over the last few weeks and put confidence in my body that it'd get me to the top.

Sal shared facts about the volcanoes: "The one we're climbing here, Azul, is actually higher than Rojo, but it's extinct. Rojo's probably the most active volcano in Mexico right now, which makes it one of the most active in North America. There's a legend that the two are brothers. Azul is cool and sensible, which is why it's been allowed to rest, but Rojo is angry and always ready to destroy anyone who doesn't worship him."

"It's crazy that we're so close to it," I said, referring to Rojo. "But I guess even from far away, it always looks like you're close to it."

"Yeah, and it looks so fucking huge," A-bomb said.

"You know why that is?" Sal said.

"'Cause of our relative height to it, right?" A-bomb said.

"Yeah," Sal said, "what's so impressive about these volcanoes is what's called their prominence. They stand nearly all by themselves in this big, sweeping plain, which is only a few hundred feet above sea level, so you can see nearly their entire height without anything else in the way. Other mountains might be higher, but they don't seem like it if you're looking at them from an elevated plateau—like when we were in the Rockies, remember?"

"Yeah," I said.

"It's all relative. And these two are just like raging earth zits on an otherwise clear face. It's so cool."

We came to a parking lot, the highest point a member of the general public could ascend. Sal led us across the pavement to a gate with a sign on it warning us to keep out. He unlocked the gate, and we walked through. Kilometers eighteen and nineteen weren't so bad, but from twenty on, I was struggling. For every twenty steps, I'd have to take a brief rest, lungs gulping in air. The oxygen was thinning, along with the evergreens, as we approached the tree line. The clouds passed through us, destroying any childhood hope I'd had to someday live on top of one. As we continued, the trees and all other plant life disappeared. All that remained were barren slopes of volcanic ash and rock. It looked like some Hollywood set of the moon. There was nothing left to produce sound except for ourselves.

"Hey, guys, stop moving for a second."

They did. Pure silence.

"Have you ever heard that before?" I said.

"What?"

"Absolutely nothing."

That nothing was filled with something long before a truck rounded the bend. The driver stopped when he saw Sal, and they spoke for a few minutes before he continued driving down the volcano.

"What'd they say?"

"Just that they're headed down to pick up some firewood," Sal said. "It's cold as fuck up there, man."

"It's cold down here too," I said.

"You know," Sal said, "I used to run this peak. I'd run down to the parking lot, then up the six kilometers back to the top. It's great exercise."

"You're insane." A-bomb exhaled the smoke from a cigarette.

Sal *was* insane. In fact, I think that's a large reason why we were friends. There were plenty of others out there who were physically stronger, more intelligent, better looking—but nobody was tougher.

We were a couple of cockroaches who'd survive any catastrophe: floods, hurricanes, TP shortages (I'd seen him use his hand once in the woods) . . . You could drop us off in the middle of the desert with nothing but a Coke and a smile and we'd crawl out a few days later. I think in some twisted way we were drawn to those deserts, and oceans, jungles, and mountains, and volcanoes. We never talked about it, most likely because we didn't even know it ourselves, but we'd push each other along, for better or worse. We were warriors, man, on a desperate and endless quest for some twisted combination of purity and revenge, and we were the fucking best. Far better than you, no doubt.

We kept going, and soon I could only do about ten steps before needing a slightly longer rest. I figured accepting this blow to my pride was better than blowing chunks, so I gave myself ample time to rest. Then we rounded the final bend, and there it was: the shimmering light in the distance was now about a hundred yards away. While I was only getting about five steps to the rest at that point, I was still doing better than A-bomb, who was about fifty feet behind and gasping for air. I passed a four-thousand-meter marker just off the trail, and A-bomb snapped a picture of me standing next to it when he caught up. It was much cooler here than where we'd abandoned the car, but it wasn't too bad.

We finally reached the lab station and went inside. There were only a few people there. One headed the Universidad's geology department. He was a short, stout man, who welled with pride as he showed us the lab's various sensors and cameras and reference materials full of information. Sal was sure to also point out the fridge stocked with beer, computer whose history was filled with porn sites, and gas stove burner where they'd lit countless joints. We stopped at a room-length window and stared at the world below.

"On a clear day, you can see the ocean," Sal said. "And on a clear night, you can see Guadalajara lit up in the distance."

The clouds continued to pass through us. I put on my sweatshirt and hat, walked around back, and took a piss on some rocks. Below me was the Cuidad Humo, whose white buildings looked like dandelions in a great field of dusty green. I'd finally done it; I'd climbed the mountain and was pissing off its top.

The guys in the truck came back and unloaded firewood in a pile under the lab. Sal, A-bomb, and I ate our lunch while sitting on a wall that had a straight drop down a high cliff. We dangled our legs over the edge as we tried to make out familiar sites in the distance. The clouds blocked our view of Rojo, which very well may have been spitting its largest plume of ash yet, but we couldn't enjoy it. We decided to leave about forty-five minutes later. We still had quite a hike ahead of us, and Sal kept muttering some crap about wanting to avoid the carretera, and its potholes, at night. We said our goodbyes, rejected an offer for a ride back in the truck bed, and started down the ashy, inactive stratovolcano.

My pocket vibrated before we'd reached the first bend. I pulled out my phone and read a text from Luz: "Where are you? I miss you." I was surprised to have service up there and took the opportunity to up my personal worth by responding honestly to her message: "I'm at the top of the volcano right now, but I'll call you soon. I miss you too, princess!"

The descent was far more difficult than I'd have imagined. In fact, I'd rather walk up than down a hill any day. When we got to the car, my knees were overjoyed. I hooked up my music to the stereo, played some Pearl Jam, and we were back on level ground about an hour later. Sal stopped at a small stand just outside the park's entrance.

"You gotta try this drink they have here called ponche. It's like a hard cider."

A-bomb and I decided to split a large ponche. The old man behind the counter dipped a ladle in a large ceramic pot and filled a mug with the brew. We paid and sat at a wooden table. The day was cool, and I was still comfortable in my sweats and hat. The sun was slowly descending, and the quiet countryside prepared for rest. A-bomb and I passed the drink and took slow, deliberate sips until it was gone. Before leaving, I walked around back to use the bathroom, which was nothing more than an unpainted plywood box with a patch of dead grass inside. I emptied my bladder while watching an enormous spider the size of a Sacajawea dollar quietly constructing a web. I said goodbye to the spider and walked back through the tall grass to the car. Nobody said much on the ride home.

Chapter 25

Mica came over for dinner that night while I was still preparing our feast. My dinner usually consisted of chicken, pasta, and whatever vegetables I had, and that night was no different. Sal was sitting under the almond trees with Paz, and the German and I joined them after eating. Luz sent me a text: "Come to Zambulla tonight. Big party! I rented us a hotel room. There's room for you and one friend."

I hesitated to ask anyone. I knew how this situation played out. I'd get excited and go, and she'd spend the whole time flirting with some greasy surfer dude while I eyed her friends, trying to determine which I'd hit on to avenge my hurt pride. Besides, I'd been trying to visit Zambulla for months and nobody ever wanted to go. Why fight it? But then again, my gut reactions were usually the cause of my misery . . .

"Hey, does anyone want to go to Zambulla tonight? Apparently there's some big hotel party by the ocean, and I can bring one person."

"Well, Paz and I were just gonna stay in and watch a movie." One down.

"I've had a serious case of diarrhea all day. I think it's those tacos by my house, Tacos el Sobrino. Don't ever eat there." Mica was out too.

"I'll go." A-bomb saved Christmas.

We took quick showers, tossed some clothes in our backpacks, and took a cab to the bus station. We bought two tickets for the next bus to the beach, and A-bomb bought the first round of Tecate while we waited for our departure.

"I don't know about this one, man," I said. "She seems too good to be true. She's everything I could have ever wanted and somehow more. This just isn't good."

"Sometimes it's just your time, buddy. And if there's one thing I've learned, it's that you gotta enjoy that light while it's shining down on you without worrying about where it's coming from or when it's gonna end, 'cause every light ends eventually. And, if you can make your peace with both the dark and the light, then it'll always be your time. Salud!"

I was glad A-bomb had accepted my invitation that night. He was a world-class companion for any event, and I couldn't imagine a better ally to have with me on that trip. Even if Luz stood me up, at least the Bomber and I could go out for a night on the town.

We boarded the crowded bus. The driver put on *Alien 3* despite the number of young kids onboard, and I cracked open one of the beers I'd snuck in with me. Christ, it was November, and I still hadn't seen Zambulla. It cost five fucking bucks to get there. But maybe a lack of loot wasn't the real deterrent? It seemed the city would blow away in a puff of smoke before our bus arrived.

We snaked around curvy mountain roads for about an hour before rounding a dark cliff and seeing sparkling lights that scattered in all directions in the distance. The first structures I could identify were a series of tall cranes overlooking the port. Though it was dark, I could sense some warmth to this place, as if the waves crashing into its distant shores were saying, "Hello, welcome friend."

The bus took us through the city, then turned onto a narrow dirt road and pulled into the bus station. We walked inside and A-bomb paid the three pesos to unlock the rotating metal arm blocking passage into the bathroom. I called Luz and bought a couple of beers. When A-bomb came out of the bathroom, I handed him a warm

Tecate, and we walked to the street. Soon, the white hatchback came tearing around the corner, and the most beautiful girl I'd ever seen got out of the passenger seat. God, and she was wearing this white cotton dress . . . Fuhgeddaboudit! I almost didn't want her to look good. But when she kissed my lips and took my hand, there was a tenderness there that drove away any nagging voices of doubt.

Luz Blanco drove us through the Zambulla streets and parked in front of a beachside hotel. We put on our bracelets, dropped our bags in our room, and walked to a bar next door called Lila, which had an enormous plastic shark hanging from a hook out front. There weren't many people inside the small bar, but the energy level was at capacity. People were up and dancing and chugging drinks. There was no roof above the dance floor. I looked up and caught a view of the stars. I was in love with the moment already.

Luz led us to a table where about fifteen of her friends were sitting. I was first drawn to the enormous Texan, who sat at the end of the table and chugged an Indio split. For some reason, he was wearing a sombrero. He tossed me a beer as I approached, and I took it down in a few hearty gulps.

"Ahh, thanks, Tex!"

The rest of the friends were from Luz's school. I'd met a few before but most were strangers. A young, attractive couple sitting at the opposite end of the table was making out and stayed making out the entire night. Next to them was one of Luz's professors, a grizzled older man who looked a little like Gabriel but with a sizeable gut and without the sizeable charm. Judging by his movements, I could tell he thought himself more a beloved leader than he actually was. He tried just a little too hard to get people up and dancing or to dispense advice to those he thought might have been drinking too much. He also spent a little too much time talking with my Luz. And each time he did, he moved progressively closer to her as the conversation continued. I didn't know if it was a Mexican custom to party with the profi, but this wasn't the first older gentleman I'd seen passing his time with younger people (I guess I had the same thing going on with the Herbster, but that wasn't a cultural thing—more a fucked-up anomaly). An all-too-eager young bartender grabbed the sombrero off Kyler's head and stuffed it on my own, then stuck a beer in my face and said, "Fondo! Fondo! Fondo!" Chanting was a great way to get me to succumb to peer pressure, and soon the beer was gone—but I took off the damned sombrero and set it on a table. Then Mr. Party Bartender tried the same shit with my Luz. He picked her up and spun her around after she took down her drink. At least he walked away after putting her down.

Most of Luz's friends were standard fare with one exception: a tall girl twirled her way across the dance floor, and A-bomb and I watched her. Luz saw us doing this.

"That is my friend Aura. She's locisma! You should go dance with her."

And dance A-bomb did. Aura absorbed A-bomb into her energy without any unnecessary mating rituals, and they twirled and shimmied together for most of the rest of the night. Luz and I bought a cubeta of Indio splits and enjoyed them while sitting together.

I put my arm around her shoulder. Despite the chaos surrounding me, she was still there, attached to me like an anchor. Again, guys tried, but she wanted nothing to do with them.

"Let's dance!"

She pulled me to the floor, and we twirled beside A-bomb and Aura, who were getting closer and closer as the night went on.

Luz's brother arrived while we were dancing. She led me over.

"Jose, this is Will. He is my teacher."

Oh, goddamn it, did she really just say that? Run away, Willy-boy!

"Hello." He stuck out his hand.

"Uh, hi . . ." I met it. Touching him made me realize that this wasn't a vacation for Luz—this was her home. *I* was the one on the run.

"Would you like to do a shot of whiskey with me?"

"Uh, yeah, sure."

We did the shot, then Luz and I were back on the dance floor. I looked up. The stars were twirling as well. I kissed Luz, and she jumped up and wrapped her legs around me, and we kept twirling. Goddamn, I was in it now . . .

The party moved back to the hotel. We hung out around the pool and the whiskey kept flowing. I could see the disappointment in the professor's eyes when Luz broke from some pseudo-intellectual conversation with him to come and rub her ass on my swelling area. In some strange way, I felt sorry for him. He left soon after that. Before leaving the bar, the Party Bartender had given me a plastic chili filled with chili powder—a gift I'd never use. I presented it to Luz and said, "Would you like my chili?"

"Shh, WILL! My brother might *hear* you!"

He did hear and shot me a disapproving glance.

"Why, what the hell's wrong with that?"

"Look at the shape of the chili. What does it look like to you?"

I laughed. "Look, hermosa, you got me all kinds of crazy right now. Let's go upstairs."

"We can't go up together. My brother is watching us. I will go now, and you come in about ten minutes."

"Okay."

I watched her walk around the pool, then through a back door. Just as she disappeared, two guys showed up with a bottle of Johnnie Walker Blue. They spoke fluent English.

"Hey, man, where you from?" one asked me.

"Buffalo. You guys from the States?"

"Yeah, we're from Compton."

"Cool. What are you doing down here?"

"There's a long story to that and a short story. Which you want?"

"How about the short story first?" I said.

"We're visiting family. My aunt lives here."

He started pouring drinks—strong drinks.

"Hey, you want one of these too?" he asked me.

"Damn, that shit ain't cheap," I said.

"Don't worry about that. Here, take one."

I took the cup, then a sip. "I think what's in this cup would cover my usual bar tab for an entire week. Thanks."

"Forget it, man."

"So, what's the long story?" I said.

Both got solemn.

"We had to get the fuck outta there."

"Yeah, one of our boys just got stabbed and things ain't lookin' so good for us."

"Shit, that sucks," I said.

"That game's getting stale, man. You get them, they get you. I just want a fresh start."

"You gonna start over in Zambulla?" I said.

"Fuck if I know. Nowadays, fuckers'll find you anywhere. I just wanna enjoy the time I still got."

"Yeah, I'm just now realizing that life's precious. You gotta live each day like it's your last."

"I heard that . . ." I held up my drink. "To living among the dead."

"Salud."

That one drink turned into several, and soon the bottle was gone. I woke up the next morning with the sun beating down on my pasty-ass face. I'd fallen asleep against a wall by the pool and still had a plastic cup in my hand. I got up, staggered into the hotel, flashed my wristband, walked up the stairs, and knocked on the door. A-bomb answered.

"Where you been?"

"I don't even know, man."

I walked into the room and lay next to my princess. She was sprawled across one of the two beds, and Luz Blanco and Kyler were on the other. A-bomb lay back down on the floor and went to sleep. I tried to wake my Luz, but she didn't move.

People started to get up about an hour later. My Luz and I waited until everyone had left the room then did what two people who are attracted to each other often do when they're in a hotel room alone.

"What happened to you last night?"

"Don't ask, cutie," I said. "I think it's important that you know early on though that, no matter what you may think, deep down I'm just a clown."

She smiled, and I kissed her. We got dressed then headed down to the buffet where the others were already eating. I hesitated to grab anything.

"Go ahead, hermoso. I already paid for everything. Eat what you want."

"You sure?" I said.

"Jes!"

That's my girl! I got some of everything: french toast, pancakes, a ham and cheese omelet, a bowl of each kind of cereal . . . Despite an empty seat at the table with all her giggling girl friends, Luz sat next to me. Her beautiful head blocked the sun from my puffy eyes.

"After breakfast, we will be going to the beach. I have arranged for us all to go on a boat, then to go snorkeling."

I was terribly hungover and couldn't make sense of much of what she was saying. But I trusted that whatever she had planned would be better than anything I could have come up with. We went back upstairs and got ready. The three gringos, Tex, A-bomb, and I, rubbed on sunscreen while watching some acoustic Ricky Martin performance on TV. It was strange hearing him sing in Spanish. Luz rubbed the lotion on my back, and soon we were out front, hopping onto a party bus. One of Luz's friends examined the red marks on my forearms.

"What happened to you?"

"Oh, uh, a bear attacked me."

Luz laughed and pushed me. I hugged her and kissed her cheek. We arrived at a small, C-shaped area of beach. It was a flawless day: no clouds, a light breeze, tropical heat and intensity. We claimed a spot under a large umbrella and hit the water. We still had about an hour to kill before the boat would take off, and we spent that time in the ocean. Luz wore a skimpy red and green bikini, exposing her tight, curvaceous body. We only swam together for a few minutes before she returned to the sand, where some of her male friends buried her up to her head. One asshole in particular added some breasts to the sand mound. He patted and shaped them with a little too much enthusiasm. Fucking chump.

Luz remained underground until it was time to board the boat, which was a fairly large two-story party boat with rows of bench seats and an aisle down the center like a floating chapel. There was a small bar and some bathrooms in back. We walked down the aisle to the front, then up the twisting stairway, and lay on the second floor. Soon the boat took off. Luz sat in front of me, pulled the hat off my head, and put it on her own.

"Have you ever snorkeled before?" she said.

"Yeah, in my bathtub."

"You will have a lot of fun."

"If the sharks don't get me."

"Don't worry, there aren't many big sharks here. See that rock over there? The one that looks like a rhinoceros? That is where we are going."

We were getting closer and closer. Soon I'd be out there with the small and medium-sized sharks.

Luz's friends kept going down to the bar and coming back with drinks. They were generous and handed me and A-bomb several plastic cups of beer.

We stopped about a hundred yards from the rhino, and the guys below threw an anchor overboard. There were three other party boats anchored nearby, and one had a sound system that was blasting a mix of Tupac and Bob Marley. There were about a hundred people snorkeling in the water and our boat's passengers joined them. I was hesitant to follow the others. I knew there must have been a lot of creatures living in the cracks and crevices in the rocks below, and I also knew those creatures would draw bigger creatures to them. I chugged my last free beer and tried to forget about certain and grisly death.

A-bomb looked at the crowd on the second floor funneling at the stairway, then he climbed the rail, and I did the same. A-bomb did a swan dive and I a cannonball. If any sharks were coming for me, I was gonna give 'em hell first. I had a crippling fear of open water, but when I hit that tropical blue, it wasn't as bad as I'd imagined. That probably had a lot to do with the beer, and the fact that there were about a hundred other people around, and the music, and . . .

Luz swam to me with a mask, flippers, and life vest.

"Here, take these."

"They're yours, cutie."

"I don't need them. Please take them."

"Okay." Now wasn't the time to be a tough guy. I put them on and continued swimming. Luz swam ahead and gestured for me to follow. Even with the flippers, I couldn't keep up. Luz glided through the water. She found a spot away from the other people and started diving. It was only about fifteen feet to the bottom, and she'd go down, grab something, study it, then come back up for a breath. Her transition between worlds was graceful and seamless. She had nothing on her but that bright red and green bikini. The fish, and sea horses, and coral accepted her as an equal, and allowed her to swim among them without fear or attack. I figured they'd all swum away from the other tourists, who were thrashing around, kicking up sand, and disturbing the peace. But they all liked Luz, and she liked them. A puffer fish swam by her, and I watched her puff out her cheeks, and blow it a kiss before it disappeared into the blue void.

"Come with me, hermoso. I want to show you something."

I removed the life vest and let it float on the surface, then dove with her. But I only got halfway before my head felt as if it was going to implode, and she continued without me. I swam back to the surface, put the life vest back on, and watched her dive. The sun was burning the back of my neck; I didn't belong there. But Luz . . . Luz remained graceful under pressure—she adapted to it. She dissolved into that water as would a fine grain of pure salt. All I could ever do was pollute. When she realized I couldn't follow, she started bringing the ocean to me, grabbing mollusks and slower-moving fish and bringing them up to my mask. Goddamn, she was beautiful. Her home was beautiful. I thought of Buffalo, but couldn't think of a single thing in that entire city I could bring to Luz that would fill me with as much pride when I shoved it in her face as she seemed to feel each time she presented me another damned stone or crustacean. The realization then came to me for the first time—the one I'd already known but had been unwilling and thus unable to see: No matter what I did, I could never be a part of this world so dear to her. And, unless I could find something of beauty in Buffalo—something that filled me with as much joy and wonder as Luz experienced swimming in that ocean—then I'd never be a part of any world. I knew that our fate was doomed. Our story already penned by Shakespeare. The best I could ever hope for was to simply enjoy the limited time I'd get with her, and I knew that, no matter how good things went, this would never change. Luz popped up behind me, jolting me from a trance.

"Will! Will! Turn and look at this." She seemed a bit too enthusiastic to get me to turn—an enthusiasm which provoked my curiosity.

"Why?"

"Just turn and look at this!"

I turned, and she had a sea horse in her hands. "He told me his name is Josecito and that he likes to swim with his friends." She laughed.

"So let him swim, baby . . ."

Luz released the sea horse and started swimming back to the boat. I looked up and watched A-bomb do another swan dive off the second floor. He'd attracted some followers. Several others were now climbing over the rail and jumping into the ocean. I smiled and followed Luz back to the boat.

Luz climbed back onboard, and I swam around to the side. I called up to A-bomb, who was now back on the second floor.

"Hey, man, why don't you dump one of those beers down here?"

"Sure thing, chief."

A-bomb dumped a cup of beer over the rail, and I drank as much of the stream as I could. I was feeling pretty good until I realized there was no more music. I looked around. The other boats were gone. In fact, I was the only person left in the water. Shit! I swam over to the steps and climbed back onboard. Christ, that was close!

I walked past the bar, down the aisle, and back upstairs. Luz was standing at the guardrail and staring at the rhinoceros. I walked over and wrapped my arms around her from behind. She accepted me and held my arms with her own.

"Hey, did you really ask me to turn just to show me a sea horse?"

"Well," she smiled, "a shark was swimming near you, and I didn't want you to see."

"Jesus-calorie-counting-christ, are you serious?"

"Jes, but don't worry, baby, it wasn't dangerous. That kind don't eat people, just fishies." She made a fish face and kissed my nose. I patted her on the pompis and walked over to A-bomb, who, despite an inability to speak Spanish, had made quite a number of Mexican friends whom he was now entertaining with hand gestures and body-told anecdotes. A girl handed us each a beer.

"Thanks! I'll pay you back for all these when we get to the hotel."

"Don't worry, they are free."

"Free?"

"Yes, they are included with the trip."

"Excuse me—"

I pushed past her, and A-bomb followed. We set up chairs just above the bar and called down for some drinks. The bartender handed them up, and we started chugging. The beers stood no chance. Every few minutes we were reaching down and pulling up more drinks. Soon the bartender just gave us full caguamas. I looked over at Luz, still standing at the guardrail. Though she was talking with a friend, she was looking directly at me; her eyes were smiling. I knew what she was thinking. I poured as much beer down my throat as possible. It was nice having A-bomb by my side. It was nice to be around people who were on vacation. They drank just as much as I did, and tipping back brews with otherwise contributing members of society made me feel like less of a worthless piece of whale shit. I did a "Salud" with the Bomber but knew the party would soon end for him. Soon, he'd be back in the Rockies helping The Man find Black Gold. Soon he'd be back on the clock, and sober. But I wouldn't. This inspired something evil inside me. I stormed over to Luz.

"What the hell are you doing?"

"Just talking to friends. I don't understand—"

"I mean, what the hell are you doing with me?"

"That is a silly question, and I'm not going to answer it."

"Yeah, well fuck you then . . ."

I turned around and walked back to my plastic seat above the bar—the throne that I knew I'd always be bound to no matter what good I'd accomplished or how far away I'd run. My soul grew dark at about the same time that the sun started dropping. I could see the concern on Luz's face; her eyes had lost something precious about them—and while they were still looking in my direction, her gaze seemed to travel right through me. I was a ghost, and now we both knew it.

The boat floated along the shoreline past beachside mansions and hotels.

"We should stay another night," I said.

"Okay," A-bomb said.

"Salud!"

By the time we got back to the beach, A-bomb and I had put a pretty sizeable dent in the bar's cooler. Before we got off the boat, Luz handed her camera to a friend and asked her to take a picture of us. Luz and I wrapped our arms around each other and the friend snapped the shot. I took a look. Christ, my hair was growing long again, and my stomach was swelling in a way it hadn't before.

We took the party bus back to the hotel. I told Luz about our plan to stay another night, and she loved it. Luz Blanco took us to find a hotel. The first place she brought us to didn't fit the bill for A-bomb: "I only get so many vacation days each year. I want to stay in the classiest joint this town has to offer." My Luz knew just the place, and soon we were sipping drinks on a third-floor balcony overlooking the ocean. The Luz's went home to get ready for the night.

"Yo, I really can't afford this, Bombersito," I said.

"Don't worry, Willy, I got it covered."

"Shit, thanks man!"

My phone vibrated as we sipped drinks on that balcony. It was Sal. "Hey, man, Paz and I are headed to Zambulla today. We should meet up."

I told him where the hotel was, and soon they were there. The dynamic changed but wasn't tainted. Paz helped balance things out. Bomber put them up too.

Luz texted me: "You hungry? I know a great seafood place near your hotel."

Sal, Paz, A-bomb, and I got to the restaurant before Luz and Aura arrived. And when they walked in the door—knockouts! Dresses, heels, makeup . . . Sal, Bomber, and I were in sandals, ripped jeans, and sweaty t-shirts. A-bomb and I had only packed for one night, so we were stuck that evening wearing the same stinkin' digs as the night before. We looked as if we'd just gotten back from a three-day Phish concert off Alligator Alley.

The restaurant was just off the beach. While it wasn't upscale, it also wasn't a hole-in-the-wall. The girls were more appropriately dressed than we were. I was pretty drunk and put all my energy into not making a fool out of myself—which only lasted a few minutes.

"The ladies are gonna be all over me tonight," I said, regarding the way I was dressed.

"If you would like to be with other girls, then that is okay. Believe me, I won't be lonely," Luz said.

"That's, uh, not what I meant . . ."

The waiter came over and saved the day. We ordered, and A-bomb randomly chose the huachinango, or red snapper, which came scales, eyes, bones, and all. Aura had to instruct him how to eat it, and he did so with a big smile.

After dinner, Sal and Paz went back to the hotel, but the rest of us went to a dance club. There was an entrance fee that included drinks, but they were weak, so Luz signaled to a guy behind the bar, and he brought us some highballs of whiskey.

Luz locked around me, and we danced as we'd done at the Feria. A-bomb and Aura danced as well. Between songs, some doofy, box-shaped gringo with a crew cut tapped me on the shoulder. "Hey, mind if I cut in?"

"Look, I know you're probably shipping out to Kamchatka or some other godforsaken place tomorrow, but I have no intention of dancing with you, so you might as well just fuck off. Although I am flattered."

He gave me a confused look, then wandered away. Luz nestled her head against my neck. There were gringos everywhere. Zambulla was a rising star in the Mexican tourism industry, and people from all over the world were buying up real estate in the best locations around town: beach lots, cliffsides overlooking the ocean, spots near the mall. The city was going up in paint-by-number housing developments and was already teeming with the bullshit: KFCs, and Burger Kings, and Pizza Huts . . . A Super Walmart was being built near a row of fruterias and panaderias that had likely stood there for decades. All of Mexico was slowly bowing to the giants of predatory capitalism. I kissed Luz's cheek and stroked her dark hair. I breathed her in deeply, trying to remember her scent, to program it in my DNA in case she was ripped from me in the middle of the night. The world didn't want us together, but I was going to fight it to the very fucking end.

We danced late into the night, then piled into Luz's truck. She drove us back to the hotel. A-bomb and Aura hopped out, but I didn't move. I had this awful feeling that Luz would disappear the moment I looked away. I stared deeply into her eyes and she into mine.

"Come upstairs with me."

"I can't. My parents expect me home soon. I will see you tomorrow."

"There might not be a tomorrow, hermosa. Spend the night with me. Please!"

"I . . . I just can't, okay? My parents would be worried."

"Well, maybe they need to be worried . . . Just one night."

She wouldn't give. But she did allow me another fifteen minutes. I knew she didn't want to go or she would have kicked me out. She smiled, rubbed my cheek with her beautiful hand, and kissed me.

Outside I knew A-bomb and Aura were okay. I could hear their laughter.

Luz and I kissed, and I got out. Aura got back in the truck, and they left.

"That girl is ruining me, A-bomb."

"Welcome to the club, buddy . . ."

We went upstairs, and I slipped into the most satisfying sleep that I'd possibly ever had. The bed held me like a gentle mother, warm and comforting. Though I hadn't had much time to reflect on it before falling asleep, I was already pretty certain I'd just lived the best day of my life. I woke up ready to see Luz the next morning.

A knock on the door, and when I opened it, she was there—again blocking out the sun. We got ready, ate, and headed to the beach—a different section this time. This section was straight and ran for miles in each direction. The sand was golden brown and the water blue and alive. I could feel its energy as it crashed into the shore. Luz found a spot just off the highway and parked her truck.

"Have either of you ever tried to surf?" she said.

"Nope," I said.

"Once when I was in Hawaii, but I couldn't even get up," A-bomb said.

"Well, I will teach you today."

We walked to the beach. A cluster of sexy, young humans lit up as Luz approached. They exchanged holas and high-fives. Luz introduced me and A-bomb to them, then ran into the water. Sal and Paz had decided to sleep in that morning but showed up a short time later. Soon we were all in the water. It was another perfect day, and the water was about the same temperature as the air—something I loved (after spending nearly twenty winters in Buffalo, I had a profound appreciation for warmth). The waves were powerful but not violent. There was some gentle cordiality in them. They weren't just trying to suck in gringos and grind them on the rocks below. A-bomb and I spent most of our water time diving head first into the waves—that is, until I saw *it*.

Just as A-bomb was about to plunge into another wave, I saw a large shadow riding it and coming straight at us. I pointed it out to A-bomb and retreated from the water like a cowardly David Hasslehoff. A-bomb followed behind.

"What was that thing?" he said.

"It looked like a huge stingray," I said.

"It was probably harmless."

"I don't know. I don't trifle with that shit."

Luz was talking with some friends and didn't see me high-kneeing it through the water. When her conversation ended, she came over to us.

"Would you guys like to try surfing?" she said.

"Sure!" A-bomb said.

"Uh . . . I don't have a board," I said.

"I have some boards locked in my friend's bar over there." She pointed to a small place on a cliff just above the ocean. "We can get them and go to surf."

We asked Sal and Paz if they'd like to join, but they declined. They were already set up under an umbrella and looked fairly comfortable. Aura pulled up, parked, and joined our party. She brought another friend with her, and soon we were at the bar. But it was locked.

"I will call my friend and see if he can come down and open it. You can go swim while we wait."

We headed back in the water, and almost immediately, I saw two dinner-plate-sized shadows circling my body. I ran from the ocean and dove into the sand.

"You okay, man?" A-bomb said.

"They're everywhere, Bomber! We're under attack . . ."

"They're probably harmless."

"Tell that to Steve Irwin."

Luz came down to the beach. "I'm sorry, but my friend isn't in town this afternoon. We can't surf."

"Oh really? That's too bad . . ." I said.

"But we can still go swimming."

Fuck! She grabbed my hand and led me to the water. "Why are you covered in sand?"

"I, uh, some kid . . . had the, uh—I'll wash it off."

We went back in the water. I swore I saw little dancing shadows everywhere.

"So, are there a lot of stingrays in the water here?" I said.

"Jes, they are everywhere, but they won't bother you."

"You sure?"

She smiled and dove through a wave. We swam for most of that afternoon. When we got out of the water, A-bomb engaged Aura and her friend in a body-conversation, and Luz and I walked along the beach. She led me to a pile of fractured boulders that had once been part of the cliff receding behind them—the same cliff that, despite erosion, still jutted about fifty feet into the ocean. She climbed on a boulder and started hopping between them on her way toward the blue. She turned to me. "Come on!"

I climbed the same boulder and hopped along behind her. We stopped at an enormous boulder that was surrounded by the frothy ocean. Luz sat and I plopped down beside her. The day was losing energy but didn't feel at all dark. A group of small, red crabs were crawling all over the base of the boulder but wouldn't come within four feet of us. I nudged Luz.

"Jes, they are very cute, aren't they?"

Her words set me at ease. A strapping young man paddled by on a surfboard. He waved at Luz. She smiled and waved back.

"Is that the guy who owns the bar?" I said.

"No, that is my friend Esteban. You should watch him surf. He is a professional—the second-ranked surfer in all of Mexico. He has been in Brazil for one year and just got back."

Christ, the guy looked like an athletic Enrique Iglesias. I stared at the big, beautiful mountains in the horizon. I wondered if I could see the volcano from where I was . . .

"Most people," she said, "when they look out there, all they see are mountains. But you can see beyond them—you see what other people don't. You asked me yesterday why I am with you. Many other boys look at me and only see a body. But you look inside and see who I really am. When I am with you, I feel valuable, and strong, and inspired, and beautiful. You have a very unique gift, hermoso. You have the ability to see the best in people even when there isn't much beauty to see. And I think it hurts you when other people refuse or are unable to see that beauty. And I think that, maybe, you get too close to things that are ugly because you want to make them beautiful. I see that you are suffering. But you have a gift. I don't think you realize how special you are."

Tears welled in the corners of my eyes. "You don't understand. I'm not right in the head. There's something seriously wrong with me. You should just go, get away. I think about it, you know. I think about it a lot—"

Luz caressed my shoulder as she watched Esteban riding a wave far beyond the shore. He was way out there, riding with sharks and stingrays and whatever else was gliding through those waters. But it didn't constrict his motion.

"Is so beautiful, no? Life . . . If I could save the world by dying, I would do it this moment. Now, as the sun is going down, I would go down with it. But I think the world needs me here."

I put my arm around her shoulder, pulled her close, and kissed her salty cheek. The crabs had multiplied and wanted to reclaim their rock. I tapped Luz's shoulder and she understood, and soon we were up and hopping boulders on our way to the sand. A-bomb was still there entertaining the girls with his essence. Some things would never change. But other things really needed to . . .

When we walked onto the sand, A-bomb approached me. He dug into his backpack and pulled out a handful of weed.

"Holy shit, where'd you get that?"

"One of Luz's surfer friends gave it to me. He just walked up, asked me if I blazed, then dumped me a handful of greens."

"You should put it in something."

A-bomb dug back into his backpack and pulled out a pack of cigarettes. There were only two left. He took one and offered the other to the girls. Luz grabbed it, lit it, and took a puff.

"I didn't know you smoked," I said.

She exhaled and shrugged her shoulders. A-bomb packed the Marlboro box to its brim with herb and handed it to me.

"Thanks, man!" I stuck it in my pocket.

We walked back to the umbrella where we'd left Sal and Paz, and they were still there—and fighting. Sal called to me when he saw me.

"Yo, where you been, Ronaldo Surf-Toe? I called you like seven times."

"Oh, my phone's in Luz's car. We were over by the bar there."

"You surf?"

"No, we were locked out."

He laughed. "Typical."

"We still had a good time."

"Whatever, let's get the hell out of here. It's getting dark. I don't want to drive—"

"—on the carretera after dark. I know."

I looked at Luz and she at me. I didn't want to leave. My life had been destroyed by blind faith, and I wanted to stay in a place where I could touch her body, hear her voice, smell her hair . . .

We walked to Sal's car.

"When will I see you again?" I asked Luz.

"I will be back in town tomorrow. I will call you when I get there."

"I'm really going to miss you."

"I'm really going to miss you too."

We kissed, and I got in the back seat. I put on my headphones, scrolled through my music, and clicked on Beck's cover of "Everybody's

Gotta Learn Sometime." My thoughts were many but not racing. It was already dark when we hit the carretera. I'd entered Zambulla in the dark and was leaving in the dark but felt I could see clearly where I was going. I looked around me at the bright full moon gently illuminating the fields and mountains in the distance. I knew something big was happening inside of me, but I still wasn't quite sure what it was. For once, I didn't fear what it could be.

Chapter 26

On Monday morning, Sal and I got up early to drive A-bomb to the airport. We piled in Sal's car while the sky was still dark and drove down some country road. Soon, we were at the smallest international airport I'd ever seen. It looked more like a county library than an airport, but it had planes taking off behind it, so I knew we were in the right spot. Sal and I carried A-bomb's bags in for him, and he stood in line. We set the bags down, and A-bomb reassured us he'd be fine. We shook hands, said goodbyes, and walked to the car. The ride home was different. The mountains in the distance seemed lonelier, and the golden light struggled to rise above the horizon. Before me was untainted wilderness, which would likely soon be covered with strip malls, and housing developments, and fast food restaurants. A-bomb had only been in Lila for two weeks, but it was enough. I already felt like a different person. As I studied the mountains beyond me, I realized A-bomb was just as much a part of my Mexican experience as were they.

When we got home, we still had about forty-five minutes before we had to leave for work. I walked into my room, locked the door, and sat cross-legged in the middle of my big bed. I wasn't tired, but even if I were I would have refused sleep. I felt inspired, but I also felt a solemn responsibility not to exploit the moment for artistic gain. I grabbed my guitar but put it down. No, now was not the time to make. Now was the time to be. I sat alone in that huge room, in that huge bed, as the overhead windows spilled a concentrated golden light upon me. A song began in my head, but I ignored it. I would soon leave for work—something I normally dreaded. But I saw work differently that morning. That morning, I saw it as an opportunity to spend time with a creative and passionate man who sincerely desired a skill I could help him acquire. Gabriel always had such positive energy, and I always felt better after seeing him. Maybe today I could give in and look forward to our encounter rather than obsess about all the little things that usually came up during the day that caused me to panic?

All the artifacts and proof of my existence were locked with me inside that room. I didn't exist beyond it. When the time came, I dressed slowly and deliberately. The cotton fabric of my button-down shirt felt soft and cool against my skin, and my shoes fit my feet just right; I wiggled my toes inside them.

Once dressed, I walked to my old room where A-bomb had been sleeping, and I noticed something on the table: two separate piles of five-hundred-peso bills, with two bills per pile. There was no note or anything—just the cash. I felt overjoyed, but not only because of the money. A-bomb always knew what to say even when he wasn't saying anything. He moved like a calming breeze. If everyone was like him there'd be no war, or poverty, or injustice—but we weren't all like him even though he faced the same obstacles as any of us. I wished I was like him but just wasn't. But I knew if I could learn to be like him, anyone could.

Sal and I went to work a short time later, cruising down jagged mountain roads. We passed trucks filled with quiet workers and passed old women standing on the roadside holding wicker baskets filled with handmade crafts or baked goods. None of these people demanded anything of me. There was no pressure here from anywhere but within. Though some eyes met mine, I didn't treat their wandering gaze as a deliberate act of disrespect. I felt no threat here as I did in the city. These people were just passing on their way to work.

It was pure. Everyone performing their necessary role. Someone would eat today because of the fruit these people picked or planted. Someone would have shelter because of the structures they built. I stuck my head out the window and breathed deeply. The mountains were covered with a thick fog, which thinned as we came across the vast fields of palms where workers collected coconuts or tended to grazing animals. We soon pulled off the carretera and parked in front of the Coca-Cola factory.

We passed through security, said hello to the secretary, and parted ways. I listened to Gabriel talk for an hour, stopping him to correct his grammar or pronunciation when necessary. And after that hour, Sal and I were back out on the highway. The return trip was always different. The carretera was busier and the day much hotter. Every so often, the police would pull Sal over and check to see if he had his papers. Sal would hand the papers over, smile, and soon we'd be on our way again.

Sometimes before going home, Sal and I would go to the fruteria or panaderia for food. Between us we'd usually get a few tomatoes and onions, an avocado, a handful of cilantro, some potatoes, a hunk of mozzarella, and one or two bolillos, or small loaves of bread. I used these loaves for sandwiches or for garlic bread when I was feeling brave enough to use the oven.

Things with Luz were starting to pick up around this time. She'd stop by whenever she could. One afternoon after school, she came over and lay on my lap while I sat on the couch. Neither of us spoke. She just lay there for an hour as I stroked her hair and observed her beautiful face. She was gorgeous from every angle. I studied her, trying to burn her image into my brain so I could recall it like a vivid photograph whenever I needed her with me. There was an immortality in her eyes that had no doubt been seen by others throughout history, drawing men to battle or new lands, or to poetry or song. Yet there she was, lying in my lap; she was as cool and firm as a lump of earth. I studied her profile and could see her front and other side so vividly in my mind. She was my three-dimensional beauty. Those times were flawless. I knew Luz would soon be gone from my life and knowing this allowed me to fully appreciate her beauty in those brief moments without the fear making us both ugly. I hugged her and kissed her cheek. Someday, I'd be long gone. But the earth would always remain . . .

It was around this time that a familiar figure wandered down our dead-end street and back into our weird lives. I was sitting alone watching TV one sunny afternoon when an arm reached through the bars of the front gate and opened the latch from the inside.

"Cisco!"

"Shh . . ." He put his finger to his mouth.

It'd been about a month since I'd seen Cisco, and judging by his dark tan and relaxed style, I could tell he'd spent a lot of that time on the beach.

"Hey, man, where's Sally?" he whispered.

"I think he's taking a nap. He's in the front bedroom now."

He walked to the door and knocked.

"Go away!"

"It's me, Sally."

"Oh shit . . ."

The door flew open. The brothers hugged then took off to get some food.

One left, another arrived—thus was the cycle of life in Lila.

When they came back, Cisco told us about his Vallarta experience.

"Yo, you would not believe the shit I've been through in the past month. I got a job laying brick. It's ten-hour shifts in the hot-ass sun, and you only make about thirty pesos a day. I've been living off beans and tortillas for weeks. And the guys I was living with—fucking scumbags. There were twelve of us packed into a two-bedroom apartment. We all just slept where we could, but there was shit all over the floor so I could never get comfortable. The bathroom was disgusting. They left shitty toilet paper everywhere. I stepped in a nutty piece one day while I was taking a shower and almost slipped. That was the day I knew I had to get the fuck outta there."

"That's crazy, man. Well, it's great to have you back," I said.

"How long you plan to be in Lila?" Sal said.

"I don't know. Until I feel like taking off again . . ."

"Well, the fair is in town. It's been good times lately," I said.

The days were again filled with Morrissey, and Joy Division, and Depeche Mode. It was good music, a good vibe, and just a general good time for me in Mexico.

Chapter 27

My newfound bliss, however, did not extend to the workplace. Lengua sucked rhino cocks. The three stooges had me locked in their dysfunctional groove when it came to scheduling. Every other time I'd come in, they'd wait a half hour before telling me, "Oh, your student called this afternoon and canceled. No classes tonight," or, "Oh, the new class starts at eight o'clock at night, not the morning. Come back tonight." It was happening far too often for it not to have been a planned effort to fuck with me.

I walked a mile in the punishing heat one Thursday for my eleven to one class with Guadalupe only to find the main door locked. I started pounding on it, but no one answered. I waited fifteen minutes for someone to come, but no one did.

I decided to leave before I did something stupid. I put on my music and took off down Madrid del Rio. I could hear someone shouting something from the street. I looked left and saw a car full of girls who were sticking out of the windows and calling to me. And one was fucking sexy. I smiled, and they pulled over.

"Hey, baby!"

Holy shit, it was Luz.

"Get your sexy ass over here!" She and her friends were all fired up. I walked over.

"Hey, hermosa, you'll never believe it. I walked all the way to Lengua—"

"Shut up, and get in the car."

Boner time! I shut off my tunes and hopped in. Luz sat on my lap and started rubbing her ass on my man parts.

"There is a BIG party going on today in a park near here," she said. "Everybody has off from school."

"Oh, maybe that's why Lengua is closed?"

There were four girls in the car with me, and they were buck wild. When we stopped at a red light, the girl in the passenger seat flashed some old guys in the truck next to us. And damn, she had nice titties.

"It's okay if you wanna stare, baby. I understand," Luz said to me.

"Whoa, whoa, I wasn't staring . . ." I wasn't either. Just caught a quick glance, but the ladies see all . . .

We stopped at a liquor store and some drunk assholes pulled up next to us in an unnecessarily large truck. They were blasting banda and were just as wild as the girls. Two of the girls and one of the guys went into the store and came out with several bottles of liquor.

We drove to a park in la Villa del Lado. Luz was right. The place was filled with young people who were partying. Some looked like high schoolers—a number of girls wore plaid skirts above knee-high white socks—but the rest looked like college students. We stopped at a picnic table where several people were already engaged in celebration. Among them were Aura and the professor.

Luz was all fired up that afternoon and showed a side of herself I hadn't yet seen. Though I wasn't fluent in Spanish, I could tell that she spoke with her friends differently than she did with me. She used lots of slang and different intonations. It was all, "No mames, whey," and "No manches." I didn't like it. She took off with a group of girl friends as I walked to the picnic table.

"Hey, Aura, how are you?" I said.

"Good. I'm happy to see you again, Will!"

Other people didn't seem happy to see me though. A large cowboy-hat-wearing shithead walked up to me. He seemed to be a leader among the other guys who were busy staring me down.

"Hola, amigo! So you are Luz's new boyfriend, no? You make sure you treat her right, or bad things can happen, man."

"You're gonna buy me a hat like that?"

He looked pissed.

"Where can I find something to drink here?" I said.

"There is a cooler behind you. Remember though, watch how you treat our friend. We've known her since she was this big." He reached down low.

I reached into the cooler. He walked back over to the five or six other guys huddling nearby. They whispered among themselves while intermittently pointing or staring at me. Luz came back.

"Hey, princess, I don't think it's safe for me to be here. It's kind of a 'Mexicans only' event, don't you think?"

"No, everything's okay. Have a nice time!"

I sat beside Aura at the table. I pulled out my music and put one headphone in my ear and the other in hers. I cranked the volume and tried to drown out the testosterone-fueled bullshit threatening to ruin my day.

Aura and I spoke for about a half hour while listening to music. It was all smiles and laughter until she spontaneously broke into tears.

"What's wrong? Are you okay?" I said.

She mumbled something I couldn't understand. I put my arm around her shoulder and tried to calm her down. Luz saw Aura crying and came over. They spoke for about five minutes before Luz ushered her to the bathroom. I put both headphones in my ears, sat back, and cranked the volume. I went after beers double time and killed a few before Luz came back out of the bathroom. Aura didn't follow.

"Is she okay?"

"Jes. This happens sometimes when she drinks. She hasn't had an easy life, and she cries."

"What happened?"

"Her mother died when she was very young. She has no brothers or sisters. It's just her and her father. And he doesn't treat her nice. Since she was little he touches her, and kisses her, and has done other things to her."

"That fucking bastard!" I spiked my beer can on the grass.

"It's okay, baby."

"Well, is he at least in jail?"

"No. She still lives with him."

"Are you fucking serious? Is the whole world insane?"

"She don't want to tell the police. Then she won't have any family left."

I reached into the cooler, grabbed another beer, and sucked the life out of it. Luz grabbed me by the hand.

"Come with me."

"Where we going?"

"You'll see."

Luz led me to the men's room. She said something, and no one responded, so she pulled me through the door and into a stall. She bent over the toilet, hiked up her skirt, and pulled down her panties.

I pulled down my pants and started rubbing my dick between her ass cheeks, but nothing doing.

"C'mon, Luz, I'm not feeling this."

"It's okay, nobody's here."

"Look, I don't want to fuck you above a little pool people shit in."

She turned around and started sucking my dick, but I pushed her head away. I wasn't diggin' the energy she gave off.

"Look, let's just go out and enjoy the party, okay?"

She nodded and soon we were back on the green field. Some new shitheads had shown up, and I could feel the tension. Luz pointed out one guy in particular: "Oh, he is always touching me and being very rough. Look what he did to me in class last week." She pulled up her sleeve and showed me a small bruise near her shoulder.

"How'd that happen?"

"I walk by him, and he just grabbed me. He always says, 'Oh, Luz, I love you, I love you, baby.'"

"What's his name?"

"Pablo."

I walked up to him. "Hey, Pablo, can I talk to you for a second?"

"Who are you?"

"I'm Luz's boyfriend. Just a few minutes . . ."

We sat on top of the picnic table.

"So, Luz tells me you like to touch her, is that right?"

He stared into my eyes. "Maybe yes, maybe no."

"Well, that's what she says. And she also showed me a mark on her arm that she said you gave her. That true?"

He rolled his eyes and looked away.

"Look, you slimy fuck, if you touch that girl again, or look at her, or make her feel uncomfortable in any way, I'm gonna hurt you."

He laughed. I got right in his face.

"I will fucking cut you open." I was ready to lose my damned mind but kept it together. His friends were looking on but didn't move.

"Is that it?" he said.

"Yeah."

He walked back to his group. More whispers and more staring. I walked to Luz.

"C'mon, let's get out of here," I said. "I don't like the way this is looking."

"It's okay. Just have fun. I'm going with a friend to get more drinks. I'll be right back."

Luz got in someone's car, and they drove away. I was alone in that park. I dug into the cooler, filled my pockets with beer, and took a walk. I came back about a half hour later and heard music. A number of people were dancing, Luz included. And she was dancing with a guy—fucking Pablo! He had his hands on the small of her back then started moving them down south. I wasn't pissed at him; I was pissed at her. I stormed over.

"What are you doing?"

Pablo dug into her arm and pulled her away from me. I hurled my beer can at his face but missed. His friends crowded around. He swung at me, but I stepped aside and countered with a shot to the cheek. He started throwing wild punches but each was telegraphed and sluggish, and he didn't land a single one. I, on the other hand, kept connecting with quick shots to the eyes or jaw. My strategy was to keep as much distance from him as I could. He was bigger, and I didn't want to get sucked into his gravity. His temper and pride got the best of him, and he started throwing haymakers. I hit him with a few more quick shots, then got in a solid right hook—that was the tamale. Blood exploded from his lip, and he dropped to one knee. One of his friends jumped in and tried to break up the fight, but I didn't care. I punched him in the face too. Pablo got up, and now I was fighting two guys at once. Luckily the new guy was as slow as his friend. I had time to dodge all their punches and hit them with a few shots as I backed away. I was doing pretty good until I backed into the cooler and fell over. I landed on my back, and they continued forward. I kicked the smaller guy's knee and put my heel in the bigger guy's stomach.

"Okay, okay, enough, you boys," the horny professor said.

Funny, he let it go on just long enough to be sure neither of his students would get a shot in. I got up and dusted myself off. Everyone was crowded around me.

I pushed past them and shot over to Luz. Her lip had been split somehow during all the commotion. I wanted to rip out her heart, but my anger subsided when I saw the blood.

"Are you okay? How'd this happen?" I said.

"I don't know. I think somebody hit me with their elbow."

I wiped the blood with my shirt. "Look, hermosa, if we're gonna be together, you can't be doing this shit. You know I'd fight the world for you, but shit like this is going to get me killed for nothing. Do you understand what I'm telling you?"

"I didn't know he would get so angry."

"What do you mean, 'he'?"

She didn't respond; she just caressed her lip with her finger.

"Look, I don't want to end up a speed bump on some country road. Can we just go?"

"Okay. Let me ask my friend Yolanda for a ride. Wait here."

She went and came back with Yolanda. Yolanda was a thin, light-skinned, tattooed party girl who'd witnessed the fight.

"Orale! You kicked those guys' asses! You are Mr. T."

"My name is Will."

"Mr. Will!"

We walked to her car, and I got in the back. Luz opened the passenger door but didn't get inside.

"I'm going to say goodbye to my friends."

Luz walked back to the picnic table and hugged her friends—including Pablo.

"What the hell is she doing with that guy?" I said.

"Who? Pablo? He was her boyfriend. They broke up last month."

"Last month? She moves pretty quickly, huh?"

"That is Luz. All the guys want her. She's so beautiful, no?"

"Not right now she's not."

Luz came back to the car. I got out and grabbed the front seat before she could. She sat in back.

"So, Pablo was your boyfriend?"

"Well, I guess he was, but just for about a week."

"You know you're going to get me killed, don't you?"

"Hey, hey, Luz, Mr. Will relax. Don't fight. It's time to celebrate."

Yolanda stopped at a red light. She dug into her torn jean jacket and pulled out four enormous nugs of weed.

"You know where I want to take you, Mr. Will? Michoacán. The land of mota. You can find any drugs you want there. I picked these off some plants growing near the beach."

"Damn, they smell delicious," I said.

"I use to have a problem with the cocaine. I went to a rehab center for six months, and I don't use anymore. I just smoke weed. I think is better for me."

"Probably," I said.

"Do you like cocaine?" she said.

"Eh, I prefer the herbal drugs."

"Cocaine *is* herbal!"

"So is strychnine," I said.

"What?"

"Never mind . . ."

She reached into her jacket and pulled out an eight ball wrapped in a plastic bag.

"Here, you take this. I don't want it no more."

"That's okay, you can keep it. I don't fuck with that shit," I said.

Luz was silent for most of the trip but eventually spoke.

"Will, I'm sorry. I should have told you we dated."

"I don't care who you dated, I just care that we're honest with each other," I said.

Luz got a call from a friend. They spoke, and she hung up.

"Yolanda, would you like to go to another party?"

"I love to party!"

"My friends are at a different park. The one where we know the police."

Yolanda nodded. They wouldn't shut the fuck up about the damned cops: about how the cops bought them drinks and drugs, how the cops did whatever the girls wanted, about how many cops had fucked their friends. I'd finally seen Luz's ugly side, and it was hideous. All I wanted was to get out of that car. And I found my escape . . .

"So, Mr. Will, you have such a nice body. Do you work out?"

"Only caguama curls."

"Can I see it?"

I looked over my shoulder at Luz, and she looked ready to rip Yolanda's head off.

"Sure." I pulled up my shirt, and Yolanda rubbed my stomach.

"Oh wow."

"So, you say there are fields of weed in Michoacán?"

"Everywhere. I will take you sometime."

"I'd like that. How about next week?"

"You know what," Luz said, "just take me home."

Yolanda turned around and dropped Luz off at her apartment.

"Later, sweetie," I said.

Luz walked to her apartment, reached her hand through a broken panel of glass, and opened the door from the inside. She entered, and the door shut behind her. I didn't know if I'd won a battle or lost something big, but either way I didn't like how I felt on that ride home. Yolanda dropped me off under the almond trees.

"Would you like me to come inside? I have plenty of mota."

"No thanks, I've got plenty of it myself."

Before she drove away, I could have sworn I saw her put her pinky to her nose. When that car left, it took a small part of my dignity with it.

Chapter 28

The next morning, I prepared myself in case the cops showed up at my door. I didn't have much of a defense: "Do I look like I got in a fight yesterday? Look at this face . . . like a baby's bottom!" But I'd been preparing for that visit for some time now. Since I'd scored that weed from A-bomb, Sal had been going on and on about how "The cops are onto you. I see them parked out there all the time—in front of Mica's too. You gotta stop givin' that shit away. The penalties here are pretty stiff, even for herb. They'll toss your ass in jail. I think they're just waiting for you guys to slip up." I had been giving that shit away but only to those cats who had that swagger in their step. I figured, why not be a friend indeed? I told Sal not to worry about it and that, for months, I'd been watching those same cops doing the same exact shit parked at the dead end. Still, he might have had a point. People were constantly coming over and blazing, and Mica's place was a regular smokehouse. It wouldn't have taken a Top Dick to sniff out that boner.

Much more so than the police, I was concerned about Luz. She was nineteen and that kind of behavior was to be expected, but still, I didn't think she was like that. We didn't speak to each other for a few days, then I got a text one afternoon: "Party at Kyler's tonight." Herb and Mica were over drinking some beers, and I told them about the party.

"Big guy from Texas?" Herb said.

I nodded. "Yeah, I think he works at your school, Herby."

"That dude's a booger-eater! I was talking with him outside my classroom a few weeks ago, then out of nowhere, he just digs in, picks out a winner, and scrapes it off on his tooth—all in the middle of a conversation. He didn't apologize or anything."

"Well, he is kind of dopey."

"Dopey? That dude's a regular loon. I swear I caught him jackin' it in the boy's room at school last week."

"Eh, who cares? I used to whack it in the bathroom all the time when I worked the maintenance crew at Buffalo Town Hall. Those government jobs, man, they pay you, basically—"

"—to whack off," Herb said. "But there's a difference between jerkin' it at some town hall and doin' it in a school full of children."

"The dude eats boogers; I don't think his judgment is exactly sound," I said.

Herb and Mica both laughed.

"So, you wanna go or not?"

"Fuck that, I'm not spending my Friday night with a booger-eater," Herb said.

"No, but you'll spend it with toothless, squirting whores," I said.

"I am already going to some beach in Michoacán this weekend, and we're leaving tonight, so I can't go," Mica said.

Sal, Cisco, and Paz, however, were in. We left later that afternoon and met the Luz's at a Kiosko on the corner of Kyler's street to buy drinks. I'd been having a great day hanging with the guys and didn't need any drama. But I could tell by the way my Luz looked at me that wasn't what she had in mind.

"I've missed you, Will." She kissed my cheek and hugged me. I broke from her grip and walked into the store, and she followed. We bought our drinks and returned outside.

"Come with me." Luz opened Blanco's back door.

"Naw, uh, I left my hat in Sal's car."

"Oh . . . okay . . ." I wanted to hug her but didn't have that kind of strength.

Both cars took off and were soon parked in front of Kyler's house. And damn was it big. It looked as if two regular houses had been smashed together—perhaps a favorable result of the 2003 quake? And Kyler was the lucky Mexican who got to live there.

Kyler greeted us at the door, and I quickly pushed past him, eager to see the house. The rooms were gigantic and nearly devoid of furnishings. White tile spanned the floor in every room and white walls picked up where the tile left off. The front rooms were vacant, but the back were filled with life. A group of about fifteen Latinos were dancing to salsa in the back room, and the rest of the partiers were just beyond them outside.

I continued my self-guided tour of the house, through the kitchen and out the back door. The tile continued with me out the door and spread into the entire backyard. No grass anywhere. A group of people sat at a table under an awning. The table was covered in empty beer and liquor bottles, cigarette packs, and whiskey-soaked playing cards. I sat and introduced myself.

I felt somewhat settled in there—that is, until Luz walked outside and sat next to me. I got up and walked into the house. I struck up a few conversations with random people in the kitchen, waiting for Luz to come back inside so that I could go back out. But she never did. I watched her through the kitchen window. She was a naturally vivacious person, but it looked to me that her every word that night was forced and flat, her every smile contrived. I hated seeing her like that—seeing the effect I was already having on her life.

Eventually, I gave in, walked back outside, and sat next to her. She started to put her arms around me, then pulled them back as if she was suddenly conscious of what she was doing. I knew those were the same arms she'd inevitably use to strike me down. I felt lost and dizzy as if I were hovering an inch above the ground, and no matter how my legs kicked and strained I couldn't control my motions. She could blow me away at any time.

She allowed her arms to break free, and she rubbed my back while speaking with someone at the table. I didn't know if this was a trap, but my brain literally couldn't take any more analysis, so I allowed her touch.

Kyler came outside.

"Did you bring it, Will?"

I patted my shirt pocket. "Sure did, Hoss."

"Follow me."

And I did—through the kitchen, up the stairs, out onto a balcony, then up a winding metal staircase to the roof. Luz followed behind but kept her distance. Kyler and I sat on the top of one of the walls at the edge of the house. A minute or so later, Luz sat to my left. I focused all my attention to the right.

Kyler pulled out an apple, took a few strategic bites, ran a few holes in it, and tossed it on my lap. I packed it, lit it, hit it, and passed it right—always looking right. Sal and Cisco must have followed their noses because soon they were there. A large Mexican woman followed behind them. Sal and I suspected that she was the one Herb complained was stalking him: "I swear, the bitch follows me around town like I was giving out Gucci bags filled with cupcakes." She seemed normal to me, so I put it out of mind.

"Yo, Roger Rayne Goosepebbles, do your Goldberg impression." Sal said this loud enough for everyone to hear, making it more difficult for me to refuse. But I had a few hits in me and felt like entertaining that night. I popped up and got into character. Everyone fell silent as I started my performance: "So I was driving through the Mojave one night with my friends after we'd eaten some peyote. I thought I saw a rattlesnake coiled around the shifter, so I opened the door and jumped out while we were doin' seventy. I must have hit the ground just right because I didn't break anything, but I rolled and kept rolling 'til I spun into a jumping cholla. It took me two weeks before I got all the prickers outta my ass."

Everyone was laughing, even those who knew little English but a lotta Herb—everyone except Luz, who just sat there staring at me with these intense, sad eyes, which looked to be doing something worse than crying.

"Do another one, Willy-boy!" someone said.

I didn't respond. Luz mouthed the words "I love you." That was it. I floated to her. The chemicals were raging through my defenseless body, and I let them do as they pleased. I sat next to her, and she leaned over and smelled my lips.

"I love the smell of marijuana on you."

I kissed her. She tasted wonderful—salty and sweet. The apple came back to me, and I ripped it twice to make up for the hits I'd missed giving my performance. Sal went downstairs to grab more beers, but instead of carrying the cans back upstairs, he started bombing them up to the roof from the backyard. One hit the ground in front of me. It fizzed and spun around for a minute before dying. Another hit Herb's stalker, but she didn't react. I caught a few and handed one to Luz. The other people were telling stories and laughing and chugging beers. But Luz and I were completely immersed in each other. Something inside of me was changing. Sometimes those changes came quickly and powerfully like an eruption from the Volcán; other times they came slowly and almost imperceptibly like the gradual shifting of tectonic plates under the earth. But both gradually and explosively, I was changing, shifting with the rhythm of nature. For so long, I'd fought these changes—was terrified by them. But here in Mexico and beside this beautiful woman, I could no longer deny my heart and soul the direction they were pulling me. I had to let go. Something colossal was loosening inside of me. Some great pillar I'd long stood upon was rocking back and forth. Soon, it was gonna fall, and I was going down with it, for better or worse.

Eventually we rejoined the other partiers below. Nearly everyone was dancing in the backroom. Paz pulled Sal onto the floor with her, and Luz pulled me. Some Latin groove rocked the place as the partiers danced in step. Luz put my hands on her hips and showed me her rhythm. She pulled me close and kissed my cheek, then she leaned back her head and said in adorable English, "Always you are in my heart and in my mind." She looked me dead in the eye. She meant it. I tried to rip myself from her grasp, but she pulled me closer. That was it. That was the moment it all came pouring in—the first moment in my life I'd ever felt it for anyone or anything:

"I love you, Luz."

"I love you too."

The walls were white, as was the floor. Luz was dressed in a white cotton dress, and I in a white shirt. We were dancing, spinning, as chemicals raced through our bodies. I felt welcomely dizzy. Why did I have to come so far for this? To find that earth is our only heaven? To understand that if I wasted this time, I wasted all of eternity? Why wasn't this something I'd already known—common knowledge passed down as a birthright? And why was she still clinging to me? This Mexican princess, this queen among girls. For my whole life, I'd been hearing from all angles that you have to love your grandparents, you have to love your neighbors, you have to love god . . . And I gave myself bloody and painful emotional hemorrhoids trying to love them all. But I didn't feel it. Didn't know what the word meant. Even at my grandfather's funeral, I couldn't cry. I tried. Everyone around me was weeping.

But now, I felt tears coming at the thought of hurting her. At the thought of letting her down. Was I still an animal like they said? Like the beast they locked in that cage? This was too dangerous. Maybe you should run? Get away!

Luz squeezed me tighter and kissed me. I decided to stop asking myself questions.

We continued twirling in that blur of white. Songs kept coming on the radio, songs I'd long forgotten but that fit perfectly in the moment. "Always you are in my heart and in my mind." Luz was my earthly angel dressed in white.

We stopped dancing a short time later. Luz and I walked hand in hand to the kitchen where Cisco was talking with one of Luz's friends, a Brazilian woman named Gabriela who was in Lila studying at the University. She was twenty-six and engaged to some Chicano tax attorney in El Paso, but she talked about Cisco nonstop like a hyperactive middle schooler.

"Oh, did you see Cisco's tattoos? Isn't he soooo dangerous?"

"Don't you think the name 'Cisco' is macho?"

And the kicker: "Cisco *has* to be gay. He's just tooooooo good-looking."

After hearing her throw around the G-word, I knew he'd be ballin' her that night. She was just toooooooo insecure.

Luz Blanco drove me and my Luz back to my house, and Sal drove Paz, Cisco, and Gabriela, back as well. I could see Cisco was jonesin' to try some Brazilian, so I split my bed and dragged half into the living room. He could have just taken my old room, but one of the extraneros, a Colombian named Jimmy, had moved in the day before. Cisco thanked me, and I joined Luz in my room and we made great use of our half of bed. After, I walked to the kitchen to fill up my water bottle and passed through the living room where Cisco was really giving it to the engaged Brazilian.

"Oh, Cisco, you're sooooooooo dangerous. UHUUL!"

I filled the water bottle and returned to my princess. In a few days, Luz was leaving on a ten-day class trip to Central America, and this was the last night we'd get together before the trip. Luz had never left Mexico and was excited. I didn't know what would happen during that time. This thing was still pretty fragile, and I knew it could easily break if not handled correctly.

"Are you going to miss me?" she said.

I was hoping—hoping with every part of me—that I'd ache for her the entire time she was gone. I was petrified to think I might not even miss her. That maybe those emotional hemorrhoids would come itchin' and burnin' back . . .

I opened my mouth to answer but kissed her forehead instead. I felt like a bird with a lead stomach.

Chapter 29

I partied like the proverbial wild man for those ten days Luz was away. She was no anchor but still left seeds of fidelity in me that were germinating slowly. Sal and Mica joined me in my quest for the Promised Land. We went to wild house parties, ripped gravity bongs, and played round after round of Soko well into the early hours of morning. We spent a good amount of time smoking on Mica's roof, rode in the bed of pickups to and from parties, and did the secret knock at the candlelit corner store to purchase price-inflated sixers or caguamas of whatever was left over after the midnight limit on alcohol purchases. We'd walk to taco stands for late-night quesadillas or to matinee showings of captioned and discounted movies—sometimes passing the billboard above the panteon showing a picture of an SUV and two smiling white gringos next to the caption, "Eres diferente." I felt comfortable walking around town, as though I was now as vivid as the tropical colors surrounding me. I walked nearly three miles a day—to and from work, to Mica's house, to the corner store, to visit the landlady, to meet with friends for lunch. I had my music, my sunscreen, my dirty running sneakers, and handfuls of pocket change. I could go anywhere I wanted. I was growing more accustomed to the heat (or perhaps the heat was becoming less intense as we approached the winter) and wasn't sweating nearly as much as I had just weeks earlier. I'd take my laundry to the lavanderia once a week and pass groups of school children who'd invariably point and stare from half a block down when they saw me coming. I'd pass fruit stands, and emaciated stray dogs patrolling the streets, and young guys zipping around on motorcycles. I walked swiftly and confidently. Occasionally a driver would honk or shout something like, "Go home, gringo!" A month earlier I'd have shouted back or given him the finger. But now I just kept going, knowing that for every one of those assholes, there were two cars full of girls honking and shouting at me for other reasons. I was learning how to take care of myself and needed the sometimes inhospitable conditions to do so. Lila was safe, but I was still a target. Every weekend some new asshole would push me like the guy at the Star Wars Bar a month earlier, and I was pushing right back. I was sick of taking people's shit just to keep the peace. I was sick of overanalyzing my every move just so I wouldn't piss anyone off. I hadn't always been like this, and I didn't know how to handle the aggression at times. I was worried that at some point I was going to go too far, but that didn't mean I avoided conflicts. In fact, I was drawn to them. I was often questioned at parties and bars about my president, about the war, immigration, and the fucking wall people back home were ever-calling to be built between us and them. Even though I agreed with most of the perspectives of those questioning me, I didn't just stand there and nod my head along like a pussy. I spoke freely and challenged opposing viewpoints. The issue of the wall was hot that month and was all over the news. I was happy to be on the other side while this was being debated. It was a hot time and a hot topic, and I followed along as much as my limited Spanish would allow. Before I'd left for Mexico, there were protests sweeping through the US against legislation that would raise penalties for illegal immigrants. Millions protested in the streets of Chicago, and LA, and Dallas, and New York . . . The images of Mexican migrant workers protesting in the US flashed across the televisions lighting up half-empty homes across the border. I wished for fluency now more than ever so I could understand what people were saying. There was heat under every Mexican's seemingly cool skin. This wasn't always apparent but had the potential to start steaming at any moment. Normally patient, affable people could be sparked into an argument at the sight or sound of some seemingly normal thing. For Juana, it was hearing a song like "Gimme Tha Power," while for others it was something as simple as seeing a shining white canvas of skin. I could understand the anger and aggression when it was directed at my country's red, white, and blue flag—I had nothing to do with that—but couldn't when it was directed at the solid-colored flag of skin draped around my body. And, because I couldn't hide this flag, I always had to be prepared for battle. In the times I felt threatened, I asked myself what would George Washington or Audie Murphy do? Or, better yet, what would my coal-shoveling, World-War-II-veteran, first-generation-Polish-immigrant grandfather do? He'd bring his iron shovel down on some fucker's head, sin duda. While I knew this wasn't the best way to handle a situation, it gave me some comfort knowing I still had a country, and a family, behind me—that if some fucker pushed me too hard, that I could push back with the strength of an army. But I preferred not to push. The heat here cooked daily. In this world, the garbagemen collected three days a week. Who was I to refuse their services?

Mica was feeling the grind as well. He was German but every bit as gringo as I was. We were riding home from el Centro in a cab one day, and the driver called him a gringo.

"I'm not a gringo. I'm German."

"No, you are gringo."

"No, I'm from Germany!"

"Yes, I know where that is—somewhere between Alabama and Georgia. I know America."

"You know," I said, "Mexico is a *part* of America."

"No," he said, "Mexico is Mexico y nada mas."

It was funny sometimes when it happened to someone else but even those funny times reminded me that I was different.

Mica also disliked banda, and we'd often fuck with the stereos at parties right as the extraneros entered the apex of dance. Just as the rhythm would climax or singer would grito, we'd switch the song to something like the Ramones or Talking Heads. We couldn't get enough of the reaction of partiers jolted out of a dance-trance by David Byrne's schizophrenic vocals.

Mica bitched about the bugs, mice, oppressive heat, inefficient Mexican business practices, the food . . . He was burning out with school, the cultural differences, with learning Spanish. He spoke it all day and only switched to English when he was around me or Sal. His Spanish was slightly better than mine, though I'd studied it longer before arrival. We taught each other new words and expressions we'd pick up on the day-to-day:

"Hey, I was watching *Beavis and Butthead* with the captions on yesterday. You know 'lograr' means 'to score'?"

"Oh, that's a good one . . ."

Mica drank every night, proving perhaps that the German body did indeed run on beer. He'd already visited a number of spots throughout Mexico—far more than I had—and seemed to be getting more from his experience here. I was nearly broke and could barely afford groceries. It was getting more and more difficult to escape this bleak reality, but something wonderful happened around this time that alleviated much of my stress. One day when I went to a cajero, or ATM, to withdraw money, I accidentally hit one thousand pesos instead of one hundred. I knew I had less than one hundred dollars left in my bank account, so when the machine started spitting bills, I was pleasantly surprised. Then I remembered I'd set up an overdraft account with my bank a few years back. I'd never used credit before and thought it to be something almost evil. Dumbass adults and saccharine television shows (think *Saved by the Bell*) had successfully planted the idea in my head that credit cards were forged by Lucifer himself. But I needed the cash, and I also needed to be far away from all of them, so I repressed the issue and started treating the cajero as nothing more than a slot machine rigged in my favor. I didn't know my credit limit, but I did know that whatever it was would buy me more time to continue living the American Dream. But something about living off credit made me realize this was indeed just a dream (yet still every bit as American as subprime lending).

Mica and I were burning out, and the heat didn't help. We'd swap stories about the racism, shitty service, our stalkers (he'd picked one up too), the unfulfilled promises of the landlady. Apparently she ran a kind of soup kitchen out of her place, and Mica ate lunch there almost every day. He hated the food, but it was included with his rent, so he scarfed it down nonetheless.

He fell in love with another "skinny one" every week, and his vain efforts to score with these chicks amused me and Sal. Mica was also developing a taste for Mexican girls but was into the lighter-skinned variety.

Mica chain-smoked cigs, burning through several packs a day, and was always coughing, pale, and sickly. Sal claimed to have seen him cough up a thick cloud of black smoke one time even when he wasn't smoking. Mica ate greasy sausages and pan-fried meats, cooked in the same pan his roommates used to fry their daily dozen eggs.

Sal and I ran nearly every other night. I could now cover six miles in about forty-five minutes without much of a problem. We always ran the same route: up our small street, right at Madrid del Rio, straight past the fruterias, library, and playground, left just before the bridge, and straight past the corner auto garage, which seemed more a graveyard for tired city buses than a hospital. We'd run at dusk when children were out riding their bikes and groups of teens patrolled the streets in their trendy clothes while playing the grab-ass games of youth. Old men and women sat in groups outside their homes, staring in silence. Their work was done. They'd sweat and toiled in the Mexican sun and survived. They deserved those moments of tranquility.

The buildings thinned as we'd near the fields of tall grass. We'd grab stones off the ground here to prepare for battle with the dogs just beyond. They'd often charge before we could even see them coming. Some days, instincts would take over and we'd charge them back, barking louder than they did. If they didn't surrender, we'd huck the stones, and they'd usually run. Only once did one get close enough to where Sal had to kick it.

We'd continue up the incline with the volcano dead ahead and the sun dropping along its side. I'd often wonder if Dr. Josh was up there taking samples and reading sensors and looking down upon us all. It made me feel safe to know that he was up there. Safe to know that it was knowledge and not faith up there now protecting me. I trusted Dr. Josh more than I'd ever trusted any of the saints.

We'd then hit the row of circus tents, where the air was filled with clouds of smoke and the low notes of the tuba. We'd take deep breaths and hold them. The dead dog still smelled every bit as fierce as it had several weeks prior. I'd probably smelled death before, but that was the first time I'd been able to identify the scent, and it was unique in its repulsiveness.

We'd take a shortcut through some tall grass before the road ran into a main one. We continued up the main road and ran past speeding cars. This was the spot I'd usually get pegged with shit, reminding me that there were still so many people out there who refused to treat curable diseases.

We'd then pass a newly constructed office complex, complete with a garden and plenty of green space. We ran along the sidewalk that winded through this park area, taking us past flowers, ponds, and a large fountain in the center. This was the spot where Sal had warned me months ago to look down while running. There were a lot of large frogs here, and it was easy to step on one. This wasn't necessarily a concern of the vegetarian's for the animals' lives, but rather a warning of the runner's not to twist an ankle on the gobs of guts that would no doubt splatter all over the sidewalk should one be squished. We breathed through our t-shirts here as walls of insects filled the air—likely what was drawing the frogs.

We'd do a few laps around that fountain, then continue up the road, and take a left at the highway running between Lila and El Campo. There was a housing development under construction here in an area that had likely once been a green field. The workers were usually still there late into the night, probably trying to squeeze in some bricking and concrete work while the earth was cooler. They'd give us awkward looks and shout platitudes: "Hey, don't work too hard, fellas!" "Why don't you run down to the store and pick me up some beer!"

Just up the highway was an enormous mall that opened a few weeks back. It was called Modaloca, and its main draw was a department store by the same name. Though nothing more than a price-inflated JCPenney's, Modaloca was all the rage among the hip socialites in that sleepy town—the ones who saw nothing wrong with paying one hundred bucks plus for an exotic pair of Arizona jeans.

We'd then make a left just past the housing development and run along the new sidewalk. A stray dog that guarded the area would always take off when it heard us coming. I thought maybe Sal had pelted it with a rock on some other day, and it wasn't sticking around as the gringos were doubling in number. We continued down this sidewalk to its end where it turned into two tracks about the width apart of a cement truck's axle. These tracks led to a wall separating the housing development from the office park. Sal and I would always split here, each taking a track, and for some reason we'd sprint the distance to the wall. It was usually a toss-up who'd win. Just beyond these tracks was a beautiful, dipping valley of tall grass and scattered trees that seemed to flow forever into the mountains in the distance. The pink sun followed its path each day, setting behind that valley. These trees would no doubt someday fall to the sprawling growth already consuming the peaceful city and be replaced with paint-by-number homes filled with the latest gadgets and appliances the stores and boutiques of Lila had to offer.

We'd take the same route home, but when we reached the deportivo complex, Sal would dash inside to run another few miles on the track. I'd jog downhill, take off my soaked shirt, and sit on a plastic chair under the almond trees. Puddles of sweat would gather and drip off my body. My stomach was growing despite the running. I was in the best shape I'd been in in years and didn't know why the muscles I'd been able to see since youth were just now being covered with a fatty layer. I'd usually sit out there and observe or read until I stopped sweating. I'd started on *Crime and Punishment* a few weeks back and was really getting into it—so much so that I had to put it down once Raskoinikov's guilt and growing insanity started to resonate with my own. When Sal came back, sometimes we'd make dinner together—I'd prepare the meat separately from everything else, then add it to my plate at the end. After dinner, I'd take a cool shower. We rarely had gas. The water's only source of heat was the sun, beating down on the tank all day. I appreciated the warmth it provided. Those nights were always so peaceful. I'd go out running but always come home, faster . . . better.

Chapter 30

Herb came over one afternoon on a day off from school, and we sat under the almond trees, drinking and telling stories: "When Sal and I were in college, we used to get fucked up, grab our music and some portable speakers, and wander around campus knocking on random doors, and when people answered, we'd say 'Dance Party Delivery.' Sometimes they'd get pissed and send us away, but most people invited inside where we'd start breaking it down in the living room or wherever. Our go-to jams were straight out of the pits of the eighties: Squeeze's 'Pulling Muscles from a Shell,' or Huey Lewis's 'The Power of Love.' Usually people would join in, sometimes coming in from off the streets. That's one thing I learned early on—if you give people something positive to be a part of, they'll almost always join in, no matter how ridiculous it is. People want to be part of something. There's something down deep uniting us all, bringing us together. I wanna find that. Discover some emotional algorithm linking all people—giving 'em something to believe in."

"You two are a coupla idiots. A fucking dance service?" Herb laughed.

"They used to call Sal 'Dance Party Sal.' He was known across campus. There was a time when he was happier—not totally happy, but happier than now . . ."

"Eh, who's happy?"

"I don't know, man . . . I think there is an answer out there—perhaps in some dark, wet vagina I haven't yet penetrated . . ."

"Well, even Wilt the Stilt couldn't ball 'em all." Herb laughed. "Hey, I got one for ya: When I first got to Mexico I started seeing this girl. Things got kinda serious, so she took me out to the country to meet her parents. They lived *out* there, man, way out in the sticks—type of place where the whole town shared one phone. Her parents were real traditional, so they wouldn't let me sleep in her bed. They fixed me a spot on some lumpy couch in the backroom. Well, I got up in the middle of the night to take a piss, but when I turned on the light, I saw something that almost made me shit my pants. There were four or five enormous tarantulas crawling on the walls. I swear, I screamed like a little girl—I fuckin' shrieked, man. She and her parents came running to see what was the matter. I took off my shoe and started smashing the fuckers, but her father grabbed my arm and said, 'No, no, don't kill them!' They were harmless and ate the scorpions in the area. He said they learned to peacefully coexist with them and that the spiders were as much a part of the house as they were. I couldn't sleep after that. I'll never forget that night."

"Fuck . . ." I'd been killing tarantulas for years. I needed to stop. "Hey," I said, "have you seen Javie at all lately?"

"Shit, he's probably crocodile food by now."

"What the fuck happened?"

"He and his *friend* Edgar had gotten into some pretty ugly shit, and I'm sorry to say that they've probably paid the ultimate price for it. It's sad. I don't think he was able to admit to himself who he really was, and he filled that gap with some nasty stuff. He'd been one of my best buddies since moving here. We'd tag teamed a few skeezers in our day, but it always seemed to me like he was just going through the motions. He and Edgar had been good friends for about twenty years, and they were both fucked in the head. Edgar was a straight meth head, and he dragged Javie into it."

"Christ! Can we do anything?"

"You can grab a shovel and start digging. It's fucking Mexico, man."

"That's terrible!"

"Yeah, it really is . . . You know, Javie grew up in a small town near the volcano. He was the youngest of eight kids. His parents caught him with another guy back when he was just a teenager. They kicked him out of the house and told him never to come back. It's a small town, man, and everybody there knows about it. They called him 'marginado,' or 'exile.' From what I know, he never spoke to any of them since. It's kinda like he had no home. A lot of places in Mexico are still in the Stone Age with that shit, and Javie suffered the ultimate price. Now I guess he's a marginado from planet earth."

"Fucking bastards!"

"Yeah. A lotta guys down here never come out—just stay inside forever. I'll never understand why people are so bad to one another."

"You ever try meth?"

"You been talking to your friend Sally, huh?"

"So it's true?"

"Yeah, I've smoked meth—but only once. It was the most intense feeling I'd ever experienced. It's like a prolonged orgasm exploding all over your body, only ten times as intense. I see why people get hooked. It's been about four years now, and I still think about it. I just try to forget it, or it'll drive me insane. I told Sal all about it after I saw that nut do it at a party one night—he freaked the fuck out the next day; he kept talking about how disgusting he felt. I figured sharing my experience with him would help him calm down, but dudes like him only see those intimate confessions as ammo that they can later use against you. About a week later, he hooked up with Paz, and that bitch just took over his life. If you ask me, he was better off with the meth."

"Fuck, I didn't know all that. I'm never touching that shit."

"I've done just about every drug you can imagine, but that's the one I can't stop thinking about. That shit's the fucking devil himself."

Chapter 31

All week, Sal had been talking about a trip he and Paz and her friends were going on that weekend to a small town in the mountains of Jalisco, called Mazamitla. He didn't invite me, but he did mention all the extra room they'd have where they were staying, which was his version of an invitation. I wouldn't have considered going had I not discovered my overdraft insurance, but now money wasn't an issue.

Kyler sent me a text that Thursday: "Thinking about going to Mazamitla this weekend. Wanna join?" It was a delightful coincidence, and I figured why fight the current?

Sal's car was full, so Kyler and I took the bus. Sal sent me a text a little after we'd left Lila: "I'm at Paz's friend's house. You gotta get here. Like fifteen girls in one spot."

I passed the message to the Texan.

"I have kind of an open relationship with Luz," he said, "so she probably wouldn't mind if I gave it a shot. Don't worry, I won't tell either of the girls if you want to give it a shot too."

I was thinking the same thing, but hearing it spoken made it more difficult to ignore.

"I'm not a cheater, Tex. I'll help you out though if you need it."

I thought about my Luz as we cruised through the Mexican countryside. She seemed to float further and further out of mind the higher we traveled into the mountains. The temperature dropped considerably, and the stone world cracked and eroded away as we entered a landscape dominated by evergreens and quaint wooden mountain-homes. The whole scene felt of Adirondack late spring.

We eventually entered a small town. The bus let us out on a street corner, and we followed the flow of traffic to the center of town. Older men rode horses as younger kids zoomed by on four wheelers.

The main square was dominated by an enormous cathedral with white walls, surrounded by bars and restaurants. There was a festival of some kind going on, and the center was filled with hawkers peddling all kinds of crap.

Sal drove down and met us; he was with Paz and the house's owner, Carlita. I'd met Carlita months back at Crystal and remembered how, while dancing, she unbuttoned my shirt, ran her hands all over my chest and stomach, then slid a digit an inch into my jeans and took an "accidental" swipe at it—but only got as far as the start of the short hairs. I swear, sometimes that shit can be better than the full-on ape grip with the cocoa butter handshake. Carlita was a sexy girl, but that was a long time ago . . .

Sal pulled me aside. "There are nine girls in that house and three guys—and one of 'em is Tito."

"Forget it, man, I got a girl now." I tried to recall the love she made me feel, but the more I tried, the more the feeling got lost in the ruts and valleys of my heart and soul. I could feel a storm approaching from the horizon inside of me.

We got some pizza, then piled in Sal's car and drove to the house. It was fucking gorgeous. Behind it was a sweeping valley with wooden homes scattered on its slopes. There was a cow pen beside the house where a cow and two calves wandered around while Paz and the others grilled carne asada a few yards away. Paz introduced me to the people I hadn't yet met, then pointed out the buffet of food on a table near the grill. I ignored the food and went right for the cooler. Tito gave me a dirty look when I pulled out a brewser.

After dinner, we drove to the town center to go dancing at a disco. Sal's car was so weighed down with passengers that its bottom was scraping on speed bumps, so I got out at a red light and jumped into the bed of a friend's truck in front of us. But as I hopped over the tailgate, the truck jerked forward, and I came down on it with my hip. I crawled to the corner, pulled a beer out of my pocket, and tried to ignore the stinging pain.

We parked and the girls looked ready to dance. My hip was sore, and I was having a good enough time just relaxing and enjoying the cold, so I nodded when Sal—after finding out about the hefty cover charge at the disco—asked if anyone wanted to go back to the house and drink. After all, the fridge was full of beer. The girls pushed forward into the night, and the gringos and Paz rode back to the house.

We lit a fire in the living room and sat around it. I put on some music and let myself relax and enjoy the cool night. It'd been so long since I'd felt the tranquility of the crisp autumn air. In pre-winter Buffalo, I'd always seen something so tragically heroic about the leaves accepting their fate for the greater good. Everything about the season brought slow, validating, accepted death. We all died together in preparation for the dark, excruciating winter. And group death made me feel less alone.

The house was beautiful. It was rustic yet modern and comfortable. Thick, splintered beams ran the length of the sloped ceiling. I wrapped myself in a colorful Mexican blanket, which was just too short to cover my feet, and drank a Modelo. Though my body remained still, my mind galloped like a prisoner through the mire after escaping a chain gang. I could hear the dogs barking in the distance. Soon I'd been caught and punished for allowing my thoughts to roam free. Though I wasn't alone in that room, no one could see or touch me. I wasn't there. I thought of Luz, but even she seemed to be nothing more than a snack for my ravenous hunger. I'd think of her, and home, and I'd smile, but that was only because I was so far from both. I was thoroughly warm. The fire did its job well.

Sal lay beside Paz. Though still, I could see his eyes shifting and hands twitching—his right foot tapping arrhythmically against the wooden floor. The waves surrounding him matched mine. We were both ringing doleful E minors while the rest of the room was humming a warm, easy C. Dark clouds stormed above our heads and in the silence I felt a burning tragedy consuming the tranquility that once so loosely held me. Though similar, Sal and I were on separate odysseys, riding the churning seas, desperately trying to thwart the sloppy and vain attempts of vindictive gods to end us—and all this just so we could return to the very place we'd inevitably set sail from once the stillness set in a few weeks after our arrival.

The dolls made their way back from the disco in clusters. Some had met boys and others returned solo. Either way, their intermittent arrivals invariably interrupted the building climax of Beethoven's hopeless "Ode to Joy" I'd forced on replay in my head. There were several bedrooms in that house, but all were claimed. All the doors soon closed, and locked, and I was left to fend for myself with nothing more than the thin, colorful blanket just too short to cover my body. I was a lead-weighted guest and knew my place was on the living room floor. I lay beside the fire and rested my head on a couch cushion. I woke several times that night after the fire had gone out, and tried to reverse my wish to experience the cold. This was another one of those terribly long nights that never seemed to end.

The next morning, I wrapped myself in every warm article of clothing I had and went outside and sat in the sun. Sofia sat beside me. I wondered why I'd never tried for her before I'd met Luz. She was the girl I normally would have gone for, but I just didn't. That almost seemed better to me than ever being with her.

Our plan that day was to see the cascadas, or waterfall, which was the main tourist draw of the area. Mica had seen them and told me how great they were. Everyone except Kyler, who'd decided to go back to Lila early that day, piled into a truck and soon we were travelling dusty country roads. About ten people, including myself, were crammed in the bed. I sat with my back against the rear window and studied the scene. Tall grass grew high over the truck walls and scraped against the backs of those seated against the sides. The deep colors of the green grass and blue sky complemented each other as they danced in the breeze.

I sat next to a beautiful woman named Alma. Alma had thick, luscious lips; straight, black hair; full, dark eyes; and bronze skin. She had her arms wrapped around Carlita's little sister, an adorable five- or six-year-old in a thick wool sweater and tiny pair of jeans. Something about sitting next to them set me at ease.

We drove past some horses on our way up the mountain. We stopped at a parking lot, and just as I hopped out of the truck, a bone-thin horse galloped by. A kid in dirty clothes grabbed the dragging reins, brought it to a stop, and punted it in the stomach. I shouted, "HEY!" but stopped myself, remembering Herb's words about being, "in his country." Though it still didn't seem right . . .

No one else in my party seemed to have noticed the kick but me. They all headed for the trail leading to the cascadas. A clear, shallow stream flowed beside the trail, guiding us along. We walked for about ten minutes before we could hear the falling water. The view of the waterfall from its upper portion was blocked by massive evergreens, so we hiked down a cliff and saw it from its lower. Most of the group walked to the pool below the cascadas. Sal and I, however, hopped between boulders until we were behind the water wall. I felt an intimate privacy there and took several pictures.

When we hopped back to the other side, I looked down and saw Alma lying with her head on a rock. I stood about ten feet above her, zoomed in, and captured a candid shot of her face.

"Hey, I was not ready," she said, after seeing that I'd snapped a pic.

"Oh, I'm sorry, I can delete it."

"No, that's okay. Take another one."

I did. I liked the first one better.

We got our fill of the falling water, then hiked back to the truck. I sat in the same spot in the bed, and Alma sat across from me. She was still holding Carlita's sister in her arms. I snapped a shot of them together. The colors of their faces were better than any of those I'd seen that day.

When we got back to the house, Sofia and I volunteered to get some supplies we needed. I collected donations, and we were out the door. I repeated the list of items so I wouldn't forget any: "charcoal, ice, toilet paper, lighter fluid, charcoal, ice . . ." We walked the dark, narrow streets lined with small stone homes that were decked out with Christmas lights and colorful decorations. Dogs barked at us from rooftops. I imagined them dressed as reindeer but knew I was far from that type of nonsense. By the time we reached the convenience store, I'd forgotten most of the items on the list. I'd been drinking heavily since returning from the cascadas and was having enough difficulty walking. The woman working behind the counter could see this. Sofia grabbed what we needed and brought it to the counter where the woman totaled our bill. I released the wads of cash in my hand, but missed the counter. The woman laughed as I bent over to pick it up. We paid and left.

On the walk back, Sofia patted her sexy, trim stomach and called herself a "gordita." Sal had told me that on numerous occasions he'd seen her take a bite or two out of an empanada or whatever, chew thoroughly, then spit it out in a napkin. Somehow, diseases like this had floated across the Rio Grande—but what the hell did I know? This shit was probably native to every population—but then again, certain social patterns probably did catalyze the process. I knew compassion was necessary to help fight against such diseases, but something about hearing her repeatedly call herself fat lit a fuse in me.

"You're not fat—not even close. And it's good to have a little cushion. Believe me, there's nothing sexier on a woman than some curves. Chew *and* swallow!" My foot got caught on a raised cobblestone, and I almost fell. Sofia started laughing.

"What?" I said.

"I think it's funny that a borracho is trying to tell me how to be healthy."

I guess she wasn't able to give any compassion either . . .

There were only a few people there when we got back. The girls had gone to the disco again. I walked out to the grill, mounded the charcoal in a pyramid, squirted on some lighter fluid, lit a piece of cardboard, and put it near the coals. Sal and Paz had also left, but to run errands, not dance. I was alone with Sofia and one of the other girls. I went inside for some meat and saw them sitting on the floor in the living room reading the Mexican version of *Cosmo* and talking about boys. I couldn't take their bullshit, so I walked back outside and took my time tossing the carne asada on the grill.

It was a gorgeous and cool night. I was thrilled to be able to wear three layers without punishment from the heat. I closed my eyes and was back in the Finger Lakes.

Sal and Paz returned, and the girls started arriving again in clusters. I'd finished grilling but didn't even care to eat the crap I'd made. Sal and I sat on a couch in the living room and found *The Shining* on some cable station. We were able to enjoy the flick for about ten minutes before Paz and the other girls sat cross-legged on the living room floor and started braiding each other's hair.

"Saaaaaal, put on something we *all* want to watch," Paz said.

"Fight it, man," I said in English. "Don't give in."

But he did. He flipped through the channels, and the girls were all appeased at the sight of Jessica Alba's smiling face. But they were paying more attention to each other's hair than their precious *Honey*, so I flipped it back to Jack.

"Heeeeeey! We were watching that!"

"No, you weren't. You were pickin' bugs out of Sofi's hair."

"Maybe you would have seen we were enjoying it if you weren't drunk, como siempre."

"Yeah, you really *do* drink too much, Will!"

"Yeah, well, maybe none of you drink enough," I said. "Look

around. We're at a co-ed party in the woods with a fridge literally full of beer. Why don't you act your age!"

For some reason, perhaps just to spite me, they got up, went to the fridge, and all cracked some beers. Now this was going somewhere. We sat in a circle on the living room floor and played some card game involving binge drinking. I sat between Carlita and Alma, and they'd stop intermittently to touch my wrist or shoulder and smile. The girls were now really going at it, chugging beers and ignoring each other's hair. Someone put on some music and a dance party began. The girls, for once, let their instincts guide them instead of their heads, and they shook their bodies in wonderful ways.

Things started to get a little wild. Alma grabbed me and started grinding. When Carlita saw this, she got on me from behind. I squeezed out of our people sandwich and walked to the kitchen for another beer. Sal followed.

"Yo, you could totally bone either of those chicks," he said.

"Don't say that. I don't even want to think about it."

"What the hell does it matter? You're not going to be with Luz forever. You'll probably be going home soon anyway. Why give up a perfectly great opportunity to live your life? None of these girls even know Luz, so she'll never find out."

"I don't know, man. I'm not a cheater. That shit's like a disease— do it once and it takes over."

"What the hell are you talking about?"

"Look, I know you fuck around with other girls all the time. Maybe Paz doesn't care. But I don't want to ruin this thing with Luz."

"Hey, whatever, man. Do what you wanna do. I just think it'd be wrong to deny yourself any real experience in life. Besides, right now Luz's probably going down on some—where'd she go again?"

"Panama."

"Panamanian man, man."

I guess cheating was an experience too. Goddamn! And, I *was* in Mexico . . .

But I just couldn't. And I wasn't sure if that was due to my feelings for Luz or due to some societal pressure. You're not supposed to cheat, even if you don't have feelings for the person you're cheating on. Cheaters are sinners. Cheaters deserve eternal damnation. And while I did believe I loved Luz, there was something off about all of it—it was as if once I started peeling back the layers, the answer to the main question below it all was a no rather than a yes. As if the yes would only come with rationalizations. But I needed that to be a yes without conditions. Is this what all love feels like? Confusion? Doubt? Forced loyalty? So far, it wasn't playing out like the shit you see in movies, but when did shit ever work out like that? Even so, when you find someone as wonderful as Luz, you need to stick with her, despite doubts. You need to ignore what's going on below to hold her up on high. You need to *worship* her. Oh god, I felt the fucking hemorrhoids coming back. And, christ were they gonna burn . . .

I walked back to the living room already feeling guilty for something I hadn't even done. Alma quickly attached herself to me, and I didn't hold back when the blood started flowing. The song ended and now it was Carlita's turn. Her hands were all over my body—up and under my shirt, then the little swipe . . . But still, I fought it. I kept my hands on her back and no place else. I could see there was a kind of playful competition between the two. The dance party continued long into the night, until Paz took control of the music and started playing some experimental techno crap.

Everyone parted ways. The bedroom doors all closed, and I again found myself alone on that cold living room floor. I felt good knowing this was my final night there, and that I'd successfully avoided temptation. But temptation didn't give up so easily . . .

About fifteen minutes later, Carlita wandered into the living room with a pillow and blanket. She set them on the couch next to me and lay down. Soon, another door creaked open, and Alma walked out. She also had a pillow and a thick comforter, which she laid on the carpet. I lay down on the comforter, and Alma put a pillow under my head, then lay down next to me. Carlita started massaging my back. I couldn't take it. I reached up, scrolled through my music without looking at it, and hit play. "No Expectations" by the Rolling Stones came on. Alma reached for me. I picked up my head and she leaned in, leading with those big, luscious lips, and kissed me. Had I been in different company, I might have pulled away. But I could feel Mick and Keith smiling in approval. They brought me through the station door, and I found myself on the other side, running my hands over the soft crests of Alma's darkened body. Though drunk, I was lucidly aware of my actions. Luz's image was vivid in my mind. And with each kiss, I wished to make her gorgeous eyes water. With each flick of my tongue, I wanted to lick open her heart. I kissed Alma with a dark power that spread through my entire being. Carlita came down and lay next to me, putting her hands under my shirt and rubbing my chest from behind, then down into my jeans. I stood no chance against them. Alma got up, grabbed my hand, and led me into one of the empty rooms in the back. She shut the door behind us, locked it, and turned off the light, then lay down and pulled me on top of her. I pulled off my black Bruce Springsteen t-shirt and threw it on the floor, then pulled her shirt over those huge breasts and that gorgeous head, and threw it beside mine. I kissed her chest while clawing at the clasp of her bra with one hand and digging into her jeans with the other. I flicked my tongue under her bra and licked her hard nipples. I got her bra open, then went after the jeans. Alma moaned and clawed at my back. I wanted to get those pants down, I wanted to crawl inside that darkness. My body was shaking; I needed my fix. I wanted to fuck her raw. I wanted to howl at the full moon. I wanted to fuck all the kindness out of me—spit in the faces of all those well-wishers and kind strangers who'd offered me subtle comforts in the past. This part of me had no lasting power. This part could do nothing but burn, burn, burn, and ash over. Give me that wet darkness, baby. I want to crawl back inside—start this whole nightmare all over again . . .

A knock at the door.

"Alma! Alma!"

It was Carlita. Alma got up and answered it. I lay on my back and rubbed my cock, waiting for the two warm bodies to lay beside me and take it inside them. But after a few minutes, I was still alone. I reached down in the dark and grabbed my Boss tee off the ground, then went outside. Carlita and Alma were both out there arguing, but they stopped when they saw me, then ran into the same room and locked the door. I thought about knocking, but fuck . . . I made my way back to the cold living room floor where I belonged. The fire was still blazing and Mick still singing, now about his "Factory Girl." I wrapped myself in blankets and smiled as though I'd just slain some Goliath in my mind. I let the music play and fell into a deep, satisfying sleep—far more peaceful than I would have ever imagined.

I woke the next morning and half the people, Alma included, were already gone. I thought back to my sins of the previous night, smiled, and made some eggs. The Tell-Tale Heart that I'd almost hoped to hear remained silent under that wooden floor. Perhaps it was buried under the tile in my new bedroom instead, and would drive me to madness on some long, hot, lonely, sober weekday night . . .?

Sal, Paz and I piled into Sal's car, and he drove us home. I sat in the back. I pulled a magazine out of the pocket behind the passenger seat and flipped through it. It was called *Rush* and had pictures of people partying in Lila's discos. I saw several familiar faces: the extraneros, some of Paz's friends, kids from Lengua . . . I was certain I'd see Luz dancing on some greasy puto like Pablo. I felt some sordid strength knowing I got her before she could get me. But I didn't see her. As for Alma, Sal and Paz spoke for several minutes about her upcoming wedding to her high school sweetheart. I guess mine wouldn't be the only floor with a heartbeat . . .

The air got warmer and thicker the closer we got to Lila. Sal tried to get us back before nightfall and made it just in time. But I didn't see any potholes in the highway on that return journey.

Chapter 32

I went to Lengua Monday night for my class with Joaquin. I sat in a wicker chair and read *National Geographic* for a half hour before Neta came over. "Oh, he canceled this afternoon. He wants to come in the mornings now."

"It's a three-mile walk here and back, you know."

"Yes, he canceled. He isn't coming tonight."

These fucking idiots were going to end me, I swear . . .

I went in the next day at eleven for my class with Guadalupe and got the same shit: "Oh, she called today and canceled. She said she won't be here the rest of the week."

Then the kicker: I woke up early Thursday morning and arrived at Lengua a few minutes before seven, the time they'd told me my class with Joaquin would begin. But when I walked to the door—locked. I slammed on the glass. No response. About fifteen minutes later, Neta showed up with the keys.

"What are you doing here?" she said.

"What do you mean, 'What am I doing here?' You told me yesterday to be here at seven in the morning."

"No, *tomorrow* at seven in the morning."

"That's what you said yesterday."

"No, I said *tomorrow*."

I laughed and walked away. Somehow, I was able to suppress

some of the rage churning inside me, and I liked that. As for Lengua, I was done with their shit. I brainstormed the best way to quit: Flaming bags of horseshit out front? Piss-filled water balloons through the windows? An anonymous tip to Mexican Immigration that they're hiring illegals? Fuck it . . . it was over. I put on my music and took off down the road.

Mica and Juana were going to Vallarta the next day and had invited me along. They'd planned the trip several weeks earlier, and I'd told them no when they first asked me to join, but that was before I'd discovered my overdraft insurance. I sent Mica a text saying I was in, and he wrote back: "Bus tomorrow, 8 a.m. See you there."

Neta called that afternoon: "I just want to remind you of your class *tomorrow*."

"I'll see you bright and early!"

I shut off my phone that night so none of the Big Three could get in touch with me the next day, but in doing so, I'd also blocked out my friends. I woke at noon the next day and had five text messages when I turned on my phone: "Where are you?" "We had to leave you!" And so on . . . I texted Mica, and he told me to just meet them at the hotel. He sent me another text a few minutes later: "White people everywhere! You've got to get here . . ." I didn't know how to respond. I hadn't been in such a population since I'd flown out of Houston three months earlier. Though I had a lot to say to those clowns, I didn't think I had the strength quite yet to say it.

I hopped out of bed, got dressed, threw some clothes in my backpack, and took a cab to the bus station. While waiting for the bus, I realized I'd left my phone in my room. I thought about going back for it, but the day was already half over, and I didn't really need it anyway, so I just said fuck it. I boarded the bus, prayed the movie wouldn't involve Tom Cruise, and enjoyed the ride. We traveled north through the mountains for about six hours before approaching the coast, and soon the city was there. The lights in the distance curled around the shoreline and looked like diamonds sprinkled on an enormous dark chocolate crescent roll.

As I stared into the endless horizon, an unfamiliar song from a very familiar band barreled into my ears. Led Zeppelin had been my default number one throughout high school and most of college. I thought I'd heard every studio and live track ever recorded. Perhaps I'd always just passed it over, confusing it with "In the Evening," but when John Paul Jones's Clavinet was all that could be heard in "In the Light," and Jimmy Page began on one of his simplest yet most powerful riffs, I knew I'd come across something special—something I'd always had with me but never before experienced. I beamed golden white light and knew I'd rip that night wide open.

Eventually, the bus pulled to the side of a busy road. I got out and hopped in a cab. Mica was right; there were white people everywhere. I arrived at the hotel and paid the driver four times what I would have in Lila. Mica and Juana were in the lobby when I walked in, and Juana was already bitching about something.

"Hola, gringo," she said.

"What up, frijolera?"

"Don't call me that."

"Well, don't call me gringo."

"Frijolera is bad. Gringo is not."

"Gringo is bad to me."

"Then what would you like me to call you?"

"How about 'asshole?'"

"I won't call you that."

"Okay, frijolera."

"Okay, *asshole*!"

Thus would be the tone for the rest of our trip . . .

I checked in at the main desk, then followed Juana and Mica up the stairs. We passed a young, white gringo family on the way. The mother smiled at me. I kept walking and made sure to say something to Juana in Spanish loud enough for Mommy to hear.

I dumped my backpack on the bed closest to the door, took a quick shower, and was ready to head out the door. Juana, however, took a shower after me—a shower that lasted at least a half hour. Mica and I found some Steven Seagal flick on a crappy cable station and passed the time by watching the master class on acting. Juana finally came out of the bathroom, and Mica and I got up to go, but she sat in front of a mirror and began the endless process of straightening her hair. Fuck! Heat, spray, comb, heat, spray, comb . . . Meanwhile the ice caps melted, and the whole world was submerged by ocean. On the TV, Seagal fired two shots and seven bodies dropped in the background. Goddamn it!

We finally entered the adolescent night. Juana mentioned an all-you-can-eat Italian place somewhere on the main strip, and we hopped on a bus. We rode for twenty minutes but passed the restaurant on Juana's watch. We got out at the next stop and walked to a busy Mexican restaurant instead. Mica and I gave Juana hell for missing the Italian place, but she gave us hell right back. There was a resilience in her that I both admired and wanted to cut out of her at the same time.

We entered the packed Mexican restaurant. There were Americans everywhere (accents, style, girth—you know what I'm talking about). A number huddled around the bar. The air was tense. We pushed through the crowd and stood at the bar. An old, wrinkled couple whose accents sounded straight from the Midwest were giving the pretty Mexican girl behind the counter as much hell as their god would allow—and their god was generous.

"Whaddya mean thirty minutes!" the wicked old woman yelled in English. "You just sat someone that came in *after* us."

"No." The girl remained cool and responded in perfect English. "They were here before you. Thirty minutes."

The old woman crossed her arms and rolled her eyes. I snorted in laughter and smiled at the girl behind the bar. She smiled back. The mid-thirties white woman sitting next to me knocked on the bar beside an empty basket. "More chips!" The girl behind the counter grabbed the basket, dumped in some tortilla chips, and tossed it back on the counter as some older man wearing a Hawaiian shirt leaned over my shoulder: "Perdon, senorita, uh, well, pa-demos, uh . . . tener? Yes, pa-demos tener una mess-a?"

"She speaks English, you know," I said to him.

"It's okay," he said, "I'm a high school Spanish teacher."

"Sounds like it . . ."

The girl behind the counter laughed.

The Spanish teacher walked away, and I squeezed between the chip monster to my left and the cantankerous geriatric couple to my right.

"Hey," I said to the girl behind the counter, "I know you're busy. What's the wait for a table?"

She smiled at me. "If you can wait a few moments, I think we have a table opening up in back."

I smiled at her. "Could I get some chips in the meantime?"

"Yes, you can have some of these." She pointed to basket in front of the snarling beast to my left. "They are for everybody." The girl pulled the basket away from the chip monster while she wasn't looking and set it in front of me. I dug in. Chippy soon noticed.

"Like I *wasn't* eating those!" she said.

"Hey, lady, she said they were for everybody."

"Those are mine!" There was no sign of life in her.

I decided against arguing. I picked up the basket and genuflected before her: "Your chips, Your Majesty."

"Why you pompous little shit!"

I dumped the basket on her lap. She shrieked.

"Oh, I'm sorry, did I purposely dump an entire basket of chips on your lap?"

"You dirty son of a bitch! Just wait 'til my husband sees! He's so much bigger than you!"

"You know, I saw some big dude blowin' a twelve-year-old Mexican boy around back . . ."

The wrinkled couple pushed into my right side. "How much longer 'til we can get a damn table?"

I turned to Grandma. "Hey, she already told you thirty fucking minutes! If you don't like it, why don't you leave, you filthy old bag of bones?"

The girl behind the counter laughed out loud. The old woman sneered at me. I turned to Mica and Juana. "Let's get the fuck outta here."

We pushed through the crowd toward the door.

"You know," I said out loud, to no one in particular, "everyone ages, but few ever mature past middle school . . . *And these people are on vacation!*"

We ate at a taco stand and walked to the main drag. Thousands of people filled the bars and strolled the Malecon, a mile-long esplanade along the beach, which was filled with street performers: mimes, human robots, magicians . . . The best part of our walk down the Malecon was seeing the small groups of people on the beach mounding and shaping big heaps of sand into castles, mermaids, shrines to the Virgin Mother . . . The worst was seeing the white assholes decked out in sombreros and party beads, stumbling around and shouting shit about "tacos" and "cerveza." If I'd had any doubt before as to why I was a magnet for Sprite bottles here, it was now gone. I'd take a million pairs of Mexican eyes staring me down daily and fight some new Mexican jack-off every weekend just so I never had to see those fuckers in the sombreros ever again. These dicks wouldn't last a second in the barrio dressed like that. And they'd break down the second they were separated from the pack and later tell their tale of horror on some contrived MTV soapbox program warning of the dangers of excess and the unknown while abroad—a show that would be followed by some old episodes of *Spring Break*. Sombrero was the bastard who always returned from places like Mexico with tales of being shaken down by the federales for pissing in some alley, then spending a chilling night in a Mexican jail cell shared with some scary guy named Pepe who had a snake tattooed on his arm. These fuckers needed that night with Pepe. I wished I had a badge myself to haul 'em in.

But more than vengeance, I just wanted to be left alone. But even if I left Vallarta, I could never leave my skin color or heritage. If Sombrero pissed in some alley and got caught, this would further perpetuate the stereotype that gringos lacked respect and appreciation for other cultures, causing every cop I passed to analyze my every moment to be sure I wasn't pissing all over his house, car, wife, and kids while he wasn't looking—that caused cops to challenge my every step, robbing me of my most basic of freedoms. Just take off the fucking sombrero, please! Wipe off the damned painted-on mustache! Wear that shit at your Cinco de Mayo frat party at Fuck-Off State!

The fuckers found me. I didn't want a fight. I just wanted to be left alone. I was so sick of hiding . . . But damn it, I think I wore a fucking sombrero at least once while walking the main strip in Cancun when I was eighteen. My head felt like it was going to explode.

Juana's constant whining didn't help: "Come on, boys, let's go dancing!"

"Just take it easy, all right?"

The German felt the same as I did, so we decided to pop into some bar advertising eighty-peso cubetas. We sat and ordered a bucket of Pacifico, and the waiter dropped a bill on the table nearly the moment we opened our first beers.

"Wait, buddy," I said, "the sign out front says these beers cost eighty pesos. Why's the bill say two hundred forty?"

"The sign is for tomorrow."

"It didn't say anything about tomorrow."

"Yes, the beers are two hundred forty pesos."

"Yo, Mica, this prick's giving us the gringo-special on this cubeta."

"Eh, just pay him. I don't feel like dealing with these people right now."

"Christ, that's all my money for the rest of the night." I turned to the waiter. "How about we give you eighty and you walk away?"

"Then I will be forced to call the police."

Fuck! We each tossed some money in, handed it over, and he walked away. I guess it didn't matter that we were traveling with a Mexican—we'd always be gringos first. A well-endowed woman wearing a skintight suit shimmied over to our table. She blew a whistle and shoved a bottle into Mica's mouth. She did the same to Juana. I refused. I knew where this was going.

"Eighty pesos, please."

"Whoa, lady," Mica said, "you forced that bottle into my mouth. I didn't ask for it."

"Eighty pesos."

She stuck out her hand, and Mica filled it with cash. We left that bar three hundred and twenty pesos shorter and hadn't even caught a buzz. That was enough to buy almost twenty-seven caguamas in Lila—an amount that could have kept us drunk all weekend. The street was even busier when we stepped onto it again, and we noticed that a lot of people were drinking out of large disposable cups. We stopped some old drunk holding one.

"Hey, where'd you get that? Does a bar sell them?"

"No, it's legal to drink on the streets here. You just need to put your drinks in a cup like this."

"Holy shit, that's great news!"

Mica and I dragged Juana to the first Kiosko we could find. He and I each bought a sixer of Tecate, and Juana got a few wine coolers. We grabbed some ice chunks from a big tub in the front of the store, dumped them in our plastic bags, and walked to the Malecon where we sat and drank.

"Hurry up, boys. I want to dance!" Juana said.

"So dance, nobody's stopping you."

"So, just the other day," Mica said to me, "I went to this burger place on Madrid del Rio with a friend from school. I asked the guy at the drive-thru for a cheeseburger and fries, and he said, 'Okay, two cheeseburgers and a Coke.' And I said, 'No, one cheeseburger and one fries,' and he said, 'Okay, a Coke and one fries.' It went on like that for another few minutes before we had to pull around to the main window to get the order right. These people, they're so fucking stupid. I don't know whether they are doing these things on purpose, but it drives me insane."

"Yeah, that's the same shit with the ladies I work for. I don't know if they're just fucking with me. Maybe it's just a translation issue?"

"Could be."

"Come *on,* boys. I want to dance!"

"Shut the hell up, Juanda! Nobody wants to dance but you."

"Ayy, cabrones!"

Juana took our advice and decided to start dancing, only with the surrealist sculptures on the Malecon. She pirouetted in front of a ladder where two children were climbing away from their mother. Mica continued with another story, but I'd had enough of the vitriol. I walked away from him and lay on my back at the edge of the concrete with my head pivoted over the side. If not for my neck, my melon would have split open on one of the large rocks scattered on the beach several feet below. I stared at the horizon with a new perspective. Though the sun had already set, there was a deep maroon hue that seemed to be glowing from the ocean. I couldn't tell what was sky or water, and lost myself in the abyss. This silence was broken minutes later with Juana's whining.

"Come on, let's go dance! I only have so many weekends where I don't have to care for my mother, and I want to relax."

"I'll tell you what," I said as I continued to stare at the horizon. "Next weekend, you bring your mom down to my place, and I'll take care of you both."

Before I had time to react, Juana had her hands clenched around my throat.

"DON'T YOU EVER TALK ABOUT MY MOTHER, CABRON!"

I ripped from her grip and started laughing, wondering whether I'd have been gushing at that moment if she'd had a knife.

"Just relax, all right," I said. "Nobody wants to fuck your mother."

"CALLATE CABRON!"

She started to cry, and I gulped down her tears—perhaps to cool some overheating system inside. But the heat was too much and boiled those tears, leaving behind only a thin sediment of misery, which continued to layer deeply inside me with each tear of hers I imbibed. And after all those years of drinking the world's sadness, my entire bottom half had calcified, and even though I wanted to run away from that damned conversation, movement was impossible with legs of stone.

"Except, maybe Herb," I said. "Whaddya think, Mica?"

"Herb would fuck blender set on puree."

Juana turned away, crying into her hands.

"Come on," Mica said, "we were just kidding."

I wanted to turn and swan dive onto the rocks below. But instead, I walked down the stairway and took a piss on the sand beside some gringo in a sombrero. I let down my defenses and allowed the chemicals inside of me to rage, and once they settled, I passed them through and into the sand. Juana had been nothing less than a great friend in the short time I'd known her, always quick to lend me her time, car, or money. I don't know why she put up with us. I don't know why she considered us friends. But then again, people have put up with far more bullshit and still kissed it on the lips.

I walked back up the stairs. Just say you're sorry. Tell her you didn't mean to hurt her feelings. Tell her she's a good friend and that you respect and care about her . . .

"Fuck it, let's go dancing."

Juana stopped crying. "No, I don't want to dance anymore. Let's just go get some drinks at the bar over there." She pointed at the place across the street blasting live rock music.

"You sure you don't want to go dancing? We'll go with you." I pointed to Mica.

"No, let's just go there."

We walked through the entrance and up three flights of stairs, and somehow found an empty table by a window despite the large, roaring crowd. I felt awful—both body and mind strangled up in this horrible, mangled spire. I could feel the chemicals rushing up my back like raging rivers. My muscles squeezed and mind raced, and neither could relax. But this was nothing new. I ordered a drink and tried to lose myself in the music. A five-person cover band burned through hits with much more skill than Rudi's trio. Most were nineties tunes: Soundgarden, Alice in Chains, Pearl Jam . . . No Cranberries or "Creep" though.

We sat next to a group of five or six rowdy Mexican guys who howled and applauded at the peaks and finales of each song. One called to me: "Hey, gringo, thank you for the music!"

"The name's Will. And don't mention it—especially since I didn't write it."

"No importa, whey. This was my favorite era of music. We play in a band too . . ." He gestured to the rest of the guys at the table, and they nodded and waved.

"I played some S.T.P. and Radiohead tunes with some other guys in college," I said. "We put together a band but never found a decent enough drummer to do us justice."

"What do you play?"

"Guitar—rhythm."

"Do you play acoustic?"

"Mostly acoustic."

"I am going to be playing an open mic at a restaurant tomorrow, and I could use another acoustic player to fill out the sound—especially one who can sing in English. Do you know any songs from Nirvana's unplugged album?"

"A few, but parts, not entire songs."

"Well, they aren't very complicated. I could teach you the other parts if you'd like to play with me."

"What time and where?"

"Just down the street. Meet me outside of here around eleven tomorrow morning."

"Eleven's a little early for me, man. If I can get up, I'm in."

"Okay, friend. Welcome to Vallarta! Let me know if I can make your stay better in any way. Mi casa es su casa."

We left a little while later. I had some trouble getting down the stairs and knew there was no way I'd be ready at eleven a.m. Goddamn, there was no way I'd be ready at any time. But at least the tension was easing. What more could someone offer than their home and their song? We decided against a cab and walked the three miles back to the hotel. Mica offered to pay, but Juana and I declined. It was important to give my pride a workout at least some of the time.

When I woke the next morning, it took me a minute to remember where I was. For some reason, our hotel door was open even though I was the first one up. I looked at the time: ten-thirty. I could still make it . . . But I reached out with my foot, kicked the door shut, and went back to sleep.

I woke up an hour later to Juana's first whinings of the new day.

"Get up, lazy boys! Let's get some food."

We got up, and ready, and followed her to the street.

"So what do you want, Juanita?"

"Anything but pollo."

Upon hearing the word "pollo," Mica and I decided that was exactly what we wanted so we dragged her along to a Pollo Frito fast-food joint.

We ate, then walked to the beach. Again we got lost trusting Juana's navigational skills, so we just followed the sound of the waves and looked for the heaviest concentration of hawkers peddling shitty beach trinkets. On the way, we passed a group of young men fixing a cracked section of sidewalk. I wondered if any of them had worked with Cisco. One looked up and stared me down. I tried to explain with my eyes that I knew one of his friends, but it was useless. While Cisco may have once broken his own back alongside these guys, he also ate in fancy restaurants and rode in planes.

Our strategy worked, and we found the beach. The hounding began the moment we stepped on the sand. A toothless sun-shriveled drunk followed us down the beach showing us shell necklaces, and rub-on tattoos, and wooden figurines of the virgin mother: "You buy, you buy . . ." He didn't leave until we'd said no to everything he had.

We found a good spot beside a guy offering parasailing rides and in front of a large resort. We spread out the towels we'd swiped from our hotel's linen closet and lay down. I pulled out my music, reached into a plastic Kiosko bag, and pulled out an ice-cold Tecate. The stuff ripped up my insides, but it was cheap . . . and my insides were already a fucking shitshow. I presented the bag to my friends. The German grabbed a brew, and the Mexican declined.

"Come on, borrachos, let's go swimming," Juana said.

"I don't feel like swimming."

"Yeah, I'd rather get drunk."

"You two are impossible!"

I put my hands to my mouth and made a loud farting noise. One of the middle-aged white women sitting under the resort's beachside palapa gave me a dirty look. I showed her my favorite finger, and she continued reading her book. *These fucking people travel two thousand miles to read a goddamned book!*

The hawkers came in waves. I swear another approached every thirty seconds, all with different variations of the same shit: friendship bracelets, hair beads, stupid statues made from coconut shells . . . Or they'd just send their dirty, innocent little kids to stick out their hands and beg for "centavos, por favor."

"Sorry, I need my centavos for beer, ninitos. Go back and beg your mother to enroll you in school." It was too much for me. "Hey, Juanda, would you mind holding my wallet and music while I take a dip?"

"Sure."

"C'mon, Mica . . ."

Mica got up and followed me to the water.

"Ayy, pinche cabrones!" She pumped her fist at us.

We walked into the brown water, which I welcomed despite Herb, Sal, and Cisco's warning that it was "some of the most polluted in Mexico." Little piles of garbage floated by: candy wrappers, plastic bottles, beer cans . . . I took a deep breath and submerged my head. Christ, the water was so warm. It was November. I thought of all the kids wrapped in layers heading to classes up the hills of Conesus. I thought about the deep winter freeze that would soon blow into Buffalo from the northwest and trap the city in several months of white wasteland. The water here may have been filthy, but it was warm. My muscles felt loose. I'd had a few beers already, and the sun was shining overhead. Did life exist if I didn't myself experience it? Did people still struggle if I shut them out of mind? I let the questions float away with the garbage. Here I was, bobbing along, swollen stomach like a buoy. Despite that swelling, I was still scoring with Mexico's best and brightest. I was drunk or stoned almost every night but still somehow managed to stay employed. And I still somehow had Luz. God, if I went under and couldn't get back to the surface for air, it'd probably take weeks before my swollen body would make it back to Buffalo. If I was going to go down, now was the time. There was no one else there I could pull down with me—it was just me and all the world's misery. I'd done it. I'd found my place to hide forever. But I could only hold my breath for so long . . .

My head pierced the surface of the ocean, and I took a deep breath. Surrounding me on most sides were wrinkled mountains jetting far out into the sea. Mica and I got out of the water and took a walk along the sand. The first section of beach was about the same: sun-reddened gringos sitting under palapas or umbrellas, sipping tropical drinks, and reading the latest shit-dump off the best-sellers list.

We walked under a stone pier and came across another section of beach, which was filled with lively Mexicans. There were people everywhere: in the ocean, jumping into waves; on the sand, playing futbol; under umbrellas, sucking down beers and laughing with family and friends.

We came to another stone pier, walked underneath, and entered another section of beach. This seemed much tamer—much like the first section. There was something different about this area though that I didn't realize until several men in pastel-colored Speedos started whistling at Mica and me.

We returned to the first section, the one where we felt we most belonged, and sank back into the water. A few minutes later, a group of about twelve teenage guys drifted toward us. We moved away, but they kept coming at their increasingly more obvious target. Soon they had us surrounded. They ignored us and spoke with one another while treading water. Then I felt a bump from behind—maybe an elbow? Then a kick. I threw one back. They continued their game of "accidentally" hitting us while talking shit about gringos. Their words were fast and coated in slang, but Mica and I understood enough to know we weren't wanted on their beach. Mica quickly gave up and headed for the sand. I, however, stood my water for another ten minutes, exchanging kicks and elbows with those bigoted shitheads. But I knew my stand was hopeless. I swam back to shore—kicking in all directions—and walked back to my towel.

Juana looked up at me with sad eyes.

"Will you go swimming with me?"

"You can go. I'm not welcome here anymore."

She ran off for the ocean. I lay on my towel and opened another beer. The parasail floated almost directly overhead and rippled in the breeze. I pulled out my camera and snapped a picture but did so just as a group of thirty-something Mexican guys walked by. One stopped, leaned in, and said in horrible English, "Oh, so you want to take my picture? Then take my picture. Take whatever you want. Take it all."

I didn't respond. I just put the camera away and took another swig of beer. I was so damned tired of it all. I felt like a billboard, immobile but still on display in the limbo before me—shadow elongating in the dying sunlight. Defeated, I just wanted to escape to a place where I was at least a customer or colleague. The sun dove beyond the mountains and the Mexicans won, emerging from all angles to reclaim their beach. I didn't fight it. I just observed what I could, and we left. This time, I didn't stop Mica when he waved down a cab. We rode back to the hotel and let Juana take the first shower.

When we walked down the stairs and out into the night, Juana hit us with the same shit: "Let's dance!"

"Later, Juanda. We got some business to attend to first."

Mica and I decided to avoid the gringo-gouging and headed to a Kiosko. We went with Sol that night to avoid the inevitable next-day Tecate stomachache. Juana bought some fruit juice and sighed when she saw us purchase a twelve pack.

We headed back to our customized beach bar. That night was almost the same as the previous. Mica and I ranted about all the shit that pissed us off while Juana danced around subconscious images cast in bronze.

"We had a house meeting with the landlady the other day," Mica said. "Hugo had complained to her many times about the parties, noise, and people constantly stopping over. It got pretty intense. He started yelling at me, and I understood nearly everything he said. I was pretty impressed with myself."

"That's crazy."

"Yeah, we had to write up a list of house rules. There are ten of them, which include: no parties, no drugs, no playing cards, and my favorite, no Turd. I insisted on that last one."

"I like *that* rule. Dude's got the charm of a dead water buffalo."

"Come on, borrachos, let's go dancing!"

We did it that night. We went to some shitty dance club with no cover charge. It was filled with the usual bullshit: "Oh wow, you're from Schenectady? I'm from Utica! Small world, right? We should exchange email addresses . . ."

Mica and I sat at the bar while Juana danced, and soon the night was over.

We got a late start the next day and walked the town for most of the afternoon before deciding on dinner. Juana knew a great seafood place near the ocean, and we were all in after she convinced us she actually knew where it was. We followed her, and it was where she said it would be: the second floor of a building above a travel agency. We walked through the travel agency and up the rear stairwell into the restaurant.

The waitress seated us at a balcony table overlooking the city. I ordered the garlic shrimp and devoured it when it came. We paid and headed back downstairs. Some middle-aged Brit in the travel agency sprang into action when he saw us. I assumed he'd try to sell us on some vacation package or some shit, but he told us he didn't work there. We walked out to the busy sidewalk and the Brit's drunk French friend approached. The dude was a scrawny, rat-faced mess of hair and incoherent conversation. He squinted his eyes and slurred his words and kept grabbing onto passing strangers as if they were longtime buddies. I thought someone was going to knock him out, but no one did.

The Brit, however, spoke clearly and rationally. "Well, friends, I had enough of the rat race in England. Life is too short and precious a thing to waste. So, I packed it all in and moved to Mexico about ten years ago. I am an expatriate, and I say that proudly. I have given up on money and the accumulation of 'things.' I don't work, but rather spend my time exploring myself and the world around me. I live on the floor in my friend's house and have found a way to survive on almost no money . . ."

Though trite, he delivered his speech with such sincerity and dignity that I kept an open mind. After all, some of that philosophical fuel pumped my pistons too. But the more he spoke, however, the more I realized how properly matched he was with his babbling French buddy.

". . . And now, finally, after fifty-three years, my life is approaching its zenith. I've just found my true love, a beautiful girl I met on the computer. Though she's just seventeen, she's already filled with a lifetime of wisdom and good karma. We're going on a soul-finding excursion in the woods next week. We're not bringing a tent or anything else with us. We're just going to live off the land for as long as nature allows. I can't wait to meet her. She's my cosmic soul mate."

All this talk about "cosmic soul mates" and sub-subsistence living got to me. I leaned in to Mica and put my hand on his shoulder: "Yo, man . . ." I said. I looked beyond Mica and saw that the Brit had his arm around the French guy's shoulder. They were telling each passing woman that she was beautiful. I took my hand off Mica's shoulder. "Let's get the fuck outta here while we still can."

We gestured to Juana and took off down the street. We'd already bought our bus tickets home and were leaving that night at twelve thirty. My stomach was burning, and I had no intention on further disturbing it, but when Mica suggested we head back to the Kiosko and spend the rest of our vacation at our beach bar, my stomach whimpered in defeat.

That night was the same as the previous two. The German and I finished our liquid dessert, and he went back for another twelve pack. It was only eleven, so we still had some time to burn. Mica came back with the juice, and we went at it. Lengua wanted me in at seven the next morning, but I was done with their bullshit. I dumped my beer down the hatch and tried to drown out any insubordinate thoughts that might push me to show up to work. Fuck them! Fuck the dancing! Fuck the wall! Fuck the goddamned ocean battles!

We crushed through the twelve pack and still had time for a caguama, so I walked back to the Kiosko, but it was locked. I knocked on the glass, and the girl behind the counter pointed at her watch. 12:01. I'd missed it by a fucking minute . . . I gave her the sad eyes, but she was oak.

I returned to the beach heated.

"No beer?"

"No beer."

"This fucking place is driving me crazy."

Meanwhile, each of Juana's attempts to get our useless asses moving were thwarted by our indifference to the situation. Mica and I were both furious yet playfully drunk, a potentially dangerous combination—the kind that can lead to felonies.

"Come on, borrachos, we need to go!"

At around twelve ten, the sober Mexican finally convinced us to get moving. Juana ran to the road and hailed a cab while we slugged along behind. The driver was a man in his early twenties. He helped us load our bags in the trunk. Mica and I stuffed ourselves into the back seat and Juana took the front. She told the driver where we were going, then said, "Please hurry!" He nodded, and we jolted to a quick start.

About a minute later, Mica asked the driver if he knew of any place along the way that sold beer. Juana turned, gave him the look of death, and pleaded with the driver not to listen to us "borrachos."

We sped through the city, down the main strip of luxury hotels and shops, and eventually returned to the Mexico we knew and loved as we drove along a desolate stretch of highway between progress and the bus station. Suddenly, the driver pulled over. I looked around. This was no bus station.

"You can buy beer here after twelve," the driver said, pointing to a small corner store.

"Ay, no, we don't have time!" Juana said.

"I'll be right back . . ." I jumped out of the cab, ran inside, and bought a sixer of something cold. I hopped back in the cab, and we took off. Juana was steaming.

We arrived at the bus station at exactly twelve-thirty. Juana ran inside and asked someone behind the desk where we had to go. Mica and I stumbled in like Raoul Duke and his attorney.

"What's the deal, Juanita?" I said.

"The bus is late. We don't leave for another fifteen minutes."

I started laughing, then opened a beer. I tossed one to Mica, but he was so drunk that it hit him in the nose, then fell into the backpack he was hugging to his chest. He grabbed it out, opened it, and we sat down. The bus came, and we boarded. Juana sat in front beside a woman with a sleeping child. I glowered at her, then pushed to the back where there were no other passengers. I cracked open another beer and watched as Mica blew in like a warm front, rising quickly and weighing down on the cool air in front of me. He was mumbling to himself.

"These people are so stupid—"

"What happened?"

"I just asked the driver what time we should expect to be back in Lila, and he said, 'eleven o'clock.' I told him that it was only an eight-hour ride, and he said, 'Well, if you knew how long it was, why'd you ask?' These people are so stupid!"

I laughed and tossed him another beer. We were two dark rain clouds absorbing all the misery around us and were ready to dump it down like a monsoon. Juana came back and started lecturing us on something, so I put on some music and shut my eyes. When I opened them minutes later, Mica was gone. I scanned the bus and saw him in the last seat in the back. I suspected he'd thought it sensible to provide a larger buffer zone between himself and humanity. I walked back there for the sake of all the kind strangers throughout my life who'd brightened my day with an unexpected smile or helping hand when I was feeling low.

When I saw Mica, however, I realized something wasn't right. Though there was a clean and fully functional bathroom about a meter to his right, Mica had whipped it out and was pissing all over the rear seat. I whipped mine out too, lucidly aware of the consequences of indulging in the darkness inside of me. But before squeezing a drop, I thought for a moment, then stuffed it back in my pants, zipped up, and walked back to my seat.

Mica rejoined me near the middle of the bus. A black hole was growing behind me, sucking at the hair at the back of my head like a vacuum. But I ignored it. Instead, Mica and I started shouting at the driver:

"PUT ON A MOVIE!"

"YEAH, I WANNA SEE TOM CRUUUUUUUUUUUUUISE!"

Mica hurled a beer can in his direction, and I threw one at Juana, nailing her behind the head. She stormed over.

"AYY, CABRONES, STOP IT! BEHAVE!"

Christ, I was an eight-year-old all over again. Soon, I passed out in my seat. I woke up the next morning to the sound of Juana's nagging. She was holding all the empties Mica and I'd thrown the night before and kept repeating something I didn't care to let my mind translate. I got up, walked past her in mid-nag, exited the bus, and walked into the Zambulla bus station where we had to make a transfer on the trip home.

I was still piss drunk and judging by Mica's half-closed eyes and general incoherence, I could see I wasn't alone. We wandered to the counter to buy tickets back to Lila. Juana ordered.

"Okay, borrachos, that's fifty-six pesos each."

I pulled out my wallet. All gone. "I spent all my money on beer last night."

"Me too."

"Ayy, cabrones!"

She put all three tickets on her card. We got the tickets, walked through security—a smiling old woman sitting beside a metal detector—and sat by a window in the waiting room. We sat with our backs to the buses outside and looked out into the crowded room. It was early and most were likely on their way to work. I wanted to disappear inside of myself, but my muscles could squeeze me inward only so much.

"I can't believe that pinche asshole from last night," Mica said. "'If you knew, then why'd you ask?' These people are all so fucking stupid."

I started laughing. Juana turned away from us. It didn't take much knowledge of the English language to know what he was saying. People must have been listening to us making fools of ourselves, but nobody stepped in to stop it. Why wouldn't they say anything? Fucking bastards. Mica kept ranting and ended each of his anecdotes with "These people are so fucking stupid," which he said louder and louder each time until it was impossible for anyone around us to pretend they didn't understand. But still nothing. It was like some evil therapy session. I looked outside and saw a young boy, wearing nothing but a diaper, hanging onto a handrail above an eight-foot drop—all in front of his parents, who stood around talking and laughing. Maybe I should have done something, but instead I looked on as would a *National Geographic* photographer capturing a shot of an injured gazelle being torn into by a lion. I then looked at Mica. Were *we* the crazy ones? Fuck, I mean, at least we were trying . . .

The time came, and we walked to our bus. Once inside, Mica and I were slapped back into reality. The bus was packed with people, and our bullshit from the previous night wouldn't be tolerated here. We walked down the aisle and found our seats. The German sat first, claiming the window, and quickly fell asleep. I sat and shut my eyes but opened them each time some asshole knocked into my shoulder on the way to their seat. The bus took off, and I lowered the window shade. This would be no spiritual experience.

I tried to sleep but felt searing pain in my stomach as if Lucifer himself was twisting his pitchfork in my gut. While I had no idea which end the crap inside me would choose to exit, I did know I'd have no say in the matter. I pondered my escape route in case of emergency. There was no bathroom on this bus, so—should the urge strike—the best I could hope for would be to cover my lap with a t-shirt, lower my pants, and release the garlic shrimp into my backpack. I tried to fight it. I tried to relax. Mica slept peacefully beside me. That bastard got off easy. My whole body shook and sweat soaked into my clothes. Inside, the magma was preparing for release. I needed the AC, but it was off. I was a raging ball of fire and growing more desperate by the moment. Fight it, Willy! At least you know when your time is up! Only another forty-five minutes. You can do this!

My moment's greatest wish was fulfilled when we arrived at the Lila bus station, and I still had a clean backpack. Somehow, the pain in my stomach subsided as we exited the bus. I was still damp with sweat as we walked to the road. We hailed a cab, and I demanded to be released first. The full load of my misery was still with me when I got out under the almond trees. I walked inside the house, dropped my bags, then the load, swore I'd never pour another Tecate through my body, and took a nap. It was noon when my head hit the pillow— five hours past my class with Joaquin. I swear I felt some dark spirit in the corner . . . watching . . . laughing. The fucking horror!

Chapter 33

When I got home from Vallarta, my bedroom door was wide open even though I always locked it when I wasn't there. Everything in my room seemed to be in order except that a picture of Luz was missing from my mirror. I'd just assumed Sal had picked the lock to get something he needed and swiped the picture to fuck with me.

Mica came over for dinner that night, and we went to his place for a small "get-together." We figured we weren't breaking house rules if we called it that and not a party. Several of the extraneros were blazing in Mica's room when I arrived, and I hopped right into the circle. My new roommate, Jimmy, showed up a short while later.

"Hey, man," I said to him, "anything strange happen in my room over the weekend? The door was open when I got back from Vallarta, and now it's dragging on the tile."

"Oh, uh, no, I didn't see anything."

"You sure?"

"Well, I did bring a girl home on Saturday, and, uh, she thought it was *my* room, so she opened it."

"Was she some kind of Amazon woman? I always lock it when I'm not there."

"Oh, haha, yes, she is strong. I think she opened your door, but then I tell her, 'Hey, wait, that is not my room,' so she left."

"Do you know if she took anything? I'm missing a picture."

"Oh, uh, yeah, I can get your picture back for you . . ."

"All right, cool, man—hey, you get a little trim?"

"Oh, yeah, she and I did it hard."

I laughed as Jimmy pumped his fist to his chest. He got in on the rotation. The story was swiss, but at least I knew I'd be getting back the picture of my princess.

I left early and followed the panteon home. When I got to my room, I shut the door, undressed, and hopped in bed. I felt around on the table near my bed for my phone so I could check my texts. Nothing. I turned on the light. No-fucking-where. I always left my stuff in the same spots, otherwise I'd lose everything, and I was pretty sure I'd left my phone on that table before I left for Vallarta. I searched all over but couldn't find it. I got dressed and waited out front for Jimmy. Soon he rounded the corner.

"So, a girl *accidentally* broke into my room, huh?"

"Oh, well, uh—"

"Where the fuck is my phone? I want my fucking phone!"

"What do you mean?"

"Don't play stupid, man. Follow me."

We walked to my room.

"I left my phone right here before I left for Vallarta. Tell me why it isn't here."

"Uh—"

"Where the fuck is my phone, you shady piece of shit?"

"I'm sorry, I'm so sorry—"

"I want my phone now, or I'm gonna beat your fuckin' ass!"

"Please, wait, I will find it. I will get it back."

I punched my closet door. "I'll fuck you up, man. Go get my damn phone!"

He started crying. I liked Jimmy—much more so than I liked the phone. He'd recently started running with Sal and me, and he always told great stories as we ran. He was also well-liked by the extraneros. He was a good guy with a good heart. But his tears sent me into a frenzy. I punched the door again.

"Please . . . I can't tonight. I will get it tomorrow . . ."

"If I don't have it tomorrow, I'm gonna hurt you and whoever took it."

"I'm . . . I'm sorry."

Jimmy left the house and didn't come back until the morning. And when he returned, he had my phone and the picture. Later, I heard some rumors that supported my suspicions: this had something to do with that prick Turd. Jimmy had thrown a party while I was in Vallarta, and that fucking weasel showed up. I didn't see much more of Jimmy the rest of that month. In fact, he moved out a few weeks later. Though Jimmy had been one of my better friends, seeing him burst into tears as he handed me that phone did nothing to mollify me. I wasn't yet sure if this was something I feared or enjoyed. I'd spent so much of my life kissing people's asses to keep the peace. Letting them violate my wafer-thin boundaries just to maintain balance. But not anymore. I was gaining a reputation among the extraneros. Nobody was going to fuck with me. Even if I'd never make another friend again, nobody was gonna fuck with me.

On the day before Luz's return, I spent the afternoon at Mica's. I was flipping through his Mexican guidebook and stopped on a picture of Palenque—that was the spot calling my name. It seemed so exotic: monkeys, and rainforest, and Mayan ruins.

"Hey," I said, "we should take a trip. I want to see all of Mexico."

"That'd be cool. But I thought you didn't have any money?"

"Got enough now . . . I just need to get the fuck outta here, man. I'm gonna seriously hurt somebody if I stay here."

"I'm in."

"We should go all the way to Cancun. I went there on spring break when I was eighteen. I want to go back."

"I have a month off school from the second week of December into January."

"We should hit all the big spots in between: Puebla, Mexico City, Chiapas . . ."

"I'd love to go to Mexico City, but everyone I know who's been there has been robbed. The Canadian and Ecuadorian just went a few weeks ago and someone nicked their wallets on the metro."

"We'll be fine."

"I have a friend who might be interested in joining us."

And so it went . . . We planned a route, researched hostels and hotels, and booked tickets to our first destination, Mexico City.

Luz sent me a text while Mica and I were making preparations: "Hey, baby, I'm in D.F. right now, and I miss you!"

"Hey, Luz is in Mexico City!"

"Tell her I said hi."

"Hey, cutie," I wrote, "what's the weather like there?"

She responded: "Very cool. It's up in the mountains. I'm wearing a jacket. I miss you! I'll be home tomorrow."

"She said it's cool! I can't wait to get away from this damned heat."

Luz arrived in Lila the next day. She sent me a text asking if I'd like to get some lunch, and I wrote back, "Yes." About ten minutes later, the white hatchback came rolling downhill. A girl I didn't recognize hopped out of the passenger door and walked to the house. It was my Luz, and she'd gotten a haircut—one that somehow altered the entire image I had of her in my subconscious. I walked to the door, leaving the cold familiarity of my dark cave behind. We hugged and our lips met awkwardly for a kiss, which seemed more scripted than spontaneous. We got in the car and Luz Blanco drove off. No one said much.

Luz Blanco dropped us off at my Luz's apartment and left. My Luz walked to the door, reached her hand through the broken glass, and opened it from inside. We walked upstairs and into her apartment, and she shut and locked the door. All at once, the walls seemed to pulsate.

"So, uh, how was the trip from Mexico City?"

"Nice."

I could see she felt it too. "And Costa Rica?"

". . . good."

"Oh, and, uh, Pana—"

"I have missed you." She looked sad when she said that—a sadness that seemed less from regret over our time lost together and more from the uncertainty of our current time being shared.

"Yeah, it's, uh, been a long time."

I pulled her to me, and we kissed. She led me to her room. She sat on the edge of the bed. I slowly took off my clothes, and trembled waiting for her subtle consent. She kissed my stomach, and soon she was lying naked and trembling beside me on the bed. She spread her legs, and looked at me with these shameful eyes, as though I were her king and she just some servant girl going through the motions of a life of unquestioned duty. I felt the urge to conquer but remained controlled.

"You know," she said, "you didn't call me once while I was gone."

"Well, they, uh, stole my . . ."

I pushed my way inside her. She bit her lip, which seemed less due to ecstasy and more as a defense to hold back on revealing some terrible secret she was keeping from me. The wetness washed away any doubts I was still her man. Though wet, she wasn't warm. I could feel her raised pores rubbing against me like sandpaper, digging and scraping into my skin, leaving thousands of mortal wounds scattered across my body, draining me slowly, and reminding me that even a king has to someday stand before his maker and account for everything. But, since I was already deep inside this sin, why not see it through? I allowed the chemicals to surge—my muscles squeezed and mind strangled. I pushed harder and harder, searching for that feeling. My heart pounded and pulse raced. Harder and harder. I gasped for breath. I could feel her body on overdrive as well. She was just a teenager, but she loved it—enjoying my evil . . . our evil? Harder and harder until it revealed itself, and I clamped down on it with everything I had, then . . .

I dragged myself off her and that rented bed and staggered to the bathroom. Luz stayed behind, resting her hand over her racing heart and staring upward into some abyss—staring as if she'd just dutifully abandoned the last bit of her youth, as commanded, and was now searching that terrible void for the meaning of her blind service and sacrifice. I'd just blown a darkness inside of her not natural to her form. I should have done the decent thing and climbed out of that bathroom window, abandoning my clothes, and shoes, and love, and never looked back.

I bent over the sink, arms bracing my body on the counter. I stared deeply into the mirror. My body was still strong, and beautiful, and every bit my own.

I rejoined Luz in her room. She had a desfile de modas, or fashion show, that weekend, and she had to meet with the show's choreographer in el Centro that afternoon to prepare.

I lay on her bed naked and watched her dress. She sang a Mexican folk song as she stared into the mirror and brushed makeup on her cheeks. Something about the song soothed me. Something about the softness of her voice eased those scathing inside me. She ran a brush through her hair, pulled it back, and held it together with an elastic band. I got up and hugged her from behind. Her clothes felt warm against my skin.

"I did miss you. I'm sorry I never called . . . It's just, I—"

She turned and kissed my cheek while hooking an earring in her ear and never missing a beat with the song. She patted my bare ass.

"Let's go, hermoso. I don't want to be late."

I put on my t-shirt, jeans, and hat, and we walked out the door hand in hand. How quickly man can forgive! I'd basically quit Lengua and had nothing to do that afternoon. Fashion wasn't exactly my passion, but at least we could get some Italian food in el

Centro afterward. We walked to the road. Luz put her hand up, and a driver stopped almost immediately. We got in and rode through the cobblestone streets as Luz and I wrapped our bodies around one another.

The cab stopped in front of a small shop, and we got out. The other models, six girls about Luz's age, were in the rear of the store trying on clothes and checking them out in the mirrors near the changing rooms. They moved with hurried and joyless energy. Luz joined them but moved at her own pace. I browsed the men's section. Each garment looked handmade. The shop's owner, a woman in her early thirties, and Eduardo, the desfile's choreographer, were busy giving the "tsk tsk" to whatever the girls were trying on. A girl would come out of a dressing room, and Ed and the woman would invariably shake their heads, skipping any sweet talk, and the girl would go back inside for another try.

Luz browsed the racks, picked out a white cotton dress, and walked into a changing room. When she came out, both Edsito and the owner were glowing.

"Yes, yes, this is perfect!"

Luz smiled. I smiled. Other girls came back out and got more headshakes. But Luz nailed it on the first try. I grabbed an embroidered cotton shirt off a rack and held it to me while looking in a mirror. I looked like a character from *Scarface*. All I needed was a pair of matching pants and a fedora. All the changing rooms were full, and no one seemed to be watching me, so I took off my shirt to try it on. When I looked in the mirror, however, I saw Ed eyeing me. He tapped the owner on the shoulder, and they approached me. Ed started pointing at parts of my body, and she kept nodding. I couldn't understand what he was saying, but did hear him repeat the word "huesos," or bones. He tried to tell me something, but I didn't understand, so he called Luz over and had her translate.

"He says you have good bone structure. He wants you to be a model in the show."

"Isn't it an all-girl show?"

"Yes, but he don't care, baby. You look good!"

"I don't know . . ."

Ed told her something else.

Luz smiled. "He says he can't pay you for this show, but you can keep the shirt if you want to. He says he can pay you four hundred pesos for our next show though."

"Four hundred? Jesus christ! All for walking down a stage?"

She nodded.

"That's about what I was making per week at Lengua."

She smiled.

I checked my schedule: no job, no more weed . . .

"Fuck it, I'm in!"

They all smiled and walked back to the rear of the store. I watched Luz in the mirror. My heart was still racing from having been intimate with her again. She turned and smiled at me as if to say she felt the same. I walked over and wrapped my arms around her. One of the girls bumped into me and gave me a dirty look. The area was too busy, so I decided to leave. But before I did, I grabbed an umbrella and did a Charlie Chaplin impersonation. The other girls looked at me as if I was just an obstruction between themselves and perfection. Luz laughed out loud. I bowed to my audience of one, then walked outside and sat on the front step where I contemplated the strange events of my weird life. I could hear the girls behind me talking about dresses and makeup. I tried to tune them out. This was easy, and the meaning of their sounds fell to the ground like lead.

Soon, Luz walked out and sat beside me. I didn't hesitate.

"I bought my ticket home while you were in Panama."

"Oh . . ."

"It's just that, I'm running out of money, and I figured if I don't buy it soon, I'll be stuck here forever."

"When do you leave?"

"Early January."

"It's okay, baby, I understand. You need to go home sometime."

"Maybe I don't? I don't know. Other than my limited cash,

I don't know why I bought it. I want to stay here. I'm just really confused."

"I know, hermoso. I was expecting this to happen sometime."

"Mica and I are going on a bus trip across Mexico in December. We'll be gone for three weeks. Come with us. Will you come?"

"Jes!"

Without hesitation . . .

Little Edsito and the Powdered Six came outside.

"Okay," Ed said, "we're heading over to the other shop now. I can fit two in my car."

Two girls followed him and the rest set off on foot. I'd had my thoughts set on lasagna and garlic bread but started moving with the herd away from el Centro. Luz wrapped her arm around my back, and I wrapped mine around her shoulder. The others walked quickly ahead. But Luz and I strolled behind. None of the others had spoken to me, but I didn't care. I had the queen wrapped around me. Goddamn, she was so radiant. She needed no coaching or special steps. Her every movement was her own. And she moved coolly despite my words about leaving. I guess we both knew this from the beginning. It was just the way relationships worked here. People blew into town and were only able to give themselves away in knowing that they'd be gone again in a few months. It was the only way any of us could give anything. The only way we'd ever allow ourselves to feel. And it fucking haunted me . . .

Luz leaned on me as she walked and I on her. I stood between her and the street: a Mexican custom allowing the man to protect his love from potential dangers from passing traffic, and far more importantly in this land of unwavering machismo, to show the world she was his. When I was with her, I walked with the strength of an army. My hands could bend steel and flesh stop bullets.

It was the same shit all over again at the other shop, so I just sat on the front steps and thought about home. I didn't miss it, except for the change of seasons and a few other things. I wondered what Josh and Paul were up to. Those guys grew up on my block. We played basketball and tackle football and pulled pranks in the neighborhood. We'd pile in Josh's truck and drive around Buffalo shining a hunting light on people we'd pass, pretending we were the cops. You'd be surprised what people will do (and confess to) when a light's on them. I remembered our pact: that, no matter how successful we became, someday we'd all be alcoholics—as if there was something noble in it. Neither of them went to college. Jake joined the Army and was in Afghanistan fighting the War on Tair (as Dubbya calls it), and Paul dropped out of high school and had been hanging drywall since. I wondered how they'd react to my Mexican modeling career: "Who the hell you think you are, George-fuckin'-Michaels?"

Eventually the girls came outside, and we walked to a car. Luz told me to get in, so I sat in the back and she on my lap. We packed seven models in that sedan: six fashion and one of how not to live your life. We pulled in front of another crappy clothes shop, and I didn't even go in. I sat on the steps and cursed into the air when I realized we'd driven beyond walking distance of my Italian dream in el Centro. Days passed, and they returned outside. Half disappeared off in boyfriends' trucks, and the other half, me and Luz included, returned to the sedan. The driver took me and Luz back to Luz's place. We walked up the steps and locked the door behind us. I wasn't getting any Italian, but I could at least get some Mexican.

The desfile was in five days. I'd planned to run each night until then to reduce some of the swelling in my ass, but I spent most of those nights chugging beers instead.

The show was part of a cultural festival going on all weekend at a convention center in el Centro. Luz told me to be there no later than seven. I spent that afternoon with Mica, a few spliffs, and some caguamas. I walked to Ignacio Sevilla around seven thirty, hailed a cab, hopped in the passenger seat, and said to the German, "Make sure you come!" I'd asked Mica to take pictures of the show, but really, I needed an ally nearby to calm the nerves while surrounded by a sea of unfamiliarity. I had no problem mouthing off to people, getting in their faces, getting roaring drunk and being the loudest prick in the room—but put me on stage, and forget it. Shine a spotlight on me, and watch that dark confidence disappear. Watch the light burn any creativity and beauty in me down to ash. As arrogant an S.O.B. as I was, I knew my place was in the shadows, the end of the line, the alleys out back—which brought those damned hemorrhoids back every time I dared imagine myself rocking an arena or acting on Broadway . . . or walking down a fucking Mexican catwalk.

"So, you are an American?" the cab driver asked in near-fluent English.

"Born and raised."

"I lived in San Antonio for three years, but I left. I don't like America. There are too many silly rules. Everything comes with rules. How to dress, how to talk, how to think, what to look like. It drives me crazy, so I come back and I am happy."

"I couldn't agree with you more."

"The name is Miguel."

"Pleasure to meet you, Miguel. I'm Will. Your English is excellent, by the way—probably the best I've heard down here."

"Thank you! I tell you this, you speak with me in English for the first half of the trip, and I speak with you in Spanish for the other. Deal?"

"Deal."

I'd made that arrangement with other drivers in the past but Miguel actually made good on his promise, correcting my grammar and teaching me some new phrases.

"Repeat after me: Repleto de ferro en el ferrocarril."

"Repleto del faro en el ferrocarral."

"Good! That is a Spanish tongue-tester that helps pronouncing the double R's. Your Spanish is very good. How long have you been here?"

"A little more than three months."

"Three months? Orale! It takes most people years to speak like you do."

"Well thanks, Miguel. I have a strong suspicion that I may have been Billy the Kid in a past lifetime."

Miguel dropped me in front of the convention center, which looked as if it had once been a church. I walked inside and was hit by a wave of energy. There were people everywhere eating, dancing, shopping at stands selling clothes, purses, toys . . . I looked at the filled cashbox at one of the stands and thought to myself, What would j the c do? But I showed a little more restraint. A group of about eight children played instruments in the back corner as a cute little girl in wooden shoes stomped to the rhythm of the song. The group was tight and drew a big crowd. There was no way my swollen stomach could compete.

I walked to the sacristy in the back where the girls and Eddie had congregated. In this once-sacred area were now racks of clothes, cosmetics kits, piles of shoes, a group of painted models, my gorgeous childhood dream, and one frantic Eduardo.

"You're late! We need to get you to makeup!"

"Whoa, makeup? No, no makeup, Eddie."

"Yes, we need to get you over—"

He gave up midsentence. I think he knew I wasn't going to listen and didn't want to waste any of his limited time on me. I scanned the room, instantly realizing my folly in coming. I started jonesin' for a brew . . . hard. My whole body trembled. Luz came over.

"It's okay, hermoso. Just relax, I'll take care of everything." She kissed my forehead. I sat on a counter and watched the chaos around me unfurl.

"Eduardo says you will be doing two passes: one in the shirt you tried on at the shop, and the other with no shirt and a sombrero."

"I'm gonna look like a fucking idiot."

"No, you look beautiful. I will tell you when you need to go."

"I think I need to go now . . ."

She smiled, kissed me, and walked away. The other girls were scrambling around, trying on outfits and stuffing shoes on their feet. But not Luz. She emerged from the bathroom wearing a new outfit, which perfectly complemented her marvelous body. She was so full of beauty it couldn't help but spill out onto her perfect skin. I loved to watch her move. While the whole world went crazy, she was always so calm, controlled, and smooth. I loved to watch her put on makeup and try on clothes. There was something so calming about her meticulous patience. Her every step made me a better person, more complete by one small increment, growing to some near-perfect end reached at the cusp of a lifetime. In a world of temptation, she remained so confidently on her path. In those moments, I felt at one with the world around me. I had no idea what the hell I was doing at that show, but I knew she wouldn't let me fail. She gathered my troubles, placed them in a basket, and carried it on her back with the strength of a thousand generations of feminine care. How could the world exist without my love? Eduardo's command jolted me from my trance.

"Okay, ladies, it's time." They gathered into the cutest huddle. I thought about joining but knew my place. Instead, I peeked around the corner and saw a pasty gringo walking through the crowd. He saw me, smiled, and held up his camera. I smiled and gave him a thumbs up. The girls broke from the huddle and lined up outside the sacristy. Each girl wore a flowing white dress embroidered with a design representing one of the six major cities in Lila. Luz was Fundido, the Lime Capital of the World, and the undisputed Meth Capital of Mexico. Her dress had two bright green limes sewn into the bottom—but no light bulbs. Eduardo checked the stage, then addressed the girls.

"We will be delayed a few minutes."

I waved the German over. Luz saw me do this and looked into the crowd. Her face beamed.

"My parents are here!"

"Oh shit!" Good, she didn't seem to have heard me . . .

But Mica did. He laughed.

The techno music started pulsating. Ed gave another command, and the girls began moving. I returned to the sacristy and backed into memory. In college, Sal and I'd played a number of parties in our band, but at each—even when everyone there was smiling and breaking it down—I couldn't so much as look at the crowd. I'd stare at my hands or the floor and avoid eyes at all costs. It was as if I'd even looked at one of them, they'd all see me, and what I was, then raid my gear and chase me out the door. You just can't play like that. You just can't live like that . . .

The girls all did a pass and came back to the sacristy. Luz called me over and showed me where to stand. If there had been any doubts before, now there were none—I was no model. Eduardo gave the command, and soon the meat line was moving. We walked out and broke into a scattered formation, which left holes between us a linebacker would dream of. The first girl walked up to the stage, wiggling her ass perfectly. I observed her movements for professional purposes and tried to remember them for my own pass. My concern now wasn't just for myself. I didn't want to fuck this show up for Luz. And her damned parents were there too . . . Fuck! This was going to be a horrible first impression.

Soon it was my turn. I walked and tried my hardest to conceal the shit-eating grin curling from the edges of my lips, but I was too nervous, and it overpowered my face. I saw Ed shake his head. I stopped at the end of the runway, Mica snapped a picture, and I walked back to the starting point. I didn't even belong in that building. I was standing there barefoot when I noticed large black footprints on the white runway. I checked out the girls' feet: all in fancy shoes. The prints led down the stage and directly back to where I was standing. Fuck!

The girls all went then we walked back to the sacristy to change. I took off my shirt and put on a gigantic sombrero, but after looking in the mirror and seeing what a jackass I looked like, and remembering that Luz's parents were present, I decided to sit this pass out.

The girls did their thing again, and soon it was over. Eduardo approached me asking if I'd like to model in the next one. Despite of my need for cash, I responded with a quick "No," then wandered to the bathroom to scrub the bottoms of my feet. I put on my torn jeans and amber t-shirt and returned to the main area. The girls were all there taking pictures, buying me plenty of time to speak with Luz's parents.

"Hello, Mr. Corta. It's very nice to meet you."

"Yes."

"Did you, uh, enjoy the show?"

"Yes."

"So, Luz tells me you work at customs for the port?"

"Yes."

The conversation flowed like that for several inspiring moments before Luz came over and saved me.

"My father looks scary, but he is very kind. He is just very protective of me."

Mica later reassured me that it looked as if Luz's father "wanted to devour your soul."

People slowly disappeared into the night. Luz invited Mica and me to join her and one of the other girls to get some drinks. Mica was pleased. He'd already fallen for this new "skinny one" and had been talking with her since the show ended. Then her boyfriend showed up. Mica was disappointed but let it go.

We walked through the cobblestone streets toward what I'd assumed to be el Centro. Luz and I strolled behind, again cruising at our own speed. The other couple walked ahead, and Mica floated between the two, carrying on with some amusing anecdote from school. I only caught the end.

". . . so I never wore *that* hat again."

Both girls laughed.

"So, where we going?" I said.

The boyfriend turned. "To listen to some rock music."

Fuck! That could only be one place . . .

We walked inside, and Rudi shot me a smile from the stage. They were in the middle of Pink Floyd's classic, "A-rotta Bleek in de Wral." The girls sat at a table in front. I fought it at first but followed the smell of Luz's hair to my seat. A barmaid came over.

"I'll take a michelada," Luz said.

"You know, I'll take one of those too," I said. I hadn't tried the beer/chili combo since Paz's b-day celebration but, eh, what the hell . . .

The barmaid left to get the drinks. Rudi had the reverb up to eleven, and it was making me loopy. The drummer, however, was right on. Despite my inclination to pedantry, I allowed my foot to tap along.

The barmaid returned with enormous glasses of beer, and Luz finished hers double time—slamming it down while I was still at half-a-huge-ass glass. My heart raced. I jettisoned the oars and let the current take me. Rudi broke into the main riff of "Break on Through" followed by a slaughtered and repeated first verse. Luz and the skinny one put up their hands and moved along to the rhythm. That was too much for me. Tapping my foot was a big enough step.

Despite the loud music, conversation flowed. The skinny one's boyfriend turned out to be a pretty cool guy. They'd been dating for over three years, and I could see why she stayed with him. He drank heavily and made fun of all the stupid crap surrounding us. He spoke fluent English, as did the skinny one, so we flipped the conversation from Spanish to English, then eventually settled on a Spanglish hybrid.

Mica scanned the room and found another "skinny one" who fit his preferred set of physical traits: dark hair, dark eyes, a medium to small chest, no penis, and light skin. He excused himself from the table and began an ill-fated conversation with her, which lasted a good twenty minutes—far longer than I would have bet had I not been deeply engaged in conversation with my own dark-haired darling to my left. We drank more beer, devoured more nuts, and enjoyed more slaughtered classics.

Soon, Mica returned to our table. When the original skinny one went to the bathroom, her boyfriend leaned in to me and Mica: "There is a party tonight. A rave at a ranch off the carretera. I know many people that are going. It's going to—"

He stopped when he saw his girl exit the bathroom. She returned to the table and asked him to take her home. Though in her early twenties, her parents wouldn't allow her to stay out past midnight with her boyfriend, and it was approaching that hour. We said goodbyes, but the boyfriend leaned in and whispered to me, "I will be back. Don't leave."

Shit, I wasn't going anywhere. Mica left again to try to score Skinny One II while Luz and I grew more affectionate with each empty glass removed from the table. In a bar full of women, my eyes didn't wander.

Soon Mica rejoined us.

"So, what happened?"

"She let me talk to her for a half hour before informing me that she had a boyfriend."

"What were you talking about?"

"Nothing much really—just Germany's role in introducing polka to the Mexican people."

"Gotcha." I smiled.

The boyfriend returned, and Luz asked to be taken home. Her parents were spending the night at her apartment, and she didn't want them to worry about her either. We paid, and I waved to Rudi on the way out. We piled in the boyfriend's brown hatchback, and he dropped Luz off in front of her apartment. She kissed me, then strolled to the front door, reached through the broken glass, and opened it from the inside. Everything about her was cool. I smiled, and we took off.

Mica and the boyfriend got along great despite sharing an attraction for the same girl. We stopped for some caguamas and chugged them as we sped down the highway. Mica put *Siamese Dream* in the CD player and cranked the volume. That took me back. *Siamese Dream* was the first album I'd ever purchased. It took me three weeks to save up enough money from delivering papers to buy it. We pulled into a dirt parking lot beside the carretera before "Cherub Rock" was even over. The boyfriend, however, had enough sense to let the song finish before shutting off the car.

There were drunk people everywhere. The ranch was protected by a huge stone wall that seemed to span forever in each direction like a number line. We started at eight and walked to zero: the entrance of the rave. The line to get inside was long and continued to grow as more cars pulled over and parked. Big security guards patrolled the main gate and surrounding fence. Techno music pulsated and every so often one of the laser lights inside would shoot out the front door and into space. The place must have been packed with honeys because there were almost only dudes waiting outside, and the boyfriend seemed to know them all. This set me at ease. Crowds like this might start gringo-bashing the second the wrong girl smiled at the white guy, but maybe he could talk them down.

"It costs eighty pesos to enter," the boyfriend told us.

"You think we could hop the fence?" I said.

"We could give it a shot."

We searched for a weak spot for fifteen minutes, then gave up. Security had the place sealed.

"It's okay, guys, I know another party down the road, and it won't cost anything."

We got back in the car and pulled over before "Today" began. There were dozens of cars in this dusty lot, but nowhere near as many as in the previous. We got out and walked to the gate. The two guys working security smiled when they saw the boyfriend. They shook his hand and opened the gate.

This scene was more relaxed . . . more sophisticated. The people here may not have been any older than those at the rave, but they exuded contrived class, making them seem so. This was an outdoor party on the property of a sprawling ranch. Sets of outdoor furniture were arranged in clusters scattered about the lawn. The coffee tables were like giant sugar cubes that glowed from the inside. This was a posh shindig thrown by those with the money to do it correctly. A thin man with a perfect smile walked over to the boyfriend. Smiley handed the bf a bottle of tequila.

"For me?"

"Of course. That is good stuff. This bottle cost me a thousand pesos. Enjoy it."

The boyfriend smiled, opened the bottle, and poured us drinks. The stuff tasted like piss, so I diluted it with some carbonated water I'd swiped from a sugar cube. I scanned the party. These were the future movers and shakers of Lila—politicians, and lawyers, and doctors, and their trophy wives whom the guys would inevitably cheat on with the next crop of eye-batting giggle-speak making their way up the power rankings. We followed the boyfriend's smiley amigo and sat at one of the couch/cube combos. I didn't like these small intimate crowds. I had terrible anxiety and never knew what to say, which is why I preferred the loud, rowdy celebrations where I could communicate with chanting, chugging, and fighting. But here, all my flaws were out on display.

"Yo, Mica, you got any herb?"

He patted his shirt pocket. "All out."

Mica and I would usually escape to the roof in situations like this and roll a few spliffs. He hated small talk as much as I did. But these guys put us at the center of the conversation.

"You know," said the guy to my right, "I am not angry about the US building a wall between us. It is your country, and you have the right to do as you please. Here in Mexico, we have very stiff penalties for illegal immigrants coming from Central and South America."

"Yeah, that's what I've heard," I said. "But aren't most just passing through on their way to the US?"

"Most, yes. It is a long and dangerous trip, though. Lots of robberies, rapes, and murders happen on the journey north that the Mexican people must deal with."

"That's terrible."

"You know, Vicente Fox was the first Mexican president in recent time who did not encourage the Mexican people to cross your border. He has great pride in his country. I just hope our next president will have the same."

To my left, Mica was engaged in conversation with another small group, but his discussion was centered on Germany. I was glad I didn't have to account for *his* country's sins. Despite the anxiety, I enjoyed the conversation. I looked around and noticed that all the people in our couch/cube group were now male, when there had been a number of females there before. I looked around the party and noticed the same change. It was at that time that the man next to me started rubbing my inner thigh.

"So, you are a model, no?"

"Easy, tiger . . ."

I pushed his hand away and gestured to Mica and the boyfriend. We got up and walked to the parking lot. While I was a strong supporter of gay rights, I loathed an ambush. The guy I was speaking with had been kissing my ass for most of our conversation. I wondered if anything he'd said was true? In a world of sex, and politics, and fear, how could you ever trust 'facts?'"

How could you ever trust 'love?'

How could the skinny one ever trust again?

Chapter 34

Sal got his pink slip from the ladies at Lengua the next day. He walked in at eight forty for his eight o'clock class. They didn't say anything—just handed him a note: "We have had many complaints about your tardiness and use of Spanish while teaching. We have given your classes to Tina. Please return your textbooks and other course materials."

"Fuck that place," he said, sitting under the almond trees.

I laughed. "So they gave your classes to that Canadian bitch too, huh?" They'd recently hired some kooky-ass "aw shucks" Canadian who'd moved to Lila after marrying a Mexican, and they'd given her mine and Sal's students.

"Guess so." He laughed too. "Fuck their books. I'm not bringin' those back. They're gonna have to come get 'em themselves."

"Yeah, I'm holding mine hostage 'til I get my last payment. That place was the most disorganized racket I've ever been part of, and I've worked government jobs."

"Teaching's the worst anyway. I don't know how you do it . . ." It wasn't long ago he'd told me "Any idiot can teach"—a platitude thrown around by countless dumbasses who never knew what the fuck they were talking about. But, because all these dumbasses had been through school and had had dozens of teachers, they felt justified in spewing this bullshit. It was easy to assume yourself an authority on something when you'd had such experience with it. But there was no comparing being a student with being a teacher. There was a feeling of intense isolation unique to the profession. Even in the most crowded room it was just you up there alone with all your imperfections magnified and open to ridicule by those too immature to understand that what they were really scrutinizing were their own damned fears and insecurities. They wanted your guidance, they needed your support—and they'd devour you in their quest for both if you let them. This was the factor most didn't consider when they spewed those platitudes. I'd had no intention of ever teaching again when I left America. But here I was, and I knew I wouldn't be able to get away so easily.

Sal's students genuinely liked him. I'd sat through a few of his lectures. He was a good teacher. He started out doing a great job: showing up on time, preparing lessons, smiling . . . But soon he started coming late—ten minutes, then fifteen, then forty-five. And when he got there, he'd just take the students on a stroll around the block, naming random objects in English: "tree," "squirrel." He called it "active learning," a shallow pedagogical strategy that he explained as clumsily as he employed. I couldn't help but think that he just couldn't stand being the center of attention anymore. They'd said nothing when they handed him his pink slip. He didn't get upset. He just filled up his two water bottles and left.

"They canned your ass too, Blowmont Roostercourage!" he said.

"I quit."

We both laughed.

I spent most of the first week of December at Luz's place. I hadn't paid the landlady yet for the month and figured if I could just avoid her until the sixteenth, I could skip town and pocket the saved cash. I packed everything in my room and stored it at Luz's in case Maria came by. Sal and I were going to Guadalajara that weekend, and I was leaving on my big trip with Mica and Luz the following weekend, so

I only had to hide out for one more week. And Luz's was a good spot to hide.

That weekend was one for trips. Mica and several of the extraneros were going to a small indigenous beach town called Matitla located in the state of Michoacán. The natives there had successfully fought off large-scale development, and the town didn't even have electricity until the mid-nineties. Mica and the crew planned to camp on the beach and hoped to see the black turtles that came there to lay their eggs in the sand.

Luz headed to Zambulla to spend the weekend with her family and left before Sal and I took off for the big city. I was excited to see Guadalajara again. I'd passed through it so quickly on my first day in Mexico and wanted more time for a proper introduction. Most of Sal's family lived there, and I was excited to be staying with them and not in some shitty hotel.

The tall grass fields outside of Lila soon gave way to the chain stores and strip malls that lined the highway to the city. Every so often the bus would stop and someone selling doughnuts or fruit would get on. An older woman boarded at a stop just outside the city and started her pitch. I didn't understand what she was saying, but Sal translated.

"She said her son is blind and that she's selling little pads of paper and pens for six pesos to help pay his doctor's bills."

I reached into my pocket and handed over the correct change, and she handed me a pad and pen.

"Man, you just got scammed."

"I don't think so."

The woman said something else to me.

"What'd she say?"

"She said the pad would bring you luck."

I smiled and stuffed it and the pen in the front pocket of my backpack.

The bus stopped outside of a metro station. We got off, and I followed Sal inside the station. We paid and hopped on a packed train. The women were gorgeous. I remembered Lalo telling Cisco that they were "the prettiest in Mexico" when he was trying to convince Cisco to visit. The sun began to drop, covering the city in soft, warm magic hour light. We got off after a few stops and walked the rest of the way to the house. Sal's aunt gave us a cordial greeting and took Sal's bag, despite his insistence that he carry it himself. The house was packed with people and decked out in Christmas décor.

"Hey, Sally, maybe we should go to a hotel?" I said.

"Yeah, that's probably best."

He said something to his aunt, and she threw up her hands and started waving them while repeating "No!"

"You need me to translate that?" Sal said.

"I think I got it," I said.

We set our things down in Lalo's room and exchanged hellos with the ten or so others scattered throughout the house. Sal's uncle was still at work. He was a Guadalajarian, born and raised, and he and his wife had three kids: Figaro, the youngest, Carmen, the oldest, and Lalo. Carmen had an adorable little girl named Nayeli, who lit up every room she was in.

Sal's aunt was a caterer and spent her days cooking soups, tacos, and other traditional dishes in enormous pots and pans on the stoves in the kitchen and garage. She used all fresh ingredients, and the kitchen was filled with big bags of ripe tomatoes, and onions, and cilantro, and celery, and the fridge was full of meats and salsas.

The other family staying in the house was also related to Sal, and they lived in LA. The parents were young and their two kids were just about to escape their teens, and they were all perfectly bilingual—a skill I envied. The older kid, a guy named Tachi, was Sal's second cousin and was apparently a kick-ass soccer player. He was being developed by the LA Galaxy. Everyone in that house was family except the shining white gringo. But, as had been consistent with my experience with almost every other Mexican family I'd been around, I was quickly made to feel at home. They filled me up with rice, and beans, and quesadillas, and surrounded me with the kind of warmth and love only felt among a gathering of family and/or close friends.

After dinner, Sal, Tachi, and I piled in Lalo's truck, and he took us out on the town. We hit a few bars, then headed to a jazz club to catch a show.

The next afternoon, the Chivas of Guadalajara were playing America of D.F. in Mexican soccer's equivalent of the Super Bowl. The game was being played in Guadalajara, and the whole city seemed to be cheering along.

The Chivas won, and the city erupted: car horns, shouting, music . . . People were parading in the streets, waving flags and chanting. Sal and I took a bus downtown and watched the celebration—endless waves of fans rolled in all directions.

Carmen met us after she got off work. Lalo wanted to come, but he was still at the office. We heard that the Chivas players were going to parade down a major street that night, and we went down to watch. Sal and I literally had an advantage over the crowd and could see in most directions without obstruction. Carmen, however, didn't. Sal picked her up and carried her on his back, and she smiled and kissed his cheek. I looked down the street in both directions— people as far as I could see. There must have been a million of them. It was the largest crowd I'd ever been a part of. Sal and I walked to a corner store and bought a six-pack. I crushed through my first brew but went easy with the second after I took a look around and saw that no one else seemed to be drinking. In fact, the celebration was pretty tame. They had the numbers but didn't use them. Soon the cops cleared the street; we could see the headlights of vehicles coming from farther down. The people cheered. The lights got closer. The first truck passed, but its bed was filled with what looked like the local news crew: toothy, waving assclowns. The next truck came and was another letdown. This one carried what looked like some hip-hop wannabe, who only affected a response from the young girls in the crowd. As Hip passed, Sal hurled an empty at him, hitting him in the side of the head. Hip yelled something at the crowd, and Sal laughed and pointed at him as the truck continued down the street. Carmen shook her head. More trucks passed, and in them more assholes, until eventually the vehicles stopped coming. The team never made a pass.

"This is the worst celebration I've ever seen," I said. "Look, everyone's going home."

"Yeah, this is pretty weak," Sal said.

If the Bills won the Super Bowl, Buffalo would be in ashes by nightfall. There'd be cars exploding, whiskey flowing, people running naked through the streets. But here it was eleven p.m., and the once-raging human river had now run down to a trickle. Sal and Carmen started walking away.

"Where are we going?" I said.

"Home," Sal said.

"Whoa, there's gotta be something happening somewhere."

"I think everybody's just going to bed."

"Damn," I said, "the Chivas must be a pretty sick team 'cause no one seems to give a shit about this championship but me. I still got enough party in me for this whole damned city. Let's go out."

They agreed to one drink. We went to a Spanish bar and watched a woman dance flamenco as two guitarists played behind her. But not even that proud performance could buy me more time. True to their word, Sal and Carmen had a single beer, and we left.

The next morning brought more beans, huevos, and tortillas. Sal and I spent the day walking the city. Lalo got off work at five, and he picked us up in the family minivan and took us on a tour of the city. We breezed past posh neighborhoods, historical sites, slums, strip malls, fruit stands, and the stadium where the Chivas had won it all the night before.

"Hey, Lalo, you should take William to that spot."

"What's 'that spot?'" I said.

"You'll see."

With Sal, I could never tell whether he was bringing me someplace special or to my slaughter. But sometimes he had a way of being kind to the very people he often so viciously tore apart. It seemed his way of making amends—even if for an offense he hadn't yet committed or had only committed in his mind.

Lalo drove through some impoverished neighborhood and pulled over.

"Okay, hop out, Willy."

Part of me expected the van to tear out of there as the preliminary phase to some sadistic training exercise Sal had signed me up for without my consent. But the other part of me . . . I got out and walked to the edge of the street. I could see some houses and buildings in the distance, but the view was partially obstructed. I needed a boost so I climbed a pile of garbage. From this garbage pedestal the city opened before me. It was enormous and seemed to sprawl forever in all directions. I couldn't believe it had taken me so long to truly see the city that had first welcomed me to Mexico—golden light on the rooftops, softness in the hills . . . It was beautiful with its blemishes. An elderly woman walked down the street behind me. The neighborhood seemed rough, but this woman strolled with a quiet confidence that made me feel secure as well. It was at that moment that I first realized that people were no different no matter where in the world you went. This idea had flashed through my mind before, but that was the first time I really understood—that this simple truth became a part of my muscles, and bone, and breath. I still had so many conflicting voices in my head, but this one seemed sincere . . . comforting.

I walked back to the van and hopped in. I didn't know if it'd been Sal's intention, but I felt changed as we drove back to Lalo's house. I'd have said with certainty that it wasn't, but there was something below his layers—some intelligence, compassion, and general understanding of things—which so often seemed to get lost on the gnarled path out of his body. But, sometimes, things just found their own way out.

Though neither Sal nor I had any responsibilities in Lila, we still decided to return there that night. We exchanged goodbyes with the family. It was nice to have spent some time in the presence of a family, with a Christmas tree all lit up in the corner and endless plates of beans and rice and tamales constantly being pushed under my hungry mouth. The goodbyes were fairly standard with the exception of Carmen's. She hugged Sal as tears dripped from her eyes, and she wouldn't let go.

"Promise you'll come see us again. We're your family and we miss you," she said.

"I promise I'll come again next weekend. I've missed you guys." He seemed to actually mean these words. But I knew from experience that that conviction only lasts so long before it fades away again into a void of shame and self-loathing where all promises are broken and all paths back home disappear. And, judging by how tightly Carmen gripped him, I think she knew this as well—but she finally released him, and we walked out the door and up the sidewalk toward the metro station. We crossed a main street where a shirtless thirty-something-year-old man was standing under a red light and spitting fire to entertain drivers. The air stank of gasoline. When we crossed the street, Sal realized he'd left his camera behind, so he dumped his things on the sidewalk and ran back to get it. I dumped mine as well. The light of the falling sun interacted with the dust and gases in the air, putting on a spectacular display of rich reds and yellows and oranges. The flamespitter continued putting on a light display of his own. Each time the traffic light turned red, he'd walk from the island into the street and do his thing. After he'd spit the flames, he'd walk between the parked cars with his hand out. I watched him repeat this cycle four or five times and only saw two or three drivers hand him change. Meanwhile, three young boys in nothing but tighty whities and dirty t-shirts played on the grassy island in the street. The boys wrestled and hit each other and ran around smiling and laughing. The flamespitter took a red light off to wrestle with the boys. I wondered if they went to school. They looked old enough. Maybe they *were* at school, learning the family trade?

I sent Luz a text: "I miss you . . ." And she sent one back: "I miss you, too, hermoso. Come over tonight." I smiled. Sal returned with his camera about twenty minutes later. We grabbed our things and continued to the station. The night was falling around us.

We hopped the turnstiles at the station—more so to save time than money—then rushed up the steps and boarded the train just as the doors were closing. There were no pretty faces that night. We got off at our stop and walked up the steps to the people bridge to cross the highway. Sal reached into his pocket, pulled out his knife, and said, "This is where tons of people get robbed. They wait 'til you get to the middle then come at you from both sides." As we reached the center, a little old lady hobbled past us; my racing heart relaxed when she didn't ask for our wallets.

When we reached the bus stop, we discovered that our bus had left while we were preparing for certain robbery on the bridge above. The buses came every half hour, so I walked to a small snack stand and bought a beer from an attractive older woman working behind the counter. She smiled when she handed over the brew, and I couldn't help but smile back. I finished my snack quickly, and it begged for release, so I walked to a pile of garbage behind the stand and let it rip. I looked down the highway in the direction of arriving buses. From this view, I saw Mexico—at least, Mexico as it was to me. Beyond the Christmas lights of the snack stand were people, quiet yet alive, waiting without complaint for their buses to come and take them back to their respective worlds. And beyond them were the lights from the city, extending as far as I could see. It was soft, and organic, and visceral. I felt alive in the darkness—alive and not alone. This was the Mexico I'd fled to see. The Mexico I'd invited to sweep me away. I could have been anything—anyone—and no one would have judged. I zipped up and walked back to the bus stop. The woman behind the counter smiled again, but I turned away from her and smiled into the night instead. A bus heading for Tijuana stopped. Though a forty-hour ride, Sal and I considered hopping on. We had no jobs, no responsibilities. The only thing stopping us from heading north was the light weight of our wallets. In those times, I could have been whatever I wanted. No one knew where I was or who I was becoming, and I had no intention of ever going back.

When our bus came, we boarded and paid the driver. A line formed behind us, but no one pushed or rushed us along. We sat near the back—I by the window. I pulled out my music and looked for something I'd never heard before. When Lou Reed's voice entered "Pale Blue Eyes," I could have cried. By the time he'd finished that first verse, I already knew I'd found something that would always stay with me.

Sal and I parted ways at the Lila bus station. I took a cab to Luz's apartment. I didn't know the name of her street, so I had to point out every turn to the driver. When we found it, I walked to the door, reached my hand under the broken glass, and let myself in. Luz met me at her door in a bra and panties. I pulled her onto me and slipped them both off. She led me to her bed where Luz Blanco was already asleep. Kyler was gone that night, and she was feeling lonely. She wasn't the only one. It's a good thing she was a deep sleeper.

Chapter 35

I had that entire week planned out: Monday and Tuesday, I had no plans; Wednesday, I'd go to a beach in Michoacán with the Herbster; Thursday, I'd pack; and Friday, I'd leave. I'd moved all my stuff to Luz's apartment. The only thing tying me to that dead-end dwelling were the keys, which I figured I could just leave with Sal.

The week started out great. Luz spent nearly all her free time with me. She'd wake at six, kiss my cheek, and sing as she got ready for class, then it'd be silent again when the door shut. She'd come back around noon and find her groggy-but-always-willing lover wrapped up like a big gringo burrito in her comforter and waiting for her to take a peek at the meat inside. This was something neither of us had ever experienced—fuck, at least, something *I'd* never experienced (I could only trust her word). I'd pull her on me, sky rockets, then we'd go for lunch. I walked so proudly with her. She could stop traffic and I, bullets. We were a fucking superhero when our separate powers combined.

Then we'd come home and wait out the afternoon heat in her bed. We'd put on movies, and she'd turn on the fan. I'd pile her pillows and stuffed animals under my arms and back, making a cushy throne. We'd sit there barefoot, sipping fruit smoothies, and laughing at subtitled *Simpsons* episodes. Luz and I shared an offbeat sense of humor. She was as weird as I was. We'd make up characters and talk to each other in accents, and make up prefixes and suffixes to words in both Spanish and English. How relaxed I was those times in her bed! It was the first time I'd realized there was no place else I'd rather be. I didn't even fuss over the possibilities—mind didn't wander to new lands. Despite the heat, despite the sun and my financial concerns, my worries melted into a pool on the floor and quickly evaporated. Though I knew with evaporation was always the inevitable rainfall. But in the meantime, I was the goddamned king.

In the late afternoon, I'd walk to the panaderia to buy bread, the fruteria to get fresh fruit and vegetables, and to the market for fish. I never felt any pressure from the masses. Nobody was looking over my shoulder or hurrying me along. I'd come home and prepare dinner. I'd start by boiling the water for the rice, then I'd add some olive oil to a frying pan, turn on the heat, and throw in the fish. I'd cut the bread down the middle and spread on some olive oil, then add some chopped garlic and freshly grated mozzarella, and put it in the oven. I'd dump the rice in the boiling water and let the heat do its thing. I'd then cut up some broccoli, carrots, and other vegetables, and toss them in with the fish. I'd heat some black beans on a back burner, then check the bread. I never removed the bread until the cheese was golden brown and edges just starting to blacken, and kept the fish on the pan until it was soft enough to fall apart in my fork. I took the rice off the heat once it'd gulped up all the water, then set the table. I had no formal instruction in cooking. I just did what seemed natural. I'd serve Luz first and pour us each a glass of wine.

I didn't speak much when I cooked, even if Luz was there with me. I meditated on the craft; sometimes poems or songs would come to me:

Lucecita
De la tierra,
Nature's mother, mother's love,
Whisperer to the lonely souls casting their shadows from the
    light above.

She's still while the earth is trembling,
Cool while it erupts its sin,
Calm when caught in the landslide,
For the mud, it softens her skin.

Lucecita
De la tierra,
A world unlike the rest.
Air a little cleaner,
Fruit a little sweeter,
To have spent a moment here, I was blessed.

I'd sing/recite these in the shower, in bed, sitting beside her at the dinner table. She made me happy in a way I'd never felt—filling gaps in time and space with no effort. Just falling, breaking apart in my atmosphere as she entered my space, a fine dust filling all my ruts and craters. And she loved me. And I loved her. And it was simple.

We'd talk and laugh and sip our wine. Neither of us was in a hurry to be anywhere. In those times, I was witty and clever and able to remember small facts and details I'd normally overlook during the day's haze. I felt I could have written any poem, acted any part, sung any song . . . When I spoke, my voice was firm and unwavering—my language was clean, lucid, and relevant. In those moments, I cared for myself and was proud of my accomplishments. But those nights only lasted so long . . .

Luz and I decided to play tennis the next day. We took a cab to the deportivo complex, slid through a chained gate, and got to business. It was hot and the sun relentless. The only relief from the heat was in the shadows cast by the net and ourselves. We volleyed to warm up.

Luz was pretty good. Though she did nothing spectacular, she was solid everywhere. I had a decent forehand, but sucked at everything else besides accidentally smashing the ball over the fence every so often. She was whooping my ass in points, but the game might have seemed even to a spectator had they been watching.

And they were watching—just not the game . . .

Halfway through our first set, a soccer ball rolled downhill and right into the fence, and two teenage boys came after it. They slowed when they saw Luz, then stopped to enjoy the scenery for a moment before grabbing the ball and running back uphill. When the scouts returned to base, they obviously spread word because more balls started rolling downhill. Soon the whole team was surrounding that cage. They began whistling and calling to her.

"Get the fuck outta here, you little shitheads!" I started smashing tennis balls at the fence.

They laughed and didn't leave until their dirty old coach got an eyeful himself and ordered them back to practice. Sons of bitches! I wasn't just angry at the assholes but also at Luz, who'd just stood there indifferently as she got eye-gang-banged by Lila's eighteen-and-under soccer league. She could have said something. She could have smashed balls with me. But fuck . . . I mean, what happened when I wasn't around? What if there was no fence there between them? I thought we were a team?

I tried to calm down, but guys passing by on foot or in cars were doing the same shit: honking and whistling as if Luz was in that cage giving a free demonstration on new and exciting ways to make a tennis racket's handle disappear. But she just stood there ready for more tennis. What a fucking experience! What an effect she had on the world! What a warped perspective she must have had. But despite the frustration, something new came to me—some new feeling of pity and despair. Perhaps she wasn't smashing balls because she was tired of it? Guys had likely been doing the same shit to her since she'd developed tits. This was her day-to-day struggle. She'd been approached to be in music videos and spread her goods for magazines—these sick fucking bastards! She was so fucking beautiful, but in a way they'd never see—so much inside of her they'd never understand or appreciate. Luz was brilliant and driven, and put all of herself into everything she did. She was passionate, and tender, and genuinely good to her family and friends. But she also had enormous breasts. She also had a face that melted hearts—that destroyed weak men. These sons of bitches! These motherfuckers! She's no goddamned ornament! Leave us the fuck alone! I would have fought to the death for Luz. That kind of beauty was worth living and dying for. But I was against so many . . .

But maybe, she didn't need—or want—my help?

Either way, we were alone in that cage together. Maybe I just needed to treat this shit with the same indifference that she was? But that would take a strength that maybe I'd never have. But maybe I could gain that strength if she and I were working together as a team? Just as I'd felt while snorkeling in the warm, turquoise ocean in Zambulla, I was again in over my head. Maybe I'd never be able to dive with her and see her world? Maybe she'd never be able to dive deep enough to see the wrecks at the bottom of mine?

We played a few more sets and left. I felt the weak glue of curiosity melting away between us in the omnipotent and punishing heat. Luz was too pure a soul to be claimed. She was merely a beautiful display in a public museum that I'd never be able to take home. I could touch her, sketch her, and talk to her all day, but at closing time I'd always be forced away by an overeager security team. Maybe Luz wasn't mine and never was? She was shared with the bricker, the hawker, and the farmer working in the Lilan sun.

Luz and I went our separate ways for dinner that night. I went to the German's for pan-fried sausages and sauerkraut. We bought some beer before dinner, and one caguama turned to two, and two to four; we sat in the living room drinking them. Hugo was shirtless, as usual, and wearing a pair of shorts tight enough to choke a six-year-old's nuts. I didn't know how, or why, he did it.

He and Mica were now back on speaking terms. They'd gotten into an argument a few days earlier after Mica commanded Hugo to

"Do the fucking dishes!" while Hugo was with a girl. Hugo waited until after the girl left to let Mica know what he thought of him. There'd been tension there since the beginning. Mica once overheard Hugo tell Eduardo that he hated how white people didn't like him and always tried to make him feel inferior. It was true that Mica didn't like Hugo—but not because he was from Honduras. Mica disliked Hugo because he was an asshole. I liked Hugo. I thought he was hilarious. Although, I didn't have to live with him. But that night, everything was fine.

Ramon, one of the Colombians, came over when we were already several caguamas deep. Ramon spoke rapid Spanish, but I picked up on most of it. I liked Ramon too. He was a cool kid and was probably as close to an unofficial leader of the extraneros as they'd had (he shared that title with the pinche fool, Turd). About ten minutes into the conversation, Ramon gave me a serious look.

"Hey, Will, I need to tell you something. It's not going to be easy to hear, but I'd want to know if I were you."

I already knew this was going to be about her.

"I was in Zambulla with a few other guys this weekend," he said, "and Luz sent Ferd a couple text messages asking him to get together."

"Wait, are you fucking with me?" I said.

"I wish I was."

"What'd these messages say?"

"One said something like, 'Hey, where are you? I want to see you.' And the other was similar. I read them myself. It sounded like she wanted to get very friendly with him."

"That son of a bitch! Did they get together?"

"I don't know. Maybe? I wasn't with him the entire time."

"Wow, I can't believe that," Mica said. "Luz always seemed so great."

I started shaking and couldn't stop. "W-where is he now? Where is that son of a bitch?"

"I don't know. But you should be mad at her, not him. *She* sent *him* the messages."

"I don't c-care. I'm gonna break that kid's face!"

"No, don't do that," Ramon said. "You'll just get in trouble with the police. What you should do is just pretend like you know nothing and see what she says about it. Just be cool."

"You're talking to the wrong hombre, hombre," I said. "I'm fire, not ice."

"Maybe I shouldn't have told you . . . I'm sorry—"

Goddamn it! I knew all girls cheated—the only dependable truth in this fucked-up universe—but why destroy it so soon? I was leaving in less than a month. All she had to do was wait a few weeks, and we'd at least stay good friends forever. I knew I couldn't trust anyone when sex was involved. It was too primitive and instinctual a desire to control. It catalyzed power struggles and rewarded the victors with flesh and pride. Wolves in slacks. Tigers in cotton dresses. There was no way to avoid it. And all hell was bound to break loose the second someone spilled blood in the arena. But I knew it sure as hell wasn't going to be mine.

But still, I didn't feel entirely like a wolf. Luz was only mine because she chose to be mine and not because I'd overpowered or outsmarted her. Goddamn! Rejection . . . it was easy to love a soul. A soul could be sincere. A soul could be loyal. But it always came with the flesh. And hers was molded all wrong for her soul. Christ, at least I tried . . .

I drank a few more caguamas, absorbed more than my fill of horrible advice from the guys, and took off for "home." I almost felt satisfied—satisfied in some sadistic way. My worry was now fulfilled, itch now scratched. I knew how to punch. I knew how to destroy. I knew how to chew the life out of all the poor fuckers who wandered too close. And I was gonna chew her to shreds.

After I got to him . . .

Team Men devised a plan before I left Mica's, and I replayed the strategy on my way back:

"Remember, you've got the upper hand. She doesn't know you know. You can bring her down from the inside."

"Yeah, just kiss her like everything's fine. Take her to bed. Hold her hand. Then break her when she lets you in."

I knew this was horrible advice, but I had no place left to go. And this plan was going to take more discipline than I'd have ever given myself credit for possessing. I tried to imagine myself as a character from a Shakespearian play. Someone disciplined, and calculating, and evil. This calmed me.

My hand shook violently as I reached under the broken glass and let myself in. I didn't even have to intentionally knock on her door. I just brought my hand up to it, and the shaking did the job. I took a deep breath and got into character before Luz opened the door. I just wanted to hold her, but she became a cactus.

"Hey, hermoso, how—"

I leaned in and kissed her on the lips. It was awkward, but filled me with a dark strength.

"Is everything okay?"

"Yeah, no problem." No problem indeed, you fucking Brutus. I was overwhelmed with the desire to pummel her with questions, but she started reaching for my pants, so I just bent her over the table and gave her everything I had.

The next day, she and I went to play tennis again after lunch. We took a cab to the deportivo complex, snuck through the gate, and started playing. Neither of us said much. In fact, neither had said much since the previous night. I took her silence as an act of subtle rebellion against our relationship. The only sound we made came from the ball.

I dropped questions, little seeds, when we met at the net between games.

"So, how was Zambulla this weekend?"

"Good. I went to the beach, saw my family, met up with some friends."

"Who'd you see?"

"Luz Blanco, unos amigos . . ."

We continued the game. A few assholes honked and shouted again as they passed. I didn't know whom to lash out at first. I felt like smashing balls in all directions. I was alone on my side of the court; a rising futility grew over me like a sweaty shadow.

A man approached us.

"Hey, did you two pay to be on the court?"

"Yeah," I said, "we paid the guy at the front desk."

"Well, I'm the only guy at the front desk, and I don't remember either of you."

"Well, do you remember him over there? Or her over there? Or—" I pointed at others running around the track or jumping off the diving tower.

"I'm going to have to ask you to leave."

"Come on, baby, let's just go," Luz said.

"Fuck you too!"

I squeezed through the gate, and she followed behind. The guy walked back to the front office. I stopped and turned.

"Would you tell me if you were ever in contact with another guy?"

"Jes, of course I would."

"'Cause I've been hearing some shit recently and it's making my mind all kinds of crazy."

"Look, I'm not with anybody else. Only you. It's true."

"So, no one tried to contact you while you were in Zambulla this weekend?"

"Maybe Luz, but nobody else."

"What about that emaciated little worm Turd?"

"Oh, yes, he did send me a message, but not to see me. He was in Zambulla and wanted to know the best beaches to go to, so I tell him."

"That sounds like a load of bullshit to me."

"No, it's true, baby. I will show you the message when we get home."

"I'm not going home."

Luz took a cab back to her apartment, and I walked back down the dead-end street. Sal was there, and so was Herb. I told them all about it as we sat under the almond trees.

"Willy," Herb said, "there's only one thing you need to know: Why did he have her phone number?"

"Maybe he got it from somebody else. She did seem surprised that he texted her."

"Of course she did," Sal said. "She's fucking with you. You need to show her who's boss."

"Yeah, like you do with Paz?" I said.

"Fuck you," he said.

"Just ask her where he got the number," Herb said.

"Yeah," Sal said, "and you can't let that German bitch get away with this either."

"Well, who should I go after first?" I said.

"I'd first find out why he had her number," Herb said. "Any reason she gives you is bound to be bullshit. Then you need to find that fucker and give him a few lumps to settle the score. Just not in a public place. You don't want the cops involved."

"Jesus christ! You know I'm the fuckin' *House of Usher* when it comes to this shit. She's gonna wear me down, man. I'm gonna ask her and she's gonna give me a reason, and I'm just gonna buy it—and I've got all my shit at her house! Fuck!"

"Well, I'll take you over there tonight to get your stuff back," Sal said. "But you gotta just get your shit and get out. If she starts talking, just ignore it and keep moving."

"Goddamn it! I hate this! I fucking hate this!"

"Cheer up, Willy," Herb said, "you're leaving soon anyway. You think it was gonna last forever?"

"Maybe . . ."

They laughed at me.

We spent the rest of the afternoon and most of the night drinking beers under the almond trees. I'd already texted Luz letting her know I'd be back that night. But I kept pushing back the time. We finally left around ten.

"C'mon, Willy," Sal said, "if I don't take you now, you're never going to go."

"Fine."

Sal drove me to Luz's apartment. I knocked on her door, and she answered. There was an innocent hesitation to her. She looked at me as if to ask, "What's going on here?" I brushed past her and stayed locked on my goal. I was fucking oak. I felt solid through and through. I went to her room, grabbed my guitar and big blue bag, and brought them down to Sal's car.

"That it?" he said.

"No, I still have to get my backpack."

"Well, do it fast. I burnin' gas here."

I went back up, pushed past Luz, and started stuffing loose items in the pack. Luz walked into the room and sat on her bed and watched me. She had the saddest look on her face. Her eyes swelled as if tears were forming behind them but none were breaking through. I wanted to ease her pain. I wanted to kiss her and tell her it would all be okay. But I continued to stuff clothes in that pack, each further item like another pin I pierced into a miniature Luz voodoo doll. I also wanted to puncture those eyes. I also wanted to see those tears. I needed those tears. But they never came . . .

I'd been prepping for this moment for a month and nothing could stop me. Her pain fueled my strength. I took out all my anger and aggression on that beautiful face. I wanted to ruin it. I had myself convinced I was Moses. I had myself convinced that my travels through the desert meant something. But I was just another junkie withering away on the streets of Lila, spitting in the face of the only person who ever really gave a damn about me. I'd never be able to love her as much as I hated myself.

I couldn't think. I knew if I stopped or slowed down she'd overtake me. I had to continue. I zipped up my bag and stormed to the front door. She jumped out of bed and grabbed me before I left.

"Please, baby, I don't understand what's going on. Don't leave! Talk to me!"

"Fuck you! Get off me."

She opened her mouth to speak but closed it. I could see her innocence. Hell, I knew it the second I opened the door.

"What would you like me to say?" I said.

"Anything. Tell me anything. Just please don't go."

"I cheated on you, you know. I kissed another girl while you were in Costa Rica."

She looked at the floor. "I know. I heard from one of my friends."

"Why didn't you ask me about it?"

"I didn't want to believe . . ."

Luz was solid—much more so than I was. I'd forgotten how young she was. At nineteen, I was even more of a train wreck. Had we switched places, I would have cracked during tennis that afternoon and signed a confession on the spot, even if I'd committed no crime. But she was solid. And I was . . .

"I will show you the messages I sent him," she said.

"No, that's okay."

"No, it would make me feel better if you saw."

I read them. Completely innocent. Something along the lines of, "Yes, the best beach here is so-and-so. I hope you have a fun trip!" Goddamn. Ramon had told me otherwise. Ramon had made it seem like Luz and Turd were ready to run off together into the sparkling sunset. Ramon was also best friends with the pinche German asshole. The same asshole who'd apparently had it out for me since I'd kissed his girlfriend in front of him a few months back. That same pinche asshole I'd suspected of stealing my cell phone. And Luz—she was studying tourism. She gave information to anyone interested in visiting Zambulla. Hell, she'd only given *me* her number after I'd mentioned Zambulla. People were texting her all the time about hotels, and beaches, and surfing spots.

I could feel the words coming from way deep down—the words I'd been holding back on telling her—the words I'd been holding back on telling myself. The ones where the language barrier wasn't so cute or funny. The ones I'd wrapped up with a tag that said, "Don't open until The Very End." The problem was that I didn't know when the end was. Every time I'd thought I'd arrived there before, the words didn't come. I couldn't let her unwrap it. I couldn't let her unwrap me. The panic and rituals and rage were the only defense I had in this world. Regardless, here we were, naked in each other's eyes. I was still oak but could feel the termites of reason and compassion chewing away at my trunk. Soon I'd be nothing but a pile of woodchips and waste on her carpet. Sal honked and shouted my name. I had to act fast . . .

"Listen." I hung my head. "My life has been like a living fucking nightmare. I shouldn't be here still. I never thought I was going to live this long. I'm so fucking tired . . ." The tears finally came, only they were mine.

"It's okay." She hugged me and wiped my eyes. Sal honked and yelled up to me. Luz shut and locked the door, and led me to her bed. Sal honked a few more times, then I heard him speed off, cursing into the night.

Luz lay beside me on the bed. Up until that point, I, like the others, would have fought to the death to convince the world I'd had a normal and happy childhood. But looking into the compassion in her eyes, I realized that was a lie. There were things I didn't talk about with people. Things so far down, I didn't even talk about them with myself. Things that consumed me every second of my every day. But the moment one came up, they all came after. I thought she'd run. I thought she'd curse me to the depths of hell like the others would have. But she didn't. Maybe she didn't understand my words? But I hit her with wave after wave of darkness long into the night, and she just rode each wave while wiping away my tears and telling me it was okay. By the time the sunlight crept in through her bedroom window, I was a pile of woodchips on her bed.

Chapter 36

I felt lighter the next morning and was elated to wake up next to the woman who'd seen my worst, yet never left my side. I'd pushed her at every angle, but she didn't budge. I guess godlike patience and compassion were necessary to date a herculean asshole. She had an enormous heart and an equally large understanding of humanity at such a young age. And I woke that morning knowing I now had a responsibility to protect this at all costs. I knew the conversation from the night before had been coming for some time. It had tried to come on many other nights. I was just relieved it was over and that she was still there, singing folk tunes and kissing my cheeks.

We were whole again and spent that afternoon together. I regretted moving my things out of Luz's place. Anything was possible in Sal's care. Maybe he'd thrown my guitar on some cobblestone street in a blind rage the night before? But I knew I could trust Luz with everything I had. At least, I was pretty sure of that.

Though I felt satisfied believing in Luz's innocence in this situation, there was still an issue that needed to be addressed. Right then, the pinche Aleman was cruising around Lila with all his bones still intact. I was prepared to change that.

Luz and I parted ways after dinner. I didn't hide my intentions. "Please, let it go, Will. It's not worth it."

I felt some responsibility to her—to listen to her. But I took a cab back down that dead-end street anyway. I had myself convinced that, while she was intelligent, there were just some things she didn't know. Like when some scrawny jack-off tried to make you look like a fool, there was no way you could let him get away with that shit. And that, no matter what went on in her wonderful apartment and her big, warm bed, there would always be strays fighting for scraps on the street just outside. I needed to keep up my guard.

Sal was sitting out front when I arrived. "Yo, that girl worked you," he said.

"You don't know that. Besides, she didn't do it—"

"Spoken like a fucking fool."

"You don't know that! How could you possibly be so certain? You don't have any of the facts!"

"C'mon, are you serious? You know what Paz's told me about her? She's seen her out with that asshole at restaurants or in the center. She's playing you."

"Fuck you, man!"

"You're an idiot."

"Fuck you!" I grabbed an almond off the ground and threw it at him, but he dodged it.

"You're crazy, just like your dad."

"What the hell's he got to do with this?"

"Your father is insane. Remember that time you called George Bush a cokehead, and he threw a flaming polish sausage at you straight off the grill?"

"It wasn't flaming—"

"And remember that time he smashed your brother's windshield with a tire iron because he got a flat in front of my house?"

"I wasn't there—"

"He went absolutely insane. He kept screaming and punching himself in the head like a wild, retarded ape. My neighbors had to call the cops."

"All right, man, I get it, my dad's nuts."

"And there was that time—"

"All right! You know what? Of all the people I've ever known, you remind me the most of him." Holy shit, I realized it was true the second I said it.

"Yo, relax, Barbeefio McTavish—"

"I am relaxed."

"Look, I heard there's a party tonight. We should go look for your friend."

"I've been thinking about this. I'd prefer to fight him in a private place, but I don't have much time left here, so I'll have to take what I can get. I think it'd be best if I just walk up to him like everything's cool, then give him a solid shot to the nose. I figure a broken nose would make us even. Then we just walk out of there before anyone has time to call the cops. I hide out until I hop on the bus for Mexico City on Friday and never come back."

"Sounds tight to me."

"If anyone jumps in, you mind holding 'em back?"

"I'll knock all those purse-wearing Euro-trash pussies out."

We drove to the party, but Turd wasn't there. I texted Mica asking him to find out if there were any more parties that night. He sent me a few addresses, and we checked them all out, but nothing. We met up with Mica at one of the parties. He'd just met another "skinny one" and was on the way to see her.

"Hey, either of you boys have any rubbers?" he said.

"Well, I guess we don't need any more abandoned children out there, do we?" I tossed him two from my wallet. I didn't really need them. I'd been giving it to Luz raw and pulling out. Not the best strategy, but I was a fucking idiot.

When we ran out of parties, Sal and I checked the bars, then the main streets, then finally rolled back downhill and got drunk under the almond trees.

"FUCK!" I really wanted to break that kid's nose. I'd have to put the plan on hold. Mica sent me a text later that night highlighting both of our failures: "I heard Turd decided to stay in tonight, but I know where he lives. Also, you can have your rubbers back."

I knew where he lived too, but something about dragging him out of his house seemed less romantic than blasting his schnoz in front of his disciples. I drank several caguamas and woke up the next morning on the big bed in my old room. Sal wandered in around noon.

"Yo, Maria was just here, and she was pissed. She saw you sleeping in your room. She asked me why you still haven't paid her your rent."

"Fuck! Did you tell her I didn't live here anymore?"

"Dude, she saw you sleeping here. You're fucked."

Damn, I was so close to pulling this off but fell just before the finish line. I only had to make it one more day. I probably should have just dropped the keys off with Sal and disappeared forever. But I was tired of disappearing.

I followed the panteon wall and arrived at her house. The thin shirtless man was there again. I asked him where I could find Maria, and he gave me the directions. I walked to Ignacio Sevilla and took Sal's shortcut down the sidewalk street. The pit bull puppy barked as I walked by, and I said hello back. He'd grown considerably since the last time I'd seen him. I came to an open square, and there, standing tall on the concrete like a messiah on a vast lake, was Maria, giving instructions to the thin men painting and scraping the outside of one of her houses. She smiled when she saw me. My pride flexed, then relaxed at the sight of her kind face. I knew instantly that this would be no battle.

"Hello, Will, how have you been? It's been too long since I've last seen you!"

"I've been good."

"Sal tells me you have a girlfriend now, is that right?"

"Yeah, her name is Luz."

"Oh, such a pretty name! You are a handsome boy, she must be very lucky."

"Thanks . . ." I blushed.

"Sal also tells me you're leaving Lila soon. Is that right?"

"Yeah, I leave on a road trip tomorrow, then I'm flying out of Guadalajara after."

"Well, you'll always have a place to stay if you want to come back."

"Thanks . . . Look, I'm sorry I didn't pay you for December, it's just I—"

"It's okay. You don't need to explain. I know people have their problems. How can we make the situation right?"

"I'll just pay you for December."

"How about you give me half? You're only here for half the month."

"Sounds good." I handed her the cash.

"I'm making dinner tonight for all of them." She pointed at the workers. "You can stop by if you'd like. Bring Luz."

"Maybe I will, Maria. Thanks . . . thanks for everything."

She gave me a hug. There was no story I could tell her she hadn't already heard. This was a woman who'd spent her life absorbing people's sadness and releasing it as positive energy. She was a steel pillar, strong and solid, tempered in the scorching heat produced under the pressure of a thousand demanding lives. She didn't seek a reward. There'd be no songs sung of her generosity or stories written on her life. She was the steel holding us together—the frame hidden behind layers of drywall and paint. I was nothing in her presence. But she made me feel like something special. And this incredible woman was the one I'd tried to cheat out of eighty bucks—the amount I could have made substitute teaching for a day back home.

I turned and walked back the same way I'd come. But before I hit that sidewalk street, I turned and saw Maria standing so solidly on that frail sheet of water that so many others had fallen through. I knew I'd never see her again, and though I'd become so callous to goodbyes, I almost cried.

Chapter 37

Icalled Herb on the walk back. We were going to a beach in Michoacán, and I let him know I was ready. He rolled down the dead-end street about a half hour later with all the gear: towels, and sunscreen, and a case of beer. I was excited to finally see Michoacán. I'd heard so many stories about it: the state seemed to be one endless field of green, where you could run in any direction with your arms spread wide and gather a lifetime fill of herb. I thought about inviting Luz, but this was one for the guys. Besides, it was probably best to get a little space from her after such an emotional week.

We piled into Abuelita, and I hooked up my music to his cassette player. We had endless tunes and the open road. We cracked open some beers and sipped them to prevent unnecessary stops as we headed southwest toward the Pacific. We rode the carretera farther south than I'd yet been, then turned onto some paved rural route and traveled through countryside extending for miles in all directions. We'd occasionally pass a small town. One in particular had dozens of chicken rotisseries set up along the roadside. Herb said the chicken here was amazing. He always had comments and advice about everything, as if he was some kind of strange life tour guide—even if it was all bullshit.

We passed through chicken town and came across some farmland where workers used what looked to be primitive tools to hack away at the thick stalks of the tall plants scattered throughout the fields.

"So, you never found that guy who banged Luz, did you?" he said.

"He didn't bang her. And no, I didn't. I looked for him everywhere though."

"They're both playin' you. You gotta wake up and smell the hog shit."

"I don't know about all that." I took a big whiff. It stank, all right—but it really stank. "You smell that, Herbstains?"

"Yeah, that's heavy. Probably a dead horse up the road."

"You sure you don't need to change your diaper, old man?"

"I'm sure. That's death. There's nothing else like it."

We drove another minute before passing a small farm. In a field just beyond lay a bloated horse with rigid, outstretched limbs. The only thing worse than that smell was the fact that the old man was right.

Herb slowed the car as we arrived at a military checkpoint.

"What's all this?"

"Well, Michoacán is like Mexico's drug breadbasket. They got checkpoints set up all over to make sure nobody's pushin' the stuff around. They get jealous when other people try to make money off it too."

"Damn, these guys look serious."

"Yeah, just set the beer down between your legs for a minute."

Herb stopped and a guy carrying an assault rifle asked some questions. Herb must have given the proper responses because they waved us through.

"God, this place takes me back. I tramped through Michoacán before I'd arrived in Lila. I met a Canadian couple out here a few years back doing the same. I brought them back to Lila and let them stay with me for a coupla days. The boyfriend asks me if I could score him some weed, so I said, 'How much can you afford?' And he says, 'About a hundred pesos.' I made a phone call, and soon a buddy of mine shows up and just dumps this garbage bag full of herb on my floor. He wouldn't even take the money, just said, 'We got this shit coming out of our ears.' Apparently they had a pretty good harvest and didn't know what to do with all the extra."

"Holy shit! What'd you do with all that green?"

"Well, the Canucks flipped the fuck out when they saw how much there was. I mean, they got seriously spooked. They only snatched a coupla nugs then took off into the night. I tried to give them their hundred pesos back, but they didn't want it."

"You still got the herb somewhere?"

"No, I just took a little for myself, then chucked the bag in my neighbor's trash can."

We both laughed. While he may have been a fuck-up, I trusted Herb with my life. He was as strange as they came, but he was a survivor and would invariably find a way in and out of any situation we could possibly encounter, even if his ends and means were dubious. We were a couple of misfits who'd turned our backs on the past and kept pushing forward—always forward—and that particular direction, on that particular day, brought us to the Pacific. We arrived at a cliff a few hundred feet above the ocean and had a panoramic view of all that deep blue water under that lighter blue sky. And it was all untainted: no cum-stained motels, or seedy bars, or vendors outside selling t-shirts with pictures of drunk frogs or some other horseshit. It was just mountains, and trees, and blue . . . and us.

Herb pulled over, and we got out. There was a shrine to the Virgin Mother standing at the cliff's edge. I caressed her cheek and scanned the scene. I already knew I could never live there, not even for a summer. This just wasn't the place for that kind of nonsense. A day trip would suffice.

We got back in the car after a few moments of silent reflection and descended the cliff to the vast beach below. There were only a few man-made structures down there: a few restaurants and a small hotel. Herb parked in front of the largest restaurant, and a few pretty waitresses greeted us. They invited us to sit, but Herb had a different idea. He walked over to the guy in the kitchen and said something to him. The guy whistled to some drunk out back, and soon the drunk was carrying plastic tables and chairs out on the sand and setting them up near the water. He grabbed a large umbrella and shovel, dug a hole, and set up the umbrella over the table. Herb handed the drunk fifty pesos, and the guy bowed his head and wandered off.

"We just bought him a couple caguamas," Herb said.

"How can you be sure?" I said.

Herb smiled. "You run a good game most of the time, but sometimes I worry about you, Will."

We went back to Abuelita for the case of beer and the rest of our supplies, and returned to the sand. One of the pretty waitresses approached and gave us menus. We looked over the fare while sipping brews. Herb recommended the ceviche and the langostina, or lobsters, which they pulled from a nearby river, but I got the shrimp due to a sudden craving of not wanting to spend double on the langostina. I knew the price of the shrimp was probably also inflated, but I didn't mind paying el precio gringo in spots like this. It was a bright, beautiful day.

"You know," Herb said, "despite all the corruption and poverty and drug problems, this is one gorgeous country. I could never go back to the States."

"I wish I didn't have to go back."

"You could always stay, you know."

"Maybe . . ."

"America has grown too smart for its own good. That's the problem there. It's an intellect-based society. People get so wrapped up in being the best, fastest, smartest, sexiest, that they forget to live— that they forget life is beautiful. But Mexico is a heart-based society. A family-based society. It's definitely got its shit too, but at least the people down here aren't born with the curse of being perpetually told since birth that their country tops the world politically, economically, and culturally. That's too much pressure for any nation to overcome."

"Would you ever go back?"

"I don't know. I mean, I've found a home here. But the drug problem's getting worse. It's eating this country away. If the people here continue to refuse to look in the mirror, it's gonna be their undoing. Maybe if it got real bad, I'd go back."

"Do you ever miss it?"

"I miss certain things—small things, but they all happened long ago."

"Like what?"

"Like, I remember when my brother got married. A few nights before the wedding, his father-in-law-to-be took us out for all-you-can-eat crab legs at some great dive spot on Lake Michigan. We ate for half the night, sucked down beers, ordered appetizers, and it ended up costing less than sixty bucks. And these were real crab legs—big ones. Just before close, the manager comes over. He sits down, we get to talking, and next thing you know we're all goofin' until the ass-crack of dawn. The guy kept the place open for us all night, drinkin' beers with us, bullshittin'. Good luck gettin' away with something like that now. Now you got all kinds of codes and regulations—the owner would probably get sued for keeping the lights on all night and disturbing the crabs while they tried to sleep in their tank, or some other bullshit . . . Life was just simpler then."

"Sounds nice."

"Back then, it seemed I knew what America was. There was something to it. Now it's just a jumbled mess of culture-bleaching corporations and free-loaders suckin' down welfare."

"Yeah, but 'back-then' had its problems too. The Civil Rights Act didn't even pass until '64. People always talk about the 'Good-Ol' Days' like they were something special, but they forget about the lynchings, and fire hoses, and oppression of women. 'Small Town America' is nothing but a fucking myth. It never existed, and it's probably a damned good thing it didn't."

"Well, maybe you have a point. But I'm done analyzing it. I have a life here now."

"That may be true—but don't you still wonder sometimes where you belong?"

He didn't answer.

The ceviche came. It was delicious. Was there a way to keep life simple while still allowing for progress? A way to achieve unity while respecting the individual rights of all people? There had to be a way. I was certain of this. But a part of me was always tearing down walls that the other part was so busy building. Did I even have a place in such a world? And if not, could it then even exist?

Herb dropped his lobster shell on his plate, shot out of his chair, and ripped off his clothes as he ran to the ocean. Hearing his words about the past made me feel as if I'd missed out on something big. But maybe that something big was the very thing he was now running from? I fought the urge to join him. Instead, I sat and observed as he splashed and dove through the waves like a smiling eight-year-old. After a while, though, I ran out to the water too. All these questions I had, I realized, would never need to find their answers as long as that beach could remain pure for the rest of eternity. What the fuck could I ever know that I couldn't touch or taste or be a part of? I swam through the water completely aware that creatures could also be swimming with me. Herb and I were the people who got eaten by sharks—not those in the six o'clock news. Regardless, we jumped through the waves on our own private beach as if we'd had no previous childhood. We were misfits. We were mutants. We'd both turned our backs on our past. I was so tired of running. I think so was he.

We swam for about twenty minutes, then decided to leave. We paid and packed up the car. We laid towels on the seats and hopped in. I hated that. The seats always got wet even with towels on them. The only way to really keep them dry was to not go in the water in the first place. I knew I shouldn't have gone in, but I have no fucking discipline . . . Fuck! I could feel one coming. I'd gone almost an entire afternoon without the slightest thing resembling a panic attack, but my realization of this rare triumph only fanned the flames. That was how they started—something as simple as putting towels on a car seat could cause the chain reaction leading to blinding panic.

But before I shut my door, I caught a glimpse of the sun falling over the restaurant's palapa roof, covering the tables and chairs in soft amber. I got out my camera and took several shots—each click of the shutter further relaxing me, like a burn victim administering their own shots of morphine. I breathed deeply and closed the door. The pretty waitresses waved, and we waved back. Just as Herb started to back up I saw the drunk popping the top off a caguama. He raised it and smiled at us.

Herb took us back up the cliff side road. The sun had already hidden behind the horizon by the time we reached the highway. I put on some more music but went for something more current this time: Wilco and Ryan Adams. I played "Let it Ride," and Herb accused Adams of ripping off Dylan: "Is this a 'lost track' from *Nashville Skyline* or something?"

I was filled with a peace as we sped through the countryside—a peace I'd only felt during a few other distinct moments in my life. One of those had come while traveling through Spain and Portugal that January with a group of friends. We drove down a highway in Portugal on our way to Lisbon that sent me to another place entirely. There were vast, rolling fields with windmills scattered throughout. People carried goods in baskets on their backs while walking along the side of the highway. I'd only seen those images before on film or in print. But in that moment, I was a part of the picture. Why weren't these scenes a part of my life? Just seeing those sights with my own eyes made me feel alive, and real. For all I knew, neither Spain nor Portugal even existed. Maybe the plane just circled Lake Erie all night and dumped us off in Southern Canada, which put on a hell of a show . . .? But that world on the other side seemed softer and more sincere than the one I'd left behind.

I wasn't driving, so I allowed my mind to wander. Everything soon settled into place. It was always in those peaceful moments when I realized that, deep down, I wasn't a cynic, or a sadist, or misanthrope. In those moments, I realized my heart was just beating too quickly to live at a normal pace, causing me to over or underreact to everything. God, I was pushing all the time, in every direction at once. It was only inevitable I'd blow if someone got in my way. Didn't they know I was out there trying to find a solution to all their problems as well and not just my own? There was an answer out there, and I was going to find it . . . and to hell with my credit score!

I could have ridden that road with the Herbster for a month. There was no way either of us was going to hit the brakes if things got too strange. We were both on a quest for the unknown, the unfelt, and the Kind, and we'd be damned if we let anything get in the way. I felt my hatred for the pathetic German melting away.

Chapter 38

I returned to Luz's place that night, and we watched a movie before heading to bed. I went back to my old place the next afternoon to get my stuff. I thought Sal'd give me shit: "Oh, well I've gotta go to school right now so I can't let you in my room to get your stuff."

"But it'll only take a second to unlock your door?"

"Yeah, but then I gotta wait for you to drag your stuff out, then lock it again . . ."

But it didn't happen like that. In fact, he was cooperative. He had this look of deep reflection and sadness about him.

"Did you finally find out Herb was your real father?" I asked while dragging my big blue bag to the door.

He laughed. "No, my mom called last night. She's sick. It sounds serious."

"Will she be all right?"

"Her doctors don't know. I'm gonna go to school this afternoon and withdraw. I'm driving back up to Buffalo tomorrow."

"Does your brother know?"

"Yeah, he's heading back too." Sal sat on the couch and took a deep breath. "You think of all these people you see each day as being so important. Think about all the friends you had in high school. How many of them would you call a good friend? How many do you still talk to? How many would even come to the hospital if you got sick?"

"I think some would."

"That's bullshit. How many guys do you still even talk to since we left college?"

"A few."

"Yeah, about what?"

"Bullshit, I guess."

"They'll probably all fade away too. There are only a handful of people that come into your life who ever really matter. Family is number one, then a few friends. Ian is one of those. You're the other."

"Shit, well, I don't know what to say . . . thanks for everything. I never would have made it down here if it wasn't for you pushing me along."

"Don't worry about it. I think this is the happiest I've ever seen you."

"The second I got down here, man, something changed in me. It feels like this is the place." It was true; something had changed, and not just in a spiritual sense. I'd had a serious physical condition that had tortured me for years, and it almost entirely disappeared the day I got to Lila. And I hadn't really thought about it much since.

"Good luck on your trip, Donny Assdrops. I hope everything works out with Luz."

"Thanks! Good luck on your trip too, Robert Spice Jackson. I hope your mom's okay."

While taking a cab back to Luz's, I thought about what he'd said. It was true. So many people who'd once seemed so important to me have all faded away. I have distinct memories of some letting me down. I also had distinct memories of letting some of them down.

I spent the rest of the afternoon relaxing at Luz's place and thinking about Sal's words. I had so many friends in Mexico whom I'd probably never see again. But I tried to ignore those thoughts. I'd done extensive travel before and knew how grueling it could be. You'd get so far out there, enter some incredible place but spend the entire time just longing for a place to call your own.

Luz packed quickly, and we waited out the sun by sitting on her bed and watching movies. My anger for everyone fell to the ground. Luz was there with me. She was always there with me. I'd known so many girls before her. So many with that distant look always in their eyes. So many who endlessly chased style, and the right shades to paint themselves, and the proper way to speak to people to get what they wanted. But Luz *was* style. She was class, and grace, and got what she wanted because she didn't want. She vibed and the world saw what she needed and gave it to her. So, she didn't have to worry about the stupid shit that burdened everyone else. That caused them to throw away the present for the past or future. She was always right there. She was the only one who said yes when everyone else was saying no. And she said it with such confidence, as if no wasn't even an option. It'd be so easy for her to have said no. So easy for her to have worn it out on her clothes. The world wanted her. But she already had the world.

If not for the twenty-four-hour cheating scare it would have been a flawless week. I was at peace with Luz, with Lila, with leaving, with digging myself into debt, and with all my hideous sins. And it was a flawless afternoon too.

Luz had another fashion desfile that night and started preparing for it early that afternoon. She left, and I took a cab to Mica's to plan our trip. Later I headed up to Modaloca for the desfile. On the way, I got a text from Herb. Apparently, Paz had thrown Sal a surprise going-away party at our dead-end palace, and Herb was heading over. After the desfile, Luz and I took a cab to the bottom of the dead-end street I still didn't know the name of and got out under the almond trees. There were people everywhere. Inside they were dancing, and outside they were talking. We stepped over a busted piñata in the street and walked into the house. Familiar faces surrounded me, all a blur. I walked over to Jose, and he introduced me to some delicious bean dip. Tito approached Luz, and they danced in a step I'd never learn. I walked to the kitchen and grabbed a beer. Paz and Sofia were sitting at the table telling stories and laughing. Sal walked over with a playful look about him.

"We should pick Jose up over our heads and just shake him around," he said.

"Okay."

We walked over, grabbed Jose, and threw him up on our shoulders. Jose laughed and clapped his hands. We spun him around a few times, then set him down. Marta walked through the front door. She saw me, stormed over, and threw a crumbled twenty-peso bill in my face. I gestured to Sal, and soon we had her up in the air as well. We didn't put her down until she was screaming and on the verge of tears.

I watched Luz dance with Tito for a song, then headed outside with the other lowlifes. I couldn't believe this was the first and only party we'd thrown. Sal had spoken of house parties all the time while trying to convince me to move there but had said no each time I'd brought it up after I'd arrived. I approached Dr. Josh. He and Herb were having a lively discussion about the use of geothermal energy to end global dependence on fossil fuels. Just past them were the three guys who'd grilled me about George Jr. on Dr. Josh's balcony during Jorg's despedida. I tried to avoid them, but they came over when they saw me.

"Hola, amigo! How have you been?" the big one said.

"Yes, long time no see," said Mama Bear.

The small one wrapped his arms around my shoulders, just right.

Such warmth. Such sincerity. Perhaps these guys weren't the pricks I'd thought they were?

I said hello, then took a look around. I couldn't believe I was leaving the next day. Lila had seeped inside of me. I could see why so many had chosen to stay here after their time was up. A bat swooped down and just missed my head. I dug through the spilled guts of the piñata on the street, grabbed a piece of candy, unwrapped it, and tossed it in my mouth.

Dr. Josh's younger brother arrived that night for a six-month stint observing the volcano. One went, another came. Thus was the cycle of life in Lila. There were already so many new people I was just beginning to meet. The semester was ending and soon many of the extraneros would be back on planes or buses home. But not everyone thrived here. Some, like Dan, signed up for a semester, but left after only a few weeks. I could only guess as to why. Luz and I hailed a cab after some more beers, bean dip, and goodbyes.

I turned my back on the dead-end house, the extraneros, and Turd. I was leaving the next day with my baby and didn't need any more baggage. If Luz ran into the prick's arms the second I left Mexico, at I least she'd chosen me while I was still around. I was ready to leave.

I woke early the next morning to run some errands before our departure that night. Herb had offered to lend me his big, green camping backpack, and I walked to his place that afternoon to get it. Herb lived in a small studio apartment just big enough for a queen-size bed, a dresser, and a couple of plastic lawn chairs. He was sitting in a chair and watching *Caddyshack* when I walked in. He handed over the bag, but I fell under Rodney Dangerfield's spell and sat down. We got to the booger scene before Luz sent me a text: "Where are you? Can you bring something back for dinner?"

"Yo, Herby, I gotta jet. The missus wants me to bring home some dinner."

"There's a shack down the street that sells cheap rotisserie chickens."

"Sounds good."

"Wanna bring me back one?" He handed me fifty pesos. I nodded and took off. I bought a couple of birds, some salt potatoes, tortillas, and a few limes. As I got closer to Herb's apartment, I saw a woman standing at his doorway. She was dressed in dirty clothing and holding a baby. Herb pulled out his wallet and handed her some money, then shut the door, and the woman left. I knocked on the door. Herb answered. He seemed flustered.

"Who was that?"

"I don't know. Just some beggar looking for change." He took a deep breath and seemed to be holding back some tears. "It's getting bad here. The divide between rich and poor is growing. Just last week a coupla little girls knocked, begging for something to eat. I didn't have much, so I just handed them a loaf of bread and some peanut butter. They walked away, and I shut the door and just started sobbing. I can't stand the way we treat each other . . ." The tears started to fall.

"Well, as long as people run the show, people will always suffer." I handed him his chicken and said goodbye. I wasn't overcome with sadness or nostalgia. With a guy like Herb, there was no need for such nonsense. We'd already said a million goodbyes in different languages throughout our lives. We were good with goodbyes. Done right, they were as valid a craft as any. And I knew I'd see Herb again. He was just too strange to ignore.

We shook hands, and I walked to the street. I rounded a corner, and soon he was gone. There he was, a potential millionaire who'd given it all up to hide out in some tiny studio in some tiny Mexican town. I didn't think much about him on the walk back except that there was no door of mine he'd ever entered that I didn't invite him through, nor any place he ever took me that I didn't agree to go.

Luz and I ate when I returned to her apartment, then finished the final round of packing. I was excited. Luz and I were a couple of bandits about to skip town. Luz was stealthy. She could move quickly and quietly, fording rivers and hopping trains. She was a great accomplice. As a kid, I'd always dreamed of meeting a scrappy girl— one who'd run away with me through some wild adventure. We'd stow away on a ship across the Atlantic, hop out on the Moroccan coast, steal our way across North Africa, and then by boat to Greece. Someone who looked beautiful in rags, who never stole a thing but to put it immediately to her mouth. There'd be no planning, no waste, just us dancing all day, and running all night. I hated anchors, and Luz was a beautiful, brilliant peacock feather.

Mica was a seasoned traveler, as well. Travel was a skill just like any other. It took skill to move quickly and efficiently from place to place without giving in to the desire to give up and go back should anything go wrong. It was a skill to know maps, to know how to ask people for directions, to know how to find what's needed should the ship be blown off course. And it always was.

Luz and I took a cab to the bus station where we waited for Mica. When he arrived, he did so with a group of the extraneros following him like some celebrity's entourage. There were tears, and pictures, and hugs, and kissed cheeks. One or two did the same with me. Others, not so much . . . Even if I'd never wronged them personally, I'd still scorned several of their leaders, and I knew most didn't have what it took to separate from the pack—even while under the influence of the dizzying emotional intoxication that often came with goodbyes—so I granted them reprieve for their cowardice and withheld any spiteful words or looks. Besides, I wasn't on the same friendship level with them as was Mica. But even if I had been, I wouldn't have cared.

The bus soon came, and we boarded. The narrow doors chiseled off the residue that had grown on us over the past few months. We found our seats and quickly fell asleep.

Chapter 39

I woke the next morning with Luz's head on my shoulder. Mica was already awake and staring out the window with the wide, enthusiastic eyes of youth.

"This place is enormous," he said. "There're buildings as far as the eye can see."

I was angry for sleeping through this but didn't stir so Luz could remain sleeping. She soon awoke, and we were whole again. Luz replaced Juana as our travel companion on this trip, and I felt the change in energy already. We were much kinder to Luz, or perhaps *I* was much kinder to Luz. We rode through another half hour of bustle before pulling into an enormous bus station.

We got off, got our bags, and walked into the station. Though it was 4 a.m., there were people everywhere. A decorated Christmas tree towered over the crowds. I was exhausted and had no idea where we were headed but knew from experience to follow those with the most confident strides. Luz walked to a taxi booth, and we followed behind. She spoke with the guy behind the counter, and soon we were in a cab riding through the Mexico City streets. I was impressed by the enormity of it all. Even the billboards and gas stations seemed to have some heroic size to them. The driver sped through a residential neighborhood, then turned onto an avenue lined on both sides by tall stone buildings, which gave the feel we were travelling between two castles. The cabbie dropped us off a little up this road, then pulled a U-turn and headed back in the direction of the faintly lit horizon. The street had the size to hold thousands, but we were the only ones on it. We opened a door in a castle wall and walked inside the hostel. The lobby was cramped and a poorly decorated Christmas tree provided nearly the only light. We checked in and lumbered up the stairs to our rooms. Mica was on the top floor and Luz and I just below him. Luz and I set down our possessions, took off our clothes, and slipped together into a deep sleep—our bodies wrapped tightly as one while the feather-weight darkness covered us like a soft, warm blanket. Mica was alone. I knew what he was feeling. He'd never had a Luz with him on a trip, and neither had I until the night before.

We woke around noon to some arrhythmic knocks at the door.

"Hey," Mica said, "you gotta check this out!"

It was still dark, cool, and quiet in our room, but all this changed the instant I opened the door. The sound of a great crowd filled the air.

"They woke me up. It's been like this since seven," Mica said.

Luz and I dressed and followed the German to the roof. There below on the once-empty street, were now thousands of people forming a raging human river flowing between the castle walls. Hundreds of vendors had set up small stands, and people were shopping or just passing down the street. There was a tremendous energy to it all. I leaned my head over the roof and felt the warmth the street radiated.

We ate some huevos and frijoles at the café on the roof, then walked down to the street. The weather was cool enough to wear a light coat. We passed several vendor stands, and I fought the temptation to buy some of the cheap crap I didn't need.

The river continued flowing into the Zocalo, one of the world's largest city squares. At its center was an enormous flagpole with a Mexican flag large enough to cover a city bus. I could feel the energy pulsing through the streets. Though the people here were no bigger than those in Lila, they seemed like giants, stomping through their proportionally large city. Street performers and pedestrians filled the empty spaces between vendors' stands. The walls of the surrounding buildings were covered in Christmas decorations. Just above those decorations was a layer of yellowish-green filth covering the city. The pollution was so bad I could taste it. It coated my mouth and likely did the same to my lungs. This place didn't fuck around. Though I was amazed with the size and intensity of it all, I remained vigilant. I knew from both primary and secondary sources the dangers: theft, kidnapping, murder. A number of the extraneros had been through here in the previous few months, and almost every one of them had been victimized in some way. Most only had their wallets pickpocketed, but one was robbed at knifepoint.

We explored the Zocalo and its surrounding area. My favorite spot was the Templo Mayor, the supposed spot where the Aztecs found the eagle perched on a cactus with a snake in its beak. Seeing this made me feel slightly more human.

Luz had recently been to D.F., but only on a connecting flight back to Lila. Other than that, she'd been there once before as a child but had little memory of anything other than the Zocalo and Teotihuacan. I was excited we'd get to explore it together. But I was also concerned. I wasn't afraid to get bruised or to throw punches if necessary. But with her here? Luz was tough, but so were they. The need to protect her thrust my already overactive senses into hypervigilant mode. I had my eyes on anybody who came near her. And this, unfortunately, kept my eyes from seeing many of the wonderful sights surrounding me.

Luz stopped at a small stand to buy some makeup. She picked out a few shades, then unzipped and reached into her purse. She grabbed out her wallet and swung her purse to the side as she handed over the cash, putting the bag on display for anyone walking by. Three men passed and each stared at it. I stormed over to her and zipped it up: "You need to be more careful. There are bad men about . . ."

We walked along the sidewalk in search of a place to eat lunch. I had my sunglasses on and watched as ten out of every ten guys we passed eye-fucked Luz from her toes to her ears. Fucking scumbags.

We found a spot, ate, and took a cab to the airport. That afternoon, Mica's friend Gretel was flying in from Germany to join us on the rest of our trip. We arrived on time. I walked to a large screen showing incoming flights.

"Yo, Mica, what's her flight number?"

"Uh, I don't know."

"Well, what airline is she flying?"

"Uh, I can't remember . . ."

Several planes had just arrived from Germany. The fucking Germans were taking the world by storm. It was as if there were some covert operation set up by an overly contrite foreign affairs minister to atone for their sins. I imagined their address to the nation: "So vee must go out into zee world, into zee homes, and hearts, and minds of all zee people of earth. And vee must show them how warm, and compassionate, and sensible vee can be. We will now begin with our daily one hour of smiling instruction, followed by a two-hour session of how to make with zee small talk. Remember people, a smile is best when it shows a mouthful of pearly whites . . ."

We checked several gates and eventually found her. We absorbed her into our group and headed into the night. We took a cab back to the hostel to get ready for the evening. Luz and I got sidetracked in the shower, delaying the process an hour and a half (what can I say, the girl's a Viking . . .). We walked back to the Zocalo. The walls on its perimeter were all lit up with Christmas lights shaped like wreaths, trees, gifts, stars . . . I took a few pictures then handed the camera to Mica, and he snapped a picture of Luz and me in the center of it all. Each time I touched her, I felt further tangled around her roots.

We got up early the next morning and took a bus to Teotihuacan. Mica had planned our itinerary for the two-week journey and had only allowed for two days in D.F. The trip to the former Aztec city that day was a part of this plan. But two days was much too short a time to even see all the sights the Zocalo had to offer, much less the city, so Luz and I made the decision to stay, and he and Gretel decided to take a bus to Acapulco that night. We'd meet in Puebla in five days, but we were together for the rest of that day.

We headed northeast. I was tranquil and, though my heart beat rapidly, my legs remained still. This ride was more than a passage between worlds—it was also my chance to observe the vastness of the city as we chugged through one of its veins deep into its heart. Even after forty-five minutes, we didn't escape the cover of the yellowish-green layer above. It rested over the mountains and valleys, well beyond the massive city that created it.

Gretel looked to be thinking about escape herself. She tapped her foot and grabbed her stomach.

"What's wrong with her?" I said.

"Has to use the bathroom," Mica said.

She struggled the entire trip, sweating, and rocking in her seat. When the bus finally pulled over in a dusty parking lot, Gretel pushed past the other passengers, shot out the door, dashed into some bushes, and let it rip while the others walked past her on their way to the entrance. She finished, and we walked to the ticket counter. Mica and Luz showed their student IDs and got the half-off discount. Gretel and I paid full price. I still didn't know what to think of her. She spoke English but didn't say much—just looked around nervously while chain-smoking cigs. I liked, however, that she had no problem with poppin' a squat just a few hundred meters from some of the treasures of ancient civilization.

"I came here with my family when I was very young," Luz said. "My father knew so much about these ruins. It made me feel like I was home."

Luz walked ahead of us down the Calzada de los Muertos as we strolled along behind. The Pyramid of the Moon stood at the end of that avenue, and the Pyramid of the Sun—one of the tallest structures in the ancient world—was to our right. Most of the visitors were climbing these pyramids. Mica climbed the steps of one of the tombs lining the avenue, and I followed behind.

"I don't think Gretel is having a good time," Mica said.

Gretel sat on a step of a nearby tomb and lit a cigarette. The hawkers went after her. She spoke no Spanish and just flailed her arms and shook her head each time they presented her with some wooden statue or other trinket she had no need for.

"I think you may be right," I said.

Luz walked alone. A hawker approached her. She shook her head and smiled, and the man walked away smiling as well.

"Luz is too nice," he said. "It bothers me."

"I don't know how she does it. I wish I did. I'd join her."

Luz ran up the steps of a tomb about a hundred yards across from us. When she reached the top, she spread her arms and twirled in the sun. I pulled out my camera and zoomed in but didn't shoot. I was tired of being a fucking tourist.

We each walked at our own pace but eventually met at the base of the Pyramid of the Sun. The pyramid was tall and steep, towering over the brown earth. Mica and I led the charge up the pyramid, which became a tacit competition between the two of us to be the first to the top. We left the girls behind and didn't look back to check on their progress. The pyramid had four levels, each littered with winded tourists catching their breath and taking photos. The steps were tall and narrow, in proportion to the slope of the pyramid. The chain-smoker and I pushed on. I pulled ahead of Mica somewhere on the second level and continued to the top without rest, despite the burning in my legs and chest. It was a hot day, and the dust in the air clung to my sweating body.

When I reached the top, I looked down on the ruins, then up at the horizon. The yellowish-green haze was still overhead. I took a deep breath. My lungs ached. Mica, Luz, and Gretel were still levels below. I waited patiently for them; it was usually during those quiet times on those lonely, sweaty summits when I realized what a fool I was. Some things just weren't a race.

When they finally arrived, Luz hugged me, then walked to the center and sat in full lotus position. I left her alone and continued to observe the world below me, imagining the daily life of the Aztecs. I got lost in a trance that overtook my reality and guided my mind to one great realization: people did exist even when I wasn't there to see them. Maybe then love too could exist even when it wasn't right there in my hands?

We descended and decided against climbing the Pyramid of the Moon. The Germans were leaving that night, and we wanted ample time to eat dinner. Before we left, I bought a colorful Mexican blanket for my aunt. We headed to the edge of the dusty parking lot and waited for the bus. I sat on a tree trunk and watched the sun as it slowly dipped below the horizon. I sat in silence. My body was tired. The pyramids and sun had had their way with me that afternoon. But I felt a deep satisfaction—the kind only felt after achieving something great. When the bus came, we paid and walked to the back. We paired off, and I melted into my baby with my eyes gazing through the window. The world was amber and moved much more slowly than it had that morning. When we got to the bus station, we took a cab to the hostel. Luz and I took separate showers that night.

We dressed warmly and stepped into the cool evening in search of a decent cheap restaurant. We found one and were seated at a table in the center. Mica and I each ordered their biggest steak, and we all got drinks. The waiter was particularly handsome and particularly good to us—too good, in fact. The room was crowded, and he spent a little too much time at our table, and a little too much time smiling.

"So where are you all from?" he said.

"Shanghai," I said.

"Don't listen to him," Luz said.

I scowled at her. I had a gut feeling this creep was inching closer to Luz or our wallets, or both. Someone at another table called him, and he walked away. I knew where this was going, but didn't want to say anything for fear of sounding paranoid. I ripped into my steak and tried to ignore him.

Luz leaned in. "See that guy?" She pointed to some older scumbag in the corner. "He keeps looking at me and blowing me kisses."

"That fat fuck in the suit?"

"Jes, him!"

He *was* looking. I held up my knife, and he smiled and kept eating. These fucking people!

The waiter came back. "So how is everything?"

They all nodded while chewing their food.

"You know, it's not often I can spend time with Americans," he said.

"Well, they're German, and I'm not interested," I said.

"Don't be rude, honey."

"No, it's okay," he said. "He's probably just got his hands full protecting such a beautiful girl in this big, dangerous city."

Luz smiled.

"You know," he said, "a friend of mine is throwing a party tonight. I'd be happy for you all to come."

The fucking creep! He was actually doing it—and they were actually falling for it.

"Yeah, that sounds great!" said my German ally, possibly forgetting he was leaving soon.

"I'd love to go to a party," Luz said.

Gretel didn't even look up. She just shoveled more food toward her gut. I sat there alone, holding back what I really wanted to tell this guy, and all of them, out of fear of sounding paranoid.

"Great, why don't you give me your number, and I'll call you . . ." he said to Luz.

"Or, why don't you give me *your* number, and we'll call *you*," I said.

"Okay." He gave me the number, and I pretended to type it in. Someone at another table called him again.

"You can really be rude sometimes, Will," Luz said. I wanted to rip into her, and the others. How stupid could they be? At best, this guy was just some scumbag trying to score with Luz. At worst, what if he worked for some big kidnapping ring? I mean, it was possible . . . And, just because I wasn't so eager to take his cock down my throat, *I* was the asshole. I fought the desire to get up and leave them—walk out into the night and find some party out there on my own. And Luz was the worst. She leaned in again. "That guy keeps staring at me and so does that other one over there." She had to be fucking with me.

The Germans had to leave, so we paid and walked back to the hostel. On the way, we stopped in the Zocalo to enjoy the decorations. The vendors were out selling hot tamales, and churros, and tacos. Luz and I bought a pancake and topped it with honey. We strolled along as we ate it. The night was cool, helping lower my body temperature.

"I was just being nice to him. You shouldn't be so angry," she told me. I opened my mouth to speak but stuffed it with pancake instead. Was this her form of an apology? If so, it was fucking weak.

A puff of what looked like pink smoke floated by. I looked up. The air was filled with clouds of it. Everyone started jumping and grabbing at these clouds. I scanned the scene and saw a teenage boy spraying cotton candy into the air from a small cart. I wondered if this was an advertisement or a sincere effort to spread sugarcoated love in the world; I took it for the latter. Soon everyone around was jumping and laughing and stuffing candy in their mouths. I grabbed a big piece. I was about to eat it when I felt a tug at my pants. I looked down and saw a small boy holding up his hand. I gave the candy to its rightful owner, and the kid smiled and ran away, wildly kicking his legs up into his ass. Luz, Mica, and even Gretel joined in on the action. I pulled out my camera and snapped a candid shot of the three. All smiles. There was an innocence there that cleansed me. I sinned every day, and only felt human in these times. And Luz, she was just a kid herself. Nineteen. And here she was in the fucking heart of it all with me—saying yes on a whim, boarding a bus, and heading out into the big, fucked-up world armed with nothing more than that beautiful smile and her sharp wits. I wished I could create these scenes and live in them. But I couldn't.

We walked back to the hostel after the Candy Christmas Magic moment. The Germans took a cab to the bus station. Luz and I went upstairs and fell asleep.

We woke around ten the next morning. I felt significantly lighter. I leaned over and kissed Luz, and she kissed me back. The Germans were probably already at the beach—the same one that I'd dreamed of visiting so many times as a kid. Acapulco. Even the name was exciting. But now I had a new cause for excitement.

The hostel was full, so we checked into a nearby hotel. We got a clean room with a balcony for a hundred fifty pesos a night. You couldn't find a cardboard box to nap in for that cheap in Times Square. We headed to a nearby café for lunch, then Luz suggested we take a tour of the city. We walked to the Zocalo and hopped on a double-decker bus. We rode down Paseo de la Reforma, D.F.'s main avenue, past skyscrapers and pedestrians in suits, then through several neighborhoods filled with posh shops and quaint cafés. The city was large and lively, but many neighborhoods had a smaller-scale homeyness to them. After the tour, we went back to the hotel, got ready, and headed to La Zona Rosa for dinner. We walked to the metro station and crammed onto a packed train. I stuffed my hands in my pockets and covered my wallet and phone. We passed a number of stops before Luz tapped me on the ass and said, "Here, sweetie." We got off and walked to an area with a number of restaurants, bars, and cafés. We picked a restaurant and were seated outside on the edge of the pedestrian-only street. I was still angry from the night before, but now I was sitting with a drink and dinner. My work was done.

Luz didn't say much over dinner. In fact, it wasn't until then that I realized that Luz didn't ever say very much. I reviewed our entire timeline together. There was always something a little off between us. Were we dysfunctional? Or was I dysfunctional? Or was I just thinking too fucking much?

I looked up. Luz smiled again. What the hell was going on in that head?

"How's your dinner?"

"Good. Yours?"

"Good."

When we finished dinner, we turned our attention to the bar across the pedestrian street whose entrance released a thick smoke and loud rock 'n' roll music each time someone opened the front door. An interesting mix of people sat out front. Men in business suits sat comfortably beside punks in ripped jeans and torn shirts.

Luz and I were dressed somewhere in between: she in a tight white sweater and jeans, and I in a button-down and jeans. We looked less a rock 'n' roll couple and more like a couple of yuppies who only pulled out their bandanas, showed off their tattoos, and smoked grass at the annual, end-of-summer Tom Petty show at the town's fairgrounds. There seemed to be a healthy balance between the rockers and the suits, but a part of me hoped for a brawl—a rebellion to spill out of that thick, wooden door and fill the pedestrian street with real sound. Part of me wanted to kick its own ass. But another part of me was glad to see these two seemingly separate worlds coexisting peacefully.

We paid our bill, crossed the street, and walked through the wooden door. A sophisticated older gentleman dressed like an English butler greeted us. The front room had the charm and class of an upscale restaurant. But rock 'n' roll blasted from the rear room. The butler showed us past the suited customers and toward the music. I dragged my hand along the wall as we walked. The polished woodwork soon transformed into what felt like stone as we entered a cave dug into the rock sediment that had accumulated over the centuries. The smoke grew thicker the deeper we went. We followed the sound and found its source when we entered a large room. This was the heart. A thick cloud of smoke was fanned around the room by banging heads and pumping fists. The creatures here were leather-clad demons, preserved in their own toxicity. They all seemed to know each other. They sat in big groups around the stage and exchanged high fives and saluds.

The butler showed Luz and me to a table in the back corner—a fitting spot. We ordered a cubeta and watched the group on stage rip through covers of Black Sabbath, Zeppelin, and Guns n' Roses tunes. Though they played others' music, they made it their own. The lead guitarist improvised on the original riffs and licks, and gave solos you'd never hear on any studio album. Every few songs, the musicians would hand over the instruments to other audience members, and they'd pick up right where the other players left off. Some guys would start on drums, then switch to bass, then to vocals. It seemed everyone there was proficient in several instruments. The second guitarist and the first singer were the best. This singer wore a torn denim vest, exposing arms with tats and tracks only gained from a lifetime of experience. If spun on a turntable, those arms could play their own tunes. I doubt this guy made a conscious decision to choose his style. It likely crawled out from deep within. He wouldn't be able to change it if he tried. I envied that.

In this room, these men had their stage. Here, it seemed, nobody'd be labeled a junky or loser for simply following their inner blueprint. They were a team—a pack of hyenas bringing down the dangerous and powerful water buffalo of convention blocking the path to creative expression. Maybe some got killed or hurt in battle, but the group ate and was able to play another night. Luz and I'd merely stumbled in as they were ripping into the carcass.

We sat beside a group of rockers seated at a long table. One, a bald guy wearing a rope around his neck, addressed me between songs.

"Hey, I just wanted to thank you for your country's music."

"How'd you know I was American?"

"I heard your accent while you were talking to your girlfriend."

"Well, I'll accept your 'thank you,' but I've had nothing to do with this music."

"You know, many Mexicans get upset with the United States, but me, I don't mind what you do. People get angry about the wall, but it is your country, you can do what you like with it."

"It's really not a bad place when you get to know it. Americans absolutely do come off as loud, arrogant assholes, but most mean well."

"I think much of the hatred and anger of the world can be solved simply by people getting to know one another and seeing they are no different."

"Well, I'm Will. Nice to meet you." I stuck out my hand and he shook it. "I agree with you. So many of the so-called 'small town values' people in my country cherish above everything, including science and reason, are the same ones people cherish here. Family, religion, hard work, simplicity. The only difference is skin color."

"Yes. Imagine if we could see ourselves as citizens of the world rather than citizens of these silly countries."

The conversation went on like that through several songs. The energy of this room was aligned. And though I felt alone, I didn't feel weak or scared, but rather a dizzying combination of both power and despair all at once, like a man who'd just won his first fistfight, but against a guy who'd banged his girl. All I ever wanted was to find my crowd. I played sports but wasn't a jock, played guitar but wasn't a musician. I was nothing but an observer and was perfectly seated at that back-corner table. If there was ever a time to get up and rip a guitar solo, now was it. But I didn't belong here. I'd been seduced by the tenets of nihilism (or lack thereof) near the end of my senior year in college, and part of me was still drawn to the philosophy of futility. But these people didn't seem like nihilists. Nihilists don't shred a guitar like these guys. Nihilists didn't talk about knocking down walls and bringing worlds together. Christ, look at Luz. Perhaps she was no more a part of me than the chair I was sitting on. But that all seemed now like bullshit. Maybe I did belong somewhere? Maybe I wasn't so unwanted here?

The current group started into "Gimme Danger" by The Stooges. Something about those opening arpeggios ripped my mind wide open, and, though the singer's voice was the weakest I'd yet heard, there was something powerful about it that called to me. I focused on the words. Christ, those fucking words . . . so simple, yet so complex. Each held a story of its own and the power of those stories grew exponentially as that voice filled the empty space of the driving guitar harmony.

I looked to my left and saw one of the bald guy's friends chatting with Luz. He smiled, and she smiled. He touched her arm.

I continued watching the band. I continued studying the power of words. Seeing that songs could be built on words and the sounds they made. Seeing that maybe I did have a place here? That maybe my clothing and style didn't fucking matter?

Luz pulled out her phone, and the guy hit some buttons and handed it back to her.

The singer screamed those last few lyrics, going for broke. Maybe he'd lose his voice?

I looked left. Now they were laughing. Maybe I'd lose mine too?

When the song ended, I got up to use the bathroom and passed the bald guy on the way. While he may have believed in a unified world, he was still a proud Mexican—a great representative for his country. I, on the other hand, was a horrible ambassador for my own. He seemed to be so sure of what it was to be Mexican. I had no idea what it was to be an American. What did it mean to be a part of something so big? So diverse? So dysfunctional? All I knew was that I'd followed all their damned rules, and the path led had me straight to heroin. But the path in Mexico seemed to have led me here to this room. But maybe both paths were part of a larger path I wasn't seeing? Maybe there was some connection between our countries? Maybe there was some connection between everything? Maybe there was some way for me to be an individual while still being part of a group? Some way for me to be a citizen yet still be permitted to pledge allegiance to myself? Some way for me to hear and understand all the beautiful words inside of me despite all the chaos and confusion screaming around me? Some way for me to release this beauty and power into the world without its pressure beating them back down inside of me? Some way for me, and us all, to feel okay? That was a world I felt I could be an ambassador of . . .

When I came back from the bathroom, the band was between songs. I looked at Luz and the asshole she was speaking with, and they were still laughing. I walked over.

"What the fuck are you doing?"

"Baby, no, it's okay."

"Don't fucking tell me 'it's okay!' I saw you get his number."

The bald guy got up from the table. "Whoa, friend, everything here is okay." He walked over to the asshole. "Carlos, apologize."

Carlos hesitated but stuck out his hand. I shook it for the sake of the bald friend, then sat next to Luz. I was having a difficult time allowing her to plead ignorance on this one. The band started up again, and she led me to the dance area in front of the stage where we grooved along. Everything was fine until I had to use the bathroom again. I did my thing, but when I returned I saw two enormous guys in suits talking with Luz. One reached out and rubbed her cheek. I stormed over, shoved him into a table of punks, and stuck my favorite finger in his face.

"Fuck you, cabron!" I said.

The guy laughed, stood, and fixed his shirt. Luz fussed over him as if he were the victim. One of the seated punks said something to me, and I shoved my finger in his face too. I knew that might have crossed the line. I knew that might have potentially upset the tender balance of the place, leading to the rebellion I'd previously wanted. But I didn't care. It was time for rebellion. It was time for war. And I was caring less and less if Luz went down with the ship. The two giants wandered away, and everyone else settled down.

"What are you doing, Will?" Luz said.

"What do you mean, 'What am I doing?' I'm just trying to stay alive here, you fucking Judas!"

"You don't understand. Those were my older brother's friends. They were eating in the restaurant and saw me. They are also very rich and were about to pay for our drinks."

Fuck! We'd run up a five-hundred-peso tab. What the hell was I doing? I needed a guide with me at all times. I paid the tab and said goodbye to my new friend, and Luz and I again entered the night. We were exhausted and decided on a cab despite our better judgment. We made it back to the hotel and fell asleep quickly. Protecting a queen in one of the world's most dangerous cities was an exhausting task. I didn't know it then, but perhaps what was more difficult was protecting myself from her. I slept well that night.

Chapter 40

The days passed, and Luz and I were on a bus to Puebla. Luz lay in my lap for most of the journey. I was still mad at her but had no idea how to respond. I pulled out my music and stuck one headphone in my ear and the other in hers. It was early and the morning was still soft. I chose "Come Away With Me" by Norah Jones. I wrapped around Luz. A tear dripped from my eye and landed on her forehead. I knew she had to have felt it, but I left it there long enough to be sure, then wiped it away. Although I didn't have many answers, I was sure Luz was still right there with me. I could touch her body, smell her hair, kiss her cheek. I believed her when she told me she loved me, even though she didn't always show it. For that, I would have jumped under that speeding bus. Our trip may have been fucked up. Our love may have been fucked up. But for years I'd been asking girls to come away with me, and Luz was the only one who'd said yes. I was beginning to see that reality, in all its painful glory, might have been a better place to live than my beautiful, gnarled thoughts. That it was better to touch love sour for a moment than dream love sweet for an eternity. That this world I was standing in could be solid underneath my legs and its air could provide sufficient oxygen for my lungs. That I could trust my instincts to guide me and not the tenets of blind love and faith and servitude. Something was happening to me on those roads. Something that maybe wouldn't have happened if I'd stayed in Lila. Something new and special. And it felt like it had less to do with Luz and more to do with me even though she had such a role in it all. I had no idea when the rage had begun. Probably grew slowly over the years. But it didn't start coming out until a few months back. Regardless of its origin, it was out and blazing and could end me at any moment. Luz was the only thing bringing me any peace—even if she did cause me so much torment—but I needed to learn how to have peace without her. I had no idea who Luz was in the past. Who she was when I wasn't around. But I did know that, in that moment, she'd altered all her short-term plans just to be with me on that bus. I had no idea what would happen to her, and us, when we said our final goodbye. But here, right now, I could finally look at the face I'd spent my entire childhood praying to meet. No matter how powerful my thoughts and dreams, there was no way I could have prepared myself for how it felt to really love someone. I needed to experience it, no matter how briefly. And maybe there was some value in having such a brief, and real, experience without having to force an eternity of blind love and service upon it? My thoughts were slowing and becoming clearer.

Hours later, we pulled into Puebla, a city of about two million. We took a cab to the town center and searched for a hotel. We walked down a crowded pedestrian-only street where several grinders cranked tunes on street organs, filling the air with a carnival-like sound. We made a left on a main street off the pedestrian street, and its fringes were lined with panhandlers, and broken buskers, and children pulling on people's pants for change. All those casually swept aside to clear the streets for commerce and recreation: the homeless, the insane, the addicted, the defeated. These people didn't share in the same spirit as those just around the corner on the pedestrian street. Nobody here was dancing for pesos. Dull, lifeless eyes gazed up from the shadows.

The thoughts rushed me: What was this spirit these people were missing? Was it indeed missing? Where'd it go when it left the body? Was it hiding out in some remote and uncharted area of the heart or brain not yet discovered by the conscious? What had broken these people, if they were indeed broken, and when did it happen? Certainly their children couldn't have been born devoid of the spirit, right? Can the spirit return to the body once it's gone?

Many couples held a child or two in their laps as they raised their hands into the street. Though their faces were pointed at us, they all seemed to be staring far beyond. And the timelines leading to those hundred-mile stares were probably just as long and likely composed of erratic chunks of memory that didn't flow coherently from one time to the next. The line itself was probably jagged, circular, or missing huge sections, and the margins above or below, a wall of graffiti, footnotes, and shorthand reminders: "Remember Life," "Try to Love," "Breathe." When did these lives go wrong?

I allowed the thoughts to ravage my brain as a kind of sacrifice for the greater good. Maybe I'd find a way to save these people—and myself at the same time? Maybe I didn't need to sacrifice anything to help them? Maybe it was precisely in not sacrificing anything that I could save us all? I was in it now—the downward spiral of despair. This desolation certainly infected my soul. Willy, you'd better be careful with all that talk about reality. It's easy to romanticize about that shit on a bus—much harder to live it walking down this street.

A little farther up, a young girl played the accordion as a young male companion sat holding two small children. Though her eyes were fixed on the street, her hands played a song that must have come from somewhere more profound than her fingertips. I glanced at her face as we walked by. It had no expression, and it seemed I could have pushed her over without her giving the slightest of resistance. Where did her song come from? Maybe the spirit hadn't left her body? Maybe it hadn't left mine either? Maybe it wasn't too late . . .?

Somewhere along the way, I'd stopped moving.

"Come on, baby." Luz tugged on my arm. God, she was beautiful. *But no matter what you think, Willy, she don't got what it takes to save you.* None of these people do. But maybe the occasional tug on the arm is all you'll ever need from them . . .

We continued down that street for a few blocks before finding a nice hotel. The room was huge, clean, had a balcony overlooking the town, and had mirrors on nearly every wall. I could see my ass from almost any angle. We dropped our loads and headed to the street. We walked Desolation Row, turned onto the pedestrian carnival street, and entered the center. Luz walked to the information booth and spoke with the woman behind the counter. Luz called me over.

"Would you like to take a tour of the city?"

"Eh, what the hell . . ."

We boarded the tour bus and walked to the back. Luz waited for me to sit, then sat leaving an empty seat between us. She turned away from me. Goddamn it! We didn't have much time left together. I didn't want to waste an afternoon playing games. Luz planned to stay behind at our next stop, Veracruz, to spend the rest of the holiday season with her sister. Tonight would be our final night together.

Puebla was a remarkable city and had Popocatepetl and Iztaccihuatl, two of Mexico's largest stratovolcanoes, towering in the distance. There were a number of legends explaining the origin of these volcanoes. According to one, the two had once been lovers: Iztaccihuatl a beautiful princess and Popocatepetl a fierce warrior. Iztaccihuatl's father sent Popocatepetl into battle and later lied to Iztaccihuatl, telling her Popo was killed, though he wasn't. Iztaccihuatl died of grief. When Popocatepetl returned and discovered his lover dead, he drove a dagger through his heart. The gods later raised the two deceased star-crossed lovers into mountains.

I looked across the valley at the volcanoes. Then I looked at the valley between Luz and me. I shifted over a seat and put my arm around her shoulder.

"Don't—"

"It's okay, Luz. It's okay . . ." I pulled her close and felt her body give. She shifted toward me. I breathed in her hair and kissed her cheek. "It's gonna be okay, sweetie . . ."

We returned to the hotel after the tour ended. Once I'd locked the door, I reached around Luz from behind, unbuttoned her pants, and slid them down her legs. Then I pulled off her shirt, unfastened her bra, and held her warm, heavy breasts. I pulled down my pants, threw off my shirt, slid off her panties, and entered her, warm and wet, from behind. I glanced around the room and saw the many angles of our physical expression of love. We were a fleshy, moving Picasso. Her skin grew cool and moist. I licked her back and kissed her cheek. That face—such emotion. It clenched and released a thousand times during those next few moments. I pulled out and came on the top of her ass. She turned and put her arms around me, pulling my head next to hers, clinging to me as she'd done the night at the fair when we'd first kissed. I felt as if we'd somehow aged exponentially in those brief moments—those moments when all pretense had been stripped away and our bodies and spirits could finally breathe and assess and come to terms with all the damage that'd been inflicted on them— those moments when our understanding and acceptance gave us the courage and wisdom to feel. I pulled myself from her grip and walked to the shower. I turned on the water; Luz opened the curtain and walked in behind me. She put her arms around me. I again pulled from her grip then grabbed the soap and washed her body.

We dressed in warm clothes and walked to the town center, where we decided on an Italian restaurant. The tables outside were all filled, but an older couple got up just as we arrived, and we were seated in their spot. We ordered a bottle of wine, then I the pesto pasta, and she the vegetable lasagna. A man played some Top 40 tunes on a sax while we ate. When we finished, we walked to the empty bar upstairs. The woman there showed us to the best seat in the house: a balcony table overlooking the center. We ordered a cubeta, and the woman brought the bucket but no bottle opener. I tried to open my beer over the edge of the table but took out a chunk of wood. Luz grabbed the bottle and opened it with her teeth. She did the same for her own beer. Smiles, saluds, and sips.

"When I was a little girl, I was in a parade. I was dressed like a butterfly. I was with many of my friends in the back of a big truck. We drove through town and everybody came out to see us. When we passed my family, I got too excited, and I started flapping my wings. For some reason, I thought I could fly." She started laughing so hard, she gasped for breath. "So, I jumped out of the truck while flapping my arms. I can't forget my mother's face. She yelled, 'NOOO, LUZ!'"

We both laughed.

"Were you okay?"

"I bruised my leg, but that is nothing. I've done worst. I used to climb mango trees when I was little. I'd climb to the very top, and sit, and eat mangos like a cute little monkey. One day, a branch broke as I was climbing, and I fall four meters into the grass. I hurt my arm, but I was okay. My mother always worries about me, but my father says, 'Let her play. She needs to bruise her knees.'"

"Do you have a big family?"

"Jes, my family is very big. My mother is the youngest of seventeen children. I have fifty-two cousins—some of them I've never met."

"Damn, I thought *my* family was big. On my mother's side, I'm somewhere in the middle of thirty cousins."

"What is your family like?"

"I don't even know how to answer that question . . . It's kinda like this." I grabbed the saltshaker at the middle of the table. "Everything is okay, until . . ." I tipped the shaker over. "Something that simple can set things off. Then, the next thing you know, a TV is going through the window or holes are being punched in the walls. And I never know what's going to cause it. Some days, spilling the salt is okay—it's funny, and we all get a laugh—but the next you're getting slapped out of your seat. It's fucking crazy."

"I'm sorry to hear that, baby."

"I just—some people are in over their heads, and they never ask for help. And if you offer it, watch the fuck out. I'm starting to see that I think I need some help. I'm so tired of being angry. So tired of being scared of all these things I can't see."

"I'm sorry you have gone through all that." Luz reached across the table and put her hand on my own.

"What do you think people think about us?" I said.

"What do you mean?"

"I mean, this . . ." I held up our interlocked hands, with alternating light and dark fingers.

She kissed my hand and smiled. "I think many people are tonto—silly fools. But you can't let them bring you down too."

"I don't want to go back, Luz . . . I really don't want to . . ."

"You can't hide in Lila forever. You need to go back and see these people. You are different from them. That doesn't make them bad people. It just makes you different."

"What are we gonna do?"

Luz pulled her seat next to me, then she put her arms around my shoulders and kissed my cheek. "No matter where you are, always you are in my heart and in my mind."

We went back to the hotel and got down, soft and slow. I slept deeply beside her. The morning came quickly, as it always does.

I got a text from Mica early that morning: "Crazy bus ride but we're here . . . What hotel you at?" I let him know, and soon they were there. Luz and I met them in the lobby.

"Ay, whey, we made a mistake going to Acapulco," Mica said. "Both the bus rides there and back were horrible. The bus got a flat on the trip last night and delayed our entry by eight hours. And, other than the cliff divers and beach, there's not much to see about Acapulco. You made a good choice in not going."

I looked at Luz. "I know."

"I know we're supposed to go to Veracruz tonight," Mica said, "but would you mind staying in Puebla another night? Neither Gretel nor I are interested in doing more travel."

I again looked at Luz. She smiled.

"That is okay. I will call my sister and tell her I'll see her tomorrow."

I smiled and kissed her.

Mica and Gretel got a room, and Luz and I reserved ours for another night. The Germans went upstairs and dropped off their stuff, then we headed to some shitty knockoff of African Lion Safari. We spent a few hours with elephants, rhinos, tigers, and other caged animals, then took a cab back to the city. We went back to the hotel, got ready for the evening, and returned to the same Italian restaurant. After eating, we headed to the bar upstairs, which was crowded that night. The same hostess found us a great table despite the crowd. A live band played Mexican rock tunes. Mica, Luz, and I crushed through several cubetas while Gretel sat back and chain-smoked cigs. At first, I figured she was a down chick but just tired from travel, but maybe this was her normal energy. Any moment now I was waiting for her to snap out of it, chug a beer, and smash the bottle over her head. But she just sat there, smoking cig after cig, only taking a break every twenty minutes or so to use the bathroom. She must have gone ten times throughout the night without putting a single drop of liquid into her body—at least, not that I'd seen. Mica, Luz, and I, however, were getting wild. Luz continued to open all our beers with her teeth, despite the bottle opener chained to the bucket. We got loaded, then stumbled back to the hotel and hung out in the Germans' room. We opened a bottle of tequila and got to work.

Luz soon left, and Mica and I killed the bottle. I started getting that feeling in my loins, so I bid farewell to the Germans and stumbled to the room. The door was locked, so I knocked. Nothing. I knocked for several minutes, and still no response. I walked back to the Germans' room.

"Luz locked me out."

"Well, you're on the same floor. Why don't you just hop balconies and go through the sliding door?"

"We're four floors up, cabron."

"Don't be a pussy."

I took a look. It was a long drop, but the balconies were only about a foot or two apart, so I again bid the Germans adieu, and started hopping toward my queen. I'd cleared five or six before arriving. The curtain was open and light on, and Luz was sprawled on the bed stomach down in nothing but her underwear. That sent me into overdrive. I tried to open the door, but it was locked, so I pounded and shouted her name. But she didn't move.

I hopped balconies back to the Germans' room.

"She's too drunk to wake up."

I walked back to the room and started pounding on the door. People left their rooms and gave me dirty looks, and security walked upstairs.

"What's the matter?"

"Man, I gotta get in there—she's in her fuckin' peach panties!"

"Who's in there?"

"I'm gonna break the door down. This is our last night—"

"You're causing a disturbance."

"I just need to get into my room."

"This is your room?"

"Yes, and I don't have a key!"

"Well, why didn't you say something?"

He opened the door, and when I walked in, it hit me: What the fuck was that guy thinking? Christ, I was practically frothing at the mouth and still sweating from hopping balconies, and he just opened the door to some young girl's room and let me walk inside. Eh, whatever . . . I ripped off my clothes and tried waking her up, but she was a log. I rolled her over, made some room for myself on the bed, and passed out next to her.

Chapter 41

We woke much later the next morning than we had the previous. We got the Germans and checked out, and Luz and I walked outside to hail a cab. One pulled up and we got in. But the Germans didn't follow. I walked back inside to get them and saw Mica yelling at the girl behind the counter.

"Twelve hundred fifty pesos? It was *one* bag of laundry!"

"What's the problem?" I said.

"This woman just gave me a bill for my laundry, and it's twelve hundred fifty pesos."

"How is that possible?"

"They dry-cleaned the clothes instead of washing them. She showed me a bill for each item. It's ridiculous."

"So don't pay—look, we gotta go. The bus is leaving in a half hour, and it takes twenty minutes to get to the bus station."

"She already has my credit card number from the room payment."

"Shit, man, that's why I always pay in cash. You talk to the manager?"

"She *is* the manager!"

"She's playin' you, man. Tell her to go fuck herself."

"I'm just going to have to pay."

"Well, whatever you do, hurry. Luz's already got a cab out front."

Mica paid, then came outside and stuffed himself into the back seat of the cab with Luz and Gretel. I sat in front.

"Why would they have accepted my laundry without mentioning prices if they were so high?"

"Because they wanted to take you for a ride, whey," I said. "Hey, would you mind stepping on it?" I said to the driver. "We're trying to make a bus."

"Sure thing, friend."

The driver was a young guy and seemed happy to have been given the go to push that cab to its limits. When we reached the station, I threw the guy an extra fifty pesos for his effort, but it was all in vain—we'd missed the bus.

"FUCK! There goes thirty more bucks I don't have," I said.

"I'm sorry for causing us a delay with my laundry. Fuck, this sucks," Mica said.

"You're fuckin' right it does!" I said.

While Mica and I steamed, Luz stood calmly in line waiting to buy new tickets. I dropped my bag, walked to her, and wrapped my arms around her, and she somehow absorbed my anger. A missed bus wasn't that bad in perspective, and at least it'd buy me more time with her. I kissed her cheek.

We bought new tickets, but the bus wasn't leaving for another six hours so we walked to a nearby mall to kill time. Mica, Luz, and I caught the latest Bond flick while Gretel sat outside and smoked. We got some dinner, then walked back to the bus station, where we sat on the floor of the busy waiting area. I sat next to Luz and had that last-day-of-summer-vacation feeling deep in my gut. I wouldn't see her again after Veracruz. We'd snuck in an extra final night together, and I knew time was already generous enough in granting us that. Mica, Gretel, and I were heading for Chiapas after Veracruz and then to Cancun, and after, I'd be taking a bus back to Lila to get my things, then hopping on a bus to the Guadalajara airport. My bags were still at Luz's, but she'd left a spare key with Luz Blanco.

The bus came, and we boarded. Luz lay across my lap and slept the entire trip. I again put a headphone in her ear and the other in my own. Even if she was asleep, this somehow made me feel less alone. I studied the scenery, and soon we arrived.

We took a cab to the town center, which was filled with navidad decorations. A giant tree towered over buildings covered in wreaths and stars and lights. We walked into a hotel, which looked to be stuck in the 1960s. It seemed everything but the furniture and employees were covered with wood paneling, and the place reeked of cigar smoke.

"Why are we staying here?" I said.

"My travel book says this is the finest hotel in town, and I wanted to stay someplace nice on Christmas Eve."

"Well, I feel bad for this town then. How expensive is this, 'Nice?'"

"The room is seven hundred pesos, but it won't be that bad three ways."

"You kidding me? For the past week I've been staying in places much nicer than this for like ten bucks a night. Who do these fuckers think they are?"

"Listen, Will," Luz said, "I've got to go. I'm going to take a cab to my sister's."

"Let me come with you!" I said.

"I don't know how she would feel bringing a boy with me."

"Can you come back later?"

"I never get to see her. I think tonight I should just spend with my family."

"But you're never going to get to see me either."

"I'm sorry. I need to go. Merry Christmas!" She walked away.

This couldn't be it . . .

The Germans and I took the elevator up to our room. We opened the door and were hit with the stench of cigarettes. Gretel and Mica tossed their bags on the floor. Mica grabbed the remote and started flipping channels while Gretel sat on the bed and added to the stench. My breathing became heavy, and I started sweating. I rushed over to the window, opened it, and stuck my head outside. I felt like screaming her name. Why'd she leave me? It was too soon . . . I sucked air into my lungs but couldn't get enough. Tears formed in my eyes, but I fought them back. I hung out of that window and stared into the horizon for a good twenty minutes.

"Hey, Willy, I got a surprise for you!" Mica said.

I pulled myself back inside and inhaled a cloud of smoke.

Mica reached into his bag and pulled out a package wrapped in brown paper. "I'd been holding out on this until the holiday." He ripped into the package, which clanged as he pulled off the paper. Inside were six beers of different German brands. "My mother mailed me these before we left Lila. It's my Christmas present."

"Damn, I haven't had a dark beer in months." I loved Mexican beer, but there wasn't much variety. The choices were either light or lighter lager. Mica tossed me a brown ale, then his lighter. I popped the top and took a gulp. It was good. I took another. Half the beer was already gone. My pocket vibrated. I checked the screen: "Would you like to eat dinner tonight at my sister's house?"

I was so excited, I could barely keep the phone steady enough to type back: "YES! How do I get there?"

Luz sent me the address. I set down the beer and jumped in the shower. I finished, toweled off, threw on the cleanest of my dirty clothes from Herb's big green bag, and ran out the door—without even saying goodbye.

I waved down a cab and gave the address. I rolled down the window and stuck my head outside like a dog. The wind felt good against my warm face. I was blazing inside. It felt as if it'd been months since I'd seen her. My body ached for her. I would have ripped through that cab door if I saw her walking by on the sidewalk. This was passion, all right, but it didn't seem healthy. Christ, was Luz now just another addiction? What was I going to do after tonight when I could no longer get my fix?

The cab rolled through the streets, taking me deeper and deeper into the inner city. The cabbie dropped me off where I told him, and I got out. In a nearby park, a group of teenagers were hurling fireworks on a basketball court. The explosions rocked like quarter sticks of dynamite—but no one stopped them.

I walked by them and stood in the exact spot Luz had told me to wait: "In front of the swings." Then she was there—swaying that wonderful sway and smiling that gorgeous smile. She took my hand and looked at me like love first realized.

"Come on, baby, I want to introduce you to my family."

We walked behind an apartment complex and over to a small duplex. A group of about fifteen people were scattered both in and outside the house: cousins, aunts, uncles, friends . . . Luz introduced me to them, but I quickly forgot their names and ranks. We sat at an enormous table in the kitchen with the other young guests. Someone handed me a beer. I knew one beer would lead to twenty, but that looked to be the same fate for the others seated around that table, so I gave in and started drinking. Then came the food. People passed plates of pasta and quesadillas and rice and frijoles. It was a pleasing navidad feast. I thought of Mica and Gretel. He was so proud of that beer, and I'd left half of the one he referred to as "the best in Germany" on a table beside the bed. I'd abandoned them without even checking with Luz to see if they could come too. The house was already packed. What were two more Germans? Christ, I mean their compatriots were every-other-fucking-where.

Luz took me by the hand and introduced me to her sister Veronica.

I kissed her cheek. "Pleased to meet you, Veronica. Thanks for letting me celebrate Christmas with you."

"It's no problem. I can see by the happiness in my sister's eyes that you are in the right place."

I smiled, and so did she. Veronica was much older than Luz. She looked to be in her late thirties. Luz explained to me that Veronica was her half-sister. Veronica's father had died, and their mother had remarried Luz's father. Veronica was also married, but her husband was out to sea. He worked an oil rig in the Gulf and wouldn't be home for the holidays.

Luz sat beside me and drank with us. They were a lively group and made me feel welcome. We killed a fridge full of beer and a bottle of whiskey.

"Who wants to go dancing?" someone asked, and we piled in a minivan and headed downtown. We stopped at a gas station, and I bought two twelve-packs of Tecate, and soon we were rolling down a beach road. Goddamn it; it was Christmas Eve. I'd missed mass and my aunt's party. The moon was full and its reflection rippled on the ocean as the waves crashed into the beach. It left a long stretch of white light, which tapered off as it neared the horizon.

I tossed beers around, and we quickly killed the first twelve-pack. We couldn't find an open bar, so we drove back to the house and sat out front in plastic chairs. The kids were still lighting dynamite on the basketball court. I sat next to Luz and Veronica. Luz walked inside and came out with something.

"I bought this for you while we were in Puebla." She handed me a long, fat Cuban cigar. I kissed her and lit it. We stayed up most of the night talking, and people started disappearing as the hours dragged on. I had no idea how I was going to get back to the hotel that night, but Luz solved that problem for me.

"My sister said it'd be okay for you to stay with us tonight."

I smiled, put out the cigar, and followed her to some couch pillows on the living room floor. We passed out in each other's arms on another extra final night together and woke up on Christmas morning. I was twenty-three and in love with Lucecita Corta.

Veronica was hard at work in the kitchen making Christmas breakfast. She provided a feast of huevos, frijoles, and quesadillas, and ate while she cooked. Mica called while I ate.

"Meet us in the town center."

I left Luz with her family and took a cab to the center, which was now alive with activity. Some kids were giving a performance on a stage under the tree, and several people watched. The sight of the hotel reminded me of the two hundred and twenty pesos I'd paid to give Herb's big green bag a comfortable night's sleep in the smokehouse. I met the Germans, and we got some lunch at a café in the center.

Luz texted me during lunch and invited us all to a restaurant for dinner at seven. The Germans and I walked the city center that afternoon, then went to get our bags from the hotel. Mica had some credit card trouble and Gretel took three trips to the toilet, and by six forty-five we still hadn't left the lobby.

"Yo, I'll just pay for the room. We gotta get moving! It's almost seven!"

"No, I need to figure this all out," Mica said.

Seven came and went. Then seven ten. By seven thirty we'd finally gotten a cab. We arrived just before eight. Luz was sitting alone on the steps out front. I ran to her and called her name, but she barely even looked up.

"I only get so much time to be with my family—" she said.

"I'm so sorry! I tried to get here earlier, but they were moving at the speed of glacial erosion . . ."

She had tears in her eyes. I could feel her pain. I pulled her close and tried to make it go away, but it wouldn't. I'd let her down. I should have just left them behind in the lobby. I held her hand, helped her to her feet, and guided her inside. Such a responsibility was this!

We ate, then walked the boardwalk behind the restaurant. On the beach, people were swimming and celebrating. I knew my aunts and female cousins were probably already drunk off wine and talking in the dining room while my uncles and male cousins were drunk off beer and watching college football in the living room. I tried to think of their faces, but everything was a blur. Luz came into focus. I pulled out my camera and snapped a picture of her. She wasn't getting away so easily.

The Germans decided on ice cream. Luz and I stayed behind.

"I've decided to go back to Zambulla in a few days," she said. "I'd like for you to meet me there. Will you?"

"Jes!" I didn't have to think about it. For months, I'd wanted to return to Cancun if for nothing other than to see how much I'd grown. But now I realized it was better to just keep growing. I leaned in and kissed her. She pulled a tangerine out of her pocket and handed it to me, then pulled another out for herself. We sat on a bench and ate our snacks while the Germans ate theirs just ahead.

We walked to the road and hailed separate cabs. I kissed Luz and smiled. We'd have several more final nights together.

The Germans and I arrived at the station and boarded an overnight bus to Tuxtla Gutierrez, which would bring us a gigantic step closer to my jungle dream, Palenque. I reclined my seat and stared out the window. Our group had lost its MVP. Luz was our translator, tour guide, and, most importantly, good friend. I was terrified of how I'd get along without her.

The trip to Tuxtla was long and had a stop in Villahermosa in the state of Tabasco, where Luz was born. The trip to Tuxtla was about thirteen total hours with the stop in Villahermosa cutting it nearly in half. We pulled into Tuxtla the next morning. Before we left the bus station, we bought tickets for the next town, San Cristobal de las Casas, then we headed to a nearby restaurant for some huevos and frijoles. After, we bought tickets for a powerboat tour of El Sumidero Canyon, which, according to Mica's tour book, was supposed to be the thing to see in town. I just wanted to sleep and followed Mica's lead.

The bus to San Cristobal left at three, giving us four hours to see the canyon and head back to the bus station. We took a cab to the canyon, then hopped into a boat and took off. I was so tired I felt drunk. The cool wind, though, was invigorating as it blew against my face. The canyon was gorgeous, but the tour lasted much longer than it was supposed to, and when two came, we were still on the boat. I thought of our missed bus in Puebla and started to panic.

"Hey," I said to the guy in charge, "the lady at the ticket counter said we'd be done by two."

"Yes, we'll be done by two."

"I guess you mean two tomorrow . . ."

The guy took his sweet time and finally got us back to shore around two forty. I jumped out and ran to the road, and grabbed the first cab I saw. I hopped in the passenger seat.

"I got one, Mica!" I turned, but Mica wasn't there. I looked down the road. They were still on the damned boat talking to some other gringo fuck. I yelled to them though I was about a hundred yards away. "MICA, LET'S GO!"

He heard me and started moving. Meanwhile, the rest of the boat passengers had caught up; some jumped in the taxi van. I had a tremendous fear of missing deadlines. I'd had recurring nightmares throughout my life of getting to the dock just as the boat was pulling away, or getting to the gate just as the plane was taking off—and everyone I knew was onboard, laughing. Fuck! Fifteen fucking minutes—but I wasn't going to miss that bus. I started coaching the driver along. "Drive down there and get them! Those two—those two white pendejos down by the dock!"

He drove downhill, and they got inside.

"What the fuck were you doing?" I asked Mica. "We have a bus to catch!"

"Oh, Gretel had to use the bathroom."

The cabbie drove uphill and turned onto the main street, and we hit some traffic.

"Look, there's a spot! You can get around there!"

The driver actually listened to me as I coached him through the wall of cars. The people behind me must have thought I was insane, but I was doing a favor for any one of them who needed to get to their destination in a hurry. Luz could move quickly. She could run at moment's notice and never look back. I was sweating, and swearing, and falling apart without her. Was this my destiny? To hustle through life, continuously pushing all those around me through roadblocks and sanity, on to some end that likely didn't even exist outside of my own head? At three, we were stuck at a red light.

"FUCK!"

We arrived at the bus station just in time to watch our bus pull away. I ran to it and shouted, but the driver didn't stop. I punched the door.

"It's okay, William, the ticket only costs forty-five pesos, and a new bus leaves every half hour."

"That's not the fucking point!" Christ, those weren't my words.

I knew Mica was right. I knew this was no tragedy. But maybe I just needed a fucking tragedy to fill the empty space where she'd once stood? Despite the reason returning to my brain, I was still steaming. I stood in a dark corner away from the Deutsche Duo, and by the time the new bus came, most of my anger was gone.

The mountain scenery helped to calm me. We pulled into San Cristobal, and I felt at home. What a beautiful town: the mountains, the colonial architecture, the cool fresh air, and friendly faces. We found a cheap hostel, dropped our bags in our room, and fell into a deep sleep that lasted late into the afternoon. I woke when it was dark and went to explore the town, leaving the Germans behind. Golden light poured through the windows of quaint shops and strands of colorful Christmas lights hung above the streets. The night was cool enough to almost be cold, and I delighted in seeing my breath as I wandered the hilly town. There were people everywhere. I could feel their kindness as they sipped tea in small cafés or walked hand in hand through the center. It was hard to imagine this was the spot ravaged by guerilla warfare just a decade back. Hard to imagine people being pushed so far as to take up arms against their country. But it happened, and it happened in places like San Cristobal.

When I got back to the hostel, we decided to get dinner. We passed several restaurants, but each time I suggested we go inside, Gretel shook her head. Finally she found a place she liked, but even though it looked all right and I was hungry, I shouted a decisive, "Nein!" just to fuck with her. We eventually settled on a spot I chose at random but insisted was the only place I'd eat. After dinner, we searched for a bar to continue our celebration. Gretel walked back to the hostel while powerpuffing cigs. That night was up to me and the pasty German. I felt some nostalgia in this.

We strolled the streets, popping in and out of every lively bar we crossed. The town was small but bursting with energy. Mica and I settled in at a hip spot where a jazz trio lathered up the suds of sound on a raised stage in front of the bar. The place was packed with tourists. I didn't want to leave Mexico, but it wasn't my home. I was stuck somewhere between life and a dream. I tried to calm my racing thoughts by citing the case of my grass vs. that on the other side, but knew that to be an exercise in futility, so I pushed through the crowd and bought a stiff drink.

There was a door in the back, and Mica and I walked through it, entering a much larger and livelier room, pulsating with rhythmic music. The dance floor was packed with ass-shaking Mexicans. My hips started to move, but Mica and I decided it best to sit at a small table just off the dance floor. While we knew we didn't belong in that room, we both felt more comfortable there than in the previous. We sipped our drinks and watched the dance as we always did. By now, I'd accepted my role as an observer and was okay with it. I had moves too, just not on the dance floor.

"Damn, whey, I can't believe it's been over four months." Mica popped a cigarette in his mouth.

"Me neither. You remember when we first got here? We could barely understand a word. We cracked the code, man. We infiltrated the secret world. I don't know how I'll be able to return to Gringo-Landia and function after this. I've seen the Promised Land."

"Yeah. Other people have come and gone so fast, they probably never experienced it. Remember the Icky-bopper?"

I laughed. "How could I forget that dude? And what about that bushy fucker, Dan. Remember that clown?"

Mica laughed.

"Herb used to say he looked like a typical Spin Doctors fan," I said.

We both laughed.

We'd done it. We were drawn to the strange, fed on the weird, and sought the unattainable in nearly every fleeting moment of our young lives. We weren't war heroes, or cancer survivors, or Noble Prize winners, or decently-rated talk show hosts, but we'd both obliterated several obstacles inside. But achievement had its costs. My savings were gone, and I crossed my fingers each time I swiped my card at an ATM. I'd learned firsthand that it wasn't wise to bet against time, and knew it best to abide its demands early on before it had to start getting more forceful. I was leaving Luz behind—I'd always known this. I'd found a new freedom in knowing this that I hadn't before. I'd let her in. I'd opened myself up. My ambition was always burning—ironically, often leaving me inert and miserable. But now I was beginning to see the subtle rewards in submitting to ambition and allowing it to guide me, rather than I it. I didn't see nearly as much tragedy and sadness wherever I looked. People seemed more content. It also seemed that fewer people were watching me than I'd previously assumed. I saw struggle as something less tragic and more triumphant. Mica and I were lost, but not dead. I loved life on the road but was beginning to see it for what it was. Constant motion was an addiction like any other, and had the same potential to destroy a life as did a drug problem. It was stillness that terrified me. But it was in stillness that I could keep the beauty inside of me in frame long enough to paint it. Life was going on as it always had in Buffalo. Nothing had changed but me.

We had a few more drinks, walked back through the gringo section of the bar, and entered the cool, crisp navidad night. We strolled back to the hostel. The only furnishings in our room were two queen-size beds. Mica crawled in next to Gretel in the one, and I under the four blankets in the other. I fell into a deep, satisfying sleep, allowing myself to rest.

Chapter 42

We woke early the next morning. I felt refreshed. We threw our stuff in our bags and walked to the street. I pulled ahead of the Germans and hailed a cab, and soon we were at the bus station. There I sat, barely awake, as that mystery person turned on the television blasting banda music. Then came the laughter. It started with one or two people and spread through the crowd. The gringos pointed at the television and whispered and giggled. I was only half-awake, but when I looked up I felt as if I'd understood something more profound about not only banda, but my experience in Mexico as well. In some parts of Mexico banda was almost sacred. And these people were laughing. It felt as if they were pointing at me. Mexico had offered me food, freedom, and friendship, and, most importantly, a place in its casa.

I reviewed my timeline of the past four months. I saw Luz's face, watched Paz and her friends dancing in the rain, saw my students in El Campo smiling while playing volleyball, sipped whiskey with Ximena, climbed the Volcán . . . I'd long thought that I was between worlds, but maybe I was just as much a part of this one as was that banda group? Maybe I wasn't as unwanted as I'd always suspected? Maybe I was already a part of something, but perhaps that something had no idea what *it* was?

The colorful history and culture of Mexico was pumping through my veins. But this didn't mean I'd rejected my own culture. I was just beginning to understand that I could choose my own path without having to feel like a goddamned traitor or sinner. I didn't think any less of the gringos laughing at the banda group—I'd done the same so many other times. But now I could see some separation between myself and them—see some separation between "myself" and my real self underneath it all. These seemingly insignificant events that morning loosened several pillars in my mind and set in motion a chain reaction leading to that one great epiphany of a lifetime. I now knew with absolute certainty: I wanted to live. I chose life. And not for Luz, or Mexico, or my family, or friends, or country, or god—but for myself.

How grateful I was that I hadn't yet done it! How grateful I was for always beating back those darkest and most sinister of shadows with a tired arm! I'd been just hanging on for so long. And as the pillars fell, the earth rose, cool and solid, under my feet, catching me just before that presumed great fall—proving there'd been something solid there all along. I'd finally touched it. I'd finally met life.

I'll never understand why these thoughts came that morning in a small bus station, but they continued long into the afternoon. We boarded the bus, and nearly everyone sat and shut their eyes. I, however, stared out the window and watched as we cruised through the cloudy mountains and farmhouse valleys of Chiapas. It was as if the sights were for me and me only. I reached into my backpack and pulled out the small pad I'd bought from the woman on the bus to Guadalajara and allowed myself to start writing the ideas for what would someday become this. I allowed myself to feel happy. I allowed myself to feel safe. I allowed myself to explore the idea that maybe I could express myself artistically. That maybe some of those raging, gnarled thoughts were just works of art screaming to be understood and released. And no one could do a single thing to stop me. I became a human being that morning. But I still had so far to go . . .

Changes usually didn't happen like they do in Hollywood. You don't immediately turn your back on the KKK and rid yourself of racism just because some black guy saves your dog. After decades of being a racist, that shit is in your blood. It's in your fiber, your marrow, your muscle and bone. The easy part is realizing it's wrong. The hard part is dedicating the rest of your life to changing. Though I'd chosen life, I still had no idea what it looked like. Though I'd chosen life, I was still living with the pain and scar tissue. Change required more than just an epiphany. It required dedication, and awareness, and humility, and forgiveness. To abandon the blind faith of old systems of thought without abandoning faith entirely. To have faith, rather, in growth, and tolerance, and love, and peace, and respect, and knowledge, and reason, and compassion. It would probably take decades of struggles and triumphs to finally be free of the darkness, if ever, but now I was on that path, and I wasn't scared to see where it would go. It amazed me that I could experience such a powerful revelation in a bus station, and on a bus, and the people around me could be so oblivious. But maybe I didn't need them to see? Maybe I didn't need them to understand this change happening within me? Maybe they were a part of it all simply by sleeping, or chatting, or daydreaming? Maybe I didn't have to be so damned furious at them all the time for continuing about their lives as I struggled? Maybe I could connect with them in other ways—perhaps by writing about these struggles and revelations?

Chiapas was a gorgeous spread of earth. The bus sped over lush, green mountains, past sprawling farms with great fields of enormous, leafy plants, and through small towns with wooden homes. In these towns, children holding baskets of handcrafted goods or treats would wait at the speed bumps and hold the baskets up to the windows as the bus slowed. A few passengers reached through the windows, grabbed a snack, or trinket, and tossed down some change, which the kids caught while smiling. Though early, the world outside was fully awake. Neighbors were up walking, talking, and working alongside one another. I'd heard much about Chiapas but rarely a thing negative. It was one of Mexico's poorest states, but easily one of the most beautiful.

Eventually, the bus arrived in the small, dusty town of Palenque. The driver dropped us off at the station. We paid a small fee to store our bags in some lockers, then found a nearby restaurant selling plates with half a chicken, spaghetti, rice, beans, and salad for twenty pesos. I devoured the first plate and ordered a second. We walked to the street when we'd finished eating.

"So, how do we get to the ruins?" Almost immediately after I'd asked that question, a man driving by in a minivan stuck his head out the window and yelled to us, "Get in! I'll take you to the ruins!"

There was something sincere in his strangeness, so we hopped in when he pulled over. The driver took us down the main road, around an island with a large Mayan sculpture at the center, then up a road lined by tall trees. I was leaving Palenque that night at eight and wanted to see as much of the ruins as possible. I'd already bought a ticket back to D.F., and it was expensive, so there was no way I was going to be late.

The driver dropped us off near the entrance of the ruins, and we paid him. I hopped out of the van and bought a ticket. I stormed ahead of the Germans and their comments—"Where is zee fire? Hehehe!"—and walked through the main gate. I was now on the other side of Mica's guidebook—the other side of *National Geographic*. Thick trees surrounded the perimeter of the ruins, providing cover for the monkeys and other animals screaming and singing in the distance. The Germans caught up, and we walked to the first temple together. Gretel stayed behind as Mica and I raced to the top. We popped inside the small, damp temple, took a few pictures, and walked back down.

We spent the next few hours wandering around by ourselves. My mind was all epiphanied-out, so I simply let it take in the sights and sounds.

I met up with Mica and Gretel. Between us, we'd taken several hundred pictures. Most were of the temples and surrounding jungle, but Mica had captured a number of fantastic tits and asses. Before leaving, we saw a small group of the extraneros. Mica spoke with them while I climbed a nearby temple. When the extraneros left, I climbed down, and the Germans and I took a cab to town.

We ate at another cheap restaurant, and I bought some trinkets from an old woman who'd walked up to our table during dinner. Now I had Christmas gifts for my sisters. We walked the streets after we finished dinner and found a rooftop bar selling cheap beers. We sat at a table overlooking the town.

"I can't believe this is it," Mica said.

"Me neither. So, what are you gonna do when you get back to Germany?"

"I'm not going back. I've decided to head to South America next month. I'm going to try to get a job teaching in Argentina or Peru. There's still so much to see."

"Tell me about it . . ."

"What are you gonna do?" he said.

"I've got some fixing to do back home, then I was thinking maybe a move down to Miami or California. I want to give America another chance before leaving it forever. It's such a beautiful country. It's worth saving."

"I think I've found my home in the Latin world. Life is just simpler here."

"Simpler, indeed." I smiled, leaned back in my chair, and put my hands behind my head. "But not too simple."

Gretel sat next to me, sucking on a cigarette. I wondered why some people struggled so much to bring home with them wherever they went.

"You sure you don't want to come with us to Cancun?" Mica said.

"I'm sure. You'll have fun though. There's nothing like that clear, blue water and pure, white sand. Christ, this is a beautiful country too."

The time came, and we walked to the bus station. I again pulled ahead of the Germans but slowed my pace to allow them to catch up. I hugged Mica outside the entrance of the bus station. While I knew I might never see him again, I also knew he'd always be a part of my history. I hugged Gretel as well. I knew she'd look back on this trip someday and remember the good times she'd spent with her cigarettes.

I turned from my friends and walked to the bus. This was the first time I'd be traveling alone for such a distance. But I wasn't scared. I felt featherlight and free. I was confident with my Spanish and my ability to get around Mexico. I tossed Herb's big green bag under the bus, boarded, and sat by a window somewhere in the middle. A pretty college-aged girl sat next to me.

"So, you are going to Morelia?" she said.

"Yeah, I'm going to stop there on my way to Zambulla. I figure I can't miss out on seeing the butterflies."

"Morelia is a beautiful city. I am going back to Mexico City. The holidays are almost over, and I need to return to my studies."

"Yeah, the holidays are almost over for me too . . ."

The conversation continued like that for several hours. She spoke no English, but my Spanish flowed with few problems. She was intelligent, interesting, and kind, and offered me a place to stay in D.F. should I need it. I fell asleep soon after the conversation ran dry, but was rudely awoken sometime later when the bus suddenly stopped and the lights turned on. The lights from several police cars flashed outside. A cop boarded and started shining a flashlight in people's faces.

"What's going on?" I asked the girl.

"I think they are checking people's identification. Many people sneak into the country from Central and South America," she said.

I started sweating. Mica had bought my ticket in his name to get me his student discount, and I didn't know whether this was a bootable offense.

The cop kept shining his light on one person at a time, inching closer and closer to me. But when he got to our row, he took a brief look at me and kept going. He stopped, however, after checking the identification of the guy sitting just behind me. The cop led the man off the bus, and soon the lights went off, and the engine started again.

"What just happened?" I asked the girl.

"That man was an illegal immigrant from Guatemala. They're taking him to the station for questioning."

"Jesus, well, I hope he's all right."

"It's okay. This happens all the time here."

"What are they going to do to him?"

"Probably send him back across the border."

In the search for illegals, they didn't even question me. I fucking hated borders. Imaginary lines separating people. I just happened to have been born on the right side of one.

I again fell asleep and woke up in D.F. fourteen hours after we'd left Palenque. I felt some intriguing kind of sentimentality upon returning to the city I'd only known with Luz by my side. When I exited the bus, the girl told me she'd help me get my ticket to Morelia. But when I looked up after grabbing Herb's bag, I saw her locked in her boyfriend's arms. They were both smiling. I decided to just let them be, knowing now what that felt like.

I walked through the enormous bus station and found the ticket area. I checked the prices of a few competing lines and bought the cheapest ticket on a direct route to Morelia. All I could think about was getting back to Luz, but Morelia was still in the way. Soon I was on an eight-hour trip through the mountains. Every mile brought me closer to her. But every mile also brought me more mental anguish. I'd never been prone to claustrophobia, but after so many consecutive bus trips, the walls started closing in on me. I kept my thoughts on Luz, and soon the panic eased.

When we pulled into Morelia's bus station, I bought a ticket back to Lila for the next night. I took a cab to the center and enjoyed the conversation I had with the young driver.

"Yeah, I lived three years in Chicago," he said in fluent English, "but it just wasn't for me. Man, you guys really love rules up there. You know, some people have a problem with Americans, but me, I don't mind. You're welcome in my country anytime, friend."

"You're welcome in mine too."

He dropped me off in front of an information booth in the town center and sped off. I walked to the booth and was greeted by a friendly woman.

"Hello, would you like to see the butterflies?"

"Yes."

She sold me on the cheapest package: four hundred pesos. Fuck! But it included all transportation and food for the whole day. I wouldn't have paid but the butterflies were the only reason I was there. She also pointed me to a cheap hotel down the street. I got a first-floor room, dropped my load, took an unnecessarily long shower, and set off to discover the town. Morelia was gorgeous, with all the charm of Puebla and San Cristobal. I wandered for about an hour until I hit an aqueduct at the end of a main street and headed back to the center. An unusually high proportion of the women here were beautiful. They wore thick sweaters, and jackets, and scarves shielding out the cold. I wandered through the town center, then to a busy café. I ordered a cup of tea and pulled *Crime and Punishment* out of my back waistband. I'd decided to give Raskoinikov another chance. But the night was too ripe for life to spend it with the deceased.

I wandered for a few more hours, then headed back to the hotel. The tour van was leaving at seven a.m., and I didn't want to miss it. I knew there'd be no refunds for this trip. I set my phone alarm, slid between the warm blankets, and fell into a deep sleep.

I woke on time the next morning. I packed Herb's big green bag, left it with the girl at the front desk, and walked back to the information booth. The town was quiet and cool. I snapped a few pictures of the square and the cathedral and walked to where the woman said she'd pick me up. Two young couples were already there waiting.

Just before seven, a blue minivan rounded the corner. The woman got out and asked us if we were hungry. When we all nodded, she said, "Vamonos." We walked to the lobby in a nearby hotel, ate breakfast, then hopped in the van. I sat against the window in the back row beside one of the couples. We exchanged smiles when we first sat, but that was it for our communication.

We drove through the Michoacán countryside, passing mountains, lakes, and several small towns. I saw Luz in everything both beautiful and tragic around me. She blew cool with the wind, rose golden with the sun, grew slowly like the forests of pine—but she also stunk like roadkill, toppled heavy like the sick trees, and crumbled small like the homes destroyed by an earthquake. She was all things; I couldn't escape her hold of my essence. I'd turn to the guy beside me from time to time with the urge to strike up a conversation but would stop myself before allowing the words to come. He was with his wife. I was envious of their age. They looked to be in their late twenties—just old enough for life to leave them the fuck alone. They'd made it past the frivolous games of youth and were now allowed to sit peacefully in the back of that van, holding each other's hands. I wished to shut off life and transport to that age—just five years; get me past twenty-seven. And take Luz with me. We could get past all the obstacles already in our way. We could have steady jobs, and a small apartment, and go to sleep each night to the sound of Mexican folk music on the radio and the smell of burning incense in the air. I wished Luz and I could hide out in one of those mountain villages—just left the fuck alone. Which is why I fought the temptation to start a conversation with this guy about the fucking weather—or worse, the butterflies: "Hey, chap, so you say the Spanish word for butterfly is 'mariposa?' Wow! Great stuff! Say, do you like music?"

I'd made such progress but still had so many mountains to climb. But which did I climb first? There were so damned many . . . Choosing life wasn't easy. I still had no idea what it looked like. Maybe it really was one long chain of mountains? But not everybody seemed to be climbing . . . And this couple looked peaceful beside me, just sitting, and holding onto one another—no mountains there. No sweat on their brows . . .

We drove through a few more towns before ascending a

mountain. The van chugged along as we winded higher and higher into cooling and thinning air. We stopped in a large parking lot and hopped out of the van. We followed the tour guide/driver along a forest trail lined by wooden shops and restaurants and continued to the gates of the Santuario de la Mariposa Monarca, or Monarch Butterfly Sanctuary. The guide took us along a path surrounded by evergreens, then up a steep stairway. The guide and I pulled out ahead of the others.

"The mariposas come every year in October and stay until April. There are millions here," she said to me.

"I'm surprised something so small can travel so far," I said.

"Yes, they come here, get their rest, and then fly home."

"Where's home?"

"Canada and the Northern United States. They weren't discovered here until nineteen seventy-five when some explorers came across them. I can't imagine what they must have thought seeing them for the first time."

"Maybe they feared an attack?"

She laughed. "Yes, attack of the butterflies!"

I stopped to take a breath. She laughed again.

"You are very high up. Maybe we shouldn't go so fast?"

"No, I'm good."

"So, what is such a young man doing traveling all alone?"

"I hopped on the wrong bus. The rest of my friends are in Guatemala."

She laughed. "And where are you going after this?"

"The coast—Zambulla."

"And what is in Zambulla?"

"That's a good question."

"Maybe a girl is waiting for you?"

"Maybe . . ."

We continued up that trail, leaving the others far behind. We were about 10,500 feet up. She was used to the altitude, but I wasn't going to let anyone beat me to the top. I took two stairs at a time, pushing through my exhaustion. She chuckled. I think I amused her.

We'd stop intermittently to let the others catch up close enough to where we could at least see them. Years back, I'd watched a documentary about the mariposas on some nature channel, and I was excited to see them for myself.

We continued climbing steps until we reached the top where we came to a green clearing. Butterflies fluttered through the air.

"Over there!" She pointed to the ground.

I looked and saw a patch of dark earth moving even though no wind was blowing.

"Aren't they supposed to be in the trees?" I said.

"They go where they please," she said.

It was a crisp winter day, but I was sweating from the hike. I patted down my body with my sweat-saturated clothing and wished for a joint. The place was marvelous. People surrounded the butterflies, taking pictures and care not to step on any. These creatures had full diplomatic immunity and rested where they pleased.

"They make the trip only once," she said, "and many will never return. Some are too weak to fly back, others will be snacks for birds."

"And others will be tossed in a Mexican prison for pissing outdoors," I said.

"No, we welcome their piss here." She laughed. "Over there you will find the crown jewel of the sanctuary." She pointed to the forest. I think she could sense my eagerness to continue. I nodded to her and walked ahead. The trees grew close to one another but had tall, thin trunks, allowing ample breathing room for the wind. I breathed the mountain air and pondered the Rucksack Revolution. Christ, what an idea. But that's all it was . . . even with real people living it.

I stepped carefully to avoid crushing any butterflies and stopped when I saw some tourists pointing at what looked like a fuzzy tree about twenty yards away. I knew there was something to it but couldn't see it at first. I had to adjust my eyes, as if staring into one of those 3D posters, and then I understood. Thousands, or even millions, of butterflies were clinging to the drooping tree limbs. Christ, alone those things couldn't have weighed more than a paperclip, but combined they had the weight to bend those massive branches. The wind blew, but the butterflies held tightly. I started thinking up little haikus as did Ray Smith and Japhy Ryder on the Matterhorn: "The mariposa remains still as the tree it clings to sways in the breeze." A butterfly landed on my shoulder. The tour guide walked up behind me.

"Don't move." She took my camera from my hand and snapped a picture. The butterfly flew away. She showed me the screen. My hair was starting to get long again.

We walked down the mountain a short time later. The tour guide and I again walked beside one another and far ahead of the others. She told me her boyfriend had recently proposed to her as they were strolling through Morelia's town square. "We came to a group of children singing Christmas songs, and he asked, and I said, yes, yes, YES!"

I thought of Luz. I couldn't get her image out of my mind. It had already been too long since I'd walked beside her, wrapped around her, felt her oils on my skin. She made walking easy. I could hear her calling me in the distance, and with every step I was falling deeper into her gravity. I called to her with words of my own—words with enough strength to climb mountains and cross streams, yet with enough agility to maneuver dense forests and enough grace to whisper softly through gentle towns, before hitting her ear thousands of miles away with an earth-filtered strength and purity.

We passed through the Santuario gates and came to the path lined with wooden shops and restaurants. We stopped in a restaurant for some roasted chicken, quesadillas, and beans. The rest of the group caught up after I'd started on my second plate. A large, leather-clad Mexican man played guitar and sang Elvis tunes outside. While watching him, I saw Dr. Josh and several of the geology students walk by.

"Hey, Doc!"

"William, nice to see you! You going up or coming down?"

"Coming down . . . You won't believe what's waiting for you up there."

"Yeah, I've been hearing how incredible it is."

"How's the volcano?"

"The same—always threatening to blow. But we'll be all right."

"I think we will . . ."

Goddamn, it really was a small world. They were losing daylight so they kept going. My group headed down to the van. I made it down first, so I sat on the rear bumper and stared into the valley below. The sun was already dying and creating vast, rounded shadows of the mountains in the distance. The day seemed older—much older than it had even an hour earlier. The others arrived, and we piled in the same seats. Again I fought the urge to pester the couple beside me with questions. My bones were tired but satisfied, filling me with an earned peace. My mind was too tired now to create romantic images of synthetic happiness and satisfaction, so I got the real thing. The ride home seemed to take much longer than the one there. But it always did . . .

We arrived in Morelia hours later and said our goodbyes as the group parted ways into the night. I went back to the hotel. I was glad to be alone. I took a quicker shower than the previous night. I was leaving for Lila at midnight and wanted enough time to get dinner, wander around, dive into a bar or two, and finish the night with some reading in the center.

I got ready, packed, and ditched Herb's big green bag with the guy at the front desk, then walked to the street. The bar next door had a Beatles cover band. I thought about it, then walked to the Italian restaurant across the street and ate a plate of spaghetti and meatballs while watching what looked to be a couple breaking up at a nearby table. The girl looked furious, and the guy looked to be holding back tears. Men rarely showed such emotion in public unless some big disturbance was smoking the life out of them, and I imagined he knew he'd be walking out of there alone.

I finished dinner and wandered again into the night. Morelia was stunning during the day and even more so at night. The city looked to have been dug out of the earth—the buildings and cathedrals carved out of exposed bedrock. I again walked as far as the aqueduct, then purposely got lost on some side streets. Eventually I found the center again. A group of young male dancers dressed in masks and wooden clogs stomped the rhythm of songs played by three or four men with instruments behind them. They drew quite a crowd. I watched for several minutes, then wandered to a bar across the center. People were everywhere. There seemed to be some kind of festival going on. There were small celebrations scattered throughout, among the much larger one surrounding us all. I wished to join in but felt I was doing so on that bar stool. I basked in the rays of energy surrounding me and absorbed their power.

"We're having a two-for-one special tonight on beers," the bartender said. "What can I get you?"

"Got any hot tea?"

He showed me a box, and I picked something that looked fruity and fun. I pulled out *Crime and Punishment* and got about an hour into it before the energy of the crowd started to surge. I slid the book back in my waistband and wandered outside. I followed the crowd to a spot near the catedral. Then, almost immediately after I'd stopped, several shots rang out in the distance. Two twirling rockets flew into space and exploded in brilliant displays of reds and blues and yellows and greens above the catedral. Goddamn, I was far from home. But I wasn't lost. Each exploding firework shattered another ancient pillar in my mind and sent it crumbling to the ground. How could I even begin to explain to anyone what was happening here? I wasn't the same. But they didn't even know the old me . . .

After the show, I walked back to the hotel, grabbed Herb's big green bag, and hailed a cab. I'd hoped my friend from the day before would pick me up, but instead I was scooped by some cantankerous old man: "Where ya headed? Come on, I ain't got all day, kid."

I'd left about an hour early so I could relax. When I got to the station, I bought a torta and a beer and sat in a corner and waited for the bus. I was so tired and had been traveling for what seemed like a lifetime. All I wanted was a safe, comfortable place to lay my head—a place I could call my own. I thought of Luz and the softness of her bed. Every passing minute brought us closer together.

Even with my newfound strength, I still couldn't shake the despair of leaving Luz and Mexico. I didn't know if I could make it back home without either. I felt good now, but I knew what bad felt like. Bad felt horrible. Bad could barely get out of bed in the morning—could barely look people in the eyes when speaking with them. I didn't ever want to feel bad again. I had so many living and thriving thoughts in me now but was returning to the graveyard of my hope, and dignity, and happiness. The spot where thousands of my former selves had been dragged out to a field, shot, and buried below unmarked tombstones; I had no idea how to even grieve for them. Some of those selves were more strangers to me now than ones I hadn't yet met.

The bus came, swept me up, and thrust me back onto the dark country roads. The claustrophobia came back. I breathed heavily, but the thought of seeing Luz soothed me, and I fell asleep.

Chapter 43

When I opened my eyes, I saw my beautiful Lila. Luz was in Zambulla with her family but was taking a bus to Lila at ten that morning to ride back with me. I arrived around seven thirty a.m. I figured I could take a cab to el Centro and hang out at a café, but I fell asleep on a seat in the waiting room while making plans. When I woke up, she was there, standing about twenty yards away.

She saw me but stood her ground, watching me as if she were trying to capture my image in memory. I left the bag and walked to her and she to me. We met somewhere in the middle. I breathed her in, and we kissed. We took a cab back to her place, got my stuff, and hopped on a bus for Zambulla.

Soon we were in the port city, wrapped together and walking as one again. We took a cab to her parents' house. We rode down some cobblestone streets and arrived at a gated community with a security guard at the entrance. Luz smiled, and the guard opened the gate. The cabbie dropped us off in front of a large one-story house, and Luz and I brought my stuff inside. Her parents had invited me to stay with them for the rest of my time in Mexico. I thought that a fitting way to finish my trip.

Luz's parents were both there when we walked inside. Her mother was a vibrant woman who spoke and smiled frequently. She walked from behind the kitchen counter and hugged Luz. Luz's father sat in a recliner in front of the TV. He was a deathly serious man and reminded me of a character from a Sergio Leone western. I walked to him first and extended my hand. He held out for a second, but stood and shook it with a vise grip.

"Hello, it's nice to see you again, Senor Corta!"

"Yes, nice to see you as well," he said, revealing a hint of warmth.

Luz's mother struck up a hurricane of a conversation with me, little of which I understood. I stared at her with a dumb grin and waited for a moment to add something more than a head nod, but it didn't happen.

"She said she's happy to see you, Will," Luz said.

Fuck, it was hard enough meeting the parents in your own country, but this shit . . .

I hugged Luz's mother and planted one on her cheek. Luz's father took my big, blue bag and showed me to the back room where I'd be staying. Two framed pictures of Luz from what looked like modeling sessions hung above the two beds.

The kitchen was full of fresh fruits and vegetables. Luz's mother made us some tortas and rice. Luz and I ate and headed for the beach. It was now tourist season, and the town was packed with gringos. We hopped on the bus and took it past the stretch of beach where A-bomb and I'd swum with the stingrays and got out at a smaller section hidden behind a field of palms. I was the only gringo there. A woman under an umbrella lit up when she saw Luz. Luz walked to her, and they hugged.

"This is my sister, Rocio," Luz said.

I hugged Rocio and kissed her cheek.

"So this is the famous Will?" she said.

I gave a bashful smile. Rocio was there with her boyfriend, Jamie, and his two-year-old son from a previous relationship. Jamie grew up in LA, but he had family in Zambulla.

"What's up, man? You want a brew?" He'd already popped the top off a caguama with a lighter before I could respond. We crushed through several caguamas and took dips in the ocean to relieve the pressure. I cut myself off earlier than I would have liked. Luz's parents were throwing a New Year's Eve party that night, and they were doing a family dinner first. I didn't want to be the guy spilling the gravy bowl all over Tia Karla's dress.

The afternoon was filled with jokes, and smiles, and soon it was over. We piled in Jamie's truck and drove to the town market. I thought I'd kept my drinking under control but realized how tipsy I was while trying to count change at the pescaderia. In fact, I was downright drunk. The market was packed with customers and shit to bump into, so I just followed behind Luz like a five-year-old as she glided between crates of fruit and tubs of iced fish.

We got what we needed and went back to Luz's place. Everyone was already dressed nicely, so I took a shower and put on the cleanest of my filthy clothes. We sat around the large circular table between the kitchen and living room. Though I'd sobered up enough to make conversation, I was still having difficulty understanding Luz's parents. Luz translated: "She asked about your family." Luz wore a flowing turquoise dress—the same color that came to mind whenever I thought of Zambulla. Luz had colors as well. She was pure white, rich mocha, tropical blue, and jet black. She helped me through the dinner conversation. Luz and her family were good people. They worked hard and cared deeply for one another. They were an important family in the town but didn't act superior to anyone. Luz's father was the head of customs at the port. He was among the wealthiest of citizens in the city. But he spoke with humility. He was born into abject poverty and worked several construction jobs to pay his way through school. He'd go to class directly from work, showing up covered in sweat and dust. But he'd risen to the top. I was humbled in his presence. I envied his courage and conviction. I envied how he could still have enough strength left to support such a beautiful family. Luz's mother was an incredible person as well. She added scintillating stories to all lulls in conversation. She was a pure and passionate woman whose words filtered through her soul, leaving nothing but sincerity and positivity for all those who had the pleasure to be around her. Luz's parents seemed polar opposites in personality, but I could tell by the way they spoke and looked at each other that there was love between them.

I felt peace sitting with Luz's family, but I also felt some discomfort. It was easy for me to ignore my sins while in constant motion on the road or in the smoky haze of dive bars or around other lowlifes. But being in the company of such honor and stability forced my inner judge to begin reviewing all my past transgressions. Inside of me, there were so many criminals whom I'd allowed to rape and pillage my own essence for so long that I didn't know which to try first.

We finished dinner and toasted the New Year, then we walked out the back door, up the steps, and onto the roof. The clock struck midnight and fireworks shot through the sky, exploding in reds, and blues, and greens, and yellows, illuminating the mountains below. I looked at Luz. She stood with her arms wrapped around her father like a little girl who still believed her daddy was the strongest man in the world. I remained several feet behind the huddled family and observed the love they shared. I felt my soul blowing in that cool ocean breeze somewhere between there and Buffalo.

The fireworks continued to light up the sky, briefly illuminating everything below that was once too dark to see. I stood on that roof watching as those explosions lit up my insides as well, allowing me brief windows of time to see the terrors haunting my gloomy interior: crumbling stone gargoyles, slippery plastic snakes, a bathtub-sized ocean full of wind-up sharks . . . Now I could see. Now I knew what they were. Here in this house of light and love.

Eventually we walked back downstairs and inside the house. The older members of the family went to bed, and the younger members headed into town. We went to a nightclub filled with gringos. I started breathing heavily.

"Let's get the fuck out of here," I said to Luz.

But she didn't hear me. She walked to the dance floor with her cousins. Some dipshit gringo in a sleeveless t-shirt tried to rub up on Luz, but she rejected him. I sat on a couch and watched. The world started spinning. Luz came over later.

"Come on, Will, dance with me!"

"I'm tired, Luz. Will you sit with me?"

She did. I fell asleep on her lap. I woke up a short time later. She was stroking my hair.

"I love you, Luz."

"I love you too."

Chapter 44

I hopped out of bed early the next morning with an intense burning deep in my gut. I ran to the bathroom, did my thing, and went back to sleep. I woke up a few minutes later, and the feeling had returned—only far more intense. I rushed back to the bathroom and did another thing, but as I released more of the darkness, the pain seemed to intensify. It felt as if someone was in my stomach stabbing my guts with a heated thumbtack, and I was growing more and more impatient with the pain each second. I visited the bathroom about three more times before Luz got up and asked me what was wrong. I ran from her and locked myself in the bathroom again, where I dropped to my knees and puked into the porcelain with such force I thought my stomach would come up with it. The room started spinning and dissolving away. I poured sweat. I spent the remainder of that agonizing morning running to the bathroom every ten minutes or so to release more evil. I tried drinking water, but anything I put in my stomach came right up. After several hours, I was starting to grow delirious. I could see the concern on Luz's and her mother's faces.

"We need to get you to the hospital."

"No, no I'm okay." I smiled, then got up and ran to the bathroom again, almost not making it. The pain was unbearable. I screamed as the filth passed through me.

"Will, we're taking you to the hospital!"

We piled in the truck and drove to the hospital. I scanned the waiting room for bathrooms, but my name was called before I needed one. Luz came in with me to translate, and soon I was on the table with my pants off. The doctor ran some tests, then said something to Luz and left.

"Am I going to live?"

"He said you're very, very sick and that you should stay in the hospital. He wants to hook you up to an I.V."

"That sounds expensive. I think I'll be fine. I haven't puked in about an hour now. Let's just go back to your place."

"My mother said she will pay for your stay. She's very worried about you."

"No, I'm fine. Let's just go back."

We left the room. I paid the bill, and we walked to the truck. I was feeling better, but then it hit me. I ran to a patch of grass at the edge of the parking lot and puked beside a tree. My body poured sweat and my eyes dripped tears—but at least I didn't shit my pants.

"I really think you should stay in the hospital."

"No, it'll pass. I'd rather spend the day with you."

We piled in the truck and went back to the house. The pain hadn't even slightly eased, and I continued with my regular cycle of puking and shitting. By four thirty, I was starting to worry. Each time my body ejected more filth I could feel my energy draining away. I tried to stay optimistic but still wasn't able to keep down any water. The day was scorching, and I was almost drained of fluids. I was overcome with a weakness I'd never felt before. I could feel the life force leaving my body, as if I was a video game character now at sixty percent health. And the worst part was that this damned disease was robbing me of one of my last few precious days with Luz.

"If you won't stay in the hospital, we will have the hospital come to you."

Luz left and returned with an older man who lived a few houses down.

"Will, this is Doctor Sanchez. He is the head medical director of the hospital you just left. He is one of the best physicians in Lila."

"Nice to meet you."

He nodded. The doctor checked me over for about ten minutes, then he said something to Luz's mom and left. Luz's mom also left and returned with some sports drinks. She poured one in a glass and handed it to me.

"He says you should drink this."

I sipped it and kept it down. She left the house again. Soon the doctor came back with a leather bag. He set the bag down and pulled out a vial and a syringe.

"We should go to a private section in the house."

The only person in the house was Luz, and she was in her bedroom.

"Let's just do it here, Doc." I dropped my pants, and he stuck in the needle just as Rocio, Jamie, and Luz's mom walked in the front door. Rocio and Jamie ran outside laughing, and Luz's mom walked past, pretending not to see. It was like an uninspired scene from a shitty rom-com. I laughed. The doctor gave me a few more injections, and I felt better almost instantly. He handed Luz a few syringes and some vials of medicine and told her I'd need a few more injections. I'm not sure how desperate my situation was, but I'm pretty sure that if it wasn't for that doctor knowing his stuff, I might have spent my remaining days in Mexico in the hospital. His knowledge brought me health. I said a prayer to knowledge and a holy! holy! to discipline!

I was feeling much better, and the concern in Luz's face eased. She'd wanted to take me to a small beach town called Punta de Santa for the day, but those plans were ruined by that horrible pain in my gut. I had a way of often changing her plans and she had a way of adapting with minimal stress or effort. I was so glad to be with her. I couldn't help but wonder how different my situation would have been had I gotten sick just a few days earlier in the company of the powerpuffing Germans. They might have helped me find the hospital, but maybe not even that much. Or what if this had happened while trapped on that bus to Morelia? Or on the boat in that river canyon? I didn't believe in fate but knew life sometimes delivered to us what we needed when we needed it the most. I'd found myself ill in the company of two wonderful Mexican women who'd nursed me back to health. I'd been sick many times before but never as I was that day. It was almost as if a lifetime of sin and darkness had chosen that very day to pass through me. And they were my earthly angels, helping to guide it through.

Luz's mother made me some caldo de pollo, or chicken soup, for dinner, and poured me another glass of red sports drink to wash it down. When the time came, Luz took me to the back bedroom for my shot. I lay on the bed and pulled down my pants but felt no prick. I turned, and Luz wasn't there. I closed my eyes and heard her mother's voice. I looked and she and Luz were there.

"No, Mom, I don't think you do it like that. You could hurt him."

"I don't know, Luz. Maybe your father does?"

Soon Sr. Corta was there as well. The three discussed how to give me the injection with my bare ass staring at them. Someone gave it to me, and I laughed as the needle penetrated my skin.

I woke the next morning feeling almost one hundred percent and was ready to spend the day with my baby. The physical pain had been replaced with another kind, which intensified with each passing moment. I was leaving for the Guadalajara Airport at midnight. Luz and I spent the day trying to ignore that fact and lived it as we would have any other. We strolled around town, took some pictures, and stopped at a café for some food. After eating, I got a picture developed of Luz and me kissing on the beach one night after a big party. I bought a frame, slid the picture inside, and wrapped it in a brown paper bag. Luz was turning twenty in a few weeks, and I wanted to give her something before I left. It was that afternoon, taking out cash for that gift, that I'd withdrawn the last fifty bucks from my overdraft account. There was no more credit for me. It was time to start repaying my debts.

I stared out the bus window on the ride back. I tried to push the small town's charm away. I didn't want to see anything beautiful. But I kept a smile on my face for her, and I think she did the same for me.

Luz and I took a nap that afternoon and woke up when it was dark. Luz borrowed her father's truck and drove us to the bar her surfer friends owned. Luz Blanco met us there. We sat at a table overlooking the ocean while some gringo played covers of Bob Marley tunes on an acoustic guitar. I sipped what would be my last beer of the trip. It didn't feel right without Mica there. I wondered how he and Gretel were digging Cancun. The Luz's laughed together like old friends. It was such an honor to have friends like them. Soon my Luz turned to me.

"You don't have to leave, you know. We could get a house together. My father owns a lot of property. We could have a place on the beach—"

I didn't say anything. I could see the sadness in her eyes, but no tears came.

"You see that spot over there?" She pointed into the darkness. "That is where I want to open up my hotel."

"Well, maybe you'll let me stay there someday?"

"Jes! But only if you stay forever."

We finished our drinks and decided to leave. I hugged Luz Blanco and said goodbye. Luz Oscura and I piled into her truck and drove to some cliffs overlooking the coast. I snapped a few pictures of Luz, and we went back to her house. I walked to the back bedroom, and Luz to hers. We both locked our doors. Then Luz climbed through her window, and I let her into my room through the sliding door in the patio. We kissed soft and slow and worked off each other's clothes. She lay on the bed and pulled me on top, but it squeaked, so I picked her up. She wrapped her arms around my neck and worked her hips and minutes later it was over. She got dressed, climbed back through her window, and I packed my things.

I hugged Luz's mother and sister and said goodbye, then Luz's father drove me to the bus station. Luz came along and sat between us. Luz's father dropped us off in front of the entrance. Luz grabbed my guitar, and I dragged in my big blue bag. We walked to security, the smiling old woman beside the metal detector, and Luz handed me my guitar. I put it down and hugged her.

I pressed the side my face against hers and whispered, "Always you are in my heart and in my mind."

I could feel her tears run down my cheek.

We kissed as deeply as time would allow, and she walked out the door, never turning back. It was from her I learned this lesson.

I boarded the overnight bus to the airport and stayed awake just long enough to say farewell to the volcano: "Goodbye. Thank you for showing me things no one else ever could. If you need to blow again, it's okay. We'll be fine. You have good people watching over you—watching over us. You're not bad. You're just as good as they are. They love you. We love you. Goodbye." I woke on a cold, dark Guadalajara morning. I carried my things inside the airport, found my gate, and passed out in a seat in the waiting room. Luckily, the final boarding call for my flight woke me. I walked onto the plane and sat in the front row of first class. For whatever reason, the cheapest flight home included a first-class flight to Houston. I pulled out the magazine from the pocket in front of me and opened to a page with an ad showing some shirtless, muscular hunk. All at once the thoughts came back: Holy shit, I need to get back to the gym! Who could ever love me looking like this?

The assholes dressed in suits behind me struck up some horrific conversation.

"Can you believe these people?" the one said to the other. "Absolutely no business sense. It's no wonder their country is such a shithole."

"Tell me about it. The only good thing about Mexico is getting to leave."

"Yeah, well, we'll close that account and start construction along the coast soon . . ."

I looked across the aisle at a white woman who was screaming at her young daughter.

"I told you if you were messing around I'd forget something! You made Mommy forget her pills! I can't believe you made Mommy forget her pills!" The little girl hung her head. The mother frantically waved over the stewardess. "Senorita, please, you need to let me off! I need to get off the plane! I can't fly without them! I CAN'T FLY WITHOUT THEM!"

I slid the magazine back in the pocket, plugged up my ears with music, and did what I did best: recede inward. I guess we all live in the land of the alacran. Tonight, I might accidentally put on my shoes in the dark. I want to be ready.

About the Author

Jonathan LaPoma is an award-winning novelist, screenwriter, songwriter, and poet from Buffalo, NY. In 2005, he received a BA in history and a secondary education credential from the State University of New York at Geneseo, and he traveled extensively throughout the United States and Mexico after graduating. These experiences have become the inspiration for much of his writing, which often explores themes of alienation and misery as human constructions that can be  overcome through self-understanding and the acceptance of suffering.

LaPoma has written five novels, thirteen screenplays, and hundreds of songs and poems. His screenplays have won over 160 awards/honors at various international screenwriting competitions, and his black comedy script *Harm for the Holidays* was optioned by Warren Zide along with Wexlfish Pictures (*American Pie, Final Destination, The Big Hit*) in July 2017.

LaPoma's novels have been recommended by *Kirkus Reviews* and Barnes and Noble (B&N Press Presents list), have hit the #1 Amazon Bestseller lists in the "Satire," "Urban Life," "Metaphysical," "Metaphysical & Visionary," and "Religious & Inspirational" Kindle categories (USA, Canada, and Australia), and have won awards/honors in the 2018 Eric Hoffer Book Award, the 2016 and 2017 Florida Authors and Publishers Association President's Awards, and the 2015 Stargazer Literary Prizes. He lives in Mexico City.

www.jonlapoma.com

Also by Jonathan LaPoma

**Hammond, The Summer of Crud, Understanding the Alacrán, Developing Minds: An American Ghost Story*, and *The Soul City Salvation* are books one-five of a loosely-linked series. Each novel can be read independently of the others.

Hammond

A group of troubled but charismatic boys in a tough Buffalo, NY neighborhood play basketball at a local park and dream winning a state high school championship.

The Summer of Crud

The summer after graduating from college, a mentally ill 22-year-old takes a cross-country US road trip with a friend, hoping to find the inspiration to reach his songwriting potential, start a band, and avoid student teaching in the fall.

Understanding the Alacrán

A 22-year-old man moves to Mexico and better understands the addiction and mental illness destroying his life.

Developing Minds: An American Ghost Story

A group of recent college graduates struggle with alienation and addiction as they try to survive a year of teaching at dysfunctional Miami public schools.

The Soul City Salvation

Not yet ready to take on Hollywood, a 26-year-old aspiring actor and writer moves to Soul City, CA and begins therapy for OCD, setting him on a ten-year healing journey that drives him to near madness as he explores the limits of his heart, creativity, and psyche.

A Noble Truth (screenplay)

Two friends set off on a road trip to explore what truths unite people in a modern America dominated by apathy and discord. It is soon clear, however, that truth is the last thing either man seeks.

www.ingramcontent.com/pod-product-compliance
Lightning Source LLC
Chambersburg PA
CBHW051208120726
47905CB00004B/1025